DEATH
AND
DUTY

BYRON WARD

"Death and Duty," by Byron Ward. ISBN 1-58939-322-8 (softcover). 1-58939-323-6 (hardcover).

Published 2003 by Virtualbookworm.com Publishing Inc., P.O. Box 9949, College Station, TX , 77842, US.

Manufactured in the United States of America.

DEATH AND DUTY

PROLOGUE

On Wednesday evening, from the flagstone patio of his opulent Westchester home, Victor Bonnelli watched his last sunset. The Sun loomed large as it descended slowly into the forested hills beyond the Hudson River. Even if he had been told in simple, specific detail the role the subsiding golden sphere would play in his death, he would not have believed it. Not in a million years.

Without a thought to his precarious mortality, Bonnelli savored his surroundings. The expansive rear lawn was level for a hundred fifty feet before dropping off toward the water, providing a magnificent view. His house, an immense brick ranch, was an unusual dwelling in a neighborhood where ornate colonials and large Victorians were the norm, but a sprawling single-story home was exactly what he wanted. Having been raised in King's County, New York—universally known as Brooklyn—and having spent most of his adult life in New York County—Manhattan—he had learned to equate luxury with space, especially horizontal space. The structure, situated on two level acres, was his perfect castle. He had made it more perfect four years previously, a year before his wife's death from cancer, by adding a thirty-five-foot long full-width extension to the north end of the house, containing nothing but a master bedroom suite.

He learned when he bought the place it was fifty years old—his age also at the time. His only child Nicky was just out of the house, learning the hard ropes of the family business, which at the time was gaining in reputation, growing sharply, and intensely exciting. Now at sixty, Bonnelli had to struggle against the notion that the best days were in the past. His business was still growing, but at a blandly predictable rate. The thrill of the deal had eroded with the competition, which was decidedly subdued, where it existed at all. Marketers were handling marketing, managers were handling management, and lawyers were handling everything else, especially the government, which had become annoying to the extreme over the past few years. Various federal agencies were constantly batting him over the head with licensing requirements, environmental regulations, tax codes, and murder indictments.

The criminal charges never went far; over the last fifteen years, he had not been before a jury, as all cases had been dismissed before any members of the public had been seated. For all his misdeeds, large and larger, he had only served a two-year stretch in Sing Sing when in his mid-twenties, long before the establishment of the diverse and powerful Bonnelli organization. It was partly due to the pressures of his enterprises that he moved to the town of Sunnyside, a quiet suburb thirty miles north of the Big Apple. Bonnelli liked his tranquil retreat, where people didn't bother him, and he did not bother his neighbors. There was one ongoing spate of business with one of the town's councilmen, but that was small and private, an interesting diversion.

As the final wisps of sunlight disappeared, he opened one of the rear sliding doors to the house and entered the sunroom. As he closed out the chill April air, he heard the lilting tones of the telephone. A moment later, his aide appeared from the direction of the kitchen.

"Mr. Bonnelli, Mr. Weiss is calling," said Marc Grunner, a combination bodyguard and butler.

"I'll take it in the library," the boss replied, not looking in Grunner's direction as he made his way to his favorite retreat.

Although Bonnelli's influence had been slight in decorating the other rooms in the house, the library decor was all his. It would have been more appropriate to call the room an armory, as it contained more firearms than books. A collection of twenty-four rifles and shotguns and almost twice as many revolvers and semiautomatic pistols adorned the thick teak walls. Retooled and rebored, each of the lethal instruments was now legally registered. Bonnelli was not aware the weapons had collectively killed ninety-four people, but he knew the number was between seventy-five and a hundred.

He picked up the receiver of the telephone that rested on the massive desk, then sat in a wide chair. "What have you got?" he demanded. He never identified himself, expecting to be immediately recognized. Few disappointed him.

"Your tax returns are ready to sign," came the reply. "There are federal and state returns for twenty-eight corporations and eighteen partnerships, along with your personal return. Close to a hundred signatures are needed." The voice belonged to Andrew Weiss, attorney at law. While not precisely a *consigliere,* he commanded some trust and more than a little respect within the Bonnelli hierarchy.

"A hundred?" the mobster questioned, annoyed. "Can't you get someone else to handle it?"

"Mr. Bonnelli," Weiss said. "I don't think you want a repetition of the signature problems we went through two years ago. These returns incorporate the other companies and partnerships, and it would take a change of leadership to placate the IRS in this matter. They take a dim view of powers of attorney when applied to tax returns, as you know."

Bonnelli acceded to the point by ignoring it. "Any surprises?" he queried. Any other head of a corporate conglomerate might have asked about the bottom line, about the total taxes paid and payable, but he already knew that amount, having determined the number with Weiss and his chief accountant months before. His tax bottom line, perhaps a single-digit percentage of the monies legally due, was the impetus to the accounting, not the other way around.

"Nothing unexpected was encountered. The figures we reviewed earlier proved to be very accurate." As always, Weiss was careful in his choice of words in deference to Bonnelli's well-founded mania that his phone might be tapped by one or two or three government agencies. The house had been swept for listening devices the day before, as it was every week, but that was just to obtain a slight edge. "Three quarters of the corporations showed losses, as did all of the partnerships, most of which are tax shelters anyway. Due largely to allowable write-offs, your taxable income is $32,400."

The figure hung in the air. It was ridiculously small, bizarre, comic—and very satisfying to Victor Bonnelli. He knew all of his enterprises had made money the previous year. Except for one, he recalled grimly, but the people involved in that fiasco had been "dealt with."

"We are still in the midst of four IRS actions from previous years," Weiss stated. "Motions have been heard, and briefs are now being presented." In the rarified financial air of Bonnelli's world, taxes were not a matter of opening a booklet and following the directions. That, lawyer and client agreed, was for the slobs at far lower altitudes. In the surrealistic arena of high finance, there were no set rules, there were only opinions of the most devious kind: legal, allowing the domestication of those creatures often spoken of but seldom harnessed by those without large influxes of cash: the Loopholes.

"Just keep guiding them around the same circle they've been treading for years. I think they sense the grass is dead, they just have no idea they killed it themselves." It was the best attempt at wit that had come from Bonnelli in some time. "Have everything at the office at ten o'clock Friday. I'll see you there." Without waiting for confirmation, he hung up the telephone.

The day's work done, he turned on the audio system built into a large, intricately carved chest, the CD changer already loaded with twenty disks of Hayden, Bach, and Schubert. The music wafted softly over the warm room as he retreated to his leather easy chair and to his literature, escaping this night, as he had the previous seven, to *Texas*.

Three hours later, the library door swung silently open. Bonnelli emerged from the room and headed down the long hall to his bedroom.

"Good night, Mr. Bonnelli." On his feet, Grunner threw the words at the retreating back of the mobster. He did not receive a reply.

Bonnelli entered his sleeping suite and engaged in his nightly ritual of preparing for bed. His cat, Messala, had already moved from its sleeping location in the sunroom to its sleeping location under the bed. Finally settled, he extinguished the light and began a two-hour sleep that would silently end in eternal rest. In the foyer, the huge grandfather clock, having completed a full cycle of St. Michael's chimes, resonated deeply as it began to toll the midnight hour.

THURSDAY
9 APRIL

CHAPTER 1

Double beeps from two watches signaled the top of the hour simultaneously, shattering the quiet inside the sedan. Having made frequent checks of the time, neither agent within the vehicle bothered to visually confirm the hour; both knew it was midnight.

Philip Roberts had put himself on point. As lead agent, he should have kept himself with the main group in this type of operation, at least that's what they taught down on the Farm, directly from the book. That had been with another organization, though, a long time ago. Now he was head of his department, albeit a small one, and there was no book other than the one in his head.

Roberts was in the Pontiac's shotgun seat, armed with a pistol; Eric Kauffman sat behind the wheel. At slightly under six feet, with a muscled build and an angular face complete with an almost Dick Tracyesque jaw, Kauffman's features were similar to Roberts', though younger. There was nothing comic about the demeanor of the men, however. Humorless and intense, they were narrowly focused on the job at hand.

Roberts glanced out the windshield. Down the dimly lit street was the target house, the residence of infamous mob boss Victor Bonnelli. Though he scanned intently, there wasn't much to see. Although he knew of sixteen motion sensitive lights to the front of the house, none were lit, and the house was barely illuminated by the crescent moon.

"Building is dark," Roberts spoke into the handset of his radio. From his lips, the message went to a communications array in the trunk, then through a satellite in geosynchronous orbit, then to the target receiver, traveling over forty thousand miles to the primary assembly area less than five miles from the point vehicle, arriving loud, clear, and secure.

"Received," replied Sandra Haines, agent, who had the additional duty of main group coordination and communications on the mission. She was sitting in one of two sedans flanking a large, windowless van in the rear parking lot of a Tarrytown office building. It was almost the perfect place, close to a major road, but hidden behind the two-story structure and high brick perimeter walls. She could hear vehicles traveling north and south along Route 9 and others turning onto the Tappan Zee Bridge.

Although it was possible they might go into action any time after two A.M., Haines knew she was probably in for a long wait. "I'm going over to check the van," she told her partner, Christopher Morrow. "Call me if any commo comes through."

She exited the sedan and walked toward the van. Three technicians engaged in conversation near the rear bumper. Their voices were not boisterous, but they were still too loud by Haines' standards. The techs might not have been schooled in security measures, she thought, but after nearly two dozen missions, they should know better. "Keep it down, guys," she admonished.

The van was a thorough compromise between the functions of the four-person medical/technical team and the six-strong operations/security team. At one point, it had been argued that two vans should be utilized, but that had been vetoed as being contrary to group cohesiveness.

As Haines entered the van, Dr. Ernest Pedrozo was checking his collection and sampling equipment stored in an overhead cabinet.

"How's everything at the house?" Haines asked.

"Everything is proceeding as predicted," Pedrozo said. "Bonnelli is in his bedroom, asleep, and his bodyguard is down the hall. The two occupants are separated from one another by about ninety feet."

"Big house," Haines commented.

"The next closest person to Bonnelli is a neighbor about a hundred fifty feet to the north."

"That's well within mission parameters. How is the surveillance equipment functioning?"

"Perfectly," Pedrozo stated. That morning, in the guise of HVAC mechanics, two members of the security team had gained access to the Bonnelli house. Even while under the constant eye of the henchman, Grunner, they managed to install telephone taps on three of the six phones in the house, as well as four other listening devices and six motion sensors.

"This is a crucial operation," Haines stated needlessly. Every member of the teams knew it was the first mission in so heavily populated an area.

"All stations are ready," Pedrozo said. "Sandra, please inform Phil everything is on schedule and that we should proceed with the final items on the checklist."

"I'll do that, Doctor," Haines said as she stepped out of the van into the dark, chilly night.

At two o'clock, the "keep away" calls went out to the local law enforcement agencies. A great deal of thought had gone into determining the proper timing and approach for these calls. Because Roberts had put himself on point, Haines should have been the person to convey the messages, but she understood that communications with the locals had to fairly reek with conventional authority, and that any assault on the preconception of male domination that abounded in the smaller departments might compromise the mission. The calls were made by Christopher Morrow, who had a voice so deep and commanding that most people took immediate notice of it, even from across a crowded room.

The ten members of the two teams then waited out the remainder of the night, conversing in low tones while reviewing their plans and contingencies. As dawn lapped at the horizon, Pedrozo monitored the call they all had been awaiting, then cut all telephone communications to the Bonnelli house. Haines relayed the event to Roberts, who immediately set his people motion with the words they had waited all night to hear.

"Move in."

———————

When he was in his teens, he had been the only one out of a group of four to survive a vicious confrontation with a rival gang in Queens. A few years later, he had experienced having the barrel of a gun shoved past his teeth and gums, so brutally that its front sight scraped the roof of his mouth and so far that its business end touched his uvula. More recently, he had sustained lacerations to his hands from a length of steel wire, the target of which had been his throat. Despite these and other incidents from a life filled with violence, Marc Grunner had never been as terrified as he was that morning, standing alone and completely unmolested in the quiet kitchen of the house in which his ex-boss had lived.

The morning had started routinely. Grunner got up, showered, and dressed well before the time Victor Bonnelli usually arose. In the kitchen, he brewed the morning coffee, then checked the house. Everything had been quiet, which was normal, but when he approached the master bedroom that, too, was quiet, which was abnormal.

Grunner knew Bonnelli to be a grand snorer, especially when on his back, which was his position as the bodyguard had gingerly entered the room. A few feet short of the bed, he observed Bonnelli's total lack of movement, then extended a tenuous hand and probed for a sign of life within the wrist of the master of the house.

There had been none.

He then backed out of the room and retreated to the kitchen. Realizing a call was inevitable, he phoned Bonnelli's chief advisor, attorney Andrew Weiss. Awoken from a deep sleep and dismayed by the news, Weiss had nonetheless acted rationally, stating he would be up after an expected unpleasant confrontation with Nicholas Bonnelli.

It was that name that struck terror into the heart of the bodyguard. He stared at the phone, wondering what horrors the son of the dead mob boss would visit upon him when he entered the house with Weiss.

Tearing himself away from the communicator of his fate, Grunner went down the hall and returned to the scene of his crime. Allowing the patriarch of the Bonnelli family to die while under his protection, no matter what the reason, was sure to be viewed by at least one member of the organization as a capital offense. He checked the body one more time. Still dead.

Grunner searched for a cause of death. There were no suspect marks of any kind. Bonnelli's face was peaceful and his hands were outstretched as if in tranquil sleep. There were no pills or needles, no sign of liquor anywhere in the room. In the adjacent bathroom, medicine containers in the cabinet were lined up normally, capped and mostly full. He sniffed the air, tasted the water from the bathroom sink, and examined the toothpaste tube on the marble vanity. Nothing. Nothing. Nothing.

The former bodyguard relaxed slightly. It was obvious that the old man died peacefully in his sleep, probably from heart failure, quick and painless. Things like this happen; everybody has to go sometime. Weiss was a reasonable man, and the only person—now—who Nicky listened to. The lawyer would accept the circumstances of Bonnelli's demise and would persuade the heir to do the same, convincing him that Grunner's sometime to go would not be that morning.

His urge to flee almost gone, Grunner walked to the sunroom to await the arrival of the limousine from New York. When the entourage arrived, they would come upon a quiet, somber scene and would quickly fall into the mood within the house, not resorting to angry outbursts, loud accusations, or gunplay.

Grunner's prediction was immediately shattered, as was the front door of the house.

The henchman jumped up and had his gun out in an instant, but when he faced the foyer, he found himself outmatched. Standing shoulder to shoulder, three large men faced him, pistols drawn and aimed. "FBI, freeze!" the biggest man shouted.

The show of force made an instant impression on Grunner. He stood motionless, one hand at his side, the other holding his automatic, pointed toward the sunroom's high ceiling.

One of the three men approached the gunman and seized his weapon. As he was being searched, Grunner saw at least six other people enter the house. Most headed down the hall toward Bonnelli's bedroom.

"Kauffman," said a man entering the sunroom to the agent who had just completed the frisking. "Take that man to the living room and lock him down."

"Yes, sir," Eric Kauffman said. "Let's go," he ordered his charge, guiding Grunner through the front entry and into the living room. After pushing his captive into a chair, he handcuffed him to a sturdy end table, then took up a watchful position in the foyer.

From the plush detention room, Grunner watched the activity. Out of the front window, he saw two Pontiac sedans and one van. People—agents—seemed to be all over the place. To his horror, he recognized two of them from the previous morning. In their guise of heating system servicemen, he had let them into the house. There must be some active FBI investigation of Bonnelli, he realized, and this was the morning they decided to make their move. *Today, of all days!* Nicky will certainly not be happy with the situation, he thought morbidly, with his father dead in the bedroom and FBI agents pillaging the house. And an unhappy Nicky almost certainly meant a briefly unhappy Marc Grunner.

Abruptly, he saw two possible futures for himself, and quickly chose the one that at least offered life. "Hey, Kauffman," Grunner ventured to the man standing by the front door, "I've been close to Bonnelli for months, seen things, heard things, you know? Maybe we can cut a deal."

The response from Kauffman was a grim smile. "Phil," he called into the adjacent room. "This guy says he'll give us lots of info on Bonnelli."

"I think we'll get everything we need without his help," came the flat response from the unseen Phil.

Kauffman turned back to Grunner. "The deal is this: you keep your mouth shut and sit there quietly, and then we'll probably let you go."

The henchman stared in disbelief at Kauffman, shocked at the response that was unnatural, unwise, and—for Grunner—probably fatal.

————————

Andrew Weiss knotted his tie and completed his fashionable ensemble just as he did every weekday. On this particular morning, however, there were two differences. First, he had arisen a touch earlier than usual. Second, the client who accounted for ninety-five percent of the revenues of his extremely lucrative law firm was dead.

It was bad, but not the end of the world, he told himself repeatedly. Though the reins of power would pass into the hands of Bonnelli's idiot son, Weiss was one of the few people who commanded a modicum of respect from the thirtysomething brat. First, though, he had to break the news to him, and that was not something he was looking forward to.

He grabbed his topcoat and made his way to the elevators. Thirty-two floors lower, he exited the front of his resplendent building. It was indeed his building, one of his major investments, funded by a Bonnelli bank. The limo was in its appointed spot, and the driver opened the long rear door at his approach.

"Nicky's place," was Weiss's greeting to the chauffeur.

He telephoned his office and told his office manager to cancel all of his appointments for the day, save one that was too important to call off via underlings. After retrieving a number from his electronic organizer, he punched a few buttons on his phone and reached his desired party.

"Alex, it's Andy Weiss. . . . Yes, I know it's early, but I knew you'd be up, eager to make the most of your brief visit to New York. I'm afraid I can't meet with you for lunch today; something's come up. . . . Yes, it does have something to do with Victor, and it might be serious, but I don't have much to go on right now. I'll call you later this afternoon with the details. . . . Me too."

The lawyer then called the house in Sunnyside and got a troubling response: a busy signal. Weiss knew Bonnelli had three lines, with automatic rollover of the calls. Maybe there was something wrong with the elaborate phone system, he considered, or maybe Grunner was calling others, in spite of Weiss's order not to talk to anyone else. He finally settled on the probability that the bodyguard had busied out the lines to prevent a call from one particular person.

The limousine glided to a stop in front of a cooperative apartment tower, and Weiss started the long walk to see Nicky Bonnelli. The anticipation did not make the trip a pleasant one. Weiss knew the heir to his father's assets was unpredictable, violent, and none too bright. His main concern was the possibility Nicky might try to oust his firm as the primary legal representation for the Bonnelli organization, despite the fact that Weiss held a tight grip on many areas of the wide-ranging conglomerate. More than anything, he wanted to avoid what might easily turn into a vicious fight. The lawyers in his firm, for all of their legal brilliance, were miserably poor shots.

In the elevator, he pushed the button to the twenty-second story of the twenty-two-floor building. When the doors opened, he was in a small hallway that led to one apartment. He straightened his tie and rang the bell.

It took more than a minute, but the door finally opened a few inches. Through the gap, Weiss saw a bleary-eyed man in need of a shave and a comb, dressed only in boxer shorts.

"What the fuck?" was Nicky's sleepy salutation. "Weiss, what the fuck are you doing here? What fucking time is it?"

Weiss had devised several possible approaches on his way to the apartment. Upon seeing the disheveled wreck of a man, the lawyer decided that Nicholas needed to be awoken quickly. "Nicky, last night your father had a stroke or a heart attack while he was sleeping. He's dead."

The statement had its desired effect. As if Weiss had physically punched him in the mouth, Nicky's head snapped back and his eyes opened wide. Unfortunately, being fully awake had no effect on his intellect. "The fuck you say!" he shouted.

"I'd like you to ride up to Sunnyside with me right now. We can talk on the way."

"Fucking right we'll talk," Nicky said before disappearing into his bedroom.

Leaving the door open, Weiss took two steps into the apartment. A few seconds later, he heard a distressed female voice. Before he had time to wonder about it, Nicky, with a heavy hand clutching thick black hair, dragged a naked, staggering young woman past him, and kicked her into the hall with a bare foot. "Get the fuck outta here! I got things to fucking do," were his parting niceties.

Weiss watched the Romeo return to his bedroom, hopefully, to get dressed. He turned to the cowering woman sitting in the hall, clutching her knees to her breasts, looking at him with anguish. He held up an index finger, mouthed the word "wait," then walked into the bedroom.

Fortunately, Master Nicholas was in his large walk-in closet, haphazardly choosing an outfit for the day. Generally around the foot of the bed, he found the woman's clothing and purse. With the items in hand, he walked to the front entry.

"Thanks," the woman mumbled through her tears as the attorney handed over her possessions.

"I think you should leave quickly and, for no one's sake but your own, never come back," he said, then reentered the apartment and closed the door.

Nicky Bonnelli soon appeared in a wrinkled ensemble. He was still in need of a shave, comb, and shower, Weiss noted. It would be a long ride up the river.

CHAPTER 2

Ending a peaceful quiet, the annoying alarm clock emitted an unearthly scream precisely at 6:00. Silencing the timepiece was the hand of Joseph Charles Hanlon, whose first conscious thought was that he was turning into a genuine hero. The realization scared the hell out of him.

Exerting himself after a moment of reluctant hesitation, Joe sat up, then stood and strolled naked to the bathroom unobserved, as there was no one else in the small, third-floor apartment. He was a morning shower person, at least he had been for the last year and a half since shortly after Janet moved in. She took her showers at night, so it had been up to him to change after a short period of experimentation during which he found that, though a pleasant occasional diversion, showering with a partner was decidedly non-habit forming. After he and Janet parted ways, he could have returned to nighttime showers, but did not, having settled into a routine. A definite heroic symptom.

After drying off, he continued his morning activities by shaving. He had to stoop slightly to get a good view; whoever installed the mirrored medicine cabinet had no consideration for people over six feet tall. A vigorous face stared back at him. The scars on Joe's body made him look older than his twenty-nine years, but there was no good age to be wounded as he was. A wide highway of purplish scar tissue eight inches long curved diagonally along his upper left forearm, and a similar but smaller gash marked his right leg just above the kneecap. An odd arrangement of old lacerations crept across one buttock, looking vaguely like overgrown and indecipherable initials of lovers carved in a beech tree. A bullet entry wound about the size of a dime was visible on his left calf near the knee; on the other side of that leg above his ankle was the larger but less obvious exit wound. After nine months of healing, his limp was hardly noticeable.

Dressed in a brown suit, he completed his ensemble with a .38 caliber pistol, then left the apartment. He descended six half-flights of stairs and exited the building into the clear spring morning. His apartment was in one of a pair of long, three-story structures that faced one another perpendicular to Route 9, more commonly known in the town of Sunnyside as Broadway. Six sets of stairs each led to six apartments in each of the two buildings. Although on the top floor, Joe was otherwise fortunate to live at the end of the northern structure closest to Broadway, along which he normally parked his car.

Joe walked down a gentle slope to the wide sidewalk paralleling the main road and made his way to a ten-year-old red Nissan Sentra. Soon, he was in the traffic along Route 9, mingling with other heroes of the morning.

Joe was feeling mildly trapped in the repetition of his work. Being a detective for the Sunnyside police, and newly promoted at that, was not a bad job, but he also thought there might be more to life somewhere out in the great beyond. Sunnyside was a quiet town with quiet problems and nothing of much note had occurred in the sleepy municipality in the three years he had been with the force. That did not count the terrifying experiences of the previous summer, of course, but those had taken place outside the boundaries of the town, and he had not had much choice in the matter. There was a saying he picked up when he was in the Army: "lead, follow, or get the hell out of the way." For the past seven years, his feeling was that he was definitely a get-the-hell-out-of-the-way kind of guy. Now, he was not so sure.

One of Joe's rebellions against routine was never to drive the same route to the Sunnyside Police Station on consecutive days. It was inefficient, as the two-mile drive straight up Broadway to a left turn at Main Street was easy and direct, but the various routes he took served to mollify his ambivalence, and that made the extra time and distance worth it.

Besides the main route to work, there were two other major and two minor circuits to the station, with dozens of subtle variations of each. Having taken Hudson Street the previous day and the avenues to the east of Route 9 the day before, Joe decided on the central residential route as the day's thoroughfare. After traveling toward the Hudson on Price Street, he turned right onto Ash, traveling smoothly north through consecutively wealthier neighborhoods until he came to Oak Street, the tree-lined boulevard at the center of Sunnyside's most affluent section.

Halfway down the street, Joe noted suspicious activity at the house to his left. Alerted into acute observation, questions began to click in his mind, one after the other. As he slowly approached number eight, he noticed four unusual vehicles by the dwelling. It was the only single-story house on the street, shaped like a backwards "L," with its three-car garage, extending out toward the street, forming the short leg of the letter. Joe was well aware it was Victor Bonnelli's house, but like the other officers at the Sunnyside station, he had never had any problems with the "reputed mob boss." Bonnelli stories were occasionally bandied about, but not one had been sited in Sunnyside. It was as if the town was the mobster's quiet oasis in the vast desert of his heinous enterprises. Up to today.

As he had driven by the residence many times in the course of his work and commutes, Joe knew all of the vehicles that frequented the house: Bonnelli's long limousines, the dark sedans of his visitors, the often-present contractor's trucks, and the small compacts of his help. The vehicles parked at the house now were new, somehow ominous. One sedan was at curbside and two other identical vehicles were parked near the house on the circular driveway, one to the front and another behind a large van. They were not the vehicles of the town police, the county sheriff's office, the New York State Police, or even the FBI, whose vehicles Joe had become familiar with the previous year.

Then the big red flag went up. One of the two men visible by the front door to the house had a drawn pistol. Never, ever had a gun been seen at the Bonnelli house; the old-timers at the station had especially commented about that. Something was up. He glided past the house and parked at the curb on the opposite side of the street after the three vehicles in the driveway were obscured by the garage. He jumped out of the Nissan and walked at a quick pace toward the house of Bonnelli's nearest neighbor to the north. In response to his ring, a feisty woman in her mid-seventies appeared at the door. Although he did not know before that moment who lived in the large Victorian, he immediately recognized the Widow Jackson.

"Mrs. Jackson," Joe said, his nylon badge case already out. "I'm Joe Hanlon, a local policeman. I was driving by and noticed that there seems to be something odd going on next door."

"So after all these years, the expected trouble," she said. "When the Bonnelli's moved in, everybody said that nothing good would come of it. Two families on the street even moved, but Horace and I stayed. For years, they were ideal neighbors; we hardly saw them at all. I guess it had to end sometime."

"Yes, ma'am," Joe said, impatience edging on his nervousness. "I'm on my way over to take a look. Would you please call my station and ask them to send over a car?"

Of course she would call, at once. Joe hastily thanked her and slipped to the south, removing his pistol from its holster as he moved. The mobster's large ranch was blind on its northern gable end, a featureless wall of brick, as was the rear of the garage. Dodging rhododendrons and lilacs, he scaled the four-foot high property line wall and maneuvered across the grass to the back corner of the house, gun at the ready.

He rounded the corner warily, his view partially obscured by shrubs. He found himself near a window and those same shrubs protected him from being seen by several people inside the house. It must be the master bedroom, Joe thought as he gazed into the huge interior space. The bed, bigger than king size, was on the wall opposite the window, facing out toward the Hudson. There were four people in the room—no, five, one being deceased on the bed. At least he had better be dead, Joe observed, because the man was lying in an unzipped bag of thick, black plastic. Two of the others were attending to the corpse and one was taking pictures. The remaining man, the only one with a gun, was at ease, taking in the room's decor.

Joe relaxed a little, but still kept a firm grip on his weapon. It was obviously a crime scene, the living men obviously police investigators of some breed. But from where? As he watched the three men and one woman at work, his certainty as to the purpose of the group evaporated. None of them wore gloves or shoe coverings. No fingerprints were being taken and no detailed search seemed to be underway. The samples they took were strange, too. One man took a razor knife and cut a six-inch square chunk out of the rug, then attacked the wall by the bed, coming away with a similar sized piece of drywall. Another man took three plastic vials into the adjacent large bathroom. He emerged a short time later, his three tubes filled. Sink water, tub water, toilet water, Joe surmised, but could not be sure. This is no crime scene, he thought, it's somebody's parody of an investigation, worse than a poorly produced TV cop show.

The situation degraded from the strange to the surreal. Because of his vantage point, Joe saw the dark lump first, far under the bed. Moments later, it was discovered by a man performing a closer inspection of the floor. As he retrieved the object, a dead black cat, his expression was one of annoyance, as if it was inconvenient to find the obviously important, perhaps vital, clue. Joe could not hear any sound through the triple-paned window, but after a short conversation between one of the unarmed men and the woman, the man holding the deceased, stiff cat placed it on the stomach of the corpse on the bed, then zipped up the body bag with man and beast inside. Momentarily paralyzed with disbelief at the bizarre techniques of the investigators, Joe's lack of motion probably saved his life.

"Move and you are dead," the voice came from behind Joe, calm and explicit and with an authority that indicated that the person meant every one of the five words. Although he did not see the man, Joe caught a peripheral glimpse of three inches of blue steel pointing at a spot directly behind his left ear.

Joe did not move.

"Drop the gun," the voice said in the same tone.

Joe opened his hand and his pistol fell three feet to the ivy ground cover.

Following other curt directions, Joe put his hands on his head and walked toward the back patio. Behind him, he heard the man pick up his gun and follow him closely.

"Halt," commanded the voice.

"I'm a police officer," Joe ventured after stopping just short of the patio.

"Pull out your identification—very slowly." The voice had softened, ever so slightly.

Joe reached into his jacket pocket and retrieved his badge, holding its case in the air just above head level. The man walked around him. It was an unhappy Philip Roberts who met Joe's nervous gaze, his jaw clenched and deep wrinkles in his brow.

Roberts took the identification, verified it, then ordered Joe to enter the house.

"Can I put my hands down?"

"Wait," Roberts said. He opened one of the large sliding doors to the house and Joe entered first.

"Who is that?" a woman asked from across the large room.

"Local cop. Name's . . . Joseph Hanlon," Roberts said, reading the ID card next to the badge. "Sunnyside Police."

"But we took care of those yokels."

"Well, we obviously weren't as thorough as we should have been. Get Morrow from the bedroom, then both of you walk the perimeter of the house. Then stay out there and cover the rear of this barn. I don't want any more surprises."

"Okay, Phil," Sandra Haines replied.

"Kauffman!" Roberts shouted, then waited until Eric Kauffman appeared in the front hall. "Take this guy and put him with the others. He's a cop, so you don't have to cuff him, just keep him out of the way. I'll deal with him later."

"You heard him," Kauffman said to Joe. Gesturing toward the foyer, he simply ordered, "Go."

They went up the hallway toward the front door, past the largest grandfather clock Joe had ever seen, then turned right through an archway near the double front entry doors and entered the cavernous living room.

"Put your hands down and sit there," Kauffman stated, pointing to the closest white leather chair.

There were two other people in the room, one man seated in a chair similar to Joe's, handcuffed to a substantial end table, and one woman, perhaps a cook or housekeeper. Although the woman was teary-eyed and trembling, Joe noticed the man appeared to be even more shaken. He had never seen such a hauntingly frightened expression.

The trio sat and waited, and Joe observed, especially the activity in and just beyond the foyer. He counted eight people from the group of visitors in two distinct categories. All of the first type were armed and intense, obviously focused on security. Members of the other group acted as if they were engaged in some kind of scientific field study.

Joe picked up snippets of conversation as his captors went about their work. "When these things get to Pope we need to. . ." he caught as two of the science types walked out of the house. "Looks like things went okay at Albany," he barely heard from the kitchen. "I'm going to get the blood samples for Dr. Z," a thin, bespectacled man told Kauffman.

"Who are you guys?" Joe asked his guard, attempting to open a dialogue.

The reply was simply "FBI," but the agent somehow did not sound convincing.

"I know a couple of guys at your White Plains office."

"We're not from there," he stated with finality, then turned his back.

No shit.

The body bag containing the remains of Victor Bonnelli was finally wheeled out of the house on a hospital-style gurney. As it passed, Joe noticed the slight bulge from the unwanted cat.

Five minutes later, there was an angry confrontation at the front door. Two men, one impeccably dressed with distinguished, graying hair, the other in his thirties and disheveled, forced their way into the house. Kauffman barred them from advancing past the foyer. "Mr. Roberts," he called over his shoulder in the direction of the sunroom. "We got visitors."

"What the fuck is this, a fucking invasion?" screamed the younger intruder, arms waving.

Joining the group was the same mesomorph that had almost blown Joe's head off at the corner of the house. Roberts.

The older visitor addressed the younger. "Nicholas, please calm down. We will get to the bottom of this right now." Facing Roberts, he stated, "I am Andrew Weiss, an attorney representing Mr. Victor Bonnelli. This is his son. I received a call about dawn concerning a mishap of some kind, so we drove up from New York."

"We're from the FBI," Roberts stated. "As part of an investigation looking into Mr. Bonnelli's business affairs, we monitored that call and came to provide assistance."

"And what 'assistance' have you provided?" Weiss asked.

"Unfortunately, when we arrived, we found Mr. Bonnelli dead in his bedroom. Although we did not find any indication of foul play, we are at present treating this case as a possible murder." Roberts sounded as if he was reading from a script.

"Bastards, you fucking bastards!" Nicholas screamed, fists raised and clenched.

"Nicholas, please have a seat in the living room. Please," Weiss said, putting a calming hand on one of his shoulders.

Violently shrugging off the gesture, Nicky reluctantly entered the living room. Marc Grunner tried to stand, but was unable to achieve an upright position because of the handcuffs that attached him to the heavy end table. "Mr. Bonnelli . . ." he began, quavering.

"You fucker!" Nicky screamed as he sighted Grunner. Taking four quick steps, he made his way to the bodyguard, shoving the man with both hands and sending him staggering back awkwardly. "What the fuck were you doing?"

Kauffman joined the fray. After pulling the men apart, he forced Nicky into a chair in the far corner.

The fracas over, Roberts and Weiss resumed their conversation. "Where is Mr. Bonnelli now?" Weiss asked.

"As part of our investigation, the body has been taken for examination." Again, there was a rehearsed quality to Roberts' statement.

Weiss, obviously not buying it, assumed his best aggressive courtroom stance. "I want to see your wiretap authorization, your search warrant, and any other documentation you might have pertaining to this case."

"Mr. Weiss, we are in the middle of an important investigation. Your requests will have to be addressed at a later time," Roberts countered.

"That is totally unacceptable," Weiss replied.

"Kauffman," Roberts commanded. "Remove all of these people

from the crime scene."

After releasing Grunner, Kauffman brandished his gun and ordered the five interlopers out of the house. Although Nicholas Bonnelli was red-faced with rage, it was Weiss who voiced the loudest protest. "This is completely illegal," he almost shouted as he was ushered out the door. "I'll have all of your stinking badges for this."

Kauffman walked outside with the group while Roberts watched from the doorway. "You can go; take the day off," Kauffman suggested to the cook. She glanced nervously at Weiss, who was, given the almost catatonic state of Nicky, the de facto leader of the Bonnelli family. He nodded his assent and she walked off in the direction of her car.

Weiss eyed Joe curiously. "Who are you?" he asked.

"Joe Hanlon, Sunnyside Police."

"Enough with the chit chat," Kauffman said impatiently. "Mr. Policeman, you stay here. I think the rest of you should get in that big limo over there and drive back to New York. Tomorrow might be a good time to return."

As the trio retreated, Roberts addressed his lieutenant. "Eric, take Mr. Hanlon here to his place of work. There you may return this to him," he said, passing over Joe's pistol. "Then straighten out those local cops. I know the word went out to them to keep clear of this entire street, and here I find one of their so-called officers right up at the house, sneaking around with his gun hanging out."

"Will do, Nick," Kauffman said, then turned to Joe. "Let's go; the front car."

"How about my ID?" Joe inquired.

"Here, take it," Roberts said with a sneer as he reached into his pocket and retrieved Joe's identification, putting his thumb irreverently on the badge as he handed it over.

Kauffman escorted Joe to the sedan parked in front of the van. Joe occupied the passenger's seat, and found himself facing some of the most sophisticated communications equipment he had ever seen.

As they pulled out of the driveway, Joe gave the agent directions to the Sunnyside Police Station. The route he described was not the most direct means to his office, however, it was the way he had originally planned to take that morning.

CHAPTER 3

Dynamically passionate about his vocation, Anthony Dempsey believed, like a Christian fundamentalist is certain of his God, that he had the best job on Earth. Today, however, though the foundation of his faith was not shaken, he had to constantly remind himself of his tenet. He had been awake since before three A.M., and had been in his office since four. Although he accepted late night calls as part of his job, the call commanding him to work on this particular morning was different. On all other occasions during his seventeen-year career, calls in the middle of the night were summonses to action, but the 2:46 call that had roused him was explicit in demanding inaction by himself and the people who worked for him.

Frowning for the forty-eighth time that day, he unknowingly exceeded his personal record for a six-hour period. Normally, he was as gregarious as he was large, and at six-three he mashed the scales at two hundred eighty pounds. He made even more of an impression in his work clothing, a police uniform adorned with a Sunnyside patch on a shoulder and the chief's badge on a pocket. He was respected by almost everyone in the small town in which he evenly supervised the enforcement of laws, but sometimes it was one of the "almosts" that could temporarily override all others. That morning it had been the grating voice of Kevin Chandler, town councilman and real estate schemer, that had provided Dempsey's wakeup call.

Four years before, after making a ghetto out of two blocks of downtown Tarrytown, a small city just north of Sunnyside, Chandler had moved into Dempsey's village to escape the blight of his own making. The year after, he announced his candidacy for a seat on the town council and, to the shock of everyone involved in the orderly running of the town, he won, primarily because his opponent suffered a near-fatal injury and withdrew from the race two weeks before the election.

It had been Dempsey's prediction that Chandler would immediately attempt to use his new position to thwart the laws of the town and move his slumlording operations to Sunnyside, but the man proved to be a far slicker operator. For almost a year, Chandler played the part of a model official, nurturing friendships and glad-handing everyone in sight. Ten months later, though, the true motives behind his public service façade were revealed. With an unknown partner, he purchased a vacant warehouse on Sunnyside's Hudson River waterfront and quietly proposed to clear the land and build high-rise condominiums. After a series of closed-door negotiations with his friends on the town council and an influx of funding from sources unknown, he was presently in the midst of seeing his plan fulfilled.

It was not Chandler the real estate mogul or Chandler the smooth politician who had made the early morning call to Chief of Police Dempsey, however, it was Chandler the very shaken man. Though he attempted to sound authoritarian, the policeman could tell the councilman was terrified as he told Dempsey to keep his people as far away from Oak Street as possible during the remainder of the day. Realizing immediately what resident of that street had promulgated the strange order, he pressed Chandler for more information. Confirming the suspicions in a quavering voice, Chandler told him there was going to be a raid on the Bonnelli house and that the FBI agents involved in the operation were insistent that there be no local interference, that they did not want to *see* a police cruiser during their entire short stay in Sunnyside.

Reluctantly, Dempsey had assented to the temporary jurisdictional change, and after hanging up the phone proceeded to the station to carry out his orders. On the short drive to work, he reflected on the circumstances surrounding the strange request. For one thing, Chandler's tone seemed to give credence to the rumor that Bonnelli was more than the developer's golfing partner and that the FBI knew it. The foray into Sunnyside would also mark the first time, to Dempsey's knowledge, that law enforcement officials would set foot inside the Bonnelli residence. Even when Bonnelli had been indicted based on evidence gleaned by the FBI's New York City office, he had been allowed to surrender himself after a limousine ride to Manhattan.

Dempsey frowned again. Although he had immediately put the word out to keep off Oak Street to the two-man night shift when he arrived at the station, and had informed his dispatcher and six other officers as they arrived for work, he had apparently failed in his directive. For some reason, the star of his force was on Oak Street and, according to the call from the Widow Jackson he had taken half an hour earlier, at the precise place he shouldn't be.

When they met three years before at an interview for an opening on the Sunnyside force, Joe Hanlon had immediately impressed Dempsey. Not quite a fresh-faced college kid, although he had received a law enforcement degree less than two months before, he was also not hampered by experiences in the NYPD, as were many of the nearly burnt-out cops looking for a change who applied for the entry-level position. Although Hanlon's resume was thin, basically indicating three years of Army service followed by college, Dempsey sensed there was some collection of hidden qualities within the affable young man. His supposition was verified when he called but one of Hanlon's references, a Colonel David Powers, who had been Joe's commanding officer. Powers not only gave Dempsey a glowing recommendation, but also stated Joe had earned the Distinguished Service Cross and the Purple Heart in an action overseas that left him severely wounded. Astonished that not only had Joe been awarded such impressive decorations but had made no mention of the fact either on his resume or during the interview, Dempsey decided the quiet man of action, a true hero, would make a superb asset to his team. He had never been disappointed.

Though the best marksman on the force, Joe had never fired his gun at a suspect while on duty. He was not on duty, however, the previous hot summer week when he stumbled onto a situation so bizarre that Dempsey still shook his head in astonishment over it. Because Joe and he were the only ones on the force who knew the details of the Saratoga affair, Dempsey took an extraordinary amount of heat the previous November when he passed over six other officers and appointed Joe to the position of department detective. It wasn't that Joe was disliked—the opposite was true—but, it was repeatedly pointed out, seniority ruled. Except in this case, Dempsey vowed, then proceeded to make it stick.

Now angry, but only with himself, Dempsey knew he should have called all of his people at home with the directive to stay clear of Oak Street, no matter what the hour. The damage had been done though, and he waited to learn of its extent. Calls to the New York and White Plains FBI offices had not yet been returned, and he elected not to aggravate his error by paying a visit the Bonnelli house himself, trusting Joe would not get himself into too much trouble before he was booted out of the area by the feds.

His intercom emitted a short buzz. "Chief, Joe Hanlon is coming in the front door," dispatcher Amy Sullivan said. "With a friend."

"Send them back," Dempsey requested. Moments later, two men entered the office.

"You're Dempsey?" the man with Joe asked sharply.

"Chief of Police Anthony Dempsey," he replied, extending a hand in greeting.

"Agent Eric Kauffman," the man stated, ignoring Dempsey's hand. "What kind of outfit do you run here? You were specifically ordered to keep your people away from our area of operations this morning, and here we find one of your cops at Bonnelli's house, sneaking around with his gun drawn."

"It was not the intention of the Sunnyside police to interfere in your operations in any way, Agent Kauffman. I took your instructions seriously and my people were being informed of your directive as they arrived for work this morning. Detective Hanlon was on his way from his home to the station when he stopped to investigate an unusual situation. Under the circumstances known to him, he did the correct thing. It was my error he was not called at home and I apologize for the inconvenience."

"I don't need to hear excuses. You are to stay completely clear of the block until we leave the area. Period."

"And when might you be leaving?" Dempsey inquired, barely maintaining his cool composure.

"About noon," Kauffman offered reluctantly. "I have to get back to the scene. I don't expect we'll be meeting again." The agent placed Joe's service revolver and badge case on Dempsey's desk, then exited the office.

The chief moved calmly around to the business end of his desk and slowly sat down. "Have a seat," he calmly requested of Joe.

"Chief, I'm sorry."

"The mistake was mine, just as I told Kauffman. You should have been called at home and made aware of our strange instructions. We'll get through this, though, and soon the only mention of the episode will be in my memoirs, *The Encyclopedia of Stupid Things I Have Said and Done.* Right now I'm on Volume 1: Aa through Ac."

They both smiled, the first time for each of them that day.

"What's up at Bonnelli's?" Dempsey asked.

"As I was driving up Oak, I saw four unfamiliar vehicles in front of the house. There were two men by the front door, and one of them had his gun out. I stopped to investigate."

"So, assuming at least a driver and passenger in each vehicle, you went alone into a situation to potentially face eight armed men at the home of one of the country's most notorious Mafia dons?"

"Er—yes, but my aim was just to do a little recon before backup arrived."

"What did you find out?"

"According to what I overheard after being detained, the feds had a wiretap operation going on. They moved in after they monitored an early morning call from the bodyguard at the house to Bonnelli's lawyer with the news that the mobster had died in his sleep sometime during the night."

"Victor Bonnelli dead; that's some news," Dempsey said, settling back in his chair. "And on the morning the FBI was planning to finally make its move against the mob boss here in Sunnyside."

"Perhaps it was just an incident in a long investigation, with Bonnelli's death coming in the middle of it," Joe ventured, as suspicious of coincidences as his boss.

"Did you catch what time the call from the bodyguard was made?"

"About dawn, the lawyer said."

"My call concerning the impending raid from our esteemed Councilman Chandler came about three in the morning. Something was definitely planned for today, dead Bonnelli or no. From everything I've heard about the man, suicide can be ruled out, so it seems either Bonnelli was murdered, or the one in a thousand event took place and he died of natural causes just a few hours before he was to be taken into custody. I don't need to tell you I don't like those odds."

"You can probably square those odds because Bonnelli's cat decided to die last night too, right under the bed. Maybe they died of poison, some type of airborne agent in the house. The bodyguard didn't seem to be affected, though."

"Whatever happened, it has been made clear that we are not involved. I'm sure the FBI will solve the mystery."

"I'm not so sure they will and I'm not sure those agents are from the FBI," Joe said in a low tone.

Dempsey sat up. "That's a statement that needs some clarification."

"For one thing, they all wore the common, dark blue windbreakers, but the only lettering on them stating they were FBI was on the front in letters about two inches high, too small to seen from any distance. I've never seen that before; it was as if they were deliberately trying to maintain a low profile."

"Go on," Dempsey urged.

"I had a chance to observe the investigative techniques of the supposed agents through the window of the master bedroom, and they were bizarre, to say the least. Although some of them appeared to be forensic specialists, they didn't wear gloves or take fingerprints. When one of them found the dead cat under the bed, it was treated as an inconvenience. They put the damned thing into the body bag with Bonnelli's corpse before it was zipped up."

"That's outrageous," the chief said, leaning forward to hear more.

"After I was discovered by their agent-in-charge, a guy named Roberts, I was detained in the living room of the house near the front door. Since this was a big mob investigation, I figured I'd see evidence being confiscated, but in the time I sat there, I saw no sign of files, cabinets, computer disks, or anything else of that nature leaving the house. The eight or ten people involved seemed interested in only one thing, and that was Bonnelli. Dead."

"Joe, you've intrigued me. I'm not convinced anything is amiss, but I want you to try to find out where these guys are from and what their mission is in my town. I know you gained a few friends over at the FBI in White Plains last year. Quietly make some inquiries and give me a report tomorrow. I did verify that there is an official investigation of some sort going on, so we will continue to follow our instructions to stay off Oak Street."

Joe rose from his seat. "Okay, Chief. Again, I'm sorry for all the trouble."

"Trouble? With our most notorious resident moving on to his ultimate reward and a minor mystery to be solved, this day might not turn out to be so bad after all. But from now on, in your lone confrontations with armed men, try to draw the line at four or five adversaries."

"I'll try, Chief, but sometimes it's tough to tell unless I go in and count them."

After nine months of mental recovery, Special Agent Richard Tobin was finally settled back into his life and his career, working regular hours out of the offices of the Federal Bureau of Investigation in the White Plains Federal Building. It was pleasant, not being shot at by various individuals of evil intent and to be finally free of the nightmares that had plagued him since the previous July. Sitting before him now, though, was the most tangible reminder of those incidents best forgotten. Although his indebtedness to and friendship with Joe Hanlon was absolute, the shadow of terror still lurked at the periphery of their relationship.

"So I was escorted to the station by this agent and Chief Dempsey asked me to quietly look into the strange goings-on," Joe said, completing his summary of his experiences that morning. "Do you know anything about it?"

"More than I want to know, Joe," Tobin began. "It's the damndest thing that's ever happened here—inside these offices, at least. What you might call the advance team invaded our quiet sanctum on Monday afternoon. There were two of them, a woman named Haines and an Agent Kauffman, whom you've met. They presented some kind of documentation to Oscar Ottoway, our new supervisor, then with his blessing kicked Carol Kowalesky out of her office, three doors down the hall. The word from Ottoway to the rest of us concerning our guests was an emphatic hands off, no further explanation provided."

"You had no idea what they were doing here?"

"I gathered they were here on a temporary basis to conduct a raid of some kind, but I didn't learn anything specific. The extent of the operation became more apparent on Tuesday, when the two outsiders were joined by about six other agents, including the supervisor of the group, a guy named Philip Roberts."

"We met," Joe said. "He's the one who came damn close to blowing my head off at the corner of the house."

"Well he wasn't much friendlier with me. Typical of every member of his group, the most I ever got out of him was a grunt when we passed in the hallway. These guys had no sense of camaraderie. They worked here a few hours on Tuesday and all day yesterday. As I was leaving last night, they were in the midst of a lengthy closed-door conference. When I came in this morning their absence was pleasantly noted."

"So they're out of here?"

"Probably not. Ottoway informed us that their lease on Kowalesky's office doesn't expire until the end of the week."

"Has it occurred to your boss he might be renting space to people who are not part of the FBI?"

"When I mentioned the possibility to Ottoway, I received a thorough ass chewing in return. Noninterference is the directive, no matter where they're from, but you raise a good point. Roberts and his crew could be part of some covert FBI Delta Force, but they could just as well be working for the CIA, the IRS, or some black government agency like the kind you read about in conspiracy novels. Got any ideas?"

"On the way over here, something did cross my mind," Joe said. "Bonnelli was involved in drugs in a big way, and probably had many international ties. Maybe the CIA learned of a plot by some foreign drug czar to take Bonnelli out, and they sent up a squad of their agents to monitor the hit, but not to interfere with it."

"That's possible, I suppose. Allowing some foreign thugs to enter the country to liquidate a citizen in his home is the type of thing the CIA would keep under tight wraps. Hell, if it's something like that, they even aided them by keeping the local law and the real FBI out of the area. Then to cover up the crime they cart the body away and explain the death as being from natural causes, perhaps taking care of the murderers later on in their own inimitable way. It's a good place to start, anyway."

"Start? You mean you're going to look into the case?" Joe asked hopefully.

"Don't take my words so literally," Tobin responded, exposing his right palm. "There is no case, and it's not my place to initiate an investigation, especially one that targets a federal agency. Any agent who thinks otherwise has a disease that is terminal to his career. I'll continue to act as I have, a passive observer to the strange comings and goings of these visitors; I'll call you if I see anything interesting."

"You know I can keep secrets."

"I surely do," Tobin replied as images of the most terrifying week of his life briefly flashed through his mind. "But my advice is to forget it. Whatever happened is over, or close to it. There might only be trouble waiting if you pursue this."

"Maybe you're right," Joe said as he stood up slowly from his chair, favoring his right side. "Still, it's an interesting mystery."

"How's your leg?" Tobin inquired.

"Better, but it still bothers me from time to time."

"Take care of yourself; I'll be calling you. And don't wait until Christmas to come up and have dinner with the family."

"I won't, Rich. Talk to you later," Joe said as he left the small office and headed toward the stairs, away from Eric Kauffman, who was watching him intently from a doorway down the hall.

Consisting of over ten thousand acres, Stewart International Airport was, in land area, the largest airport in the Northeast and featured one of the world's longest runways. The airport was home to the 23rd Wing of the New York Air National Guard, the members of which were responsible for eight of the world's second-largest aircraft, the C-5B. Nearly as long as a football field and capable of transporting a payload of a quarter of a million pounds, the C-5B was a record breaker in more ways than one, as the contractor that built the huge planes overran the original two billion-dollar budget by nearly three billion dollars.

After crossing the Hudson River at the Tappan Zee Bridge, just north of Sunnyside, the four-vehicle convoy made the trip up the New York State Thruway to the Newburgh exit in less than two hours. In formation, it sped along a three-mile stretch of Route 17K and turned into Stewart at an infrequently used gate, held open by a reluctant reservist detailed to the task. The sedans and the van quickly traversed the open plain of grass and concrete to the C-5B awaiting them. Not at all hidden, the behemoth plane was nonetheless inconspicuous among its eight sister ships of the New York Guard.

The convoy split and the van and two sedans drove up the open ramp into the mammoth interior of the airship while the remaining Pontiac came to rest a hundred feet from the fuselage, close to the tip of the plane's left wing.

The lone occupant of the land-bound car exited the vehicle and waited patiently. As the airplane's ramp closed, a female figure appeared at the passenger hatch.

With determined haste, the woman descended the access steps and walked over to the man. "All vehicles and personnel are secured," Sandra Haines said. "The pilot says skies are clear all the way down; we'll be leaving in five minutes."

"You look tense, Sandy," Philip Roberts replied. "Try to relax over the next three hours; they'll be enough to worry about after you land."

"I wish you'd reconsider your decision, Phil," Haines said, the chill wind rippling through her short black hair. "You know I'm capable of handling the tail jobs here; I've done it before, and it's in the plan. I don't see any reason to change the mission parameters at this late stage."

Roberts turned his back against the brisk breeze whipping across the tarmac. "If I didn't have every confidence in you, Sandy, you wouldn't even be a part of this team, to say nothing of my second in command, but I have to be where I think I'm needed most, and right now that's here. I know your keen instincts played a big part in your successes when you were with the Secret Service, and now I'm asking you to trust my intuition about this case."

"Something wrong?"

"Specifically, no; everything has played out well, but some minor points seem just a little askew. I have the feeling there might be a little more work to do up here than we figured. But that's what intuition is all about, isn't it?" he asked Haines rhetorically, offering her a closed-mouth, crooked smile.

"The cop?"

"He was just a minor annoyance, although we need to pay more attention to site security on future missions. No, I'm worried about the mob lawyer, Weiss, and Bonnelli's heir, that wild cokehead. In different ways, they each came on a little too strong." Behind the agents, the four huge turbofans of the transport began to whine. "Looks like your taxi is about to leave. I'm counting on you to deliver our package and take charge of things until Eric and I return. I hope to be back tomorrow evening; I hate it when missions cut into the weekend."

"Okay, Phil," Haines replied above the growing swell of the engines. "Take care."

"As always," he nearly shouted at her back as she strode back to the airplane. Within five minutes, the twenty-four tires of the Galaxy, nicknamed "Moby Jet," began to roll toward the runway. A few minutes later, when the plane was just a dot in the clear afternoon sky, he entered his vehicle and picked up his phone. Seemingly at his touch, the device buzzed, indicating an incoming call.

"What is it?" he answered.

"Phil, are you at the airport yet?" Eric Kauffman queried.

"Yes. The flight just left and I'm starting back now."

"We have a problem."

CHAPTER 4

"**I**n fact, prior to this morning, I had had no previous opportunity to enter the residence of Victor Bonnelli." Detective Joseph Hanlon entered the words on his computer keyboard, stared disgustedly at the monitor, then deleted the sentence that comprised the totality of his report to Chief Anthony Dempsey concerning his early morning adventures. Though he knew it to be technically acceptable writing, the double use of the word "had" had always struck him as awkward.

"There he is," boomed Michael Overton, the rugged face of Sunnyside's oldest policeman simultaneously appearing around one of the gray partitions that made up Joe's small back office. "Joe Hanlon: Dragonslayer." In low tones, word of Bonnelli had obviously made its way around the station, ending up with the affable but not-so-quiet Overton.

Joe allowed himself a tight-lipped smile. "Not this time, Mike. Today, I was only a simple peasant who unwittingly stumbled upon a group of royal wizard-coroners attending to the corpse of the dragon."

Overton settled himself into the chair next to the desk. "And they were pissed?"

"I think if they had had their way, I would have been immediately beheaded," Joe replied, suppressing a wince at the verbalization of the same mistake he had just eliminated from his computer.

"Those feds can be tough, especially with something that's as high profile as this. So he's really dead?"

Joe eased back in his chair, dismissing his lingering doubts that the occurrences of the morning had been an elaborate ruse, a choreographed production to whisk Bonnelli off to incarceration, or even protection. "He's dead. Let's hope there's nobody out there to replace him."

"Come now, young pup! The line of scum itching to sink their claws into even a small piece of Bonnelli's organization wouldn't fit on the Tappan Zee Bridge, and you know it. The best we can hope for is that none of them chooses our fair village to live in. Bonnelli may not have ever caused trouble around here, but I am glad he's gone. He has a son, I hear, but let's hope our small community doesn't fit his lifestyle. I don't know that he's ever been up here."

"The little psycho was at the house this morning," Joe said. "It didn't seem he would fit in here."

"Not one to keep a low profile?"

"If he moves to Sunnyside, I can see a substantial increase in our workload."

"Maybe we need a little more action around this sleepy burg," said a grinning Russell Mullin as he joined the men. In his early thirties and outfitted in an impeccably tailored uniform, Mullin was one of the Sunnyside force's more recent acquisitions from the NYPD, strongarmed by his wife into seeking employment up the Hudson after hearing one too many graphic tales of derring-do.

"Yes, Russ," Overton said sardonically, not turning toward the interloper. "More action. That's what we live for."

"Well something is obviously needed to wake up our tight-assed town fathers," Mullin said seriously. "I'm tired of the petty bullshit that goes on every time our force and money are mentioned in the same breath. A little more criminal activity might just shake loose enough change to replace equipment that can't be seen anywhere else except *Adam-12* reruns and get the station moved to a building that doesn't have the novelty of having three 'eights' in its cornerstone. I know my views don't exactly toe the company line around here, but what has garnered this department the most publicity over the last three months? The Gloria Strong case. What a fucking joke."

"What kind of joke?" Joe asked, exchanging the briefest of glances with a grinning Overton. The older man had seen it before and had understood without explanation Joe's subtle goosing of that one element of vacuous speech.

"Huh?" mouthed Mullin. Along with similar utterances, repeating the statement, and ignoring the question, it was one of the standard replies. Joe had never received a sensible answer to his queries concerning the employ of the universal adjective of the lexically impaired.

"Gloria Strong has finally been overshadowed," Overton said, turning toward Mullin. "I guess you haven't heard what happened over on Oak Street this morning."

"Yeah, what kind of shit was that? The first thing this morning I get this order to keep away from there. What goes?"

"You won't be happy, Russ," Overton said. "Our village's criminal population was reduced this A.M. The FBI carted away Vic Bonnelli."

"Christ," uttered Mullin, then recovered quickly. "He'll be back. I followed Bonnelli's activities for years down in New York, even had some personal confrontations with a few of his goons, but his organization is so layered that we never got close to the Man himself. That guy is slippery as an eel."

"He'll have a tough time wriggling out of his current predicament," Overton replied. "The feds took him away in a hearse."

"You are shit-ting me," Mullin exclaimed, his astonishment returning in force.

"Ask Joe," Overton said as he gestured across the desk with a broad sweep of his arm. "He was there."

Frowning, contemplating the plane of his desk, Joe could feel Mullin's amazed, envious glare upon him. The surveillance van at the mobster's house—it was a hearse, he realized with a start. Packed as those types of vehicles normally were with all manner of electronic marvels, no undercover van he had ever seen had been spacious enough to provide much comfort to its living occupants, much less be commodious enough to accommodate a recumbent corpse on a wheeled stretcher. And it couldn't have been standard procedure—even for the FBI—to mount a surveillance effort with a bulky gurney, completely accessorized with a body bag, could it?

"What the hell happened?" demanded Mullin, snapping the detective out of his reverie. "Was there a gunfight?"

"It wasn't anything like that, Russ," Joe related. "It was all very quiet. Bonnelli apparently died in his sleep last night, spoiling plans to apprehend him."

"Shit," exhaled Mullin. "Why didn't we hear about this raid earlier? How'd you get detailed to represent us at the site?"

"The first one to hear from our federal friends was the chief, whose instructions were to keep *all* of us out of the area," Joe said. "Apparently, everyone got the word but me; I stopped to investigate the activity at Bonnelli's on my way to the station."

"What went down?"

"I didn't see much," Joe sidestepped, not anxious at that point of the investigation to go into the details of his encounter with anyone but Dempsey. "They hustled me out pretty quick."

"So the chief's fair-haired boy is in trouble?" Mullin asked, following his question with a thin smile.

"Less trouble than you were in after you shoved your gun in the face of that eighty-year-old shoplifter," Overton said in a voice two notches higher than his normal conversational tone.

Mullin shifted thirty degrees and faced his challenger. "Hey, who knows these days? She could have been armed."

"Yeah, with a loaded salami," Overton muttered.

"Excuse me, fellas," Joe interrupted. "Take it outside. I have to write a report, and I've yet to put down word one."

"Okay, Joe," Overton said. Buoyed by the lively deliberations, he fairly leaped out of the chair. "Let's go, Howard Hunter." He urged his fellow patrolman through the gap in the partitions that substituted for an office door. "I happen to know our friend has been tasked to coordinate the support for the Memorial Day parade, and I'm sure he'll want to get to that immediately after he completes his current chore."

"Thanks for the news," Joe said as his co-workers beat a retreat. Shrugging off the thought of yet another additional duty, he positioned his computer keyboard dead center on his desktop and began to pound the keys.

"Prior to this morning, I had never had the opportunity to enter the residence of Victor Bonnelli. . . ."

"The fuckers are all over the fucking place. What the fuck am I supposed to do?" demanded the voice of Nicholas Bonnelli.

"Nick, please calm down. Like it or not, representatives of the media have a right to be on the sidewalk outside your building, but you don't have to talk to them. Please pull your men inside and lock the doors. Roughing up reporters in broad daylight and with cameras rolling certainly can't help matters, and might give the authorities an excuse to enter your offices. Stay where you are and take it easy. Lie on the couch and turn on the TV. I'll be over as soon as I can break away."

"You fucking better be," said the now-eldest Bonnelli, not at all sounding as if he was about to recline on his workplace sofa and take in some tube. A rough click terminated the conversation.

Andrew Weiss was alone in his office, larger than the footprint of a Levittown tract home, with a striking view of Manhattan through the window wall behind him. Telephone receiver still in hand, he pressed the intercom button. "Sheila, please ask Karl Kastner to come see me," he said.

The lawyer eased back in his chair and contemplated the vast teak plain of his desk. It was bunk, he thought, the oft-told fable that Alexander the Great, having conquered the known world, died largely due to a lack of new challenges. At his death, Alexander had more plans for the expansion of his empire than he had victories behind him. So it was with Bonnelli. Although twice as old as Alexander at his death, the mobster had died in his prime, quietly conducting grand campaigns of expansion and implementing far-reaching schemes of consolidation while giving the appearance he was content in semi-retirement. Perhaps he didn't think he would live forever, but the main trouble for those left behind was that, like Alexander, Victor Bonnelli thought he would be around for a much longer time than he was, and died without anything resembling a competent heir. The mob version of the Wars of the Diadochi was about to begin.

Twenty feet in front of Weiss's desk, the door opened and a young man entered. Sporting wire-framed glasses and an ultraconservative three-piece suit, Karl Kapral Kastner was an intelligent and innovative flexor of the law, one of the rising stars in the firm of Weiss and Associates. He eased the door closed and approached his mentor.

"Karl, you know our problem," Weiss began. "Things are going to be—interesting around here for the next few weeks as we confront the changes that will take place because of Bonnelli's death. I hope you don't have any plans for your nights and weekends over the next month."

The young lawyer stood in front of the desk, heels together. "My plans are to be right here, Mr. Weiss," he replied.

"Right now, I need someone to go over to Bonnelli's building on Forty-first Street." Weiss looked straight into the unemotional eyes of his minion. "It's a mess down there, Karl. Somehow, the press learned of the death, and reporters have laid siege to the offices. Nicky is inside with a few of his men, and you know he is not generally a happy boy under the best of circumstances. The situation has to be diffused, fast."

"I'm your man," Kastner said flatly. "Any specific instructions?"

"I don't know what those reporters have learned, but I want you to make a statement. Tell them Bonnelli, a man advanced in years, quietly passed away in his sleep last night at his home Upstate, far away from the city. No big deal. Downplay it so much that they'll have to look in the gutter to find a story, which they no doubt will do, but at least you can quell the frenzy that exists there now. Take a few questions and give innocuous responses. If anyone asks you about the FBI being on the scene this morning, you don't know anything about that."

"FBI agents were in Sunnyside?"

"You don't know anything about that," Weiss repeated. "It might be nothing. I'll fill you in later if it's warranted."

"I will probably be asked about funeral arrangements."

"Plans have not yet been finalized. Period." Weiss winced slightly at the reminder of yet another of his many problems: locating and re-covering the corpse of Victor Bonnelli. "After you make it clear to those journalists that nothing more can be gained from hanging around the building, go in and gage the atmosphere around Nicky and his clan. Try to calm them down and strike up some conversation. I know you've defended Nicky at least twice, and there will probably be three or four others who you've sat beside at the defendant's table. They won't buddy up to you, but at least they'll accept you as a familiar face. Again, downplay it. Things will be fine; it will be business as usual in a few days." In other words, lie, Weiss didn't say.

"How long do you want me to stay?"

"I'll be over to see how things are faring in a few hours. The goal is to keep Nicky inside tonight, as incapacitated as possible. This is one night we don't need him to be out on the town, being his usual *fucking* self."

At the reference to the mobster's favorite word, Kastner's lips moved ever so slightly, briefly forming his unique version of a smile.

The older lawyer continued after a pause. "Make sure there's plenty of booze on hand, and order out for some whores if you think it might help." Catching a subtle, quizzical look in his employee's cold eyes, Weiss answered the unspoken question. "No, you don't have to go out in the street and arrange for the girls personally, just make the suggestion to the sanest-looking thug in the bunch. I'm sure every man there is skilled at handling that type of negotiation. Now get going."

Another crisis averted, Weiss thought as the click of the door latch signaled Kastner's departure. Maybe. With many more to come. The Bonnelli Empire was going to fall, as inevitably and completely as the empire of Alexander, the attorney thought. He realized his major ad-vantage in making the best of the situation was not that he was more knowledgeable about Bonnelli's diverse activities than any man alive, but that he was the first, by what would certainly be a very narrow margin, to foresee the unavoidable demise of the far-flung network of operations. Only for a moment did Weiss fantasize that he might be-come the next Bonnelli don, dismissing the notion after briefly consid-ering his lack of experience in the dirtier aspects of the business, the massive legal exposure, and his penchant for avoiding the prospect of being—did they still use the term?—rubbed out.

Weiss swiveled his chair through a half circle and took in the view of the great gray edifices beneath his feet. No, he recognized, his strat-egy could not involve an attempt to hold together the doomed empire, but to carve off the dying behemoth as many assets as he could. In this, Nicholas Bonnelli was the main impediment. The megalomaniacal Victor had largely ignored his son's business education, and because of this Nicky was not even the equivalent of a middle manager, but a kind of foreman, relegated to grunt work in several of Bonnelli's smaller enterprises. Being the sole legitimate issue from the loins of the mob boss, though, he was the official heir to the empire, and therein lay the problem. Nicholas had remained largely an unknown quantity to those who now mattered: the major officers of the various divisions, the family's allies, and its myriad, ruthless competitors. If they were to gain sudden knowledge of the lack of experience, character, and intellect of the new head of the Bonnelli family, however, Nicholas would be nothing but a bloody, bullet-ridden corpse within a day and his inheritance would disappear like a pile of dust in a gale, leaving the attorney with nothing but three tons of useless legal paperwork.

Assuming he could keep Nicky sequestered for a few days, Weiss shifted his thoughts to a more perplexing problem. He knew everything depended on his preparation for and conduct at the Funeral, the traditional Mafia linchpin between what was and what will be. Any meetings concerning transfers of power would be either preludes to or follow-ups from the Funeral, but in reviewing the countless details surrounding the event, one fact stood out, omniscient and annoying: the Funeral could not take place without the Body. Weiss swung back to his desk and punched a button on his telephone, activating an interoffice link.

"Yes, Mr. Weiss?" a middle-aged voice responded to his boss's distinctive signal.

"Scott, what's the latest on Bonnelli—his remains, I mean?"

"It has been four hours since I petitioned the District Court for the release of the body, but the judge has yet to respond. I have a man waiting on site, but I'm afraid writs of this nature do not warrant top priority." Simultaneously, both lawyers lamented the irony that habeas corpus did not apply when the person held was a true corpus.

"I need very good news on this by tomorrow morning at the latest," Weiss said.

"Understood."

"Anything new from the FBI?"

"I finally got through to the assistant special agent in charge down at Federal Plaza about an hour ago. After dropping some tantalizing facts concerning what happened at Sunnyside, I sensed surprise from him, although he tried to cover it. He then put me on hold for seven minutes; when he came back, he stated only that he could not comment on the case while it was still under investigation. Click. He might have been out of the loop on this one, but this guy is the number two man at the field office, and anything involving Bonnelli has to be a big deal down there. My gut says the agents you met this morning were not from New York, which means they were probably imports from Washington."

"You're probably right; there was something different about those guys," Weiss said. Hunched over his desk, he rubbed his forehead with three fingers.

"Everything else seems to make some kind of sense. The FBI conducts a surveillance operation on the house, as they have at least a dozen times, they monitor the call to you about the death, then seize the opportunity to 'help.' That's probably just the way it happened."

"Possibly," Weiss said, his headache worsening. "We'll talk about it more tomorrow morning. I'm going up to Sunnyside first thing to assess the damage. Be on hand for a meeting in my office when I get back. I might have some of Bonnelli's personal files to share, but I doubt it; I'm sure our friends were their usual thorough selves. And keep working on locating the body."

"Yes, sir," was the last thing Weiss heard before he terminated the call with his left forefinger. He pressed his shoulders back in his chair, the growing pain between his temples bringing forth the thought that it might be madness to attempt to control the dissolution of the empire, that at any point along the torturous path he could be stopped cold—as in the icy finality of his own cadaver cold—by any of scores of potential adversaries. Still, the notion did not deter him for a moment from the realization that he would have to see the situation through to the end. Pushed by the fact that both his practice and personal finances were in extreme jeopardy, Weiss was equally drawn by the opportunity to take advantage of his intimate knowledge of the network of enterprises painstakingly fashioned by the late mob boss.

Used to dealing with legal cases of extreme complexity, Weiss was nevertheless daunted by the delicate, precise choreography in which he had begun to engage. To be successful in his dance, he knew that when it was over, every one of the myriad characters encountered had to be left either satisfied or powerless.

———————

Even after months of working on the project, Elizabeth Brooks was still amazed that such garbage could generate so much money for so many. By any aesthetic standard, it was the worst real property she had ever brokered, but the transfer of the 472-unit mobile home park—Putnam County's largest agglomeration of trailers—was a lucrative deal for all involved. The sellers, a rough-hewn codger and his delicate bride of forty years, would be able to make a cash purchase of a retirement home in one of Florida's poshest new communities and live comfortably on the substantial income provided by the mortgage they would hold. As seventy-five percent of the trailers were park property, the new owner, a real estate investment trust, would benefit from apartment-grade rents as well as income from space leases. Overshadowing this, the REIT would be tallying up massive tax write-offs made possible by the accelerated depreciation of the substandard, non-real property units for a full decade, at which time it would take advantage of the appreciated value of the 150-acre site as it was put to a higher and better use. Payne and Nelson Realty, a commercial real estate enterprise, would glean large profits from the sale, management, and ultimate improvement of the property. Finally, Elizabeth was looking forward with some giddiness to the settlement of the transaction that was not only the largest sale she had made in her four-year career, but which would also result in her first six-figure commission.

At ease in her small office in the Payne and Nelson Building, a modern, four-story structure on a busy thoroughfare two miles west of White Plains, the young broker gently caressed the thick file that represented over a third of her long work hours over the previous four months. The late afternoon sunlight warmed her, in stark contrast to that memorable trip the previous December when she saw the property for the first time.

Jolted out of her reminiscences by the demanding bleep of her telephone, Elizabeth picked up the receiver and mouthed the perfunctory business greeting.

"Hi, Babe," the male voice returned.

Briefly, Elizabeth flashed on the uniformly dismal history of her attempts at romance, despairing of ever having a relationship with anyone with a rating on the masculine scale higher than "jerk." Until now, she knew, smiling inwardly. "You're a sexist pig," she joked, pleased to hear from her lover.

"Oink. Care to join me at the trough tonight?"

"Sorry, can't. I have a late meeting with Ralph Payne to discuss tomorrow's closing, and he promised me dinner. It'll be good schmoose time; I seem to be moving up a little around this male-dominated dominion."

"As you should; that was one hell of a deal you put together. I don't like the idea of another man going out on the town with my girl, though."

"Strictly business. Anyway, I'm sure getting involved with another female is the last thing on Ralph's mind right now. He's been out of the office for the past two days attending to his divorce, and I also heard that things are not going so smoothly between him and his middle-age-crisis-relieving blonde, either. I don't understand it. He had a lovely, devoted wife, three great kids, and a huge new house in Somers, yet he threw it all in the crapper for that bimbo barely out of her teens. What makes a man act like that?"

"We each go insane in our own way, El."

El. It was Joe Hanlon's unique invention, this nickname for his lady, fashioned from compromise shortly after they met. When after two dates Elizabeth said that everyone addressed her by her full name and she took offense whenever anyone called her "Betty," "Beth," or "Liz," Joe told her he could not abide having a four-syllabled girlfriend. Although slight annoyance lingered, she now accepted the sobriquet as a special feature of their loving relationship. "You haven't lost your mind yet," she said.

"Maybe not, but I reserve the right to go insane any time I want to," Joe replied. "Perhaps tomorrow night."

"Don't even think about it," she stated firmly. "I'm worried enough about the unexpected from your parents; I don't need anything strange suddenly oozing out of you." Given the couple's closeness, the first encounter with Joe's parents was inevitable, but Elizabeth had more misgivings about the impending visit than she did about the possibility that some disaster would occur at the settlement table the next morning.

"Just joking; everything's going to be fine. I'll pick you up at your place about six; we'll be there before eight."

"They still don't know about the Big Issue, do they?" Elizabeth asked with trepidation. "I have to know, Joe."

"Let's just leave things the way they are. I think you'll be pleasantly surprised."

"I doubt it."

"Wait," Joe asked. "Okay, Mike, I'll be right there," he stated in a voice away from the mouthpiece. "El, I have to go," he said, back on the phone. "Mike Overton is giving me a ride to my car, and when he works the eight to five shift he wants to be out of the station no later than thirty seconds past the hour."

"You really should spring for a new car. How many miles are on that red devil?"

"A hundred thirty, but it's not in the shop this time. I had to leave it in front of somebody's house this morning."

"What happened?"

"I can't go into it now, but if your meeting doesn't run too late, you might want to check out the eleven o'clock news. I played a small part in the situation. I'll give you all the details tomorrow night on the drive up to Marlborough."

"Now I'm interested, but I'll wait," Elizabeth said.

"Have a good night, and stay calm; it'll all be over tomorrow. The trailer park sale, I mean; for my parents, hey, we have all weekend."

"Three strikes," Philip Roberts muttered from the passenger side of the sedan as the car slowly made its way along Elm Street, one of Sunnyside's quiet residential byways. "The asshole has three strikes."

"So he's out," responded the driver, Eric Kauffman, in a matter-of-fact tone, though they both knew it was a wild understatement. The subject of their conversation was *way* out in the game played by the agents, where one strike was seldom tolerated and two, never.

"First, the circus this morning. The asshole marches right through our security and screws up an otherwise decent operation," Roberts said, relating his irritations as if he were picking at a scab. "Then he goes to White Plains—way out of his jurisdiction—to see what he can learn. About us. After we told him and the chief of that backwoods operation, more than once, to butt out, in all caps and underlined."

"He couldn't have picked up anything from that agent—Tobin, his name is. Nobody in that office knows anything, not even the head guy, the . . ."

"Senior resident agent, White Plains Resident Agency. You have to do better on the nomenclature if you're going to continue to play FBI agent, Eric," Roberts reprimanded. "Then tonight. What the hell was that action?"

"I was as surprised when I saw it as you were when I told you about it. I go over to the house for one more look-see and—*bam*—there he is again. But I still think he was just picking up his piece of crap of a car," Kauffman said.

"But he was questioning the neighbors."

"I don't see it as much of a problem. This death is big news, so a couple of neighbors approach a local cop to pump him for information. But the cop, this Hanlon, doesn't know anything. What could he tell them, that Bonnelli is dead? Hell, it's been on TV since noon."

"That's another aspect of this case I'm uneasy about. The news got out way too quickly," Roberts said as he stared out of the window, searching for house numbers. "You're probably right about Hanlon, Eric. He's just a dumb shit local cop who stumbled onto something, and now he has a few questions as well as a knack for being in the wrong place at the wrong time. If his entire force did nothing except investigate the death for the next six months, I'm sure they would uncover precisely squat. But always remember, Eric, there is a huge difference between someone having a negligible chance of uncovering anything and someone having a zero chance. That's why we're here, still working at ten o'clock, instead of getting a well-deserved night's rest back at the hotel."

"Are we there yet?"

"According to the numbers we just passed, the house should be two doors up, on the right," Roberts said.

Two dwellings and a hundred yards later, Kauffman eased the Pontiac to the curb.

"Okay," Roberts said. "Let's get this done, take care of the few remaining details, and we're out of this state by tomorrow noon."

"Sounds good to me," Kauffman responded as they exited the sedan.

Roberts rang the bell. "Morrow made the call to him this morning. Apparently, he was cooperative and did exactly as he was told. We're not here to praise him, though."

A few moments later, a frail hand opened the heavy door. A nervous, shaken man faced the two agents. Barefoot, he was dressed in baggy pants and an unbuttoned white dress shirt. In a state he referred to as "currently between wives," he lived alone.

"Kevin Chandler?" Roberts asked sternly, receiving a hesitant nod in return. "I'm Philip Roberts, FBI. We need to talk."

The few remaining corpuscles of color drained from Chandler's already ashen face. Awoken from a deep sleep at two o'clock that morning by a call notifying him that federal authorities were aware of his misdeeds with regard to his waterfront development, he later learned that the financier of the project had died. Feeling caught between the heavy rock of the FBI and the unforgiving hard place of Bonnelli's mob, he had been assailed by a progressive nausea since before dawn.

Almost extending his arms out to receive handcuffs, he instead ushered the two agents into his large living room.

Chandler collapsed into a sofa and gestured toward two chairs. Roberts availed himself of the seat directly opposite the master of the house, but Kauffman remained standing, striking his most intimidating pose a few feet from the subject.

"You screwed up big time, Chandler," Roberts began. It was a speech, memorized and rehearsed, but in its delivery the agent tempered his tone, realizing the quivering man before him didn't need any more softening up. "You had nice, simple instructions to keep your two-bit police force off of one street for one day, and you blew it. Bad."

The councilman looked up in anguished surprise "Wh—what?" he stammered. "But the word went out; Dempsey told me everything was set."

"I guess you two don't talk much. You know a cop named Joseph Hanlon?"

A spark of recognition flashed in the old man's terrified eyes. "Yes. . . . We met a couple times . . . young . . . good cop . . . rising star, everybody says," he rambled.

"Well not only was this star on Oak Street twice today," Roberts related, "but this morning he was in the house."

"Jesus . . . Jesus what a mess," Chandler whined, covering his face with his hands, completely crushed by the myriad, damning facets of his predicament. "I should have gone down there personally. I could have . . ."

"We're not here to talk about what you could have done," Roberts interrupted. "I'm here to tell you what you will do."

"Go on," Chandler responded weakly, totally resigned.

It was way too late for a work night, Joe thought as he stared at the starkly lit bedroom ceiling, hoping his need for sleep would quickly triumph over the questions that kept assailing him from odd directions. If Bonnelli was killed by a CIA hit squad, or maybe a team from the firm of Carver, Gunmann, Garrote & Hemlock, then why was the body taken? Proper procedure for that type of operation must certainly be to get in unseen, do the job, then make a hasty, undetected retreat, leaving the task of wondering what happened to others. Oh the other hand, if the discovery of the corpse was a surprise to the agents, then why did they bring the equipment to handle it? Above all, he wanted to know why the unseen Fates kept dragging him into impossible situations.

"But not this time," the detective vowed firmly to the empty apartment, attempting to force the accumulated detritus of his conjectures on the case from his consciousness. Whatever happened, the evidence was gone, as were the agents, whoever they were, probably never to return to Sunnyside. It was over, or would be within the first hour of the following day when the report to Chief Dempsey would be finished. He did not have the time, the authority, or the inclination to pursue the investigation further.

The questions would remain, he knew, long after he filed his report and attempted to file the incident into the seldom-visited recesses of his mind. They spanned the entire spectrum of Investigation 101's five W's now. What exactly happened at the house? Who were those strange agents? When did they know about Bonnelli's impending demise? And where did they come from? Finally—new to the picture—why the blood tests?

He hadn't been looking for this most recent twist, he had merely been picking up his car. He found the vehicle where he parked it, across the street from Kathleen Jackson's home. As he opened the Nissan's door, he heard a shout from a figure strolling across a nearby lawn. It was Thomas Keener, whom Joe had met the previous summer while responding to a call concerning a possibly rabid raccoon in his backyard. Joe and Keener had just reacquainted themselves when Keener's neighbor to the south joined them.

Expecting the two citizens to question him in a general way concerning the departure of their infamous neighbor, Joe was caught off guard when they related worries of a more personal nature. One of the agents that morning, at least one of the technicians assigned to the armed team of investigators, had taken a blood sample from each of them. Upon further inquiry with other neighbors, Keener had discovered blood had been taken from every occupant of the two houses adjacent to Bonnelli's, along with the residents of the houses across the street. There was absolutely no cause for concern, the technician had told them, which of course resulted in worry by all. Was Bonnelli killed by a contagious virus or perhaps poison gas?

Assuming his role of mollifier of the populace, Joe had answered reassuringly that, although he did not know exactly why Bonnelli had died, his neighbors almost certainly had nothing to fear. After all, he related, he had seen the bodyguard, the man who had been in the house just a few feet from the mobster when he died, and he appeared to be fine. He did not mention the dead cat under Bonnelli's bed.

In his own bed, Joe blinked twice to disperse the illusion that the ceiling was descending upon him. The unsolvable case was baffling to irritation. What perverse procedure was it that made fingerprints at a possible crime scene irrelevant, but which necessitated the collection of blood samples from people three hundred feet away? And if some type of poisonous agent was suspected, then why was there a total lack of protective equipment among the investigators? Full chemical suits should have been standard in such a situation, but those in the house seemed so unconcerned with whatever killed the two mammals in the bedroom that they didn't even wear dust masks or gloves.

Disgusted with the perplexities and contradictions of the case as well as the lateness of the hour, Joe searched for something that would put both mind and body to rest, settling on a dog-eared novel he had read some months previously. Tomorrow, he promised himself, it would all be behind him, and his shift would quickly evolve into another day of heroic routine, serving the Sunnyside populace in quiet ways that would never make the local paper, much less the regional TV news.

Ah, this is it, he thought as he turned to a random chapter and began to read. Replete with cardboard characters and mindless plot twists that could be seen many pages away, it was the perfect somnifacient. As if the book weren't annoying enough, Joe recalled after a few minutes, the author had incorporated into his story some kind of code involving the first letter of every chapter. *What a cheap gimmick* was his final criticism of the novel as he drifted off. Shifting slightly to gain a more comfortable position, he displaced the book from the bed. Befitting the apartment's stark decor, it was the soft thud of the volume as it contacted the carpet, not chimes, that tolled the midnight hour.

**FRIDAY
10 APRIL**

CHAPTER 5

Chin dropped, eyes wide, the young police officer's expression would not have been out of place at the site of a multi-vehicle accident or the scene of a bloody convenience store robbery gone awry, but Buford Burks' look of dismay on Friday morning was promulgated by the jolly bulk of his mentor opening a door. Slipping uneasily to the edge of his seat at the front desk of the Sunnyside Police Station, the man watched intently as Anthony Dempsey stepped through the glass entryway and entered the building. It was an act he had seen his chief perform over a hundred times in the previous six months, but only once had it been as early, and yesterday, he recalled with chagrin, had not been a good day.

Dempsey crossed the reception area and was at the front desk in half a dozen energetic strides. "Nothing," he said, grinning, in answer to the question asked only by Burks' grim countenance.

"Sir?"

"Nothing," he repeated. "I am not here to perform any nefarious tasks or to aid in any covert operations. Quite the opposite. My wife has given me gracious leave to take my first fishing trip of the spring this weekend, and I'm here early because I'm leaving early. I intend to be across the Tappan Zee Bridge and well on my way to the Ashokan Reservoir long before rush hour yuppies choke up the Thruway."

"Oh," Burks replied, greatly relieved.

"So, Buford, how goes the night shift?"

"Quiet as usual," Burks replied. "Only one call, from a woman who thought she heard someone outside her house. Martin responded and came up empty except for a cat that jumped from a windowsill as he drove up to the house. Later, he ticketed two late-night speeders on Broadway."

"How are things at the house of our recently departed friend?"

"Martin made two passes down Oak Street, and reported all was dead quiet at Bonnelli's—if you'll pardon the expression."

"Pardoned with pleasure," the chief replied with a wry smile. "I suppose the 'family' will sell the place now and we can return to our tranquil lives."

"Actually, it was always quiet there, except for yesterday. It's ironic that the only time we ever had trouble at the place was when the FBI had control of it. It still irks me that they excluded us."

"I'm sure they had their reasons," Dempsey said. "At any rate, it's over now; once again, we are in charge."

The slight squeak of a police cruiser's brakes took the attention of the two officers outside. Moments later, the mobile half of the department's night shift had negotiated the front steps and was inside the building. Upon sighting Dempsey, the expression that formed on Martin Coleman's face was more quizzical than worried, but it asked the same question posed by Burks' grimace a few minutes earlier.

"Nothing to be concerned about, Martin," Dempsey said calmly before relating the reason behind his premature presence. "I hear all sectors were quiet during the night, Oak Street included."

"Yes, Chief, but I don't know how long that's going to last," Coleman said as he removed his hat, exposing a pate of thinning brown hair. "On my way here, I made one last pass through the neighborhood, and as I was coming off Oak, a big limo was turning in. For all I know, it could have been headed anywhere, but I'll lay four to one it's parked in Bonnelli's driveway right now."

"I won't take that bet, but even so there's nothing unusual about that," Dempsey replied.

"Before yesterday, I would have agreed," Coleman said. "But now, with Bonnelli dead and the FBI involved, I don't know what to think. I sure didn't expect those agents would have treated us like they did. I guess being part of the top law enforcement agency in the country gives them some bragging rights over members of a twelve-man local force, but the way they totally excluded us went beyond arrogance. This must have been an operation planned well in advance so why the last-minute notification? Something stinks in this picture."

"We were just discussing that very . . ." started Dempsey before he was interrupted by the insistent buzz of the desk phone.

"Sunnyside Police, Officer Burks speaking," the policeman answered. A long pause followed, during which the look on Burks' face turned to concern. "Yes, sir, I know he's not at home, but I don't have to page him, he's here at the station. Please wait a moment and I'll transfer you." The officer punched the machine's hold button and looked up at his chief.

"That would be for me," Dempsey stated in a light tone, attempting to break the tension. It didn't work.

"Chief, it's Councilman Chandler. He's not happy, and I think he's a little drunk. If you'd like to talk to him in your office . . ."

"I'll take it here," the chief said, extending a meaty hand. "I wonder what *this* morning's drill is." Burks passed the handset and hit the hold button. "Good morning, Councilman," Dempsey greeted. Four "yes's" followed by an "I'll be here" was the extent of his end of the conversation. He returned the telephone to Burks.

"New orders?" Coleman asked.

"No. I don't know what he wants, but he's coming right over to personally impart his wishes to me."

"Any instructions?" asked a wary Burks.

Dempsey confronted the desk officer squarely. "Buford, very shortly, an enraged and intoxicated Kevin Chandler will appear at this station. I'd like to think he won't drive here, but he probably will. Greet him courteously and usher him back to my office. I'll handle the situation from there."

"Yes, sir."

"Looks like another full moon," Dempsey muttered as he disappeared down the hall. From an old Gary Larsen cartoon captioned "The Tidy Bowl Family at Home," the oft-used department slang was the comment by the tiny man floating in a toilet bowl. The Sunnyside Police Force was about to be shit upon.

In the apartment of Joseph Hanlon, the same annoying alarm clock emitted the same unearthly scream at precisely the same time it did every morning. After completing his rising rituals, however, the detective decided to depart from his routine by taking the same route to work two days running. As he negotiated the car up Broadway and down Price Street, he noted no differences from the traverse of the area he had taken twenty-four hours before. He almost convinced himself that the duplication of his journey would affirm the normalcy of his life, but quickly discarded the notion as a pure self-deception. What he really wanted was the confrontation with the shadows of the unknown he somehow knew was awaiting him on Oak Street.

Finally sighting the large house of the dead mob boss, Joe almost didn't stop. The scene was certainly different. In place of four vehicles of unknown origin, there was a single, dark limousine. Two men stood by the front door, ominous but at ease, like occupants, not invaders. Logically, there was no way he could expect to gain anything for his report from a confrontation with the men. A few grunts in response to his questions, he knew, would be followed by strong hints that he make a quick departure. Still, there might be something to be gained. "What the heck," he finally decided, then maneuvered the Nissan into the driveway, coming to a stop a few feet behind the limo. No sneaking around *this* morning, he thought as he killed the engine; these guys were obviously mobsters.

The eyes of the men were on Joe the entire distance of his short walk. He recognized one man as the prisoner of the living room, although the he had lost his wild-eyed expression.

"You're no mover," Marc Grunner threw at Joe. "Who the hell are you, another fucking reporter?"

Joe paused, then gave in to temptation. "What kind of reporter?" It was clear he wasn't going to gain anything, anyway.

Grunner stared dumbly at the visitor, not comprehending the question. "Wait, I know you; you're the cop from yesterday. Whaddaya want?"

"I have a few questions about what happened here. Remember, I was kicked out at the same time you were."

"Well you should've stayed gone," Grunner said. "There's nothing you're gonna get here." The man next to Grunner punctuated the comment with an icy glare.

If looks could kill, thought Joe, before recalling the vocation of the two men.

"Well, it's Officer Hanlon, isn't it?" asked Andrew Weiss as he stepped out of the open front door. Dressed in a well-tailored suit and holding a sheaf of papers, he was smiling.

"Yes, Mr. Weiss," Joe acknowledged. "We spoke briefly yesterday."

"An unpleasant situation," Weiss said. "As I recall, you were treated rather roughly by our visitors. I take it you were not part of the investigation?"

Joe hesitated, not entirely sure he should reveal much to the lawyer, a de facto resident of the opposite side of the legal fence. He realized the game was going to be one of give and take, however, and the burning desire to learn more about what had gone on the day before prevailed. "Sir, the local police were ordered to stay completely out of the area early yesterday morning. Before I learned of the order, I noted some unusual activity here and stopped to investigate. As you saw, I was quickly made aware of my error and ushered from the scene."

"Yes, indeed, as we were," the lawyer said. Ignoring the two henchmen, who stared at him in amazement that he was saying even two words to the local cop, the lawyer continued. "It seems you know as little as we about the situation. What is it you want?"

There's no way this guy is going to give me squat, Joe predicted, but he decided to attempt the impossible anyway. "Sir, as my visit yesterday was more or less an official one, I have to file a report. I would like your permission to look around in an effort to make this report more complete."

Weiss pondered the request for a full fifteen seconds, lifting his right hand to his chin as he did. "Okay," he finally consented.

"Christ almighty, Mr. Weiss!" Grunner exclaimed with such vehemence that his entire body shook.

Weiss exerted his authority over the failed bodyguard. "Grunner," he said sternly, "I want you to escort Officer Hanlon through the house—the north end only, to include the master bedroom."

"Yes, sir," Grunner replied through clenched teeth.

Weiss then faced off with Joe. "Please accept this gesture in a cooperative spirit; I hope you can shed some light on several unanswered questions concerning what happened here. You may look, but do not take anything, not a sheet of toilet paper, not a drink of water, without my permission. When you are finished, please see me."

"Thank you, Mr. Weiss," Joe said, not believing his luck.

"Grunner, when the inspection is complete, you will find me in the library," the lawyer said. He then opened the rear door to the limousine, retrieved a large gray briefcase, and walked back into the house.

Following Weiss's retreat, Grunner turned to his companion. "Watch for the movers, and some carpet guys are supposed to be over later," he said gruffly. "Anybody else, you get rid of—quick." He threw a sneer in Joe's direction. "We don't need any more tourists."

"Okay, Marc," the man acknowledged.

"I'd like to see the bedroom," Joe requested.

"Sure, now that you got the run of the place," Grunner responded sarcastically.

"Your arm okay after the blood test?" Joe asked as they entered the house.

"I'm fine," he muttered, his left hand moving briefly to his right upper arm.

Joe followed Grunner down the long, wide hallway to the master suite. Nothing appeared amiss; there were not even wheel marks in the plush carpet from the gurney that must have traveled down the hall on its way to the front door.

"Here it is, for all the good it'll do you," Grunner said when they were three steps inside the bedroom. "I think the assholes actually cleaned the place."

Joe's eyes swept the space. The exquisitely decorated room did indeed look clean. Except for a few details, it looked as if was awaiting a photographer from a fancy homes magazine, but those details were telling. For one thing, the bed had been divested of all sheets and blankets. For another, there were holes in the carpet and the wall behind the bed. Joe wondered if there was some significance to the pieces removed, or if they were they just random samples. He noticed the carpet showed a remarkable lack of matting for a room that had been under intense scrutiny by no less than four people the day before. There was evidence in the form of slight indentations from himself, Grunner, and one or two others, but that was all.

"We don't have all day," Grunner vocalized impatiently.

"Have you vacuumed in here since yesterday?"

"Hey, buddy, I don't vacuum," Grunner said disgustedly. "The room was cleaned on Wednesday, but that's it as far as I know."

Joe had trouble believing it. He walked up to the large dresser and examined a highly polished silver box. As expected, it was free from fingerprint dust, but there was more—or less. He recalled seeing the armed attendant to the technicians idly open the item, yet there was no evidence of the act. To test a theory, Joe tapped the top of the box with his thumb, and a visible latent print appeared, dust being unnecessary to reveal prints on surfaces with such a sheen. The box had been cleaned.

"One more minute, please," Joe implored Grunner in response to a grunt. A quick survey of the huge bathroom revealed nothing except an immaculate floor, spotless fixtures, and clean wastebaskets. He then opened the door to the closet a few inches. "Where do you keep the vacuum cleaner?" he asked across the room.

"What's all this about the goddamn vacuum? I told you I got nothing to do with the vacuum; it's in a closet next to the kitchen."

"Well if this is it, it's not there now," Joe said, opening the large closet door fully, revealing to his escort the upright cleaning apparatus in the middle of the floor.

"No way is it kept in there," Grunner said, surprised. "I told you the bastards cleaned."

"I'm done here," Joe stated. "There's nothing." Although not once had it been mentioned in his police or military training, the word that came to his mind as he strolled across the room was "sanitized." Did the word even exist outside of bad novels and worse television? Even if it did not, its definition was all around him.

The two men walked down the hall. "Anything else, master?" Grunner queried, sarcasm coming fully to the fore.

"I'd like to take a look outside."

"Your wish is my command."

At the foyer, Joe took the lead. He exited the front door, turned left, and passed through the corridor that separated the garage from the residence, then stopped at the corner. Maybe it was here Roberts had first spotted him, he postulated. Being seen, and subsequently allowing the agent to sneak up on him were mistakes that under slightly different circumstances might have been lethal. It was his wish to avoid other such failures that had brought him outside.

"What the hell are we doing out here?" Grunner asked.

Ignoring his tail, Joe walked slowly along the north wall. Arriving at the corner of the house, he saw at once it was a bad position, as there was a huge blind spot in the direction of Roberts' approach. And all of a sudden, there was a gun to his temple, Joe recalled with chagrin. So what would have been a better solution? he wondered, stepping back from the house thirty feet to take in the entire scene. A superior position might have been behind the large elm about a dozen feet from the corner. . . .

"Enough of this bullshit," Grunner grunted. "It's past time you left."

"Fine," Joe said, but as he spoke, he caught a glimpse of something on the roof six feet above Grunner's head. Gray and amorphous, the lump was lying on the edge of the shingles, almost obscured by the gutter. Intrigued, he advanced toward the house.

"Great," Grunner muttered at Joe's approach. "Let's go."

"There's something on the roof," Joe advised the man.

"What now?"

"I don't know; it might be important. Do you have a long stick or something?"

"Shit," was the reply. Grunner shuffled toward the large swimming pool on the other side of the yard and returned with an extendable aluminum pole with a plastic net on the end. "Knock yourself out," he said, thrusting the shaft at Joe.

Manipulating the pole to its full length, Joe stood back from the edge of the house and attempted to snare the elusive object. Not quite caught in the net, the lump was dislodged from the roof and fell straight down to the ivy that had received Joe's gun the day before.

Grunner reached it first. "Very goddamn important," he said as Joe joined him. "A dead squirrel."

"I'm ready to go now; I believe Mr. Weiss asked to see me before

I left," Joe said calmly, though his brain was screaming, *Dead Bonnelli! Dead cat! Dead squirrel!*

Joe followed his escort through the wide sunroom doors, and was directed to sit. Grunner then disappeared. There's no way, Joe thought, no way could there be a connection between what happened in the bedroom and the dead squirrel. The rodent could have lain there a week, or could have died that morning. But what else did he have to go on? A dump truck load of diddley.

"Well, Officer Hanlon, how did we make out?" asked Andrew Weiss as he strolled into the room. He seemed even happier than he had been earlier.

Joe stood up. "I'm sorry, Mr. Weiss, but I didn't find anything in the house. Mr. Bonnelli's bedroom appears to have been cleaned before the agents departed. They didn't leave a thing."

"Cleaned?" Weiss challenged. "As in swept up and wiped down?"

"It appears so."

"Isn't that highly unusual?"

"It would be for us," Joe acknowledged, "but I am unfamiliar with the procedures the FBI follows in such cases." It was almost a lie. Although he was not privy to most FBI procedures, the bizarre activities of Roberts and his people were certainly not from any book.

"I'm sorry you didn't come up with anything that might help clear up the situation," Weiss lamented.

"There is something outside I'd like to take with me," Joe said. "It's a ridiculous long shot, I'm afraid, but I'd still like to have it checked out."

"Let's take a look," Weiss said, slightly intrigued. "Front or back?"

"This way," Joe directed, gesturing in the direction of the sunroom doors.

They walked outside, followed at a discreet distance by Grunner, irritated almost to the point of apoplexy.

"What is your interest in this?" the lawyer asked Joe as the two stood over the small gray corpse.

"As I said, Mr. Weiss, it's probably nothing, but it's the only thing I found that could possibly be tied to the case."

Still undecided on a course of action, Weiss turned toward the third member of the group. "Grunner, please retrieve a bag of some sort for us from the kitchen."

The red-faced henchmen retreated without a sound.

"Where was it?" inquired the lawyer.

"On the edge of the roof," Joe said. They both looked up. High in the branches of the large elm, they sighted a cluster of leaves and twigs slightly over a foot across.

Weiss scanned the tree and the roof, then focused again on the tangle of sticks. "That is a squirrel's nest, isn't it?"

"Yes," Joe verified.

"Was the body right under the nest?"

Joe backed away from the house and considered the question. "Yes, directly beneath."

"I don't see any branches closer than a dozen feet or so from the roof," the lawyer observed. "Isn't that a little too far for a squirrel to jump?"

"I see where you're going," Joe said. "The squirrel would not have normal access to the roof. It probably died in the tree and fell from a point at or close to its nest."

"That's how I read it," Weiss sighed. "I can't conceive of any scenario that might tie in the demise of this little fellow with Mr. Bonnelli's death or the subsequent intrusion by the odd federal agents."

"You're probably right, but I'd still like to have it analyzed," Joe persisted.

Grunner rejoined them. "Here," he expelled, thrusting the paper shopping bag nearly into Joe's face.

"Be my guest," Weiss said disinterestedly.

Joe retrieved the pool net and with it urged the squirrel into the bag.

"You're a little young to be a detective, aren't you?" inquired Weiss as the trio made their way back to the sunroom.

"It's a rather involved story, but I was promoted somewhat early."

Lord knows why, the faces of Weiss and Grunner expressed simultaneously.

After they reached the front entry, Joe turned to Weiss. "I appreciate your assistance, Mr. Weiss," he said, still not quite believing his good luck.

"Although I don't expect there's anything to this—evidence," Weiss stated, gesturing to the bag in Joe's hand, "I would appreciate it if you would notify me if any other developments arise with regard to this case. Please accept my card."

"I would be happy to help you," Joe stated, exaggerating wildly. He took the white rectangle from the lawyer's outstretched hand, then left the house.

Weiss watched the policeman place his odd parcel in the trunk of his Nissan, then turned and went down the hall. As he entered Bonnelli's library, he frowned as the euphoria he had felt for much of the morning was tempered by thoughts of the possible negative consequences of his gamble. Maybe he was being stupid to attempt to control the collapse of Bonnelli's empire, stealing what he could in the process, but so far things had gone extraordinarily well. The first item of good news had come via telephone to his office late the previous afternoon. Perhaps due to his petition in federal court, FBI Agent Sandra Haines was very helpful regarding the remains. The preliminary determination of the just-completed autopsy was that Bonnelli had expired from heart failure at approximately two in the morning, she told Weiss, then informed him that the body would be delivered on Saturday morning to wherever the lawyer directed. The vitally important funeral could finally be planned. He had learned about the second bit of good fortune upon his arrival at the house less than an hour before. Expecting with absolute certainty that all of Bonnelli's personal documents would be absent from the safe in the library, Weiss was astounded to discover that nothing had been taken, or even perused.

It might have been a flaw in his lawyerly character, Weiss knew, but he had his reasons for being so permissive with the Sunnyside cop, Hanlon. Primarily, he was ecstatic to find everything in its place within the safe and was thus much more charitable than he normally would have been with a cop asking permission to look around. He also hoped Hanlon might help him find out just what kind of agents mount a massive raid on the home of one of the nation's top organized crime figures, but come away with nothing except the corpse of a man who died of natural causes.

Weiss walked across the den to the large safe recessed into a niche in the south wall, then dialed the four-number combination he was sure was known to no other living soul. He opened the heavy door and checked, for the third time, the interior digital displays that monitored the state-of-the-art depository. Extremely sophisticated, the electronics kept a date, time, and event record of not only openings and closings but of attempted openings as well, noting every time the combination dial was rotated more than five hachures in either direction. The readouts verified that the last activity had been a closure at 6:07 P.M. Wednesday, shortly before Bonnelli's last conversation with him. Nothing followed, no openings and no "ATTOPs." With absolute certainty, Weiss knew the agents had not touched the safe.

The old adage was if you are going to break into a house, steal something, even if you are there for something else. In Bonnelli's house, the federal agents must have known the safe was the only place to go. It wasn't as if they were unable to locate it. Even if they didn't notice the large hinged panel in the wall, there was a two-foot diameter concrete support column smack in the middle of the basement, the gray base of the vault clearly visible at its crown. By making no attempt to confiscate the documents, the agents telegraphed the fact that their motivations lay elsewhere.

Dabbling into the mystery would have to wait, however. Weiss removed a large file box and his briefcase from the safe and placed the items on the desk. There was far too much paper, he noted, displeased that Bonnelli had not heeded his advice to let his office be the repository of the documents, as attorney-client privilege would have provided more protection than any safe. All items were going to the office now, though not to Bonnelli's benefit. Of particular interest was the unrecorded mortgage on his apartment building. With that one slim sheaf of papers in hand, Weiss's already substantial wealth was almost doubled.

Weiss glanced toward the room's wall decorations, the firearms that had been lethal to so many, and reminded himself of the dangers involved in the game he was playing and of the single, severe penalty he would face should he lose. His overriding emotion, however, was exhilaration at the prospect of victory, which buoyed him more than his most exciting courtroom confrontations.

Firmly grasping the briefcase, Weiss stepped out of the library and spotted his driver. "Grab that box from the desk and let's go," he instructed as he took off at a quick pace toward the foyer.

Weiss paused and took one last look at the furnishings. If everything went his way, more than a few treasures from the residence would end up as conversation pieces in his apartment. He particularly had his eye on the Renoir that presently exuded its radiance from the living room, but such personal luxuries would have to wait until the dust settled from the explosion that had not yet occurred.

CHAPTER 6

As Joe negotiated his Nissan into the small parking lot directly across Main Street from the Sunnyside station, he saw Russell Mullin about sixty feet away. Headed toward his police cruiser, the officer glanced over and moved on. Immediately, Joe recognized there was some kind of message in Mullin's manner. It was not any one thing, not the slight movement of his head or the tenuous change of his gait; it wasn't even in his eyes. It was the subtle combination of a multitude of separately indiscernible gestures that told Joe some big shit was up. With him.

After parking the car, he danced with the morning traffic and leapt up the wide steps of the station. At the door, he met Mike Overton, headed out. With scant inches separating them, the older policeman looked up at the detective.

"Joe, I . . . Jesus Christ," Overton sputtered as he looked away, his face more grave than Joe had ever seen.

"What is it, Mike?" Joe asked, attempting to regain eye contact with the distraught cop.

"It's . . . it's bullshit, that's what it is," Overton replied, looking across Main Street at nothing in particular. "The bastard. . . ." Slipping quickly past Joe, he walked somberly away, head bowed.

"Amy, what *is* up?" Joe asked the officer behind the desk in a sober voice as he crossed the tile floor.

If anything, Amy Sullivan's face looked more tormented than Overton's. "The chief wants you to go directly to his office," she said. "It's not good news." Not one to be moved to tears, she was obviously on the verge of making an exception.

With a terse nod of acknowledgment, Joe skirted the desk and took the few steps necessary to reach his destination. At the far end of the long hall stood the immobile figures of Buford Burks and Martin

Coleman. Normally in a great rush to leave the building after the end of their shift, the presence of the officers was unusual, as was the position of the door to Dempsey's office. It was closed, in contradiction to the chief's open door policy that was both figurative and literal. The door was shut only when something serious was astir.

After a short pause, Joe knocked.

"Come in," Anthony Dempsey said in response to the two raps. "Please close the door, Joe," he asked after their eyes met. The two were not alone. Resplendent in his best cheap suit, a grayish-green affair accented by a garish tie, was Kevin Chandler. Turning from the councilman, Joe apprehensively faced off with his boss.

The police chief shuffled some meaningless paperwork before looking up. "Joe," he said gravely, then paused, clearing his throat. "I don't know how to tell you this . . ."

"But I do," Chandler snapped. "You're fired."

Dempsey jumped up. "Councilman Chandler, that was not at all necessary," he almost shouted. He placed his palms flat on the desktop and leaned toward the object of his wrath.

"I don't want to spend my whole morning here. You would have hemmed and hawed for another ten minutes."

"I'm sorry about this, Joe," the chief said.

"I don't understand."

"It's simple," Chandler explained. "You interfered with a federal investigation, endangering the lives of several FBI agents at Victor Bonnelli's house. Then you went over to White Plains to poke your nose further into places where you held absolutely no jurisdiction. Finally, your questioning of Bonnelli's neighbors last night proved to those agents you were up to no good. You're finished."

"But we do have some authority over Oak Street and its residents," Joe countered, attempting to grasp why his actions warranted so severe a penalty as his termination.

"No, you don't," the councilman stated. "When the FBI tells you, more than once, to stay out of their business, they mean it."

"This comes from Philip Roberts, doesn't it?" Joe inquired.

"The actions of Agent Roberts are entirely appropriate. He could have made things much worse."

Joe wondered what could be worse than his career ending over a minor and unintentional violation, but did not speak.

"I'll need your badge and gun, Joe," Dempsey said.

"Okay, Chief," Had it been any other person, Joe might have been angered by the request, but Dempsey was a man to whom he could refuse nothing. Deflated, he laid the symbols of his lost career in the center of the desk.

Unmoved by the ceremony, Chandler broached the next item on his list. "Hanlon, Dempsey tells me you're writing a statement concerning your escapades."

"Yes," the ex-detective advanced tentatively, not wishing to bring the chief into the sinking boat with him.

"I have to insure all copies of the report are destroyed," the councilman insisted.

"There are no copies. The statement exists only as a file on my computer."

"Well it needs to go," Chandler said.

With its youngest member in the lead, the trio went to the cubicle of the department detective. Within two minutes, Joe had activated the necessary computer files and the first page of his report filled the monitor. "This is it," he stated.

"Get rid of it and forget it," Chandler said.

With several quick moves of a mouse, the file was gone.

"Now clear out your desk and get out."

"Chandler, you got what you came for, now I would appreciate it if you would leave my building," Dempsey said. "Officer Hanlon has been a loyal employee for three years, and I would like to have a private conversation with him before he leaves."

"All right," Chandler said begrudgingly, "but I want him gone within the hour. Cross me, Dempsey, and you'll be out on your ass even faster than this ex-officer. Believe it; I can make it happen."

As Chandler disappeared around the corner, Dempsey grabbed Joe's nameplate and moved around the desk. After opening the largest drawer, he deposited into its yaw the nameplate and various papers, knick-knacks, and office supplies from the desktop, clearing the surface of everything but the computer and a telephone. He then attacked the pushpins stuck into the partitions, freeing a calendar, three pages of notes, and a photograph, likewise relegating the items to the drawer. In less than three minutes, the office looked like it was awaiting its next occupant.

"Chief, I should be doing this," Joe protested.

"That's all the desk-clearing you need to do today," Dempsey announced easily. "Lock it and follow me."

Curious at the change in his boss's demeanor, Joe secured his desk and turned off his computer, then tailed Dempsey back to his office.

"Close the door and have a seat," the chief said as he claimed his own chair. "What a prick; God, am I glad he's gone. I just wish we had the resources to investigate our esteemed councilman and send him up the river for his criminal business deals. That asshole is so greedy he'd print space helmets on dry cleaning bags if he thought there was a buck in it."

"What's this about?" Joe asked after surrendering briefly to his mentor's ability to make him smile.

"I doubt Chandler has enough friends on the council to get rid of me, but he might. That possibility, however, was not the reason I restrained myself from kicking his bony ass down Main Street when he demanded your dismissal. We had a long, unpleasant talk before you arrived. Apparently your friend from yesterday—Roberts?"

"Philip Roberts," Joe replied, regretting he'd ever heard the name.

"Apparently Mr. Roberts told Chandler if you were not ousted from the department, you would be brought up on charges for obstructing the activities of the FBI. I don't think the threat should be taken lightly, and prison is something you could well do without. Observing Chandler's manic attitude this morning, I believe you were not the only one threatened with incarceration."

"Where does that leave me?"

"You're in a serious situation, but your reputation with this department is intact. You aren't fired, but for the time being that's just between you and me. As far as everyone else is concerned, and that includes our co-workers, you no longer work here. If anyone asks, I'm in the process of filling out the paperwork and cutting your final check, but I have other priorities to attend to first."

Torn between relief and concern, Joe shifted in his seat. "These guys are playing for all day, Chief. I can't ask you to go out on a limb like this."

"You're *not* asking me, I'm *telling* you how we are going to proceed. Your actions were entirely proper. I should have contacted you yesterday morning to make sure you didn't drive down Oak Street, and I was the one who asked you to look further into the matter."

"Well, I appreciate it," Joe said. "This is something you don't have to do."

"You are exactly wrong, Joe. There are too many others who think like that, who justify wrong courses of action with all kinds of aberrant logic. There's no choice for me here; it's simply something I have to do."

"Okay, Chief. What's the next step?"

"What one option should always be considered when making a decision?" asked Dempsey, reverting to his role as instructor.

"Doing nothing," Joe answered, having learned the lesson years before. "That's what you're saying I should do now?"

"I think the situation will blow over if we only give it a little time. Doing nothing for a few days may be the smart thing to do. At least two members of the council are out of town today, and Roberts and his gang probably won't be around for long."

"He's scheduled to leave sometime today according to Rich Tobin," Joe said.

"When they return after the weekend, the councilmen can temper Chandler, and I believe Roberts will take care of himself."

"How's that?"

"You may have ruffled his feathers, but come Monday my guess is he'll be at least three states away attending to other matters. He simply won't care about the employment status of a small-town cop hundreds of miles away. And if you're right about his being a member of another federal service, he won't want to risk exposure by utilizing FBI contacts and the court system to pursue such a trivial matter. I think Roberts was blowing smoke so far up Chandler's ass it fogged up his eyeballs. I could be wrong, of course, in which case we'll both be looking for new jobs by next Wednesday."

"So I get the rest of the day off?"

Dempsey smiled. "I'm going up to the Catskills this afternoon to engage in some long-awaited fishing, and I think you should do something similar. Get away from this mess, go out of town, try to relax. There will be enough to worry about next week."

"Chief, I discovered a few more things about the case, and I found something . . ."

"It'll wait a few days," interrupted Dempsey, holding up a wide palm. "We'll take it up on Monday."

"I don't know what to say, Chief," Joe said with a grim smile. "Thanks."

"Don't thank me yet, Joe," Dempsey warned as they shook hands. "You may be fired for real next week."

———————

Oscar Ottoway did not care much for his job as the head of the White Plains Resident Agency, although he received a promotion to get it. As the senior resident agent, Ottoway was in charge of the FBI's presence in six Upstate counties, but in the three months since he had assumed his post, he had been plagued by two major frustrations. First was his unease at being thrust into a leadership position after fifteen years as an administrator in the New York Field Office, where he had avoided making any except the most trivial decisions. His second disappointment stemmed from the workload of his office, comprised almost entirely of routine background checks and painfully inconsequential investigations. Anything important, he learned, always seemed to have ties to cases originating outside of his office, and his jurisdiction was constantly usurped by teams of agents from the south that considered interactions with personnel assigned to White Plains to be nothing except an unwanted inconvenience.

Before Monday, the invaders had all come from his old haunt in New York. The first day of the week, however, brought a new breed of agent into his domain. He had not known any of the twelve people of the visiting cohort, and they brought with them mannerisms that made the worst gestures of his previous visitors seem like a heartfelt embrace. Additionally, the authority for their intrusion came from outside the state. Even the assistant director in charge, the high-ranking head of the New York office, was not aware of the team's mission, at least that was the impression Ottoway had come away with after a telephone conversation with the ADIC on Wednesday. No, the instructions to be a gracious, unquestioning host had come directly from one of the FBI's elite in Washington.

It had therefore been his main task to greet and bid farewell to the temporary tenants of Carol Kowalesky's office while insuring that the permanent occupants of his small boat did not make even the smallest ripple in the bureaucratic waters extending all the way to the nation's capital. This morning, however, he had been made aware that one of his agents had been jumping up and down on the gunwales of his vessel, and he was decidedly unhappy about it.

In front of the supervisor at a position resembling the military stance of attention was Richard Tobin: agent, wave maker, career threatener. "Tobin, do you know why you are here?" Ottoway asked harshly.

"I have no idea," the junior agent said. "My cases, such as they are, are all up to date, and you have reports on the status of each."

"It's your extracurricular activities I'm concerned about. You know a cop over in Sunnyside, name of Hanlon?"

"Yes, we met last year," Tobin answered, slightly uneasy.

"I just had a talk with Agent Roberts. He's had a great deal of trouble from this Hanlon, and informs me that you were talking to him yesterday. I need to know the details of that conversation."

"Yesterday, Joe Hanlon stumbled onto some kind of operation being conducted by our guests; I needn't tell you where. After he was hustled out of the area, he came to see me to find out what was going on, as the men claimed to be FBI agents."

Ottoway glared at his subordinate. "Let's put that little issue to rest right here, *mister*. The agents temporarily using our facilities are from and acting for the Bureau on an assignment of the utmost priority."

"Yes, sir," Tobin replied.

"What did you tell him?"

"Other than the fact that Agent Roberts was making use of one of our offices, I didn't tell him anything. I couldn't have given him any information if I wanted to because I didn't know anything, and still don't. It was Joe who informed me of Victor Bonnelli's death."

"What else did he tell you?"

"He told me he found the procedures of our visitors to be somewhat foreign to him," Tobin answered. "Of course, he's just a local cop, untrained in our techniques."

"Well he's not a local cop anymore," Ottoway said. "His interference with Agent Roberts' investigation was completely unwarranted. He was dismissed from his post this morning, and federal charges against him are being considered."

"What?" Tobin exploded. "Of all the stupid, asinine things. . . . Joe Hanlon is the finest law enforcement officer I've ever met, in any branch. You'll never know what he did last year . . ." he started, then caught himself.

"What he did last year is irrelevant," Ottoway stated in a voice almost as loud as Tobin's. "It's what he did yesterday that counts, and he screwed up big. You are to have nothing to do with him again. Ever. Period."

"Of course, Mr. Ottoway, you're right. I'm sorry," Tobin forced.

"See that you follow these instructions, Tobin," Ottoway concluded, not convinced of the agent's sincerity. "Foul up, and you'll be joining your friend on the unemployment line. Now get back to work."

"Yes, sir."

Another crisis averted, Ottoway hoped, wishing for a quick departure of Roberts and what remained of his crew before anything else happened.

———

"It wasn't the kind of end to his reign we had planned for him," the well-dressed, middle-aged man behind the podium stated.

"So you're saying you were close to bringing him to trial?" asked one reporter within the dense crowd of journalists that stood before Lucian Sonner, the deputy director of the FBI's New York Field Office.

"That determination would have been made by the federal prosecutors," Sonner deflected above the low din of clicking cameras and jostled equipment. "I also cannot comment on an ongoing investigation. Victor Bonnelli's death did not bring about the demise of his organization."

"When's the funeral?" was the query that struck home among a volley of simultaneously shouted questions.

"The body will be released to Bonnelli's next of kin tomorrow morning," Sonner stated. "As far as specific burial arrangements, you'll have to contact the family."

"Mr. Sonner!" a petite female voice shouted, winning the agent's attention over several of her male colleagues. "Why was the body taken in the first place? Shouldn't the local medical examiner have been informed?"

Just for an instant, the deputy director frowned. "The Bureau has the best forensic facilities in the world," he stated, fumbling slightly. "Given Bonnelli's history, it was decided to investigate the matter in-house. As I stated at the start of this press conference, there was absolutely no foul play involved in the death."

"What happens now?" was the gist of variously worded questions that assaulted Sonner from several directions.

"This office is firmly committed to putting an end to organized crime in New York. We have made great strides over the past few years, and we intend to diligently pursue all illegal activities until this goal is achieved." Sonner then thanked his rowdy audience and retreated from the room, ignoring a chorus of attempts to seize his attention.

The scene abruptly terminated to a glassy gray surface that reflected the plush decor of Andrew Weiss's office. Weiss set the remote on top of the television but did not close the oak doors that normally hid the electronic device, sure that more material of interest would be spewed from the box before the day was out.

"Quite a performance," remarked Karl Kastner from a nearby chair. "What do you make of it?"

"Political grandstanding, that's it; they have nothing," Weiss stated confidently, joining his assistant at the conference table. "Something happened, the media is in a frenzy, and the feds have to say something, so they resort to the same tired lines."

"I guess they'll be gunning for Nicky now."

Weiss's brow furrowed at the mention of the person who was both the most annoying impediment to his plans as well as the catalyst who could see his dreams fulfilled. "How is the gentle heir doing?"

"He finally collapsed on the couch about an hour after you left.

When he woke up this morning, he was still shaken, agitated, and acting like he wanted to bust a few heads, but a little breakfast and a lot of talk calmed him down. Nicky's currently cool demeanor is probably not going to last long, though."

"I know," Weiss agreed, already planning to take advantage of the fact when the time was right. "I want you to go back and sit on him for a few hours. You shouldn't have much of a problem controlling him; he's definitely a nocturnal beast. I'll be over about three to gage the situation and talk a little business."

"I'll try to keep him sedated, but not too drunk." Kastner replied as he departed.

Weiss walked to his desk where the large briefcase containing the booty from the Bonnelli house awaited his pleasure. With more than a little anticipation, he sat down and opened the treasure chest.

Scattered about the interior of the gray case were bundles of the least valuable commodity within: cash. To clear the way to get to the more interesting articles, Weiss created a rectangular parallelepiped of the banded bills by his telephone. The total of $135,000 was barely enough to buy a decent car.

Next to the currency, the lawyer placed eight plush cases of various sizes and subdued colors that contained what was left of the jewelry collection of Bonnelli's late wife. The discovery of the items had been a pleasant surprise; he estimated the value of the irregular stack to be ten times that of the adjacent cash.

Delving into the documents, Weiss caressed the mortgage papers for his apartment building before setting the sheaf aside, then examined the other contents of a thick folder that held a variety of real property and chattel mortgages and both business and personal loans. Finally, the truth is revealed, Weiss thought as he mentally compared the documents with the records his firm maintained for Bonnelli.

One unexpected discovery was the last document in the folder, a large personal loan to Joey Messina, one of Bonnelli's soldiers. Messina was almost an unknown to the lawyer; briefly, he wondered if he constituted a threat. There was also a handwritten agreement with a man named Chandler, whom he had never heard of.

Weiss finally opened the file that contained information on Bonnelli's most guarded assets: his offshore accounts. Although he was aware of the existence of about half of the two dozen accounts through previous transactions, Bonnelli had never made him privy to the figures or activity involved. "Wow," he verbalized as he educated himself on the vast amounts of money represented by the papers.

After placing the empty briefcase on the floor, Weiss sat back and took in the whole of the trove that adorned his desk. Had the authorities confiscated the items from the Sunnyside safe, it would have been the end, he realized. There was enough information to give the FBI a hundred new leads, forestalling any plans he might have to exert some control over the huge organization. "The fools," Weiss said with a mixture of relief and bewilderment.

He extracted a yellow legal pad from his desk and began to plan his next actions. There was much work to do before his meeting with Nicky that afternoon, and before the funeral, now set for Tuesday. After two pages of notes, the lawyer paused to take in the hourly television news. Pleased to learn Bonnelli's death had already been supplanted as the lead story by a minor crisis in Israel, Weiss knew it wouldn't be long before it was totally out of the public eye. Although not an advocate of all of the Mafia's methods, he was a supporter of the concept known as *omerta*, the code of silence which among other things meant the less publicity the better.

If this is the worst thing that's going to happen to me all day, I'll accept it with pleasure, thought Elizabeth Brooks as she sat in her Oldsmobile at the edge of the northbound lane of the Bronx River Parkway. Though the speedometer showed the vehicle was not moving, it had moments before been pointing at the hachure indicating sixty-three, at least according to State Trooper Hal Balser, who was documenting the fact on an oft-used form. After estimating that the ticket might deprive her of eighty dollars, she calculated she was still $144,920 to the good for the day.

The settlement on the trailer park had gone surprisingly smoothly. Minor points were quickly and amicably resolved by the attorneys representing the sellers and purchasers, and for once the bank was fully satisfied in all respects. Most importantly, the owners made no move to hold the broker's commission hostage, a sport that was becoming increasingly popular with sellers and their lawyers.

"Here's your paperwork, ma'am," stated Balser as he handed Elizabeth her driver's license and vehicle documents along with the ticket. "Please drive carefully."

"Thank you," Elizabeth said, feeling exceptionally generous. She retrieved her cellular phone, punched in a series of well-known numbers, put the car in gear, and pulled back onto the parkway.

"Yo!" answered a familiar voice after three rings.

"Joe, it's Elizabeth. I called your station a few minutes ago and

Amy Sullivan told me you took the day off. That's unusual for you, and she sounded upset. Is anything wrong?"

"It hasn't been a good day," Joe admitted. "I'll tell you about it when I see you. How did your closing go?"

"Great! I'm headed back to the office now, and then I'm going to the bank."

"Good for you, El. I know you worked hard for that one."

"None of them are easy."

"El, do you think we can get together earlier than we planned?"

"I'd love that. Have you had lunch?"

"Nothing other than half a bag of chips I found behind the couch."

"Wonderful," Elizabeth scolded. "I'll meet you in an hour at the Italian restaurant on Central Avenue. My treat."

"You made my day," Joe said. "Just when I didn't think I could love you any more, you offer up a free meal."

Elizabeth hung up the phone and focused on the upcoming confrontation. Consciously restraining her foot, she traveled the remaining eight miles to the Payne and Nelson Building under sixty miles an hour. Inside, she found Ralph Payne waiting for her.

"Elizabeth, I heard everything went well in Manhattan," Payne said cheerily, a big smile covering what looked like a third of his face.

"Come on in Ralph," Elizabeth said, as she walked into her office. "We can make each other happy today."

"How's that?"

"As you recall, we discussed the commission split last night. At the closing, I had the seller's attorney cut two checks to the brokerage in accordance with those figures. I would like my money right now."

Payne dropped his smile. "You know that isn't the way we do things here, Elizabeth."

"There's nothing wrong with doing it this way," Elizabeth said firmly as she took two blue rectangles from the folder she held. "I know I'm just the agent. Both of these checks are made payable to the brokerage, as required; you merely have to endorse the larger one over to me, and the deal is done."

"But we have to account for the money," Payne countered.

"You know very well you can account for all funds from the information in this," Elizabeth said, handing the man the folder. "It includes copies of the checks, of course."

"You don't trust me?" the broker asked.

"Greed makes people do strange things. That fact was verified with you when I found out what you were doing when we first met in Scranton."

"I remember," Payne said. " I was scouting out locations for that burger franchise."

"Except the corporations that purchased the lots were your own shell companies. The fast food enterprise—your client—ended up paying double the original price for the parcels, plus commission, plus your fees and expenses."

Payne relaxed and emitted a two-syllable chuckle. "Yeah, that was a sweet operation," he admitted. "I still don't like what you're doing."

"Of course you don't; we're talking on the same level," Elizabeth said. "Ralph, I'm the best salesperson here. You don't need to hold onto my money for three or four months to motivate me to work harder, collecting interest you don't deserve in the process. Here's your check, over a hundred thou; now let me have mine."

Payne surrendered smiling. "Okay, Elizabeth, you win. Let me get my pen."

"Here's one," she said before he took one step away from the desk.

"I can see that in a couple of years we're going to have to rename this place Payne, Nelson, and Brooks," he said as he endorsed the check.

"I hope you remember that," Elizabeth said. "Otherwise, I may have to find another broker."

"I wouldn't like that at all; I'll remember," Payne stated with commitment. "Just keep commissions like this coming in."

"You know I will," she said as they walked into the hallway.

"Where are you going?" Payne asked.

"To the bank," Elizabeth responded with a flourish. "Just as I planned. See you on Monday."

CHAPTER 7

The digitized voice was indistinct, muffled and broken. "Well, Off . . . Han . . . how . . . we . . . out?"

"That's as good as I can get it on this equipment," Eric Kauffman said as he manipulated the controls of one of the electronic boxes attached to the dashboard of the sedan. "Next time we should consider keeping the van on site if we're planning to do this kind of thing. Not only would the voices be clearer, but we wouldn't have to wait until the end of the surveillance to filter the conversations."

Philip Roberts wasn't listening to his partner's suggestions concerning what should be done on future assignments; the current case, it suddenly seemed, was very much alive. "Play it again," he ordered.

"Sure sounds like our buddy Hanlon came back for more," Kauffman observed as they listened once again to the barely intelligible words.

"Incredible," Roberts said angrily. "What's it going to take to get this kid out of our hair? Let's hear the rest of it."

For several minutes, Kauffman ran through four iterations of the conversation, finally ending up with a product somewhat illuminating in its content despite the fact that its quality was severely lacking. "Hanlon is talking with a guy named Weiss," he said. "You know him?"

"Yes. You saw him, too. He's the mob lawyer who was at the house yesterday. He filed a motion for the release of the body in Manhattan, but we haven't heard from him since Sandy phoned him with the news that the corpse would be in his hands tomorrow."

"Sounds like they're talking about our cleaning of the house," Kauffman noted.

"They can make of that whatever they want," Roberts said. "What was that at the end?"

"There . . . something . . . take with me," the recorded voice of Joe Hanlon said.

The agents listened intently to the rest of the muffled dialogue. "He found something outside of the house, then both of them went out to look at it," Kauffman said.

"I app . . . assistance. . . ." Joe's voice came.

"I don't . . . anything. . . evidence. . . ." Weiss replied.

"Whatever it was Hanlon found, he took with him," Kauffman said after they listened to the rest of the parting words.

"We need to know, Eric," Roberts said. "We need to know why this asshole was back at the house again this morning, despite our best efforts to keep him away, and we need to know what it was he took with him."

"Christ, Phil, whatever he found, it can't be anything related to the operation. It's just us two up here now; we don't have the manpower to undertake an investigation like this."

"It's time to improvise," Roberts said. "Too many things have already gone awry with this mission. No real damage has been done yet, but we can't afford to overlook the possibility that this new development might bring trouble. One thing for sure is that I am completely fed up with this local cop."

"Ex-cop," Kauffman corrected.

"That's right. What time was Hanlon at the house?"

Kauffman checked the digital readouts. "He arrived after seven this morning, and was out just before eight."

"Okay. See if you can coax anything else out of the recordings; I'll be inside making a couple of phone calls. I'm going to push back our departure time another twenty-four hours. Sorry to break into your weekend."

"No problem, Phil."

Roberts exited the sedan, parked in the lot adjacent to the White Plains Federal Building, and made his way to his temporary office on the second floor. The day had begun routinely enough, he recalled as he ascended the stairs. Kauffman went to the Bonnelli house to check the effectiveness of their new listening devices and to gage the atmosphere of the household in the aftermath of the death. Although a sweep of the house by Bonnelli's people the previous afternoon had uncovered three older devices, Roberts was pleased that all four of the newer gadgets had not been found. He was displeased with their range, however. Kauffman had been on a road down the hill from the house near the Hudson River, and the quality of the audio was decidedly lacking at a mere two hundred yards.

It had been enough to uncover yet another twist in the operation, however, Roberts knew as he entered the office. He retrieved a notebook from his pocket, grabbed the telephone, and punched in a number.

"Yes?" a tired voice answered after three rings.

"Chandler, it's Agent Roberts."

"What can I do for you now?" a submissive Kevin Chandler inquired.

"Tell me what happened this morning," Roberts demanded.

"It didn't take long," Chandler related. "I read Chief Dempsey the riot act concerning his wayward officer, then Hanlon joined us a few minutes later and was fired."

"What did he say?"

"He wasn't happy, but he didn't say much of anything. He handed over his gun and badge, then we went to his computer. He was in the process of writing some report. I had him delete it."

"Did he bring anything in with him or mention he found something at Bonnelli's?" Roberts asked insistently.

"When I saw him he was empty handed," Chandler replied. "And, no, he didn't say anything about his activities at the house. Look, I've done everything I can. Can't you guys lay off?" he asked, exasperated.

"Chandler, it'll be over when we say it's over," Roberts said harshly. "Stay by your phone; we may need more from you before the day is out." He terminated the conversation with a forefinger. His next call was answered on the first ring.

"Haines."

"Sandy, I need you to push off our flight another day," Roberts said. "We also might be in need of some computer support; we're a little lacking up here without the van."

"Of course, Phil. Anything wrong?"

"A minor annoyance," Roberts said. "It's that local cop, Hanlon. He's been buzzing around our operation like a housefly since yesterday morning. No matter how many times we've swatted at him, he keeps coming back."

"Do you need assistance?" she queried. "A couple of us could come up this afternoon; we could even bring the van."

"That's not necessary, Sandy. With our schedule as tight as it is, I don't want to waste the manpower, and the van has to be readied for next week's mission. This guy is nothing but a small irritation, probably as harmless to our operation as a fly. He certainly has no more information about what we were doing up here than an insect, but we have to check out everything, no matter how small the threat."

"Okay, Phil. We'll be here for you."

"You can start by getting us the home address of this Joseph Hanlon. He probably lives in Sunnyside or one of the surrounding towns."

"I'll get right on it."

"I believe it's time to have another face-to-face with this guy," Roberts thought aloud.

"We don't need menus," Joe said, holding off the young waitress with a gesture of his hand. "Just bring us two orders of haggis."

"I don't know if we have that," the perplexed girl informed him.

"It's the minced heart, liver, and lungs of a sheep, mixed with suet, onions, and oatmeal, all placed in the stomach of the animal and boiled to tasty perfection."

"We don't offer anything like that," the waitress stated as her face scrunched up in a look of disgust.

"Well I hope you offer entrees just as delectable," Joe stated with a straight face as he relieved the girl of her two-menu burden.

"You're bad," Elizabeth said with a grin after they were alone. She had experienced the haggis routine six times since they mutually discovered what the dish consisted of on their third date—from a dictionary, not a restaurant.

"Someday, we're going to walk into a place that will call our bluff, and we'll find ourselves facing plates piled high with stuffed stomach."

"You can pick up that tab."

"So how's the car?" Joe asked, gesturing out the window in the direction of the adjacent transmission shop.

"According to the experts, it only needs minor repairs," Elizabeth answered. "Of course, their definition of 'minor' is in the range of three or four hundred dollars. They said I can pick it up first thing Monday, which is convenient for work, but I'm not looking forward to a long trip in your old car."

"Hey, no cracks about the Nissan," Joe said, feigning offense. "It's provided reliable transport for years. Whose car is in the shop now, anyway?"

Interrupted by the waitress, they both ordered light lunches of sandwiches and salads.

"Why the sudden change of plans?" Elizabeth asked. "It's not normal for you to take an afternoon off."

"I got in a bit of trouble this morning; the time off was mandated."

"What happened?" she asked, concerned. "It's been all over the news about Victor Bonnelli's death, but I didn't hear anything about the local police being involved. Does it have something to do with that?"

"You are a bright one, El. Yes. The activity surrounding the death was definitely the FBI's show, so much so that they did not appreciate it when I stumbled onto their odd operation."

"Tell me everything," Elizabeth said, her eyes alive with interest.

The waitress delivered their repast and between bites Joe related his experiences over the previous two days, though he did not detail his suspicions concerning the agents and did not go into his discovery of the dead squirrel.

"Damn, Joe, it sounds like you might be looking for a new job."

"I doubt it," Joe replied as calmly as he could. "I can't say I'm not worried, but I trust Chief Dempsey. I believe he's right and that things will blow over. I'm going to take a few days off, but everything should be back to normal by about next Wednesday."

"I hope you're right," Elizabeth commented as they stood to leave.

Joe retrieved his keys as the two of them reached the Nissan. After opening the trunk, Joe set Elizabeth's case between his own bag and the small paper parcel he had acquired earlier that morning, then turned his attention to the spare tire.

"What are you doing?" she asked after catching the intense look on Joe's face.

"I always check the spare," Joe said. He shut the trunk, turned around, and embraced his girl. "I love you, El," he said after several warm kisses. "Let's get out of here. I've looked forward to being with you all week."

"I'm ready," she almost whispered in his ear, "but I'm worried about meeting your parents."

"I'm sure everything will be fine. Besides, they're hours away. Let's forget what's here and what's there for a while and just enjoy the ride."

Within minutes, the car was on the New York State Thruway. After crossing the Tappan Zee Bridge, Joe took the first exit and headed north. "We're taking the scenic route today," he announced.

"I don't like the sound of that," Elizabeth said with mock dread, having experienced one of Joe's circuitous and ill-defined "scenic routes" during a trip to Connecticut two months before.

"We can hardly get lost today. We're actually traveling the shortest possible distance, although the two-lane road can't compete with the thruway for speed. This is Route 9W, and except for minor detours we'll be taking it all the way up. I grew up just two hundred yards from this road."

The miles went by quickly as the car wound its way through the greening hills of the Hudson Valley, through quaint villages and large, undeveloped parks abutting the river. At length, they came upon an exquisitely appointed castle tower rendered in granite standing in the middle of the road.

"What is that?" Elizabeth asked in surprise.

"Probably the most ostentatious guard shack in the United States Army," Joe replied. "We're entering West Point, once an important Revolutionary outpost, now home to the U.S. Military Academy."

As they drove down the main road, Joe explained to his companion various features of the military installation, dividing his narrative between the area's prominence in the Revolution and its status as a renowned school.

"You seem to know quite a bit about this place," Elizabeth commented, as Joe parked the car by a level, wide expanse of lawn known as the Plain.

"I was stationed here for a few months at the end of my military service," Joe said. "The orders that brought me here were based on the post's proximity to my home of record and its medical facilities." He gestured across the grassy Plain at the post's largest building, a wide stone structure consisting of a central edifice flanked by six-story wings. "That's the main cadet barracks—the student rooms. In the center is the mess hall, where they feed all four thousand cadets at one sitting, three times a day."

"Quite a place," Elizabeth stated.

"Yes it is."

Elizabeth caught a subtle inflection in Joe's voice and turned. "It sounds to me you might have wanted to go here—as a cadet, I mean."

"Ancient history," he responded in a slightly melancholy tone. "I thought about competing for an appointment in high school, but decided against it. A few years later, there was another opportunity, but things didn't work out then either."

"That's too bad," Elizabeth comforted.

"Is it? As a West Point graduate, I would probably have been an Army captain in Korea, or Germany, or some godforsaken desert outpost like Fort Irwin about the time I was giving out a speeding ticket to a certain beautiful woman. We would have never met."

"And I would have saved sixty dollars," she recalled.

Following a long stroll around the grassy, ordnance-enhanced grounds of Trophy Point, the pair resumed their car trip. "That's the building where I spent most of my time here," Joe commented as they passed the post hospital, a layered, gray building that looked remarkably like the superstructure of a battleship. Shortly after, he turned right just past West Point's northern exit. "This is Route 218," he said. "It served as the main route to civilization from West Point back in the 1920's; now it's just a secondary route to Newburgh."

"Newburgh isn't civilization?"

"We're unavoidably going through the city on our way up to Marlborough. You can decide for yourself."

Paralleling the river, the road wound pleasantly for several miles through the trees. Having hiked the hills extensively, Joe pointed out several features of the area, including the overgrown entrance to Stock-hamfield. At one time one of the finest estates on the west bank of the Hudson, the land attendant to the abandoned ruins had been incorporated into Storm King State Park. Soon, the road began to climb and was soon clear of the trees. "This is Storm King Mountain," he said. "This stretch of road always reminds me of those cartoon mountain roads depicting a sheer wall of rock on one side and a straight drop on the other."

"I can see why," Elizabeth responded as her eyes moved from the nearly vertical rise to the left of the car to the precipitous drop on the right, thankful for the low stone wall that separated the car from a potential plummet that was quickly approaching four hundred feet.

"We're in luck; there's nobody at the overlook," Joe announced as he maneuvered the car into a tiny roadside parking area barely capable of handling two vehicles.

Braving a brisk breeze, Elizabeth joined Joe on a rock outcrop on the perilous side of the protective wall. "Wow," was her only comment as she took in the scene, a sprawling view of the Hudson greater than a hundred eighty degrees in breadth. Topping off the vista was a small island sporting a large castle. "There must be some story behind that," she commented.

Joe followed her eyes and smiled. "I've been there. Officially, it's called Pollopel Island, but to most it's known as Bannerman's, after the arms dealer who improved the property with that six-story castle. It's an abandoned ruin now, but once upon a time, the island was home to the world's largest private arsenal. It's a great place, romantic, even—magical."

Elizabeth turned to Joe and caught a sparkle in his eye. "I take it you were not alone on your previous trip there," she surmised.

Joe reached out and warmly embraced Elizabeth. "That was long ago, in a different world, and things ended . . . badly. It's you I love, El. Everything else is so much baggage."

Elizabeth hugged him back, tightly.

"Well, El, we have dinner waiting," Joe said softly. "Time to meet the parents."

"I'm ready, although my stomach's a little uneasy," Elizabeth replied as they turned away from the river.

"Speaking of stomachs, I asked my mother to prepare a particular meal for this special occasion," Joe stated with a smile.

"You don't mean . . ."

"She flatly refused, of course."

———————

Though it was less than a mile from his downtown office suite, Andrew Weiss seldom ventured to the squat brick building that served as rude headquarters for half a dozen small construction companies. Intensely undistinguished, the flat-roofed, two-story box was once a uniform ivory white, but water and wind, sun and smog had taken their toll on the twelve-year-old paint job, and there was not a single square foot of its exterior surface that was not chipped, faded, or discolored by rust or dirt. Though one of the businesses sharing the building was a four-man painting firm, the only thing the resident painters had done to the façade in a decade was to spray paint rough, angular characters to either side of the front entry, in crude imitation of the colorful graffiti that adorned all other structures in the neighborhood. Though the building's owner had wanted to blend in, the area's gangs, having knowledge of the affiliation of the construction workers within, were loath to accommodate him.

"I'll be about half an hour," Weiss informed his driver. "Pull down the street or drive around to stay clear of the riffraff. I'll call when I'm ready for pickup."

"Yes, sir," the chauffer acknowledged.

Briefcase in hand, the lawyer went between two parked cars and made a beeline toward the gray steel door. As expected, five men accosted him before he had gone ten feet.

"Could you tell us what is going on in there?" shouted one man. "When's the funeral?" asked another. "Mr. Weiss! Who is going to take over the Bonnelli family now?" The questions came one on top of the other as each of the reporters competed for attention, desperate for any tidbit of information.

Without a word to encourage the continued cacophony, Weiss reached the door and, as if responding to a mental command, it opened. He entered the building and within seconds was separated from the reporters by two inches of steel. In the dimly lit hallway, he faced the man who had awaited his arrival from his post at the peephole.

"Mr. Weiss, I'm Sammy Capizzi," the doorman greeted. "We met maybe two years ago at one of Nicky's trials."

"Of course," Weiss said, vaguely recalling the man who aided the defense by providing a convenient alibi.

"Nicky's upstairs, but Mr. Kastner asked that I take you to see him first. He's just down the hall."

"Lead on," Weiss said.

As he followed Capizzi down the long corridor, the lawyer noted only one other person on the ground floor, a mousy-haired receptionist who occupied a position behind a metal desk awash in telephones. After passing three more offices, Capizzi motioned Weiss into a room marked on the door with the name of an asbestos removal firm, then returned to his post.

"Mr. Weiss, good to see you," Karl Kastner said.

"Give me an update."

"The atmosphere here isn't good. Nicky's still on a binge, and nobody knows what's going to happen when it ends, and according to his co-workers it always ends after three or four days. As for business activity, the fellows here are just going through the motions, just marking time while waiting for something to pop."

"I need you to stick close to Nicky until the funeral; I think a clear direction for the future will be outlined within two days after that."

"I'm glad to hear it," Kastner said. "I think Nicky needs to go home tonight. Among his many demands, it's the one he's vocalized the most."

"Agreed, but I want him to have a bodyguard. Anyone here capable of handling the job?"

"Capizzi, the man you met at the door. He seems to be Nicky's most loyal lackey, and I think he's done the work before."

"Okay. Stick around until Nicky is out the door, then go home and get a good night's rest. We'll pick things up first thing tomorrow morning."

"One more thing, Mr. Weiss," Kastner said. "Quite a few men work out of this office, and I've had nothing much better to do than to watch them for the past couple of days. Most act about as expected, rough in manner and speech, constantly engaging in gabfests about nothing in particular, but there's one guy who doesn't fit the mold. He's reserved, but he subtly elicits a great deal of respect from the others. I don't think anybody acknowledges him as a leader, but he gets things done."

"What's his name?" Weiss asked, intrigued, having wondered for some time who really was in charge of the branch of the Bonnelli family officially headed by Nicky.

"Joey Messina. Before yesterday, I never heard of him. We've never defended him, and he was never used as a witness."

"You may have discovered the person who has kept Nicky out of trouble for all these years," Weiss said.

"That may be going a little too far, Mr. Weiss. Nicky has been our biggest headache as far as criminal litigation."

"You don't know him like I do; things could have been a lot worse. I'm going up to see the young heir now and have him sign some papers. Stay down here and fill Capizzi in on his duties tonight. You can notarize the documents back at the office sometime over the weekend."

They left the office and found Sammy Capizzi in rapt conversation with the receptionist. Kastner motioned him away from the desk and the two retreated down the hallway as Weiss started his ascent to the second floor.

Weiss reached the top of the stairs and took in the scene. The men who lay within his vision did not impress him. All sitting or supine in the numerous overstuffed chairs and couches scattered around the large room, none of them looked like they were engaged in anything remotely worthwhile. With beers in hand and empties on the floor around them, two men in one corner engaged in low conversation. Near them, oblivious to the smoke-permeated surroundings, a beefy man lay diagonally across a sofa, deep in sleep. Nicky's condition was not apparent, as he sat slumped in another couch in front of a television, the back of his head barely visible. Only one man looked at him with a disinterested glance. Dressed a bit more nattily than the others, the footsteps on the stairs pulled his attention away from his reading material, a paperback edition of *Humboldt's Gift*. Without a doubt, Weiss knew the man was Joey Messina, apparently the de facto head of Bonnelli's enforcement squad.

As Messina was closest to the lawyer, Weiss knew it would not be out of place to approach him. "I'm Andrew Weiss," he addressed the seated figure. "I'm here to see Mr. Bonnelli."

"He's over there," came the cool volley back. The man gestured in the direction of Nicky with his thumb, but said no more.

Weiss walked away from Messina, wondering how he might better approach the low-profile mob soldier who probably was so much more.

His eyes half closed, Nicky seemed to be mesmerized by the moving pictures on the electronic box before him, currently airing a rerun of *The Beverly Hillbillies*. He took no notice of the man directly to his front until Weiss leaned over and turned the television off.

"Hello, Nicky," he said.

The inebriated mobster, unable to shift and refocus his eyes, moved his head slightly in the direction of the greeting. "Oh, look, it's my fucking lawyer," he said in a drunken slur. "Find some legal fucking loophole that brings back the dead?"

"That's pretty cold, Nicky. Your father was a good friend, and I'm as upset as you over his death." Weiss spoke slowly, carefully enunciating each word to assist his client's alcohol-soaked brain to comprehend his speech.

"Weiss, I'm tired of hanging around this fucking shithole," Nicky spat. "I want the fuck out of here."

"It's being arranged, Nicky; we'll have you home tonight, but first we have some business to do. Weiss sat down and removed a fistful of papers from his briefcase. "A lot of people depend on you now, Nicky. These papers have to be signed."

"I don't fucking feel like signing no fucking papers," Nicky barely managed, his breath befouled by a variety of hard liquors and cheap wine.

Ignoring the olfactory affront, the lawyer coaxed and coddled his client, finally managing to get a pen in his hand and the empty briefcase on his lap. Keeping up a running encouragement, Weiss fed him a stream of documents, withdrawing each after the young Bonnelli anointed it with his rabid scrawl. Standard corporate resolutions, assumptions of partnership interests, and signature pages of tax returns made up the bulk of the pile, but scattered in among the last two dozen papers were a liberal assignation of power of attorney, deeds to several choice pieces of property, and a will. Although the two of them were left alone during the process, Weiss could feel he was being slyly observed from across the room by that new enigma, Joey Messina.

While it was considered ostentatious by many to give picturesque names to modern estates, few derided, and many celebrated, those with historic appellations. The exact year of Idlewild's construction was unknown, but the house was featured in designer Calvert Vaux's illustrated architectural tome *Villas and Cottages* in 1857. Barely visible over a rise from its entry pillars on Route 9W, Idlewild was built on a plateau that rose gently from the west, but descended sharply for several hundred yards to the east, providing a magnificent view of the Hudson River.

"That's quite a place," Elizabeth commented to Joe as she attempted to make out the details of the residence through the rapidly deepening dusk. Like soldiers deployed for eighteenth century battle, the windows of the house were spaced perfectly, rank and file. Seven windows on the second floor were positioned directly over the front entry foyer and groups of three casements to either side of the door. At the flanks of the main body were more lighted trios, evidence of single story wings.

"Looks like all the lamps are lit in honor of this special occasion," Joe said as the Nissan closed to within a hundred yards of his old home.

More imposing to Elizabeth than the house was the prospect of meeting its residents. Her relationship with Joe had been a month old when she learned Albert Paul Hanlon was in a business associated with her own, heading a firm that was among the top hundred construction companies in New York State. Although she tried to resist stereotyping Albert, her dealings with people of his stature had been unpleasant. Without exception, she found them arrogant, severe in their judgment, and quick to make known their prejudices concerning those who did not meet their standards.

Joe eased the car into the turnaround in front of the house circling a perfectly round, grassy island, at the center of which stood a flagpole displaying a large American flag illuminated by spotlights from four directions. There were no other cars in sight. "Looks like my sister and her husband won't be making it tonight," he commented. "I'm sure they'll be over tomorrow. I think you'll like Charlotte, but Mike Fleming is something else. He has a passion for killing deer. If he's not hunting right now, you can be sure he's either preparing for a trip or regaling his buddies with tales of past conquests."

"What about sleeping arrangements?" Elizabeth asked, vocalizing the last of her many concerns as the Nissan came to a stop.

"Our visit brings up a situation which has no precedent," Joe pondered aloud, having the effect of both comforting his lover with the knowledge that calls on his parents with girlfriends were not a regular occurrence and causing her anxiety about yet another unknown. "Although the folks are fairly conservative, we are adults. My guess is we'll be ushered toward the north end of the house, where there are two bedrooms, and left to deal with the situation on our own."

"So do we muss up one bed or two?"

"Neither. It's one of the unwritten rules of Idlewild, a meticulously maintained abode, that all beds be made up before breakfast." Smiling, Joe reached over the console and caressed her left hand with his right. "To answer the question, I think one bed will suit us just fine. Ready?"

"Let's do it."

Close together, they walked from the car and ascended three wide steps to the front porch. Joe rang the doorbell, and after a long fifteen seconds, the right-hand panel of the double doors opened, revealing the lord and lady of the manor, a distinguished couple in their mid-fifties.

A barely perceptible half second of silence followed, a subtle, suspended moment in time which served to completely dispense with the Big Issue, astonishing Elizabeth from that point on.

"Come in, you two," the woman said gaily, ushering the pair into the spacious foyer.

"Good to see you, Joe," the man chimed in, grinning.

"Mom, Dad, this is El—izabeth," Joe introduced, at the final millisecond bowing to his lover's wish that he utilize her full name when introducing her.

"It's a pleasure, Elizabeth. I'm Rose. Joe has told us so much about you."

The man, holding a drink of amber liquid in a crystal tumbler, extended his free hand. "Al," he said as he engaged in a warm handshake with his guest. "Heard about your sale. Hell of a deal."

"Thank you," Elizabeth managed, nearly overwhelmed by the hospitality and the decor. Magnificent twin staircases led up to the second level from the sides of the high-ceilinged foyer. Straight ahead was an elegantly decorated sitting room, and beyond that, through a rear wall of glass, she could see the sparkle of lights from homes on the opposite shore of the Hudson.

"Can I get you a drink?" asked Albert Hanlon of the couple.

"Of course," Joe answered immediately for both of them, having knowledge of the local mores that forbade a refusal. After taking an order from Elizabeth, he joined his father in a trip to the living room bar while the women headed toward the kitchen.

"How's work?" inquired the father of the son as he poured himself another scotch.

"Could be better," Joe understated wildly. He retrieved a bottle from the small refrigerator under the mahogany countertop and filled two glasses with chilled Chablis. "How are things here?"

"Business hasn't been as good in years. Even Milton is showing signs of growth," Albert said, referring to the tiny village a few miles north of Idlewild that had experienced its share of economic bad times. "You know about the renovations we're doing at the winery, and just last month we landed a contract to build a big addition to the bottling plant."

"Sounds great."

"We're always looking for good people," Albert ventured.

Joe looked at, through, and beyond his father all at once, contemplating the events of the recent past and his uncertain future. "Dad, I'll think about it," he said seriously. "I don't think it would work, though. We're just too much alike to get along with each other."

"Let's go join the girls," Albert suggested, obviously satisfied with the response. They found Elizabeth and Rose in the kitchen putting the final touches on the evening meal. Renovated two years before, the room now boasted yards of granite countertop, a small forest of cherry, and major appliances that were difficult to locate, as the refrigerator and dishwasher featured the same carved panels as the ample cabinetry.

"Joe, perhaps you can show Elizabeth around the house," Albert suggested. "I'll help your mother finish with dinner."

"Sure," Joe agreed. "We're eating in the dining room?" he asked, noting that the informal eating table was bereft of utensils.

"This is a special occasion, son."

Joe caught the double meaning and walked out with Elizabeth beside him.

"What's going on?" Elizabeth inquired after they were two rooms distant.

"I just told Dad I would think about taking a job with his company, and he took my unqualified 'maybe' as a 'yes.'"

"So you're going to work for him?"

"I don't think so, but by this time next week I may not have much of a choice. Excuse me for a minute. I have to use the can."

"You're so eloquent," she gently chided as she watched him retreat toward the powder room located down a short hallway off the foyer.

As Elizabeth rarely remained stationary for long, Joe knew he had a search in store for him as he exited the facilities. The quest for his ladylove did not last long, and he found her just a few yards away.

Though the paneled, book-lined den functioned as a male retreat, the room's decor, like all of Idlewild's interior, was a product of Rose Hanlon's meticulous attention to detail. To Joe's slight embarrassment, Elizabeth was examining the room's only wall hangings, a line of weighty oak frames, each surrounding a foot-square pane of glass that covered a cornucopia of military badges, insignia, and medals. Set into the base of each frame was a brass plate engraved with a name, the five surnames being identical.

"What's all this?" an intrigued Elizabeth asked.

"The 'Military Review,'" Joe explained sheepishly. "It's one of my mother's projects, documenting five generations of government service. Dad and I think it's a bit over the top, but in this house none dare touch what she installs."

"Tell," Elizabeth urged.

"Charles Hanlon, my great-great grandfather, was a captain in a regiment of New York volunteers during the Civil War, settling here in Marlborough after the conflict. Charles, Jr., his son, was a farmer like his father, but in his early twenties served a three-year stint in the Navy. He was a seaman on board the cruiser *Raleigh* under Admiral Dewey at the battle of Manila Bay. His oft-told tales of life at sea inspired my grandfather to attend the U.S. Naval Academy. His display is the one in the middle."

"What's this?" Elizabeth asked, pointing to the topmost decoration within the most copiously filled frame, unique in that its ribbon was much larger than any other and sported embroidered stars instead of stripes.

"That's the Medal of Honor. My grandfather, Sheldon, was a submarine commander in World War II, a very successful one. After the war, he purchased Idlewild, then added the wings and renovated the rest. We all lived with him here until he died, nearly twenty years ago."

Five seconds of silence followed, a reverent pause.

"My father comes next. He served in the Marine Corps and was in Vietnam during the early days of the war. The last one's mine; I served three years in the Army."

Elizabeth scrutinized the last frame in the row. Slightly darker in finish than the others, the wide wood square surrounded a variety of colorful mementos. Not knowledgeable concerning things military, she recognized only one medal, which lay within the frames of both Joe and his father: the Purple Heart. As she was about to make further inquiry, they were interrupted by a figure at the doorway.

"Dinner's ready," Rose Hanlon said cheerfully.

"Thanks, Mom," Joe acknowledged, then turned to Elizabeth. "Go ahead, I'll join you in two minutes. I have to make a phone call."

"Don't be long," Elizabeth said, obviously disbelieving the time estimate.

CHAPTER 8

Excruciatingly confused, Kenneth DeLuca was adrift on a vast sea of ambivalence, the vessel of his soul awash with a caustic mixture of enviable blessings and haunting curses that he found incomprehensible. To most, he was the brilliant Dr. DeLuca, gregarious as the most good-humored extrovert and generous as Scrooge reformed. No Marlborough resident knew the dark reasons behind his flight from a promising career in medical research, and few wondered, so fortunate did they feel to have such a superb doctor serve the community as a general practitioner. Nor was he ostracized from the side of his profession he had distanced himself from. Still respected as an authority in several esoteric fields, he performed intermittent consulting work and occasional peer reviews, checking and questioning the work of cutting-edge researchers far younger than his nearly seventy years.

Chilled by a moderate breeze that wafted across the rear deck of his residence, built on a gently cresting high point along aptly named Ridge Road, DeLuca stared into the indigo night that all but hid the hundreds of acres of pear and apple orchards abutting his two-acre lot. The four-bedroom house at his back was much too large for him and his companion, but it had been the perfect size when his family had moved in two decades before. His son had moved out first to become a doctor, though the specifics of the career choice had deeply anguished him. His wife was taken from him a few years after. Though he had nursed her through several bad illnesses, when she died his medical expertise had been useless, as he did not even have an opportunity to attempt to save her. Right on the heels of the death, his daughter left him, first in spirit, then in body to further her schooling and enter a career. Over the years, he had come to regard her ivy-league education as a tragedy; only after nearly a decade of hesitant, faltering efforts was he able to reestablish a bond of affection with her.

Abruptly detached from his reminiscences by a nuzzle at his leg, DeLuca looked down to find the expectant furry face of the other occupant of the house. "Yes, Edson, it is well past your dinner time," he acknowledged to the cocker spaniel. "I shall rectify the situation immediately." He walked across the deck and entered the house through the rear French doors, followed closely by the anxious pet.

DeLuca retrieved a large bag of dry chunks from a kitchen cabinet and filled one of the two empty bowls on the floor by the sink. Sweeping up the other bowl, the doctor filled it from the tap. "Looks like you'll drink tonight," he said, an offhanded reference to the low water pressure from the town main under Ridge Road. Though complete outages were rare, when they occurred they were extremely irritating.

The chimes of the front doorbell resonated through the house and the dog emitted a bark muffled by the bowl that encircled his snout. He left his meal and joined his master in the foyer as the door opened, and barked once more before recognizing the figure on the front stoop.

"Joseph, my boy, it is good to see you," the doctor greeted, exuding a genuine kindness. "How is that leg of yours?"

"As good as new, or nearly so," Joe replied with a smile, recalling the kind care of the doctor during his recuperation the previous year. "I still have a slight limp, but it's quickly fading."

"That's good to hear."

The dog anxiously circled the two humans. Joe reached down and gave the animal a gentle pat with his free hand. "And how's Edson doing?"

"Surprisingly agile for a beast his age," DeLuca answered. "He has dinner waiting in the kitchen, but seems more interested in that bag in your hand. I assume that's the item you mentioned on the phone."

"Dr. DeLuca, I know this is an odd request, but I'd like to have an expert's opinion as to a cause of death," Joe requested as he opened the top of the paper receptacle.

The doctor peered into the bag and recognized the inert figure as a deceased gray squirrel. "The strangeness of your request is dependent entirely on the circumstances," he replied. "As to expertise, you've come to the right place. Although it has been some time, in my research days I autopsied thousands of lab animals, including cousins of your little friend here."

"It's probably nothing, but there's a chance the death of this squirrel might be related to something I'm looking into. I found it . . ."

"Say no more," DeLuca interrupted. "Let's see what I can uncover on my own. Let's go downstairs."

Joe followed DeLuca down a long run of stairs after he closed the door to prevent the dog from joining them. After finding the way blocked, Edson returned to his meal.

Except for a small restroom and a smaller utility area, the basement was entirely taken up by DeLuca's extensive laboratory. Serving patients, consultees, and peers alike, the surprisingly complete facilities also provided the doctor with his chief form of recreation. Although the basement lay entirely below grade, it boasted a large sliding glass door that opened onto a gentle earth ramp extending up to the level of the rear lawn.

"This is some place." Joe commented.

"It's not much compared to the big labs," DeLuca replied, lamenting the fact that despite intense efforts he never made one discovery he considered substantial.

"Where would you like it?" Joe asked as he lifted the bag slightly.

"The table to your right," DeLuca answered, gesturing to a wide white surface cluttered with a variety of equipment. He donned a pair of plastic gloves, gently hefted the corpse out of the bag, and began his examination.

"I see no sign of trauma and no blood," DeLuca noted as he manipulated the animal with his skilled hands. "Neck isn't broken; no fractured bones at all as far as I can tell. From the configuration of the body, it appears the animal fell from some height, either after it was dead or shortly before it expired, but it didn't die in the fall. From the blood settlement, it looks like it lay undisturbed on an inclined surface after death, with its head near the most elevated point."

"From what I observed, you're right on in every detail," Joe said admiringly. "Any idea how long it's been dead?"

"Did you find it outside, in the open?"

"Yes, but it's been in the trunk of my car since early this morning."

"Given the weather we've been having, I would say it has been removed from the world of the living at least a day but not more than two, two and a half at most."

"That fits," Joe said.

DeLuca picked up a fine-toothed instrument and combed the flattened side of the body. "Along with fine threads of organic matter, there are some curious particles," he said as he picked up a magnifying glass. "They appear to be manmade." He put his tool down and turned to Joe. "Given what I already stated about the body resting on an incline, I would tentatively conclude that these granules are from asphalt roof shingles, but I'd have to test them to make sure."

"There's no need for a test, Dr. DeLuca. The squirrel was recovered from a roof. Asphalt shingles."

The doctor completed the external examination of his subject by checking its head and tail orifices. After finding nothing amiss, he turned to his visitor. "Joe, I don't know why this little fellow died, but I will. My next step is to cut him open and go into various procedures that are somewhat time consuming. I probably won't have an answer tonight."

"I appreciate whatever you can do, Dr. DeLuca."

"Fill me in on the circumstances that brought you here."

"I discovered the squirrel at a house in Sunnyside this morning. Yesterday, two other bodies were found in the vicinity. I think it's possible that the deaths of all three are related."

"Were the other two bodies humans or animals?" DeLuca inquired, his curiosity piqued.

"One man, one cat."

"That was some news out of Sunnyside yesterday. Might I know of this man?" DeLuca pressed with a sly grin.

"Well . . ."

"No," the doctor recanted. "We can get into the details when I call you with the results of the examination. Will you be in town all weekend?"

"I'll be at my parents' house until Sunday afternoon."

"Good. I will call you at Idlewild, Sunday morning at the latest. Let's meet again before you leave."

"I'd like that," Joe said.

"I heard through the grapevine you were bringing up a girlfriend on this trip."

"Uh . . . yes," Joe admitted, uncomfortable.

"Well, you better be off to rescue her," the doctor joked. "There's no telling what mischief might be afoot without you there to protect her from your parents' wiles."

They stood up and shook hands warmly. "Doctor, I . . ."

"Don't say it. I'm glad to help, and I didn't have anything planned for this weekend except the dreary task of attending to my taxes. You've presented me with an exciting mystery, one I'm going to return to right now. Can you find your own way out?" It was a rhetorical question; Joe had been to the house dozens of times.

After another minute, the doctor was alone again. Distracted from the unremitting pain of his life, he launched himself into his work.

The irony of the situation was not lost on Philip Roberts: had he not gone out of his way to have the current bane of his existence fired, Joseph Hanlon would have been much easier to find. Among other things, the agent's actions had freed the ex-cop from the requirement to keep members of the Sunnyside Police Force informed of his whereabouts.

A visit to the station by his fish-on-a-hook, Councilman Kevin Chandler, produced next to nothing. It was expected that none of the officers present would be cooperative with the person who had ordered the dismissal of their co-worker, but Hanlon's personnel file was missing as well. Presumably, it had been taken for administrative outprocessing by the head of the force, but Chief Dempsey was off to parts unknown for the weekend and over a dozen attempts to page him were fruitless. Chandler did manage to pry Hanlon's unlisted phone number from the recalcitrant officers, but by the time he got it to Roberts, it was old news.

After contemptuously dismissing their reluctant ally, the agent and his assistant began their work in earnest, Roberts manning the computer in his temporary office in White Plains, and Eric Kauffman running down numerous leads in the field. Hanlon's address had been easy enough to find, but when Kauffman drove to the apartment building, he found no red Nissan among the vehicles in the vicinity and no visible activity within the third-floor residence from the street. The junior agent then entered and searched the premises, but came away with nothing.

Roberts next launched into an intensive search of Hanlon's telephone records. He discovered that over two-thirds of the fourteen calls made from the apartment during the previous month were to one number, the residence of an E. Brooks. After a call to the number resulted in a woman's voice on an answering machine, Roberts noted the address and dispatched Kauffman cross-county to the site. A short time later, Kauffman reported that, although the apartment was unoccupied, the status of the woman as Hanlon's girlfriend was verified by a photo of the man on her dresser.

Kauffman next visited the real estate brokerage of Payne and Nelson, only to find that Brooks had taken off for the weekend after she received a large commission check. In a lascivious tone, Ralph Payne informed the agent that she was probably with Hanlon, whom he had seen at the office twice before.

Encouraged that they had a good reason to spend money, Roberts then embarked on an exhaustive computer search of the finances of the pair. Several reports led the agent to a string of credit cards issued to one or the other, two of which had been used that day. Not buoyed by Hanlon's use of a Visa card to make a gas purchase at a local station just before noon, Roberts was slightly encouraged to find that one of the woman's cards had been used at a nearby restaurant early that afternoon. Kauffman verified Hanlon and Brooks were together from the waitress that served them, but learned nothing else from a disjointed tale regarding a request for an item not on the menu.

Convinced the people he was searching for were out on a weekend jaunt, Roberts kept cycling through credit card records all afternoon, monitoring the two Visa cards, a MasterCard, and a Discover card the couple held between them.

Roberts became less sure of his assumptions as the tedious afternoon ended and darkness descended. More than once during the frustrating hours, he contemplated enlisting the assistance of the agents that worked in the rooms around him, but resisted the temptation. Almost six hours into the vigil, Roberts discovered another possible destination. From Chandler, he learned that part of the benefits package for town of Sunnyside employees was a life insurance policy, and after a long and convoluted process Roberts now had the details of Hanlon's policy on his computer screen, complete with beneficiaries: Albert and Rose Hanlon. An address was listed, and minutes later Roberts discovered its location was less than two hours north, in rural Ulster County.

"Taking your girl to meet the parents, maybe?" Roberts said to himself, then considered his next step. After punching up the records of the phone company, the agent noted the number of Albert Hanlon in Marlborough, New York, then picked up the telephone receiver on his desk and punched in a set of numbers.

"Haines," the woman answered.

"Sandy, it's Phil," he greeted his fellow agent.

"Phil, how's it going? You found your man yet?"

"Not yet, but I have a lead I'd like you to check on. He might be at his parents' place for the weekend, about fifty miles north of here. I need you to find out if he's there. He knows my voice and Kauffman's, too, and I don't want to tip him off."

"What's the plan?" Haines asked.

"I'm going to fax you a copy of Hanlon's life insurance policy, along with the number to call. The parents are listed as beneficiaries. Play insurance agent. Ask whoever answers if Joseph Hanlon is in, and if he is, ask him if he wants to continue making payments on the policy. The life insurance was free to him as part of the benefits he received as a town of Sunnyside employee, but since he was fired this morning he'll have to make payments personally if he wants it to remain active."

"I understand."

"The fax is on the way," Roberts said, turning to his computer.

Less than ten minutes later, Roberts' phone buzzed. Grimly, he listened to the results of Haines' inquiry. "Okay, Sandy, that's interesting news," he said.

Roberts turned to his radio. "We missed the son of a bitch by five minutes," he informed Kauffman. "He was at an address two counties north of here and was supposedly going to be there all weekend, but his plans suddenly changed. Still, it looks like we might have him shortly."

"How's that?"

"Word is he's headed our way. He should be back in Sunnyside within two hours."

It was Joe that finally broke the brooding, almost palpable silence that had existed in the car for the previous thirty minutes and thirteen miles of travel. "One more time, just so I get it straight," he said with a forced calmness. "We left my parents' house because you had an argument with my father over—flag burning?"

"Yes."

"And that floodlit flag atop the forty-foot flagpole in front of the house did not give you a hint your views on the topic might result in some controversy?"

"It's something I happen to feel strongly about."

"Okay, maybe I agree that too much time and too many taxpayer dollars have been wasted on such a non-issue, but thankfully the ridiculous debate has quieted over the years. I haven't heard a single reference to flag burning in months. Until tonight."

"It may be ridiculous to you, but I think the standard politician's stance is downright dangerous," Elizabeth stated, seizing the opportunity to divert the discussion away from the immediate problem. "After criminalizing one freedom of expression, it wouldn't be long until the entire First Amendment was out the window."

"As I said, I'm with you on this—the general issue, anyway," Joe said as he pulled the car onto the New York Thruway and pointed the Nissan in the direction of Westchester County.

"Then we're basically in agreement with whoever said 'I disagree with what you say, but I will defend to the death your right to say it.'"

"It was Voltaire, and, yes, I do agree with the sentiment, although my personal version of the quote omits 'to the death.' You didn't seem

99

to be defending whatever my father was saying when I came back to the house, though. What happened?"

"We were discussing various topics in the living room. I don't remember exactly how the subject of flag burning came up, but he made a comment and I felt obliged to speak up."

"Uh huh," Joe muttered, though it sounded more like "uh oh."

"His reply was absurd, and I said so. Things went downhill from there."

"Where was my mother? She usually acts as a mediator in those discussions."

"On the phone in the kitchen," Elizabeth recalled. "I think she was talking with your sister."

"Then what?"

"We volleyed increasingly louder points of view at each other. I was upset with the scene and with your father and by the time you walked in the door I was more than ready to leave."

"Dad sometimes has a strange effect on people that don't know him well," Joe said. "I suppose it could have gone better, but you should regard what happened tonight as a success."

"What do you mean?" Elizabeth asked, incredulous. "It couldn't have gone worse."

"Dad actually enjoys getting into these tiffs once in a while, which invariably take place after he's had a few drinks. It gets his blood flowing, he explained to me once. He's very reserved about discussing controversial topics with anyone except family or close friends, though. Even my brother-in-law doesn't qualify. You two must have hit it off. I think he likes you. A lot."

"You have got to be shitting me," Elizabeth said, ending the sentence devoid of breath.

"He didn't insult you personally, did he?"

"No, he didn't," Elizabeth recalled after a moment's contemplation. "He just countered my arguments with the most outrageous statements."

"He does have a penchant for hyperbole," Joe explained.

"Why didn't you tell me this might happen?"

"I didn't think things would go so well. I expected a dull weekend of polite conversation. This changes everything."

"So what do we do now?"

"We're not far from Sunnyside and it's getting late. I think we should go to my place for the night. In the few words I had with my mother, I told her we might be doing exactly that and to expect a call in the morning. We can head back up after breakfast, if you're willing."

"I trust you," Elizabeth said.

The remainder of the journey went smoothly, as the night was clear and the traffic sparse. Fifteen minutes after they crossed the Tappan Zee Bridge, Joe pulled the Nissan into a parking space along Broadway by the narrow, wooded incline that led to his apartment.

"Shit!" Joe exclaimed almost simultaneously with the clunk of the driver's door of the Nissan as it seated itself into the frame.

"What's wrong?" Elizabeth asked over the car from the sidewalk.

"Today must have stressed me out more than I realized. I locked my keys in the car."

"I have a key to your apartment. Do you have an extra car key up there?"

"Yeah, somewhere," Joe stated, exasperated, searching in vain for an easier way to retrieve the keys that dangled from the ignition.

"There's nothing in my bag I can't live without until morning," Elizabeth said. "Let's go on up."

"I guess if all else fails, I can have one of the guys from the station come over tomorrow with a Slim Jim," he said. Close together, the couple negotiated the adjacent steep driveway, then entered Joe's building and climbed the stairs.

"You certainly were out of harm's way when I was engaged in battle with your father. Where did you disappear to?" Elizabeth asked as they entered the apartment.

"Visiting a friend."

"Something to do with whatever was in the paper bag?"

"Yes. I'll tell you about it when it's over. It's probably nothing. Right now, all I want to do is relax; it's been a long day." He dropped into a wide recliner and kicked off his shoes.

"I hope you're not too tired to do a little snuggling," Elizabeth cooed, advancing toward the chair.

"I think I could fit it into my schedule," Joe said gently. Extending an arm, he encompassed her waist and pulled her into his lap.

Elizabeth settled in, placing her head on his shoulder. "Do you really think everything's going to be all right?"

"I'm optimistic, but from time to time I feel like I'm in a classic novel."

Elizabeth recognized his foreboding tone. "And that isn't good?"

"All my favorites end tragically: *All Quiet on the Western Front, Nineteen Eighty-Four, A Farewell to Arms, From Here to Eternity.*"

"Well this is reality; it isn't scripted."

"Everything does seem perfect now," Joe said, thoroughly enjoying the moment. "I'm looking forward to a good weekend and an even brighter week. Everything's fine; you'll find out when we travel back up to Marlborough tomorrow."

"Okay," she replied, comforted.

They kissed, almost tentatively at first, then more fervently as they closed themselves off to the world and succumbed to the intense passions born of true love.

"I could get used to this, El," Joe said as he caressed Elizabeth's dark hair.

"Me too," she replied as her free hand roamed her lover's body. "It looks like Mr. Happy is awake," she observed.

"You do have a knack for arousing him."

"Perhaps we should continue our discussion in the bedroom."

They extracted themselves from the chair. "You set me on fire, El," Joe said as they walked down the short hallway, hoping she would pick up on the allusion.

"If you were a flag, I know someone who'd have me arrested," she obliged.

"I can't think of a better time to bust this guy's door in and take the asshole down," urged Eric Kauffman from the driver's seat of the sedan.

"If that was the plan, you'd be absolutely right," stated Philip Roberts as he turned a knob that slightly reduced the distinctive, guttural sounds of passionate lovemaking transmitted to the car courtesy of an electronic listening device. "I have something else in mind, though."

"Christ, Phil, we've been looking for this guy all day, and now here he is, ripe for the plucking," Kauffman said, gesturing out the windshield in the direction of Joe Hanlon's apartment building, a hundred yards distant across the street.

"I think there's something more to this guy than meets the eye, and I think a period of discreet surveillance will yield more than a session of harsh questions. If he landed anywhere else for the night we might have approached things differently, but right now he's perfectly positioned for us to gather a little covert intelligence."

"I guess he's not going anywhere," Kauffman agreed as his gaze dropped from the building to the red Nissan parked across Broadway less than fifty feet away. "Locked his keys in his car; what a moron."

"Never underestimate the enemy," Roberts warned. "He's been surprisingly persistent and resourceful, and whether by chance or choice, he managed to elude us all day."

"But he can't know anything, not anything important," Kauffman protested.

"You're almost certainly correct. We could probably turn our backs on the guy and never suffer the slightest consequence, but there is a slight chance he could do the project some harm."

"One in a million, if that."

"And there are wider implications," Roberts said. "Remember our ultimate goal is to be out of field work altogether, to be thousands of miles away when a death occurs. This is an opportunity to find out what might be discovered when we no longer have the luxury of being in the proximity. I want to know what he took away from that house that so intrigued him. It might help us in our planning."

"Do you think it was the thing in the bag the girl mentioned?"

"There's a good chance. We may have to make a trip up the river with them tomorrow to find out."

"How's that going to affect our timetable?" Kauffman queried tiredly.

"I want to get the hell out of here as much as you, Eric. It's been a long mission, and there's plenty of work waiting for us when we get back. My plans are to still make tomorrow afternoon's flight."

"Whatever it takes, Phil," Kauffman said, resigning himself to a full day of activity following his ninety-seventh all-night stakeout.

"Sounds like they're finished," Roberts observed. He turned up the volume on the equipment and the men listened intently to the ensuing conversation.

"Love you, love you, blah, blah, blah," Kauffman paraphrased. "Looks like we're in for a long night of nothing."

"Probably," Roberts said. "But how many times have you been surprised on one of these things by phone calls in the middle of the night or visitors at two A.M.?"

"A few," Kauffman admitted. "Three other times, I've had guys talk in their sleep, but only one was intelligible, and it didn't help with our case."

"Keep listening for voices in the night," Roberts instructed. "I'm going to recon the perimeter."

"Okay, Phil," Kauffman said.

When Roberts was halfway out of the car, a single, deep bark of a big dog in the distance failed to cover the beep of his watch indicating that midnight had arrived.

SATURDAY
11 APRIL

CHAPTER 9

Damn it to fuck, where the fuck am I? was Nicholas Bonnelli's first thought of the day as he opened his eyes and attempted to focus on the bleary surroundings. Heedless of the ache that had entrenched itself in his brain, he shook his head vigorously and sat up. In moments, his addled mind registered the location. He was in bed, in the place he referred to, with a favorite adjective, as his place, barn, or dump, depending on his mood. His environs naturally illuminated in a manner he seldom saw, he knew by the angle of the sunlight that it was early. Too fucking early.

Forcing his legs to find the floor, Nicky stood up and shook his throbbing head again, attempting in vain to drive away his hangover by sheer force of will. He was still dressed in the clothes he had worn the previous day, now tinged with the combined odors of smoke, alcohol, and sweat. His shoes, however, had been removed and placed by a nearby chair and the contents of his pockets now lay in a jumble on top of his dresser. The evidence was clear he had been assisted in his nightly ritual of drunkenly staggering to bed, but his attempts to draw from his fogged brain the identity of the helper proved fruitless.

Whoever it was still seemed to be in residence, Nicky noted, jerking his head at the faint rattle of paper that emanated from outside the bedroom. He retrieved his 9mm pistol from between two empty bourbon bottles on his bedside table and advanced toward the sound. Noiselessly swinging open the door, his eyes immediately met those of Sammy Capizzi, who sat facing him on the living room couch. Dressed in a rumpled suit, the mob soldier was holding Nicky's substitute for a coffee table book, a year-old issue of *Penthouse* with a pictorial featuring one of his many former girlfriends.

"Good morning, Mr. Bonnelli," Capizzi greeted, attempting with some difficulty to ignore the pistol pointed at his head.

"What the fuck you doin' here?" the mobster spat. Though displeased, he lowered the pistol to his side upon hearing his subordinate's respectful salutation.

"Mr. Weiss suggested and Mr. Messina agreed that you should have a personal assistant, sir," Capizzi answered. His last word, a seldom-utilized form of address, hung momentarily in the air.

"I don't need no fucking bodyguard," Nicky snapped.

"It's much more than that, sir. You are now in complete charge of your father's businesses, and because of that, you're probably the most powerful man in New York. It's a lot of responsibility, and people like you need others to take care of the more menial tasks."

Nicky grunted an acknowledgment and retreated to his bathroom, then cast off his clothes and stepped into the shower. As he lathered his aching head, he contemplated Capizzi's words. It was true, he realized, he was a man of great power. Gone were the shakedowns of recalcitrant debtors and the weekly collections from minor drug dealers. Others could attend to those tasks, to his benefit. The concept was appealing: less work and more money, more power, and more prestige.

But just how big was the fucker—the organization—over which he now held supreme dominion? Nicky wondered as he stepped out of the shower and seized a towel. Although he had been called upon occasionally to violently emphasize certain rules of protocol that had been trampled by men associated with other Bonnelli enterprises, his exposure to those operations had been brief, his tasks small. He cursed his father with a well-worn word for keeping him ignorant of information that had suddenly become vital to his future.

He walked naked to his closet, examined his wardrobe, and frowned. Items of clothing that had the day before been superior finery became at once just so many rags hanging pathetically from a stick. Disgusted, he settled on a black suit he had worn three times before, to the funerals of five of his colleagues. After donning a silk tie, an act he had performed less than half a dozen times over the course of the year, he accessorized his raiment with a pistol and walked into the living room. "Let's get the fuck out of here; I'm fucking starved," Nicky commanded, not considering for a moment that he should alter his locution along with his manner of dress.

"Right away, sir," Capizzi acknowledged.

In the hallway, Nicky took a last look inside his inadequate residence. Making a mental note to vastly change his living accommodations to match his new status, he closed the door.

"Mr. Weiss asked that you stop by his office later this morning," Capizzi said as they entered the elevator.

"The fuck I will, the fucker can come to me," Nicky snapped. Fucking *Weiss*, the mobster sneered inwardly. Why the fuck didn't the lawyer treat him better? He actually acted like he had some power. Well that would change, and quick. Weiss and all the other distinguished, educated suits he had occasionally seen talking in serious tones with his father would quickly learn to respect the new man in charge. Or else.

In the lobby, Nicky made his way to the main entrance and stepped outside. Following closely, Capizzi caught up with his boss at the curb of the narrow, one-way street by the building's loading zone, which was clear of vehicles for its fifty-foot length.

"The Caddy is just down the street," Capizzi said, gesturing to his right.

"Let's use a fucking limo from now on," was Nicky's last comment to his assistant.

The two men were standing abreast on the sidewalk when the midnight blue sedan moved quickly from its parking place to their left and stopped abruptly in front of them. Capizzi was the first to notice the dark muzzle of the automatic rifle as the front seat passenger swung it around to meet them. Acting on instinct, the mob soldier drew his weapon and stepped obliquely off the curb, blocking his charge. The one round the bodyguard managed to fire shattered the back window of the vehicle, but injured neither gunman nor driver as his aim was degraded by the impact of six bullets that stitched themselves across his chest faster than anyone could count.

Deflected by the ribs and sternum of his assistant, the three bullets that made exit wounds did not strike Nicky, but did cover him in blood. In an enraged trance, his weapon already in hand, Nicky grabbed the slumping corpse and advanced toward the killers, feeling as he went impacts from automatic fire that attempted in vain to penetrate the flesh-and-bone shield. As he shoved Capizzi's body at the car from a distance of four feet, Nicky brought his gun to bear on the vehicle and fired three quick rounds, silencing its occupants. Though both of the seated mesomorphs suffered from ugly head wounds, they were still alive.

"You . . . can't . . . do . . . that . . . to . . . me . . . now . . . you . . . fuckers," Nicky screamed at the attackers, punctuating each word with a bullet to one or the other. The immediate crisis over, he briefly wondered who they were, having not recognized either of his attackers in the moments before he fired. Now, they were not recognizable to anyone.

Shaking more with rage than relief, he turned contemptuously, then bent down and retrieved a set of keys from Capizzi's pants pocket, further soiling his jacket sleeve with blood in the process. He proceeded in a steady walk down the middle of the street, located the Cadillac, and drove away, leaving behind several startled witnesses to the carnage to breathe in his exhaust.

The first thing Joe Hanlon saw that morning as he opened his eyes was the naked chest of Elizabeth Brooks, enjoying the last moments of a restful sleep from a position beside him on the bed. He watched her skin undulate in response to her soft, somnolent breathing, then his eyes moved leisurely up his lover's body to her face, serenely resting on the pillow they were sharing. Elegant, knowing, and familiar, it was a face he knew he could get used to waking up next to for a long, long time.

As if she could feel Joe's visual caresses, Elizabeth opened her eyes.

"Good morning, Breasts," Joe said, smiling.

"What kind of comment is that?" Elizabeth asked, returning the expression. She pulled her share of the rumpled sheet around her exposed body, not as much to block Joe's view as to gain some protection from the brisk spring air that infiltrated into the room.

"I'm applying synecdoche," Joe replied in a matter-of-fact tone. "It's a literary term in which a part references the whole. I was greeting you, El, by referring to one—excuse me, two—of your attractive assets. All the great poets use it."

"Very romantic," she responded in good humor.

They exchanged a brief kiss, both aware that first thing in the morning was not the ideal time for such a display of affection.

"I've never had much of an opportunity to look at this room in good light," Elizabeth said as she gazed around the bedroom, unevenly filled with several pieces of unmatched furniture and decorated with an odd assortment of wall hangings.

"You like it?" he asked. "I tried to capture high style in a true eclectic vein."

"You failed," she informed him. "What's with this picture?" she asked, slightly twisting to gesture at the large reproduction that hung over the bed.

"A genuine classic. I think it ranks on a par with the *Mona Lisa*, Michelangelo's *Creation of Man*, and Van Gogh's *Starry Night.*"

"Dogs Playing Poker?"

"You have to look deep to fully appreciate its underlying meaning," Joe said, only half in jest. "Within the picture you can see the whole of humanity, the activities, hopes, and emotions of Everyman. See those two in the front? Deviousness, stoicism, and camaraderie, all symbolized by the ace of clubs."

"And those?" Elizabeth asked, nodding toward four unframed panels that hung on an adjacent wall in a vertical column. A progressive series, each scene contained a golden boat carrying a person who advanced in age from a baby in the first panel to an old man in the last.

"Another allegory, much less famous," Joe explained. "That's my life, presciently depicted by an artist of the Hudson River School a century before I was born. It's called the *Voyage of Life: Childhood, Youth, Manhood, Old Age.*"

"You identify with that?" Elizabeth asked. "But there's an angel in every scene. You're not a religious person."

"I've had more than my share of angels," Joe explained. "Loving parents, caring teachers, and bosses who evolved into true mentors—a process that has little in common with the faddish crap about mentoring flying around these days."

"I like them. Where are the originals? You might take me to see them sometime."

"Washington, the National Gallery," Joe replied. "Sounds like a good weekend trip, and I'll bet there won't even be a line. In their heyday, though, back before the Civil War, these paintings were the equivalent of a new Spielberg movie; people sometimes waited hours to see them."

"Well, I'd rather see some good paintings any day over some of the junk we've seen on the screen lately."

"No argument here," Joe said. "Though there's not much I like better than seeing a good movie, I'm getting tired of wading through the cesspool of highly touted crap to find one. It seems almost every writer in Hollywood starts a screenplay by asking, 'what old, tired storyline that's been done to death and beyond can I trot out yet again?'"

"A definite lack of imagination," Elizabeth agreed.

"It also seems most writers consider it a necessity to have their films inducted into the FCC."

"What's that?"

"The Fucking Century Club, the not-so-elite institution made up of movies that manage to work in the word 'fuck,' in its various forms, at least a hundred times over the course of two hours."

"Unfortunately, I know what you're talking about. Some movies seem to qualify within the first fifteen minutes. But enough erotic talk," Elizabeth joked as she slid out of bed and started to gather the various pieces of her apparel scattered about the carpet. "I guess I can wear these clothes for a couple more hours, but you'll have to get that trunk open before we go back to Marlborough."

"You're feeling better about that?"

"Yes, but we have to call your parents before we go. We have a busy day ahead, so I suggest you get your ass out of bed," she said cheerfully. "I am, of course, employing the literary term Schenectady."

Joe didn't correct her mistake substituting the town for the term. She might ask for specifics and although he might know the correct spelling of one or the other, he sure as hell couldn't spell both.

———————

Except for the naked corpse of Victor Bonnelli lying on the mortician's slab, Andrew Weiss was alone in the great white room that took up over half of the basement of the Tessla Funeral Home, the finest establishment of its type in midtown Manhattan, catering to the needs of dead mobsters since 1929. This would not be Ennio Tessla's toughest job, the lawyer considered as he examined the body, not by a long shot. Although violated by long, irreverently cut autopsy incisions, the body of his former boss was not shot, knifed, bludgeoned, or missing limbs. The head was still attached to the torso, too, Weiss noted, completing the catalog of things he had seen in that very room.

"Mr. Weiss, the doctor is here."

The lawyer turned toward two men descending the white, wooden stairs. They made an odd twosome, the nervous sycophant Tessla, a wiry man pushing seventy who sported a great shock of white hair, and Dr. James Swanson, whose girth was as large as his boisterous personality. He was generally referred to as the family doctor, though never to his face.

"Weiss, how the hell are you?" Swanson boomed as he reached the floor.

"I've been better."

"Hell of a thing," Swanson said.

"Mr. Tessla, I would like to continue our discussion concerning the arrangements in your office. I will join you in a few minutes," Weiss said. "You may start your work down here as soon as the doctor is finished. How long might that be?" he went on, addressing Swanson.

"Less than two hours," the doctor replied as he set down a small case.

"Yes, sir," Tessla acknowledged, then retreated up the stairway.

After the door at the top of the stairs clicked shut, Swanson faced off with Weiss. "So who's in charge now that our benefactor has gone to his reward?"

"Officially, it's Nicky" Weiss replied grimly.

"God help us," Swanson muttered. "I've saved that kid's life twice, and he never acknowledged my efforts with anything better than a 'fuck you.' What is he going to do now that he has some real power?"

"There will be changes, but I think everything will settle down within a short time," Weiss said encouragingly, as much to himself as the man standing before him.

"Maybe, but I sense a storm before the calm."

"We can discuss possibilities later. Although my priorities are centered on Monday's funeral, I want you to examine the body before it's prepared. I'd like to know if anything is amiss."

"You suspect something?"

"No, but the interference of the FBI does motivate me to examine the possibilities."

Swanson stepped up to the corpse and inspected the autopsy scars. "Looks like someone else examined the possibilities."

"That's government work," Weiss explained. "I need separate verification. For starters, how was his health?"

"About par for a man of his age. I advised him that cutting down on his alcohol intake, tempering his consumption of unhealthy foods, and starting a regular exercise program might be prudent, but I didn't expect he would follow my advice. He didn't. He had some problems, but nothing I considered life threatening."

"Do you consider the death suspicious?"

"I need more information to answer that accurately, but on its face I would say no. It's not the norm for a man in his condition to drop dead without warning, but it happens all the time. You didn't bring me here to speculate, though; I'll find out for certain if there's anything wrong."

Swanson opened his case, revealing a wide variety of medical paraphernalia, sample vials, and protective gear. "When did the body arrive?"

"Less than an hour ago," Weiss said, recalling the incident. The two agents that delivered the body to the funeral home were not exactly apologetic, but their demeanor was surprisingly courteous. "He was delivered in that," he went on, gesturing toward what appeared to be an elongated footlocker on the floor against the wall.

"That certainly won't do for the funeral," Swanson joked. "Still, it looks like a fine travel case. I'm surprised they didn't want it back."

"The couriers seemed more intent on getting out of here than they did on saving taxpayers a few dollars," Weiss said. "On their way out, they also left this." The lawyer walked to the case and picked up a large manila envelope.

"This is amazing," Swanson noted with a grin as he leafed through the contents of the thick package. "This is the preliminary autopsy report, complete with photographs and x-rays. Thirty-five pages, plus exhibits; those government doctors must have knocked themselves out to finish it so quickly."

"Anything interesting?"

"It will take time to go through it, but the preliminary findings are right here on page one. It states Bonnelli died of heart failure due primarily to arteriosclerosis, though vasospasm is suspected."

"I'm a lawyer, not a doctor, Jim."

"Arteriosclerosis is the buildup of fatty tissue on the walls of the coronary arteries. It's very common, and many heart attacks are caused by the blood flow being completely blocked by the buildup. A vasospasm is a spontaneous contraction of an artery, usually one affected by arteriosclerosis, and results in heart failure even though fatty tissue does not completely block the blood flow."

"And?" Weiss urged.

"Vasospasms are a relatively recent discovery, and many aspects of the phenomenon are still unclear. By bringing up the possibility, it indicates the doctor who performed the autopsy did an extensive amount of work to find the cause of death. Under normal circumstances, I would accept this report without question."

"The activities surrounding this death are hardly normal," Weiss stated with a frown.

"You needn't tell me again," Swanson replied as he donned a pair of surgical gloves. "Everything will be checked, rechecked, and verified conclusively. If there's anything wrong with this report, if Bonnelli died of anything other than what appears to be a run-of-the-mill heart attack, I'll find out."

"The funeral cannot be delayed."

"No need to concern yourself; I'll be here only an hour or so. The real work will take place in the lab. We'll be at it all weekend, and you'll have a full report by the time our friend is laid to rest."

"Please call me if you discover anything of interest before then," Weiss requested. Eager to return to his primary mission at the funeral home, he ascended the stairs. He found Tessla behind his desk, busily engaged in planning what was to be, for them both, the funeral of the year.

"Any of these would dignify the ceremony," Tessla said as he handed Weiss a folder containing several illustrated casket options.

"This one," Weiss said after a minute's perusal, handing back the folder opened to a laminated page with a description and photograph of the Aidoneustian, a weighty bronze box with ornate gold embellishments.

"There are also many choices available for the stone," Tessla said as he proffered another collection of samples.

Weiss waved away the folder. "I'll leave the decision of a monument up to you," he said, not the least bit interested in the headstone, which would be placed some days after the burial, never to be visited by anyone of importance. "Let's move on to the agenda."

Several minutes into a detailed discussion of the schedule, Weiss heard the front door to the funeral home open. He turned his head, and saw an imposing, insistent figure framed in the doorway.

"Mr. Weiss, we have to talk," Joey Messina said.

The lawyer excused himself, then walked down the wide hallway with Messina. "What is it?"

"Somebody just tried to whack Nicky outside of his building."

"Tried?"

"Capizzi's dead, along with the two guys that made the attempt. I'm not sure how Nicky made it out of there alive, but he did. He's holed up in one of our bars in Brooklyn."

"Dr. Swanson's here, in the basement," Weiss offered.

"Not needed. Nicky walked away from that massacre unhurt. Some kind of miracle. From what I hear, he doesn't seem quite right in the head, though. I mean more than usual," Messina added after catching the lawyer's expression that clearly conveyed, "So what else is new?"

"What's the situation with the authorities?"

"I managed to get close to the scene just before coming over here. There's a cop convention outside the building, and I gather there were several witnesses to the shootings. It's certain they're looking for Nicky right now."

"Let's go see him."

———————

Click. Call from the apartment terminated.

"Isn't that sweet?" Eric Kauffman said. "The girl made up with Hanlon's father. I still have no idea what the hell their argument was about."

"IDM, my friend: it doesn't matter," Philip Roberts stated from the other side of the sedan, well into the eighth hour of its occupancy of the Broadway parking space. "Nothing they've said since we've been here has mattered much, except that we can plan to follow them up to Marlborough in a couple of hours, after breakfast."

"Yeah, their breakfast," Kauffman groused, still unsatisfied from the coffee and handful of donuts from a nearby deli an hour earlier.

"Eric, I think you're losing your touch," Roberts gently chastised. "You're complaining about having to listen to normal conversation, you didn't provision the car for the stakeout, and you let your shaver battery run down."

"Sorry, Phil; I'll do better next time. It's been years since I've been on one of these all-nighters that didn't involve a specific objective."

They paused their conversation long enough to listen to more transmitted dialogue that enlightened them not at all.

"It's good to hear that everything went well with the delivery of the body," Kauffman said after the receiver went silent. "I still would have felt more comfortable if Sandy and Chris had stuck around; they could have taken the flight out with us later this afternoon."

"Separate part of the operation," Roberts said. "Our improvised hearse was designed for one thing: secure transport for the bodies related to our missions. I don't want it being used for unscheduled field work unless it's absolutely necessary, and that's hardly the case in our current situation."

"Well it would have been nice to have another person yesterday. We're involved in a billion-dollar project; I think somebody could spring for a few more resources."

"We could, except twenty or thirty more agents would be counterproductive, widening the risk of a security breech. I'm comfortable with our current dozen-person arrangement, despite its occasional inconveniencies."

"Okay, Phil," Kauffman conceded. "I know everybody's busy, especially with this month's schedule."

"I'm going out to take a leak," Roberts said as he grabbed the door handle.

"Here's the pee bottle," Kauffman said as he grabbed an odd plastic contraption from the floor of the sedan.

"You know I hate those things," Roberts objected. "And it's completely dry. You've been taking advantage of the great outdoors, too."

"Yeah, during the night, but it's morning now."

"Eric, one of the benefits from the hundreds of thousands of tax-payer dollars expended on training me in clandestine operations is the ability to take a piss unobserved, no matter what the circumstances."

"Okay, have at it," Kauffman said with a chuckle.

"Be back in five," an almost relieved Roberts replied.

After his partner's departure, Kauffman turned his attention back to the sounds brought to the sedan courtesy of the listening devices three hundred feet away.

Ring. Call to the apartment coming in.

CHAPTER 10

The transformation Dr. Kenneth DeLuca had undergone over the course of the previous twelve hours was unlike anything he ever experienced. Still plagued by the constant mental pounding of his regrets and failures, he spent the first four hours more bemused than intrigued at the task he had undertaken at the behest of his young acquaintance. During the next four hours, however, the eternal hangover of his ambivalences dropped away as the autopsy of the dead squirrel fully consumed him, bringing forth skills he had not employed in years. The final four hours began with dawn breaking over the Marlborough house, but the light that streamed through the sliding door went unnoticed by the doctor, as his attention was fully focused on a discovery that was ever so slowly revealing itself. As he finished, DeLuca was certain he had found something that was not only new to him, but unknown to medical science. Now he was three rings into his second phone call of the morning, his body weary, but his mind awake with an excitement that almost overwhelmed him.

"Yo," a man said before the fourth ring.

"Kenneth DeLuca calling; is that you, Joe?"

"Yes, Dr. DeLuca," Joe Hanlon replied. "It's a lucky thing you caught me; I had the door open, heading out for breakfast."

"Joe, I have to see you immediately; it's vitally important."

"Well, Dr. DeLuca, since you called this number, you know I'm in Sunnyside right now."

"Yes. I called your home, but your mother told me you left last night. Is anything wrong?"

"My father got my girlfriend to engage in one of his famous debates while I was visiting you, and she didn't take kindly to it," Joe explained.

"On her first visit? Al must have taken a liking to her right off."

"I explained that to her during our drive down here. We straightened out everything this morning and we're heading back to Idlewild in a couple of hours. We should be there by noon."

"Well as soon as you arrive, dump her off and come over here. I have to see you."

"'Dump her off?'" Joe asked. "That doesn't sound like you. You seem excited."

"Indeed I am, my boy. I've found something very intriguing with that dead squirrel of yours."

"Already? Dr. DeLuca, don't *even* tell me you've been up all night with our fuzzy friend."

"Yes I have, and they've been some of the best hours I ever didn't sleep through."

"Please give me the details."

"Your squirrel died of heart failure," DeLuca began. "That was evident within the first two hours of my investigation, as was the approximate time of death: sometime between one and five A.M. Thursday. It took a bit more work before I discovered that the myocardial infarction—heart attack—was caused by a failure of the sinoatrial nodes, the fibers that send impulses to muscles of the heart, normally in a steady pattern. It's the irregular operation of these nodes that is corrected in humans by the installation of a pacemaker. If a human were affected by node failure in the same manner as this squirrel, though, no pacemaker would be necessary, because that person would be dead. What happened to that animal was catastrophic, occurring in a matter of minutes, maybe seconds. You with me so far?"

"It's not over my head yet, Dr. DeLuca," Joe answered. "What could have caused the failure in such a short time?"

"My next task was to determine the answer to that very question. I performed many conventional tests on the remains to pinpoint a cause, but the results were not enlightening. Not willing to give up so easily, I then delved into the various chemical processes that aid the function of the sinoatrial nodes, and finally ended up examining the several enzymes that support the reactions. One of these enzymes was inexplicably missing—*absolutely absent!*—and that caused the death."

"Dr. DeLuca, it's obvious that you found something very interesting, but you managed to lose me."

"Okay, Joe, let me try again," DeLuca replied with a mixture of weariness and joy. "In order for the sinoatrial nodes to send the proper messages to the heart, several chemical reactions must take place. These chemical reactions cannot occur effectively without the aid of enzymes acting as catalysts. In the particular case of your squirrel, every bit of the enzyme phosphofructokinase was missing, so the enzyme did nothing to promote a chemical reaction necessary for the sinoatrial nodes to function. Since the nodes stopped working, the heart ceased beating and the squirrel died."

"So no enzyme means no reaction means malfunctioning nodes means heart stops and death," Joe paraphrased in one long breath.

"That's basically it," DeLuca allowed.

"I don't know much about medicine, but that sounds pretty obscure, maybe even to other doctors."

"You're right, Joe. I found the solution only because I was engaged in some specialized research into mammalian cardiovascular enzymes with several colleagues years ago. You were extremely fortunate to come to me with this problem; there probably aren't half a dozen doctors in the country that would have discovered the obscure cause of the squirrel's demise. It was also lucky you brought the body to me in such a timely fashion."

"Why's that?"

"After death, phosphofructokinase molecules break down at a very predictable, arithmetic rate. No matter what size the animal, they are completely dissipated within seventy to seventy-four hours. My team was never able to discern a reason for this, but documented the fact thoroughly. If you had brought the squirrel to me twenty-four hours later, the role of the enzyme in its death would not have been revealed, as I would have had to assume its absence was due to this postmortem phenomenon."

"On thing still puzzles me, Dr. DeLuca," Joe said. "I follow the reasons for the death from the heart attack back through the chemical reactions and the enzyme, but what caused the premature destruction of that substance? Was it some external force?"

"That's the key question, Joe, but it remains unanswered. I found no evidence of toxins, the animal did not suffer from any kind of disease, and there was no trauma. The replacement was also okay. As far as I can tell, the squirrel was normal in all respects before it suddenly lost a few vital molecules and died."

"Do you have any theories?"

"At this point, the cause could be anything: chemical, bacterial, viral, or genetic; I don't know, but I am certain that this discovery may lead to an important advance in medicine. The affected enzyme is common to all mammals. Whatever killed this rodent may be killing dozens, maybe hundreds of people every year, except no one knows about it. Even if a victim of this new unknown were to be autopsied, the examining doctor would not have any idea what to look for, because the results of my team's findings were never widely disseminated. Research into what I've found over the past few hours might result in the discovery of the extent of this malady, its cause, and a cure that could potentially save thousands."

"I can see why you're excited. You certainly found a lot more than I ever expected. There are other things you should know about this."

"That's why I called," DeLuca said. "You need to tell me about the other victims."

"The details are rather extensive," Joe replied. "I'll be up to see you in a few hours and I'd like to tell you then."

"That's fine, Joe; I'll be looking forward to it. One last thing: I haven't told anyone else about this discovery and I would prefer it if you would keep this between us for the time being. I have to recheck everything and the possibility exists that my findings might be based on a laboratory error. I'd hate to appear an old fool."

"Your secret is safe with me."

"If everything checks out, I'm going to contact several of my colleagues on Monday. I think something of a fire may be set by all of this."

"It sounds exciting, Dr. DeLuca," Joe concluded.

"Get it out of here. Now," commanded the man as he inspected the Cadillac, parked twenty degrees off parallel on the narrow Brooklyn street. There were not many civilians that could order around a made member of the Bonnelli family, but at that particular time and specific place with a certain mob soldier, Andrew Weiss could not only get away with it, but was treated with respect in the process.

"Yes, Mr. Weiss," acknowledged Joey Messina, four feet behind the lawyer with a cell phone to his ear. "I have a man on the line now. He'll be here in about three minutes." While Messina relayed his instructions, Weiss made a brief inspection of the car. He opened the driver's door and was hit by the stench of sweat and blood as it intermingled with the brisk morning air. The perusal of the interior found the keys still present in the ignition and dark crimson smears on the black leather driver's seat and the steering wheel.

"Let's go see him," Weiss said, suddenly doubting Nicholas Bonnelli had come away from his recent violent encounter uninjured.

They walked down the sidewalk to a narrow brick building sandwiched between a coin-op laundry and the neighborhood bakery. Messina pounded on the gray steel door of the establishment, identified as "Vito's Bar" in two-inch block letters just above the peephole. After a long minute, the sound of heavy bolts being thrust aside was followed by an oscillation of the doorknob. The door opened slightly, not even enough for its thickness to clear the jamb. Sensing that the scant movement was the only invitation to enter forthcoming, Weiss pulled open the door and stepped into the building, followed by Messina.

"I don't like lawyers," Vito Umbrera grunted as he re-secured the door, thrusting the set of bolts back into their keeps with an intent viciousness. Dressed in a soiled white T-shirt, stained slacks, and frayed slippers, the wiry old man looked as unpleasant as he sounded.

"We won't be long," Messina said as the three men moved down the hallway paralleling the street, built to prevent any sunlight from penetrating into the bar.

It took some time for the eyes of the visitors to adjust to the painfully subdued illumination of the small main room provided by a smattering of incandescent bulbs, the light of which barely penetrated the yellowed plastic lenses of the inset ceiling fixtures. Not that there was much to look at. A floor-to-ceiling array of bottles was protected by a long, stained slab of oak on the left side of the room. On the right was a scattering of rude chairs and round tables. The ghosts of several pictures in the form of rectangular discolorations on the walls indicated that some attempt at decoration had been made in the past, but the wall hangings had long ago been discarded as unnecessary to business.

"He banged up the place a bit before I managed to calm him down with a few drinks," Umbrera sniffed. "It's gonna cost you."

"We'll take care of you," Messina promised as the trio made their way to the rear of the building.

"Who the fuck is it?" came the unmistakable bellow of Nicholas Bonnelli through an open door beyond the last set of chairs.

Messina was the first one through the doorway. "It's me, Nicky. I have Mr. Weiss with me."

Nicky sat at a small table in the only unbroken chair in the room, a half-empty fifth of bourbon in one hand and a half-filled tumbler in the other. A dripping explosion of liquor on a wall and shards of glass on the floor gave evidence that his anger had been vented on more than the furniture. "I don't need a fucking lawyer," he protested loudly. "I want all our fucking guys over here now! I want those fuckers dead!" he ranted and spat, screamed and belched, all at once.

Messina walked to the table and placed both hands on its edge. "Jesus, Nicky, are you all right?" he asked, getting a good look at the mobster's blood-spattered face and crimson-smeared hands and clothing.

"I want the fuckers dead!" he repeated before downing a large mouthful of liquor, then punctuated the order by slamming the glass hard on the table.

"Sure, Nicky," Messina said calmly. "What happened?"

"Fuckers come out of nowhere and fucking start shooting. They got Capizzi, but I fucked them up good."

"They're dead, Nicky. Who were they? Where did they come from?" Messina asked, stating each word firmly and clearly to get his boss's attention.

"I don't fucking know," he said dejectedly. "Could be any of a thousand fuckers."

"Listen, Nicky," Messina pleaded in a steady, calm voice. "We'll find out. It might take a little time, but we'll hit them harder than anybody's been hit before. Right now, though, we have to get you to a safe place."

"There's more to worry about than the people who tried to kill you, Nicky," Weiss said, imitating Messina's easy tone. "The police are looking for you; they'll take you in if they find you."

"But I didn't fucking do anything," Nicky protested, for once not violently.

"It was self-defense," Weiss said. "I know that, but they'll want the details on what happened. They'll want to know about the weapons involved and why you left the scene. It's my job to insure you don't see the inside of a police station over this. I think Messina is right; you should lay low for a couple of days. You are too important to be tied up with this right now."

The last comment hit home. "Fucking right."

"We'll set up operations at the Farm outside Albany," Messina said. "It'll be a good place to get cleaned up, relax, and plan our next move."

Glassy-eyed, Nicky sat immobile for a moment, then nodded, drained his glass, and stood up.

Weiss was pleased. The Farm was the perfect place to get Nicky out of the way for a few days, and plotting revenge would occupy his time. The lawyer was also aware, however, that his chief rival's ability to extricate himself unscathed from a situation that by all odds should have left him a bloody corpse on the concrete was a sure warning that Nicky might prove dangerous to his plans.

"Put the gun down, Phil," urged Eric Kauffman. "Put . . . the . . .

gun . . . down."

Scarlet-faced, hands trembling, Philip Roberts checked his 9mm Sig-Saur for the fifth time since he had listened to the playback of the telephone conversation between the man who had immediately taken several quantum leaps in status—from a minor tactical annoyance to a global strategic threat—and the doctor who identified himself as Kenneth DeLuca. "This can't be happening," he said, then immediately discarded the notion and turned to his partner seated beside him in the sedan. "When was this?"

"About ten minutes ago," Kauffman replied. "Three minutes after he hung up the phone, Hanlon and his girlfriend were down here on the sidewalk, headed up the street."

"And you didn't do anything?" Roberts queried harshly, his temper quickly eclipsing his professionalism.

"I did what I should have done under the circumstances, Phil: I stayed here. If they had gone for the car it would have been a different story, but they walked away from it, headed to some local joint for breakfast. They'll be back, probably in half an hour or so."

"You don't know exactly where they are?"

"They're not far, I can guarantee that, but no, I don't know their precise location. I couldn't have followed them, Phil; I would have been alone and you would have returned to an empty car, wondering what the hell was going on."

"Take a piss and everything goes in the toilet," philosophized Roberts, calmed slightly by the explanation. "This has a good chance of blowing the lid off of the entire project."

"I thought it might be a threat, although I didn't understand most of what that guy DeLuca was talking about."

"It's serious—unbelievably serious. By all odds, it's impossible this could have happened. Of all the goddamn luck!" Roberts exclaimed, then went silent, brooding. "Okay," he finally said. "We have to salvage the situation. You're right, Eric, they'll be back. We know they're going back to his parent's house this morning, and we know she wants a change of clothes. Hell, he hasn't even started looking for his spare key has he?"

"There's been no indication."

"Fine. Then we know exactly where they'll be and what they'll be doing. We've even got a little time to prepare."

"Jesus," exhaled Kauffman. "I can't believe it. This thing was supposed to be so foolproof, so undetectable, and now the shit has hit the fan because of this know-nothing cop."

"What is, is," Roberts proclaimed as he holstered his weapon. "We have to deal with the situation as it stands." He reached for the door handle.

"Don't do it, Phil," Kauffman pleaded. "What's your plan? To blow them away while they're eating?"

"Relax, I'm not going anywhere near them; there's a better way to deal with this. I'm going for a short walk—ten minutes tops—and I'll lay it out for you when I get back."

"We seem to be circling the subject like two cats around a bowl of some strange new food," Elizabeth said, slightly tensing her arm around her companion's waist.

"Oh? What subject is that?" Joe asked in mock surprise, as if he were not as involved as she in the heady content of the long conversation that had begun over breakfast. They were at the midpoint of their journey along the Old Croton Aqueduct, which acted as a level, grassy thoroughfare between the restaurant and the rear property line of Joe's apartment complex. "Seriously, El," he said, stopping in the middle of the path, "I feel strongly about you, about a need for—change."

"But you're not sure what kind of change?"

"I didn't say that," he replied, hugging her tightly.

"Well if you aren't going to say the word, I guess it's up to me," Elizabeth said, staring into her lover's eyes. "Would you like to get married?"

"To who?" Joe couldn't resist. Before she could react, he tightened his embrace and brought his cheek to hers. "El, I love you. I can't think of any better fate than to spend my life with you. I want to say yes without hesitation."

"But you have reservations?" she asked. "Does it concern your parents?"

"Hell no, they'd be thrilled. My father likes you; I hope you know that now after this morning's phone conversation. Mom took to you also, and she's been angling in her own unspoken way to get me married for some time. No, it's all the crap that's happened over the past two days that has me thinking twice about our future together. I might still have a job next week, or I might be out on my ass."

"So you end up an unemployed bachelor for the rest of your life," Elizabeth said softly. "Or do I know you better than that?"

The gentle reprimand hit home. "Sorry, El. I'm just a little intimidated by changes, and it looks like some kind of change is in the wind. Certainly, I'll get back on my feet, no matter what happens. I don't suppose you'd want to recant your proposal because my present prospects are somewhat shaky?"

"Not in the least."

"Then let's do it, and I will say the word: Let's get married."

Tightly embraced, they engaged in a single, long kiss of lifelong commitment to one another, an exhilarating, exhausting expression of their passions and fused desires. No formal ceremony, no matter how long or intricate, could ever match that moment.

Firmly bound to each other, they at last resumed their walk.

Joe broke the silence after they traveled fifty yards. "When would you like to get hitched? I'll leave the date entirely in your hands."

"Oh, it will take at least six months to make all of the preparations."

"I take it, then, that you wish to have a wedding with all the ceremony and associated accoutrements?" Joe asked with a slight frown.

"It's the dream of most girls, me included," Elizabeth responded, somewhat perplexed. "Why?"

"Okay, El," Joe said cheerfully, then stepped out in front of her and, with a broad sweep of his arm, bent deeply at the waist. "I bow, without reservation, to society's vision of the wedding day. I will joyfully engage in whatever machinations you will have planned down to the minutest detail. I will play my part, and my performance will be superb. It's just that I really can't get excited about the day. I've been to too many splendiferous weddings steeped in ritual resplendent with flowers and gaily costumed participants, with music and poetry filling the air, whirling about the two main participants fairly jumping over one another in their varied and numerous expressions of love forever. In my experience, though, 'forever' is between three months and three years for over half of those eternally joined lovers. I suppose I've acquired a jaundiced eye, but in my opinion the wedding day pales to insignificance to the months and years—the five decades—ahead of us: forever, in good times and in bad."

"You may have a point," Elizabeth replied, looking straight into his eyes. "But get this straight, buster," she went on in a sincere tone interlaced with good humor, "I want the day, too."

"As I said, no argument here," Joe replied, raising his hands in mock surrender. "I'll be a good boy."

They resumed their stroll, hand in loving hand. "So you only give us fifty years?" Elizabeth asked as they approached the rear wall of Joe's apartment complex.

"Till death do us part. My goal is to reach the age of eighty. It's an arbitrary definition of the length of a good life, just something I use to gage the passing of time. If I live beyond the goal, I'll happily embrace the bonus days; if I fall short of being an octogenarian, I don't think I'll care much—after the fact. You'll outlive me, of course."

"Because I'm a woman? Are you stereotyping me?"

"Maybe a little," Joe replied as they ascended the short flight of concrete stairs to the walkway leading to Joe's unit. "But I really don't want to think about living without you. Maybe by our golden anniversary I'll finally get used to some of your annoying quirks."

"Like what?" she asked, giving her lover a gentle punch on the shoulder.

"For one thing, you drive too fast," replied Joe, fondly recalling their meeting.

"I'm in the real estate business," she defended. "Half of my work is being out on the road, and the quicker I get around the better. Besides, that happens outside of the house, unlike some of your irritating peculiarities."

"Like what?" he asked in the tone she had used, returning the shoulder tap.

"The word is 'hello,'" she stated. "Why must you answer the phone with a 'yo?'"

"It's an old habit, picked up from a good friend years ago. I'm sure you'll meet him at the wedding."

They arrived at the apartment building and Joe opened the door. Side by side, they began the climb up the five half-flights of stairs.

"This is one thing that's not going to survive past the wedding day," Elizabeth panted after thirty steps. "With my recent earnings, I'm going to invest in a house, preferably a ranch."

"Better wait until I have a secure job," Joe warned.

"You'll be fine," she replied. In front of the door to the apartment, they embraced, their mouths meeting tenderly. "This really is the beginning of something," Elizabeth whispered as her head rested on Joe's shoulder.

"We'll have a great life together," Joe promised.

The sound of a phone ringing reached out into the stairwell from the apartment. Gently breaking away from Joe, Elizabeth retrieved her key. "I hope that's somebody who's going to get your car open," she said, holding the key up to Joe before inserting it in the lock. "This is the last time I'm going to do this."

"I'm aware of the priority," Joe said, smiling.

"If I'm going to be a Hanlon, I guess I better get used to answering the phone like one," she laughed as she opened the door and skipped to the telephone.

Joe closed the door quickly and made a beeline to the device, but lost the race by a good six feet.

As she picked up the receiver, Elizabeth dropped her smile by necessity as she did her best imitation of Joe's deep-toned greeting, "Yo."

The blast that disintegrated the telephone receiver was not especially loud, muffled as it was by the flesh of Elizabeth's hand and face.

CHAPTER 11

One instant, then everything was irrevocably changed. Joe Hanlon would never remember what took place in those first few moments. Before, he was moving from the front door toward the woman who was to become his wife, looking squarely at her when he heard a pop and saw a small black cloud form instantaneously around her head. The next thing he knew he was kneeling, holding that broken head in his hands, in his lap, with no expression on his face, but tears pouring uncontrollably from his eyes, tears of anguish and loss and powerlessness.

There was no doubt Elizabeth was dead. The entire right side of her face was a bloody mass of blackened, torn tissue. One eye was open, staring straight up at him; the other one just wasn't there. Joe had seen death before—many times and up close—but never like this, in his own quiet home, never with such unexpected suddenness, never with someone he loved so much.

Disjointed thoughts raced through his mind. Where was the phone? He had to call for backup, for help, for an ambulance. Where was his gun? Maybe whoever did this was close. And why? Why would anyone want to kill this beautiful person, who was the best thing that had happened to his life since—well, it had been a long, long time. What happened? Was it a shotgun or rifle blast from some sniper? He could hear more shots in the far distance. Bang. Bang. Bang.

No, it was someone pounding on the door. The sound of Elizabeth's head bursting had carried through the walls to a nearby apartment.

"Go away!" Joe yelled, hating himself for doing it, but he said no more. There would be time for others, for responsibilities and questions, reports and explanations. Right at that moment, however, he just wanted to be alone, fervently wishing that he was not alone, that Elizabeth was still with him.

If not a rifle shot, then what? he wondered, forcing himself to look down. The phone was there, or what was left of it; the cord from the carriage that should have ended at the handset led to a burned and splintered chunk of plastic the size and texture of a chestnut husk. The rest of the handset was—just about everywhere. Pieces of the ivory plastic, the wire and various components were strewn around the room. Most were scattered along the floor but some were embedded in the ceiling and many shards could be seen sticking out of the red masses that once were the face and right hand of Elizabeth. If he cared, even a little bit, Joe would have wondered why he had not received the slightest scratch.

The fact raced through Joe's mental maelstrom and found a temporarily placid spot: it was a bomb. A bomb in the phone. He recalled those last moments. She was playing a game, grabbed the lethal phone and answered as he did, mimicking his "Yo." Whoever was calling would have thought, for a moment, that it was him. Some asshole, Joe thought, came into the apartment, set a bomb, then made a call to remotely kill his target.

"That target being me," he said to the room, experiencing a moment of fear that was instantly overpowered by racking regret at the realization that Elizabeth's murder was a mistake. "A mistake someone is going to want to fix," he said, speaking again to the empty apartment. Shaking himself out of his torturous reverie, Joe began to think of suspects. But there was only one suspect—or rather one group—to consider: those agents, or spies, or goons, or whatever they were. Over the last two days they had held a gun to his neck, detained him, tailed him, and had him fired, at least as far as they knew.

He gently laid Elizabeth's head on the carpet, then stood up and walked to the front entry. The bastards will pay now, he thought. Big time. New York has the death penalty; prepare to face it.

Joe opened the door and came face to face with Philip Roberts and the big, black gun he was holding. Thanks to Roberts, Joe did not have his.

The eyes of the two men locked for a millisecond, then with surprise, fear, and rage all boiling within him, Joe lunged at the long-barreled pistol, or rather the gun to which a silencer had been attached. The first round spat out the instant he grabbed it; the bullet ripped through the left side of his pants and grazed his thigh before it embedded itself deep within a plaster wall. With a grunt, Roberts twisted around savagely, disengaging his target from the weapon. Joe slammed against the wall, then hurtled backward down half a flight of stairs, finding himself in an awkward crouch at the corner of the landing.

Confronted with the classic question of survival—fight or flight—and with but a fraction of a second to decide, Joe was fortunate that there was only one viable option. Unarmed and nine open steps below his adversary, the only rational path led down to the outside exit. He continued his descent just as another bullet impacted the plaster where his head had just been.

Joe leaped down the stairs, taking three and four steps at a time, grasping the railing at each turn to sling himself further from his pursuer. Almost a lifetime later he reached the entry landing, ripped open the door, and stumbled outside, leaving behind the quick ticking sounds of rapidly descending shoes. To his left, across a narrow access lane, a rough wooded downgrade led to Broadway—straight to his car, less than a hundred yards away.

Joe took off sprinting toward the vehicle. Just as he reached the pavement, he heard the distinctive crack of a brutally opened door, followed quickly by a pop very close to his right shoulder—the tiny sonic boom of a bullet. Thus urged on, he set his sights on the red Nissan, clearly visible through the sparse vegetation. The muffled *thunk* of a large bullet hitting hard wood—the oak tree to his left front—reminded him of the closing of a car door, and he had a vision of a set of keys hanging impotently from an ignition. Without a doubt, Joe realized, he was a dead man, but the momentum of his downhill strides kept him moving steadily away from his pursuer and toward his doom. Cursing between desperate gulps of air, Joe approached the wretched car. A bullet kissed Joe's right cheek, traveled fifteen additional feet, and shattered the front passenger window of the Nissan.

Joe seized the opportunity and dove through the broken window, scattering thousands of glass pebbles in his wake. He reached out, grabbed the steering wheel with both hands, and wrenched his body into the driver's seat. He grabbed the key and the trusty engine started at once; within seconds he slammed his way straight out of the parking space, clipping the rear bumper of the Volvo parked to his front and cutting off a Buick in the travel lane. Two pings of lead meeting red-painted sheet metal comprised his pursuers' literal parting shots.

———————

Shaking from rage and exertion, Philip Roberts stood at the crest of the rough slope leading down to Broadway, staring at the empty parking space that had held the car of his adversary less than a minute before. We had the bastard and had him again but still he escaped, he fumed. For now. For perhaps the next twenty minutes. But there was too much to do where he was, so others would have to be recruited. At least one volunteer was on the way now, he realized as he heard a siren in the distance.

Moments later, a breathless Eric Kauffman was at Roberts' side. Upon hearing the struggle to the front, he had come around the building from his position covering Hanlon's fire escape. He managed to fire off a single round at the Nissan, which struck but did not stop the car.

"We can still catch him," Kauffman told Roberts.

"Don't be an idiot," Roberts snapped, his mind working triple time attempting to form a workable contingency. Things had gone wrong, but were not yet out of control. What he wanted most was reliable backup, but within five hundred miles all he had were the local cops, the state police, and the FBI. "Just put away your gun and bring the car up here."

The Sunnyside patrol car arrived first, climbing the access road to the complex swiftly before jolting to a stop. Patrolman Dan Bouton, the youngest rookie on the Sunnyside force, nervously got out of the car, his gun drawn and pointed skyward.

Roberts walked up to the officer. "Philip Roberts, FBI," he stated with stern authority. "Glad you're here. There's a bad situation upstairs and we need all the help we can get."

"I received a call about a shooting," a nervous Bouton said. "What's going on?"

At that moment, Kauffman pulled up and parked directly behind the Sunnyside cruiser. Roberts walked to the passenger side of his car, then opened the door and seized a radio microphone. Facing Bouton, he held up his left hand as a silencing gesture while he keyed the mike with his right, reaching the White Plains FBI immediately. "White Plains, this is Sierra Four Five, Special Agent Roberts. Please dispatch all available units to the vicinity of South Broadway, town of Sunnyside, to pursue fleeing murder suspect by the name of Joseph Hanlon, description to follow. Suspect was last seen driving south on Broadway in a red Nissan Sentra, New York license ORX-360."

Bouton's eyes widened as Roberts spoke.

"Suspect is armed and has fired at agents," Roberts lied. "Suggest all local and state authorities be notified. Over."

The reply from the radio was positive.

"Sierra Four Five out," Roberts concluded.

"*Our* Joe Hanlon?" Bouton asked, startled.

Roberts turned to the officer. "Contact as many of your people as you can. Let them know what's going on, then come up to Hanlon's apartment. It's the first set of stairs in this building," Roberts said, gesturing to the structure nearest them. "Apartment 3B."

Bouton nodded, put away his revolver, and turned to his radio.

Kauffman followed Roberts up the stairway. They were both unsure of what had happened, but Roberts did glimpse a body when Hanlon opened the door. It was Roberts who made the call and put an end to his major annoyance with the punch of a button—or so he thought. But it *was* him that answered, wasn't it? Roberts vividly recalled.

"I guess it wasn't him," he mused as they entered the apartment and encountered the mutilated body of Elizabeth. The bomb had worked perfectly, but the mission was a failure. What went wrong? After the telephone went dead, he sat with Kauffman in the car and attempted to analyze the situation. At first, Roberts thought that both of them had been killed, but he knew the explosive charge wasn't that powerful. It didn't need to be when the victim would be holding the bomb against his—her—head. They then heard soft weeping. That was something, but he had expected screaming and the sound of the front door opening as the girl made her escape, but who could predict what women would do? The mystery was solved with the pained and unmistakably masculine "go away" response to the neighbor's knock, and he knew that somehow he had missed his mark.

The neighbor that knocked—from 3A perhaps? But there was no answer. Being a top end unit, the next closest apartment was directly below—2B.

Roberts descended the stairs and knocked on the door, which elicited a timid "Yes, who is there?" A woman.

"FBI, ma'am," he replied. "I'm holding up my identification." He was rewarded with the sound of a door chain being removed and in another moment was face to face with an elegantly dressed woman in her late fifties, fright evident on her face.

"Agent Philip Roberts," he said. "I need to ask you a few questions, starting with your name."

"Josephine Gavin," she replied. "Please tell me what is going on."

"Do you know the man who lives directly above you, in Apartment 3B?"

"Yes, Joseph Hanlon; he's a policeman."

"He *was* a policeman. Did you know he had been fired off the force yesterday?" Roberts asked in an ominous tone.

"I had no idea," she replied, concerned.

"Could you please tell me what happened here over the last hour?"

"Well, everybody around me usually goes out early on Saturdays, and today that included Joseph and the black girl. I don't remember her name; we met only once, briefly, in front of the building. That was two or three months ago, I think. They came in late last night, and I think she stayed here. Not that I approve, but . . ."

Roberts let her ramble; he had sometimes gained valuable tidbits of information from such disjointed monologues.

". . . and I didn't expect them back this morning, but about thirty minutes ago I heard them coming up the stairs. Then I heard them upstairs; you can hear voices through these floors, but can't tell what people are saying. I then heard a short scream, and that got me concerned."

Roberts nodded, recalling the playful shriek.

"A few seconds later, I heard a bang, then something fell against my ceiling. I thought there had been an accident, so I went up to see if I could help. After all, he is a policeman—or was. When I knocked on the door, Joseph answered, but he told me to go away in a very angry tone. It wasn't like him at all. So I came down here and called the police; I thought if Joseph needed help, his policeman friends could help him better than I could, but if it was something else then they could handle that, too."

Bingo, Roberts smiled inwardly. He had guessed right; she had been the one that both knocked on the door and called the police. "The bang you heard was Hanlon shooting his girlfriend, and the thud was the young lady's body falling to the floor. She's lying dead upstairs."

The woman gasped in horror, put both hands to her mouth, and retreated two steps into her living room. "God . . . no!"

"Ma'am, just a couple more questions," Roberts said as she sat down on her couch, shaking. "Did anyone else go upstairs besides Hanlon and his girlfriend?"

"N . . . no," she managed. "It was quiet, it was only those two until afterward, until the fight . . . and the running. Did the police get him?"

"No, he escaped. We're trying to find him."

"What can I do? What if he comes back?"

"Please stay right here. There will be more policemen around to talk to you, and they will probably ask you to tell them the story again from the beginning. Just tell them what you told me."

"Yes . . . of course."

As he left the apartment, Roberts heard someone on the stairs below, coming up. He reached for his pistol, then relaxed. It was the boy cop. Let's see if I have this kid pegged as well as I did the old lady, he thought. "The crime scene is up one flight," he told the young officer. "It seems Hanlon and his girlfriend had quite an argument. Follow me."

Kauffman was waiting in the apartment, standing over the grotesquely sprawled corpse. Roberts entered first, followed immediately by Bouton, who took three steps into the room, observed the body, the blood, and the obscenely mangled face, took three steps out of the room, and vomited in the stairway.

"Beautiful," Roberts whispered, then addressed Kauffman for Bouton's benefit. "Hanlon really made a mess of things. Looks like a single head shot; hit the phone by her face at the same time. A witness says there was a violent quarrel beforehand; she was probably trying to call for help."

Roberts joined Bouton on the stairway, still bent over but slightly more composed. "Listen, kid, you don't have to go back in there," he said kindly. "There are a lot of frantic people down in the courtyard and on the street who are wondering what happened, wondering if they're in danger. They need to be calmed down. In my experience, just telling them the simple truth is the best thing to do. Don't try to cover up the fact there was a murder or that Hanlon was involved; a lot of people saw him running away. Just tell them it's all over and that he's gone, at least for the time being."

Bouton quietly took the advice that would have outraged any law enforcement official with even slightly more experience and descended the stairs.

Roberts reentered the apartment and locked the door. "I don't like splitting up, but there's no other way; I have to take care of that other matter," he said, rummaging through Elizabeth's purse. "Clean this place up and get rid of any evidence of the bomb; stick to the story about the nasty head shot and the fact that Hanlon still has the murder weapon with him. With luck, the cops will save us the trouble of having to kill him in custody."

"Whatever you say, Phil," Kauffman replied as he scraped debris off the floor.

"Damn women's purses, full of so much crap," Roberts muttered before grunting in triumph. "Here," he said as he tossed Kauffman a jingling mass. "One of these keys fits this door. Keep it locked and don't let anyone in. Because Hanlon was a cop, some of the locals are going to try and push their way in here, but don't let them in. Be demanding, be an asshole, be a tyrant; we're FBI, remember? And when the real feds get here, keep them out as well; we have a special dispensation. Put them onto the chase to catch the dangerous killer; they'll like that. Only let in the guys who will bag and remove the body. Make sure they work quickly, and seal it up tight. Then go with them after you finish cleaning up."

"Got it," answered Kauffman.

"I'll contact you this afternoon," Roberts said. He was at the front door, but, suddenly inspired, turned and entered the apartment's small kitchen. He opened the refrigerator and after inspecting its contents carefully removed a half-full two-liter bottle of Dr. Pepper.

"What's that?" inquired Kauffman.

"A minor detail," came the reply. "A little grain of payback for all this aggravation."

Aside from those actively involved in mortal combat, seldom had a period of mourning been so forcibly curtailed after so brief a period. Aware of Roberts' inexplicable influence over the powers that were, Joe knew without a doubt he was being hunted for Elizabeth's murder. He also knew that Roberts could not produce evidence for a trial and so was depending on the expedient method of closing a case from which there was no appeal: a dead perpetrator.

Joe was surprised he had escaped so easily and kept looking back through his rear view mirror for a glimpse of one of the accursed white sedans he had first laid eyes on just two days earlier. At one time or another over the previous hour he had been headed toward all points of the compass and was presently traveling north towards White Plains on New York State Route 100, a commercial strip. His head hurt, his arms ached and his left thigh felt as if someone had stuck a fiery poker through it. And he was cold; April was not the ideal month to have a window shot out. The remaining shards of passenger-side window were also attracting too much attention. Or was it something else? Then he remembered, and realized that no matter how violent America had supposedly become, it was still considered unusual to drive around with bullet holes in one's car.

He turned into a shopping center, an archaic, open affair with several shops and a small department store. He pulled the Nissan next to a retaining wall at the far end of the asphalt, then got out and inspected the damage done by the bullets, both to the car body and his own.

After noting that the nearest person was over fifty feet away, Joe unbuckled his pants and glanced down at his wound. The grazing bullet had cut an ugly four-inch gash along his thigh, angled down from front to back. At its deepest, a little over half the diameter of the bullet had cut into his flesh. Although bleeding, the flow was not extensive, the speeding bullet having cauterized the wound somewhat. It wasn't life threatening, but it hurt like hell. He hiked up his pants and checked them. He was fortunate; the entry and exit holes of the bullet and the blood that had soaked through were hidden by his windbreaker.

He knelt down and examined his cheek wound in the side-view mirror. If the bullet had been a millimeter to the right, it would have missed him completely. Effectively a bad bruise, it was the size of a dime and slightly swollen.

The Nissan was not so lucky. Joe opened the front passenger door and twisted the window crank. Pebbles from shattered safety glass cascaded to the pavement, but many clung to the doorframe, caught in the rubber seals. He closed the door and heard the rustle of broken glass. The rear door was decorated with two 9mm holes about eight inches apart.

Joe adjusted his clothes and smoothed back his hair, then checked his wallet and muttered a low curse. Four dead presidents stared back at him: twelve dollars in cash. He debated whether to use one of his credit cards but decided quickly against it, having discovered in his work that one of the main features of the computer age was the ability to use people's money against them. Limping slightly, he entered the store and began to search for the most economical scissors, gauze, and red vinyl tape he could find. The total came to $8.34, plus tax, which left him with two singles in currency plus some change. At least he had a half a tank of gas, he considered as he made his way back to the car. He could go quite a distance in the Nissan with half a tank.

He then turned his attentions to mending the car and himself. The car came first. He cut two small strips from the roll of two-inch wide red vinyl tape and placed them over the bullet holes. The color match was good. With the scissors, he then carefully cleaned around the rubber seals that still held remnants of the shattered window until they were clear of glass. An open window in April was a little odd, but nothing most people would take note of.

Joe moved around the car and sat down in the driver's seat. He glanced around furtively, then pushed the tops of his trousers and jockeys to mid-thigh. Blood continued to slowly ooze out of the dark furrow on his leg, the edges of which were blue-black. He laid one, another and finally a third layer of gauze on the wound, then secured them with several lengths of red tape. After tucking and zipping, he started the car and pulled back into the stream of traffic.

Just the radio call was the most exciting thing that had happened to him all day. State Police Trooper Hal Balser should have been home taking it easy on his thirty-third birthday, but as sometimes happens in an organization that remains active all day, every day, he was stuck with Saturday duty.

It was two hours before the end of his 7:00 A.M. to 3:30 P.M. shift, and so far everything had been routine, dull even. A quick response to a silent alarm call at a convenience store had done nothing except to shake up the young clerk who had unknowingly tripped the swing-down alarm switch while she was putting a stack of bags under the counter. Other than that, there was a fender-bender just outside the main gate of the Sunningdale Country Club—cleared in fifteen minutes—and a citation for an illegal left-hand turn at the Yonkers-Hartsdale line.

The radio had been quiet, too, not communicating any events more remarkable than his own. Until this most recent call, about a murder of all things! In Sunnyside of all places! With a suspect, armed and dangerous, on the loose! The name—Joseph Hanlon—was one he knew. Could it be? thought Balser. No, it couldn't, he concluded quickly. It was just a coincidence, two people with the same name, each working on opposite sides of the law, or maybe a mix-up of the names of the reporting officer and the suspect.

Though it was something to hone his senses on, the chance he would see any action from the warning was extremely slim. Still, he would keep an eye out for the suspect car, even though it could be any one of tens of thousands of cars in the area. Like that one, he mused, mentally noting a vehicle heading toward him a few hundred feet ahead. The car was a compact, possibly a Nissan, he noted. The car approached steadily. It *was* a Nissan, and a red one at that, but he knew perhaps half a dozen people in his neighborhood with one similar. And it had New York plates, too. Big deal. With numbers reading . . .

Officer Hal Balser jerked up in his seat so fast he nearly dislocated his back. "Jesus, Mary, and Joseph!" he exclaimed, staring through his rear view mirror at the receding car, "That is it!" The street was wide and the traffic sparse, so in making the U-turn he thought he was not posing any danger to the public. He would find out later that day that letting the suspect remain free was considered by his superiors to be very dangerous to the community.

In a way, Joe was pleased the police car had done a one-eighty and was now headed in his direction. He had seen the cruiser approaching from a distance. Head forward, teeth clenched, he did his utmost to feign disinterest to the vehicle, all the while following it intently with his eyes as it drew near, passed within thirty feet, then receded. At that point, the crisis had just begun. If he had followed proper police procedure, the state trooper should have immediately grabbed his radio mike to quietly summon all available forces to the area, all the while traveling innocently along until he could discreetly turn around. By the rash U-turn, the uncertainty was over. He would have thought the move was made by a rookie if he did not recognize Hal Balser in the driver's seat.

Acting quickly and decisively, Joe sped up and moved deftly to the right in front of a panel truck, then moved east onto a side street between two block buildings. The neighborhood was a mix of older residential homes built close to the streets and small commercial properties. He was not familiar with the specific neighborhood, but knew the type, and became wary of possible dead ends. After an immediate left followed by another right, he drove straight for three blocks, then ventured a look back, catching a glimpse of the cruiser as it started to go straight through the intersection. Good. At the last possible moment, it abruptly turned toward the Nissan, its left front tire jumping the curb before regaining the pavement. Not so good. Joe hated car chases; he hated them even more when he was on the end where the bad guy should be.

As he made three more quick, random turns, Joe briefly entertained the thought of just stopping, getting out of the car, and carefully approaching Hal, arms in the air. After all, he was his peer, his coworker. The situation was a bit confusing, but things could be worked out. Then he thought again. "No way—no way in hell," he said. He accelerated, opting for more distance and less turns. The pursuing police car was, for the moment at least, no longer in sight.

Joe knew he could endure the unpleasantness of being arrested and jailed if he could expect to enter the justice system he knew so well. For all of its problems it did work, at least most of the time. But now he was in a Twilight Zone of justice stood on its head, where the legal system was suddenly and inexplicably crowned with murderous goons.

After briefly reconnoitering the wide road from a convenience store parking lot, he crossed Route 100 headed west, and was rewarded with the sight of a police sedan from the Hartsdale force turning off the road a few blocks away—headed east. It was a good sign, but he didn't consider himself safe yet.

Joe crept up the county, crossing major roads as a jungle patrol might cross open streams in enemy territory. It was similar to a jungle, actually. If there had been any reason behind the original layout of the Westchester road network, it had been lost between the Revolutionary and Civil Wars, and subsequent attempts to improve the transportation arteries had, like tax law reforms, only led to more confusion.

The Nissan skirted the Kenisco Reservoir for a short distance, then Joe turned west, now eight miles from his pursuers. The initial pursuers anyway, he thought. Not aware of how wide the net had been thrown, he wondered how many of the dozens of village, town, and city departments had been alerted and were now out in force looking for him. Presumably, even his own Sunnyside peers were out on the search as well. He desperately wanted to know the source of authority for men who could chase a police officer in broad daylight, guns blazing, and then call out every arm of the law to hunt him, when it was they who killed his—fiancée. It was the first time he had thought of the word in conjunction with Elizabeth and the blissful events of that morning, but that was, and would always be, Before, and now it was after Before and that was far too late. He shook off his tears and faced the cold reality that he had to concentrate on saving his own worthless hide now.

CHAPTER 12

Minute in comparison with any other city within seventy miles to the south, Peekskill's heyday was fully a century in the past. With commercial river trade all but gone, and with its predecessor, the railroad, in sad decline, the small municipality had stagnated. Once-bustling roads wound up from the Hudson in odd patterns to what had been the central business district, but was now more than anything else just the central district. Suburban encroachment had resulted in housing developments to the east and south, but Peekskill proper was still an agglomeration of low, old buildings, narrow streets intersecting at strange angles, and quietly frustrated people. A good place to stop, Joe thought.

For the first time since . . . Before, he was thinking not just about what happened, but why. There was a progression in the actions of Roberts and his people: they detained him at the Bonnelli house, then they had him fired—as far as they knew—after he went back the next day. After that, his only connection with the case had been peripheral, involving the dead squirrel and DeLuca. Then he remembered the call, the penultimate call on his phone. Kenneth DeLuca's explanation of the cause of the rodent's death was confusing, but one thing became abruptly clear: it meant something; it was a reason to kill.

Suddenly, communication took urgent precedence over escape, and Joe began to search for a telephone among Peekskill's twisting streets. From this point on, he knew, every call would have to be evaluated against the possibility it might be traced. Landlines and even cellular phones could now be almost instantaneously pinpointed with the proper equipment, he knew, but only through reading about it. The Sunnyside force did not have access to things that modern and expensive, but he was certain that those most eager to find him did.

He spied a phone in front of a mid-block liquor store, the windows of which contained taped-over cracks and were covered with wire mesh. Joe did a full circle of the block, analyzing the urban terrain, searching for anything potentially threatening, then parked the Nissan on a parallel street, or at least as parallel as a street could be in Peekskill. With care, he went up the alley to the north side of the liquor store and approached the pay phone.

In Croton, another river town miles to the south, Joe had stopped briefly at a convenience store. As it was unheard of anywhere in New York State to ask for change, he had purchased a can of Dr. Pepper with two singles. The change, along with another two dimes and a quarter he discovered in a dusty corner of the Nissan, was all the money he had in the world. He retrieved the coins from his pocked and dialed.

He was being rung through, but no. The line was busy, the one response he had not expected. His mind grasped for reason. Everyone had call waiting nowadays, didn't they? Perhaps the line was already in use, with another call on hold. That would result in the terrible tones he was listening to, or would it?

The street seemed more ominous as he hung up the phone and the coins jingled down to daylight. He stared down at the silver, reluctant to touch the symbols of his reaching out to help that had been so impotently returned. He resolved to find another way to warn Dr. DeLuca.

The man was not yet thirty but was the supreme commander of powerful armies, victorious in many battles. His current campaign was taking his forces north into Lauredor to attack the treacherous Selentines. From the sea, a force led by one of his veteran heroes attacked Jessarton and quickly dispatched the defending garrison, a unit of light infantry. The vanquished city not being crucial to his plans of conquest, he razed it. Bells of victory rang out.

And continued to ring. Stephen White reluctantly turned away from the computer screen and answered the phone. "Yo!" he greeted.

He heard a pained utterance, followed by a short silence. "Steve, it's Joe," the distressed man finally managed.

"Jesus, man. What's wrong?"

"Deep shit; shit so foul you can't possibly imagine."

"Where are you?" It was an innocent question; Steve didn't know how threateningly it was received.

"It doesn't matter. I'm not calling for me. I need your help with Dr. DeLuca. I need you to tell him to get out of town. He needs to hide." The sentences came in quick, staccato bursts.

"Whoa, old buddy, slow down," Steve said, trying to take it all in. "If the doc's in trouble, why don't you call the cops? Hell, you're a cop."

"They won't be able to help with this," Joe replied.

"You want me to call him?"

"NO! Just drive by his house to see if he's in. If he is, plead with him to go somewhere—anywhere—to a place nobody can find him. If he's not in, just drive straight by his house like nothing's up."

"I can tell you if he's in right now. I can see his place from here." Steve lived in Marlborough on Route 9W in a rambling clapboard farmhouse into which eight small apartments had been crammed. Located on an upgrade just north of the Royal Winery, the house had a view of portions of Ridge Road, which paralleled the state highway three quarters of a mile to the west. The DeLuca colonial was located on the crest of the ridge. "I've seen that old Volvo of his in the driveway plenty of times." He headed toward the door.

"Wait! What's that?" Joe asked as static encroached on the connection.

"What, the interference? It's this damned cordless phone," Steve explained, opening the door. "It's impossible to find a good one, and even in my small apartment, I keep losing it under the desk, in the chair, you name it. It would be nice to have it attached to the base unit with something. Like a cord. Next time . . . oh my God! Damn!"

From the small landing of the stairway that led to his second floor apartment, Steve looked to the west. In the distance stood the DeLuca house, surrounded by vehicles. "I heard the sirens about twenty minutes ago but I didn't pay attention to them. But now . . . and you calling . . . Jesus!"

"What's going on?" Joe demanded.

"The DeLuca house is on fire! Completely fucking ablaze!"

I am sick to death of New York; I never want to set foot in this state again as long as I live, Philip Roberts thought as he drove south through the Hudson Highlands, not paying any attention to some of the most picturesque scenery in America. He had taken a wrong turn in a pesthole of a city called Newburgh, and was now seemingly in the middle of nowhere.

Roberts was exhausted, the two-day mission having been extended by three days, during which time he had not slept for more than four hours at a stretch. And things had gone so spectacularly wrong. That some punk cop from a two-bit town could so foul up such a simple, well-planned mission was almost beyond comprehension. It wasn't that he expected perfection. Some minor mistakes were bound to occur, some contingency plans activated. The level to which the seemingly minor blunders had been elevated, however, had him baffled. At least the essential part of the operation had been completed successfully. The technical team had completed whatever alchemy it was they did with the body, and it had been returned without a hitch. Only he and Kauff-man had remained behind to tie up the simplest of loose ends, one of which involved keeping a punk cop out of the way for a few days. But he just wouldn't stay gone, Roberts thought, his rage intensifying. Now two people were dead because of Hanlon, killed sloppily, inconveniently, and the bastard was still loose. He had just verified that fact with the FBI—the real FBI—which had assumed the lead in the search.

He sped on through the mountains, urgently taking the winding curves that had long been a hallmark of Route 9W. A lonely sign proclaimed his entry into the "Town of Highlands." Crazy goddamn place, the man pondered disgustedly. He hadn't seen a building for miles and there was still nothing in sight but trees, the road, and the sign. "This is a town?" he cried to the interior of the vehicle. "Let me out of here."

The car negotiated a long downgrade. Ignoring the panoramic view of the United States Military Academy to his left, Roberts picked up his cellular phone and punched a button. "Have you got everything ready?" he asked Eric Kauffman.

"It's bagged and ready to go."

"I'm picking you up within the next two hours. We'll take the package with us." That was the plan: they would stuff the body of Elizabeth Brooks into the trunk, then would fly her, still within the car, out of the accursed state.

"I'll finalize the arrangements. We'll have a plane at Stewart standing by in three hours," Kauffman said.

"You find out anything about her?"

"Let me get my notes," Kauffman answered. "Elizabeth Brooks, 30, local real estate broker, verified as the girlfriend of the suspect. Parents dead, no relatives in the vicinity."

That was good luck, Roberts thought. "Any late word on the search for the suspect?"

"Nothing," Kauffman reported. "It's been six hours now."

"I'll be there soon. Out." Roberts punched another button and tossed the phone onto the passenger's seat.

The car passed through Fort Montgomery, a tiny village in southern Orange County. A local police officer, his ticket book drawn, was standing by a mini-van just to the front of his unmarked sedan. "There are better things to do, asshole," Roberts muttered as he drove past.

Finally, he sighted a sign for Westchester. He maneuvered the car three-quarters of the way around a traffic circle and moved onto the Bear Mountain Bridge, a two-lane suspension span. It took less than a minute to cross. As he was turning south, he caught sight of a small car on the same road, moving away from him to the north. Another red compact. He had been seeing them all day, eyeing each suspiciously, looking for broken glass and bullet holes. They were everywhere, the puny crimson demons, an unending profusion of admonitions for his failure.

"Yeah, that's him," Roberts said with dejected sarcasm. He continued on to White Plains.

———

Of the two options open to him to traverse the rolling, rocky mountains north of Peekskill known as the Highlands, Joe had chosen the road along the Hudson. There were other routes that led north farther to the east, but he was running out of gas and had fifty cents to his name. When he had at last spied the towers of the Bear Mountain Bridge, he debated whether to cross the span, a quick hop across the river, but then thought the better of it. For one thing, the bridge led to Fort Montgomery and its inevitable, local income-producing speed trap, a tax for the unwary. For another, a little farther on, Route 9W passed unhindered through a portion of the 17,000-acre reservation of the United States Military Academy. In a class necessary to get his law enforcement degree, that very stretch of road had been used to illustrate cases where two agencies—in this example, the West Point Military Police and the town of Highlands Police Force—might hold purview over a single area. Although mildly interesting at the time, the concept of dual jurisdiction held absolutely no appeal to him now.

So he moved on to the more sparsely populated lands of the river's east bank, passing the spot where the Appalachian Trail disappeared into the rugged hills after crossing the Bear Mountain Bridge. He was relieved to have reached Steve, one of his oldest and closest friends, but still a safe call. He had considered calling others first, though. Special Agent Richard Tobin would have stood by him, but Joe didn't have his home number. Chief Dempsey, another unwavering ally, was also out. Though even a few words of advice would have been welcome from that underrated Nestor, he was currently navigating the Ashokan Reservoir in the Catskills, questing for an elusive blue trout. His parents were also out, out, out. There was no way he wanted to involve them, phone tap or no, and it was almost certainly yes.

Racking his brain for others, Steve had come to mind. Though he had not called him for what seemed like forever, he vividly remembered the number, as Steve had once remarked that his last four digits spelled out a female body part. Joe still thought it extraordinary, both for the fact and that a person would spend his time figuring out words that could be made with a telephone number.

Joe ended the conversation with the plea that Steve quietly—so quietly—gather more information about Dr. DeLuca and the fire. The doctor might still be alive. The house fire could have been an accident, one of his tests gone awry. Those pursuing Joe might not know anything about his last conversation with DeLuca.

Not bloody likely.

Joe gripped the wheel and averted his eyes from the remnants of a squirrel—or something—just to the left of the road's center stripe, its entrails reaching almost across the yellow. The Nissan sped on toward a rendezvous with another telephone, its location unknown.

Nauseous, his stomach twitched, his last meal—Before—churned. The car passed through the short tunnel piercing Breakneck Ridge. He turned on his headlights, the tunnel reminding him it was near dusk. To his left, Bannerman's Island and its huge, burnt-out shell of a castle loomed menacingly. Burned like DeLuca's house; a shell like what was left of his life.

Joe glanced at his watch and increased his speed slightly. He had arranged to call Steve at seven o'clock, and wanted to make that appointment as if his life depended on it.

At last he arrived in Beacon, another stagnant river city much like Peekskill. After parking a block away, he walked to Main Street and up to the telephone he had seen a few moments before, the liquor store this time being across the street. He dialed, and dropped his last two quarters—his last money—into the contraption. Never before, since his mother received a fifty-dollar U.S. Savings Bond in his name from a congratulatory relative—he was two days old at the time—had he been absolutely broke.

Please don't say it, he prayed silently as the phone rang, but of course Steve did.

"Yo."

"It's me. Let's talk."

As a firm rule, the young woman was meticulous in her appearance. Consistently, she bought the best in clothing. Her shoulder-length blonde hair was always brushed to perfection, and a weekly appointment with her hairdresser was maintained religiously. She had taken courses in cosmetology at night, but had applied the knowledge learned to but one person. All of this served to ameliorate her radiant good looks which had been turning men's heads even before she started her rigorous program of beautification.

She now would have now been receiving overlong glances for a different reason, however. She was a mess, not having looked this much of a wreck, inside her apartment or out, for years, maybe forever. Her clothes were disheveled—even a pocket of her tailored jacket was torn—and her hair was hopelessly asunder. Her face reflected a blind madman's attempt at makeup application, and two well-manicured nails were broken. Susan DeLuca didn't give a damn.

She had been out on a Saturday afternoon shopping trip at an upscale mall on Washington Street, searching for something suitable to wear to an upcoming stockholders meeting. Between shops, her cellular phone buzzed. On the other end was her brother, having been given her number by one of the poor souls at her workplace with weekend duty.

Visibly shattered by his news, not at all displaying the proper composure expected of well-dressed Bostonians, she attracted many eyes. Having heard more than she ever wanted to, she attempted to remove the accursed electronic messenger from her sight, but the fine fabric of her jacket ripped when she attempted to jam it into her pocket. Joining her two packages, the black device clattered to the floor and she ran away from the crowd, leaving the onlookers to ponder the ownership of property so abandoned.

She had driven through her tears to her apartment, threw a few random items of clothing into the back seat of her Taurus, and was now on Interstate 90, chasing the Sun that had receded under the horizon a few minutes before.

In many ways Marlborough was still home, Susan thought. She had grown up there and it was the home of her parents of course, but she was also subject to the whims of society, which held that, unmarried and living alone, she had not yet settled down, had not earned the right to call her current abode a home.

There had never been any single issue fatal to her associations with men, no thread of cause to generally explain her love life. Her first love, far in the past, was her greatest. Deep and consuming, at the time she did not even imagine it would not last forever. Since then, she had been close to love, but something always prevented her from grasping it, perhaps grasping for it. Though there were more good times than bad scenes, termination was always the result. On occasion she had put an end to the relationships, more rarely he—the he at the time—ended them, and twice the dissolution had been preceded with a period of drifting so drawn out that the assignation of either party's role was impossible.

Though romantic love had bypassed her, she had loved her mother, so long dead but still in Marlborough in spirit, and she did love her father, but he was missing, and his house—her home—was on fire. What precipitated her frenzy, however, was the added fact elicited from her brother that the Volvo was still in the driveway.

Susan's brother was a doctor, ten years her senior, but he had not quite followed in his father's venerated footsteps. Christopher DeLuca lived on a five-acre mini-farm in Milton with his wife and two young sons, a scant eight miles north of the Real Dr. Deluca, a sobriquet often used when Kenneth and Christopher were referred to in the same conversation. A chiropractor in Poughkeepsie, Christopher was by most definitions a success, but his father disapproved of both his craft and his vigorous use of radio and billboard advertisements to promote his practice.

It was almost certainly because of her brother's career decision that her father had frequently urged Susan during her last two years of high school to attend the best college she could find. Remarkably, he didn't lead her in the direction of any one institution. There had been one serious, memorable conversation when, like a king commissioning an explorer to find gold for the realm, he generally outlined his requirements. As treasures of knowledge could be widely located, geography had not been an issue. As long as the school was reputable, she could go anywhere in the contiguous forty-eight, he told her, except Florida, where there were too many distractions, or North Dakota, where there was absolutely nothing. After months of intermittent searching, weeks of constant consideration, and days of final agony, she offered up Smith to her father. She would always remember his terse nod of approval.

After the appropriate interval, Susan was ushered out of Smith with a degree in political science. After another nod, she entered Harvard Business School, taking mental classes in the Establishment and the Politics of Big Business simultaneously with her scheduled course load.

Upon that last graduation, she remained in Boston, accepting a position with an information services company, and since then had been promoted twice. Her first promotion occurred after only a few months, coming about due to a combination of her recognized ability and the fact that her immediate manager, a man, was being aggressively moved out due to several sexual harassment charges. Although he had attempted liaisons with Susan, she had successfully rebuffed him, then assumed a low profile and let others act as the whistleblowers. Society considered her beauty to be an asset, but she had not always found that to be true. Certainly, it had helped her career. Her comeliness and manner of dress made her appear to be a successful woman going places, which greatly aided her to be both successful and going places. In romantic spheres, though, she did not view her appearance in the same way it was billed.

Although she wanted to think that most men were not like her former boss, her experience had not proven that true. She knew she possessed the Look that drew pigs like flies, those nothing-to-lose guys whose attitude was that it was better to take a chance than to lose the opportunity to pop someone who looked like her. Like telemarketers, the fact that these little-head thinkers had some small percentage of success kept them going. That she had to worry so much about her trappings and yet still be subjected to the attitudes she had to distastefully deal with every day, Susan thought as she drove through the night, was crap. Bullshit. *Menkus.*

The Newburgh-Beacon Bridge stretched out straight in front of Joe for two miles like a gigantic model's runway. Although he didn't know if there was an audience waiting for him in the darkness to either side, he was aware he was sporting the latest and most sought-after fashion: a red Nissan Sentra, New York license ORX-460.

He maneuvered the car down the onramp and mingled with the traffic on Interstate 84, praising whatever gods might be that only eastbound travelers crossing the Hudson River were tolled. He passed the wide toll plaza on his left, and nearly choked when he saw a state policeman standing to the side of the tollbooths glance in his direction. Fortunately, the trooper held his ground, and Joe finally lost sight of him over his shoulder. Obviously, the uniformed cop was also an uninformed one. After traversing the bridge, he took the second 9W exit—the one leading away from Marlborough—and entered the city of Newburgh.

Of all the old river cities along the Hudson, Newburgh was the only one that consistently struck dread into the hearts and minds of those in the know. While places like Beacon and Peekskill had stagnated over the decades, Newburgh had continuously deteriorated to a point that it was considered a place without hope. Joe turned the Nissan into the most blighted section of the wretched, ruined metropolis.

He rode on pitifully maintained, trash-filled streets, past old brick buildings that sixty years before might had served as the residences of doctors or lawyers, but had since been brutally sliced up into four, five, or six apartments. They look abandoned, but most were not except by all who might perform repairs.

Lander Street, commonly known as "Crack Alley," was where Joe decided to bid farewell to his Nissan. Of certainty, no police would be prowling Lander Street anytime soon, and the car would probably be removed from circulation permanently within hours. He rolled down the driver's side window, thought briefly about the incident that made rolling down the other window unnecessary, and got out of the car. He opened the trunk and retrieved two bags. Though he needed only one, Joe could not bear abandoning the possessions of his beloved Elizabeth on those mean streets. Finally, he took the car key and threw it onto the front seat. At least somebody is going to get a break today, he considered before turning his back on the vehicle.

Prepared at any time to use his skills of escape and evasion learned and practiced years ago while in the Army, Joe walked west up Third Street on the broken, heaved sidewalk, traveling uphill, away from the river. At an intersection, a voice accosted him from half a block away: "Hey white boy! What are you doing here?" Joe ignored the taunt and continued to ascend the slope. Four blocks later, he crossed Route 9W, the border between the worst parts of the city of Newburgh and the rest—the bad and worse sections.

Quickening his pace, limping slightly, Joe traversed several more streets and entered an area of professional offices, one of which was the firm of Brent Parmenter and Associates, Architects. Steve White was one of the associates.

There was one car in the rear parking lot, far in the corner. A figure leaned nonchalantly against the vehicle, an old Dodge.

"Steve," Joe called in a voice as high as he dared from the entrance to the small lot.

"Yeah, Joe?" the figure answered in a voice just as low.

The two friends met with a warm clasping of four hands. In short order, they pulled out of the lot, headed north. "It's a lucky thing I still work there," Steve said to provide a brief respite to the tension. "Last summer, the firm almost went under because of a lawsuit. Some general contractor in Rockland misread one of our drawings for a mall design and installed an escalator between the wrong floors, because in lower case letters 'up' reads the same as the abbreviation for 'down,' 'dn,' when turned the wrong way."

"What happened?" Joe asked tiredly, content to hear a friendly voice.

"After massive legal arguments, and the lawyers' attendant massive fees, they lost because there were other drawings that clearly showed the escalator between the entry level and the first floor, not between the first and second floors."

There was a brief silence in the car as Steve passed Blue Jay Drive and crossed over Route 32. "Find out anything new?" Joe finally asked. While in Beacon, Steve informed him the DeLuca house was still burning, firefighting efforts being hampered by low water pressure on Ridge Road, and the doctor was missing, although his Volvo was still in the driveway, or rather what was left of it after its gas tank ignited.

"Nothing much," Steve said. "Everybody's searching for the doc, but by now most people think they know where he is. The flames have died down, but the place was still smoldering when I left. We haven't had many fires in the area, so I don't know what the procedures are, but there sure are a shitload of police around," he went on, making it clear that other forces had greatly augmented Marlborough's tiny fleet of three police cars. "Do you know anything? What the hell is going on?"

The car, uneasily at times, covered eight country miles as Joe related his recent experiences.

"Jesus fucking H. fucking Christ!" exclaimed Steve in one quick breath, echoing his passenger's sentiments, if not his vernacular. "I still don't know what's going on! That this could happen to Mr. Eagle Scout War Hero Goody-Goody Top Cop is . . . more than unbelievable. It's . . . unthinkable. Alien."

Joe was flattered, having never known his old *compadre* respected him so much. "I don't get it either, but it's true. It happened."

"You need help. Isn't there anyone you can call?"

"I called him."

It took a moment to sink in. "Jesus," Steve swore at the responsibility. "What do we do now?"

"First of all, there doesn't have to be any 'we.' I'm not going to lie and say I don't need your help, but these—goons are killers, and they're not going to stop anytime soon and the police are unknowingly but wholeheartedly on their side. You can let me off at any time."

"That was really a pitiful speech," Steve said. "Don't be such a martyr. Sure it's a bad situation; shit, I couldn't imagine a worse one, but we're old buds, right? I'll do whatever I can, just don't let me do anything stupid."

Joe saw his friend's hands shaking on the wheel. "Okay, but I don't like it." Given the circumstances, he didn't like much of anything. "What's the situation at your apartment?"

"Quiet. The house has eight units, but I live in the back on the second floor. There aren't any lights on that side of the building, but you'll have to be careful going up the outside wooden stairs."

They continued discussing their plans. Just outside Dawesville, population 43, they stopped on a lonely stretch of Plattekill Road, next to a sign indicating the town of Marlborough line. The both exited the car, Joe having opted to complete the trip within the confines of the vehicle's trunk. He winced as he contorted himself to fit the small compartment.

"What happened to your leg?" Steve asked.

"We'll have show and tell later," Joe replied before the lid closed.

The circuitous route was completed without mishap, but several bystanders observed Steve as he entered the more populated sections of town, justifying Joe's uncomfortable berth. Wary of prying eyes, Steve parked in his apartment building's small gravel lot and unlocked the trunk, then the two men crept up the stairs. Joe allowed himself one glance back toward the DeLuca house. The flames were extinguished, but smoke swirled around the flashing lights of uncountable fire and police vehicles at the site.

The cramped residence was commonly called a studio apartment, "studio" being synonymous with "little piece of crap" in most of Joe's experience, and he was not now prone to change his mind.

"Welcome to Shitville," Steve said quietly. They did not need a reminder to keep their voices down.

It was bliss being anywhere, though, Joe thought as he settled into a frayed easy chair, the largest piece of furniture in the room. The bed was a thin, narrow camping cot mattress, sans cot. Steve sat in the only other seat in the apartment, an old office executive chair. "In my snooping around this afternoon, I ran into Cheryl Clarke. You might remember her from her job at the Stewart's up the road."

Eyes closed, Joe nodded, not recalling the convenience store clerk.

"We went out a couple of times last year, and she's the biggest gossip around. Matter of fact, I didn't continue the relationship because of her constant prattle. With this fire being the biggest news in years, she was really into it, so I casually mentioned that she give me a ring if she found out anything. Looks like she hasn't called yet," Steve observed after he glanced at the unblinking light of his answering machine.

Joe opened his eyes and pondered the risk. Was it safe? It sounded okay. He wasn't sure. He wasn't sure of much, anymore. "Okay, but if she doesn't call, let's lay low until the morning."

"Whatever you say." A pause. "Let's take care of whatever that is in your pants." Blood had soaked through Joe's jeans, outlining his wound.

Joe stood wearily and dropped his trousers, revealing the make-shift red vinyl bandage, other, darker red now adhering to it. Steve cleaned the injury and dressed it with white strips liberated from a T-shirt and liberal quantities of adhesive tape.

"How'd you get that?" he asked as he was completing his ministrations, gesturing to Joe's right cheek.

"I got nicked," Joe replied as if he had cut himself shaving. Then he went into the details.

"Shit," was the only response.

The phone rang and Joe jerked violently in his chair, the memories of the last time he had heard that sound immediately inundating his mind: the smiling face, the fatal bang. He had to restrain himself from grabbing the pealing phone and flinging it unanswered into the darkness. But he did hold back, and braced himself for the next word, so necessary because it was normal, and Steve had to act normally.

"Yo."

It was Cheryl, Steve indicated to Joe by a thumb. "Yeah, it's late, but I was up. . . . You called how many? . . . Well, some people can sure talk." Steve's caller entered into a long monologue, punctuated by Steve's random "yes's," "yeah's," and "uh huh's," with an occasional "wow."

Achingly fatigued, Joe stopped trying to follow the one-sided conversation, settled back into the old chair, and closed his eyes.

"Hey buddy." Steve said, gently nudging his guest.

"Umm."

"Listen." Steve paused. "There's no other way to say it. It's arson and murder. They put out the fire and pulled DeLuca's body out of the basement about an hour ago. They found his dog near him. I don't know the details on the doctor, but the dog was shot, right between the eyes. Susan was at the scene too."

So much, and now so much more. Elizabeth and DeLuca and his new status as fugitive. Now Susan, too, and those Things from the dark past. Joe shut his eyes, trembling, and acid tears began a continuous journey down his face.

The friends sat unmoving in the still, dingy room for several minutes. As there existed no words of comfort for his friend, Steve finally said, "You look like shit. Get some sleep."

"No. . . ."

"Look, it's midnight, the end of a long, crappy day. You take the bed; I'll sleep on the floor."

Too weary to argue further, Joe assented to his friend's suggestion, and was asleep in an instant.

SUNDAY
12 APRIL

CHAPTER 13

Yesterday, she had seen it in person, and it seemed just as real when depicted within the sheaf of papers before her. She didn't know which she detested more, the bold, black headline, or the large, full-color picture beneath it. No, she didn't know; she was incapable of making a decision on anything.

Susan DeLuca, awake but numb, was in a large eat-in kitchen overly decorated in a country theme. The place looked vaguely familiar, but she did not know from where. She was wearing a nightgown that someone had given her, but she had no idea who. The thoughts left as quickly as they came as her entire being focused on the horror within the newspaper that had been left on the table, tragically unattended.

She found herself sitting, holding but not feeling the paper. The *Times Herald-Record* was printed in tabloid format, with the daily headline and one large photo on the front page. This sunny Sunday morning, the paper boldly proclaimed "Murder/Arson Suspected in Marlborough Fire." Susan stared at the words, half disbelieving them, but the half was immediately dispelled by what lay beneath the banner. She saw her house—home—in its final agony. Vivid orange and red flames leaped high into the night sky through the maw where the roof had been as fire and smoke escaped out every window opening. Glinting in the firelight, not yet consumed, was a large gold "D" on the front door.

Unseen within the picture, she realized, was her father, dead inside the burning cauldron. Waiting for help. Waiting for a rescue that, like her arrival, came infinitely too late. The photograph having been seared into her mind forever, she turned the page. As all of this newspaper's lead stories began on page three, Susan was facing the article, "Dr. Kenneth DeLuca Dead in Marlborough Blaze," accompanied by a picture of her father. She was familiar with the photo. It had been taken about twenty years before, just after the family's move to Marlborough, when a reporter had visited to write a much different kind of article.

Through bleary eyes, she began to read. "Late Saturday afternoon, firefighters rushed to—"

The words blurred as the page rose rapidly. She saw other articles, but couldn't make them out, and caught the barest glimpse of another photo, somehow familiar, at the bottom of the page.

The newspaper disappeared and was replaced by the grim face of her brother. "You don't need to be looking at that," he scolded.

Susan snapped back to the present, becoming more aware. She was in the house of her brother and his wife, on their farm, or what used to be a farm and was now another doctor's residence.

"And what do I need to be doing?" She honestly didn't know.

"You don't need to do a thing; we will take care of you," came the answer from behind Christopher DeLuca. It was Pamela, his wife of thirteen years, a heavyset woman in her late thirties. She joined the siblings at the table and put a kind hand on Susan's shoulder. "We know what you've been through," she said, a touch too gaily. "Please try to relax; I'll get anything you need."

Head bowed in grief, Christopher turned away and walked slowly from the room.

"You must have something to eat; I don't suppose you've had anything since you left Boston," Pamela said, taking command of the kitchen and her guest.

Susan nodded. As she emerged out of the haze, she recognized her sister-in-law's need to fawn, and it was better for her to lavish her attentions on food than the alternative.

Booger, the family cat, entered. Noted for its missing tail, it used to have a nightly habit of climbing up and sleeping on the warm engine block of Christopher's car. Except for the last time, Booger was always up and about before the chiropractor went to work.

As her gaze wandered from cat to sister-in-law, now busily preparing a meal, Susan recalled it all in unblinking harshness. From Boston, after two breaks for gas, her third stop had been at the police barricade on Ridge Road. The young policeman who stepped out of the darkness reluctantly let her pass, her pleas to know prevailing over his desire to protect her from things she should not see. She parked just short of the house and ran up the road, being detained near the driveway entrance by strong arms while around her voices hushed to a whisper and several fingers pointed in her direction. The daughter, they said silently. She could see the smoldering, stinking ruins of the house in the spotlights, and saw four sooty firemen standing shoulder to shoulder at the edge of the foundation, now the uppermost portion of the house. They were pulling something, roping up from the depths of the basement a heavy, inert object covered with black plastic. The men then carried the dark object to an ambulance, a vehicle for those in distress, but it took her father away instead of her. Christopher was there and helped as much as he was able after she collapsed.

He had helped her to here, Susan considered. To this quaint kitchen with its matron attending to her cooking, moving almost merrily from boiling pot to frying pan. Helped her to where everything would be taken care of. Helped her to helplessness.

There was one other thing, she recalled. A name from the past, overheard from a distance as she stood before the fire, coupled with the picture on the bottom of page three. In the fleeting instant she had seen it, she thought she recognized that face. It looked like—but could it possibly have been?

"There, now," Pamela said, placing a large, unwanted plate of heavy breakfast selections before Susan. "You must be famished. Can I get you anything else?"

"Pam?"

"Yes?" she answered, slightly apprehensive.

"Does Joe Hanlon have anything to do with . . . this . . ." She didn't know what to call it. This thing? This soul-wrenching debacle? This totally screwed-up life-ruining shit?

Pamela DeLuca seized the pause. She looked quickly around the room and spied the cat in a corner. "Booger, you must be hungry, too. Let me get you something." She turned away and walked to a cabinet on the far side of the room. As she removed the plastic container of Kat Kibbles, she addressed Susan. "I called some of my dearest friends before you got up; they should be over in about an hour. I'm sure you'll be comforted by them. They're very nice, and we get along very well; I think it's because we're so much alike."

It might have been a bedroom at one time, but the bed had been replaced by a desk. Now it was a library, usually a place of relaxation or quiet study, but on this morning its sole occupant was anything but relaxed or quiet.

Standing behind the desk was Ronald Louis Hightower. In his mid-fifties, his athletic build had not diminished perceptibly over the decades, and his gray hair only enhanced his distinguished appearance. Stiffly agitated, he shouted into the receiver of the larger of the two telephones on the desk. "I just talked to Irwin and Wainwright and they told me you pulled some real shit in New York."

"Wait one goddamned minute," the voice demanded. "We had some problems, but the situation is under control. I took my lumps from Wainwright last night when I got in, and took another ass chewing from Irwin this morning. I told them both what happened, but neither of the sons of bitches was in a listening mood. And I didn't tell them everything; I was waiting for this pleasant conversation." Philip Roberts was not happy.

"Okay," Hightower answered, slightly calmed. "Give it to me."

"The operation went fine, straight down the checklist. Then this punk local cop stumbles in. We boot him out, but he comes back. We have him fired to get him out of the way, and he comes back again, dragging in another person, a doctor. We had to take quick action to address the problem before it spread."

"What happened?"

"We had the bastard, we were sure he was dead, but we got his girlfriend instead. Now he's on the run, charged with her murder."

"Jesus wept."

"I took care of the other end, the doctor, personally," Roberts said. "There was no doubt about that one."

"I never wanted people killed like this; I never authorized you to go that far."

"You hired me to provide security for this project—total security. I did what had to be done. Sometimes people have to be killed in ways that don't involve clean hands and white coats, but look who I'm talking to; you've blown away more people than I ever thought of killing."

It was true, but Hightower ignored the reference to his activities many years in the past, back when he was in his twenties. "What was this threat to the project that was so big that two people had to be killed?"

Roberts told him.

"Fuck." It was not a word Hightower used often. He sat down at the desk. "That could have blown everything."

"That's why I took the action, so give me a little credit and call off your dogs Irwin and Wainwright."

"Okay," Hightower said. "What's the danger now?"

"Minimal risk, just a lot of additional work down here. I checked the doctor's phone records and there were no calls in or out after the one. With him dead and the place destroyed, the only loose thread is the cop, name of Hanlon. He has one obscure reference to our activities, and it's probably the last thing on his mind now."

"Where is he?"

"If I knew that, he'd be dead," Roberts said. "He's probably hiding in some hole, like a rat, and the cats are all around. I jumpstarted the FBI, and I'll be monitoring their activities and feeding them information from here. The locals are in on the chase, too, and will probably become more involved when they find the little present I left at the doctor's house."

Hightower didn't want to know about it. "What do we do when they catch him?"

"I'll pay him a visit, then he won't exist anymore. In the brief time he's out of our control, he won't be able to tell anyone anything that will be believed or understood."

At the mention of more killing, Hightower told himself he didn't approve, but remained silent.

After ending the conversation, he sat at his desk, quietly contemplating the situation that had the capability to put his major responsibility in a tailspin, a downward spiral that could end in an abrupt crash. After a few minutes, he rose from his chair, unlocked the door to the library, and stepped out into the open entryway of his large home. Looking up, he spied his wife descending the stairs.

"Dear," she said, joining him, "you know I don't like it when you work on Sundays." It was a light scolding; she did it every week.

He took it just as lightly. "I'm going out now. What will you be doing this bright day?"

"Planning for the party." The gala affair celebrating the occasion of their thirtieth wedding anniversary was two weeks away.

"I'm sure it's going to be a smash. I'll be golfing with the guys, but I'll be back by mid-afternoon." He pecked her on the cheek.

"Have a good time," she said. "You know, I still have a hard time getting used to the identity of those 'guys.'"

It was a dazzling, crisp spring day, the cloudless blue sky meeting the gently rolling sea at the horizon in all directions. A lone vessel sailed upon the vast expanse of ocean; upon the afterdeck stood a bold, proud man. He was captain of the kran, a wooden sailing ship of the type peculiar to the naval forces of the Kingdom of Carin. Desirous of an empire, the mighty King Hissop had personally charged him with clearing the seas of all enemies. His eyes scanned the horizon. Nothing—no, something. From the west, a squadron of large warships flying the detested blue and white banners of neighboring Har was headed straight for his ship, impossibly quickly. He turned, and turned again. From all directions, it was the same; dozens of ships surrounded him, closing fast.

The fight, if it could be called that, was over quickly. Clouds of arrows descended, covering every square foot of the vessel. Catapult boulders smashed its planking and fireballs ignited the resultant kindling. Already sinking, the ship was rammed in three directions at once. His body smashed and bleeding from countless gaping wounds, the captain was hopelessly wedded to his ship by tangled ropes and broken timbers. Still conscious though he could not breathe, he was carried deep into the ever-blackening water by the wreck of his kran.

He opened his eyes. Davy Jones' Locker was a very dingy place.

Then Joe remembered, all of it. Back to the land of the living, he thought morosely, a reality worse than his deadly dream. He could think a little more clearly, though his heart still had a constant ache for his dead wife-to-be and the doctor who had served as mentor in many ways, killed less than a mile away.

"Wake up buddy, time to face another day," Steve said in a tone both sympathetic and encouraging.

Joe sat up, then stood slowly. His thigh still ached, but the only blood near the ragged holes in his pants was dry.

"I decided to forego a shower today," Steve said. "You need one a hell of a lot more than I do."

"Thanks." Joe moved toward the small bathroom, grateful to his friend and comforted that Steve was savvy enough to realize the sound of only one shower should emanate from the apartment that morning.

The bathroom had been a small walk-in closet when the rambling building served as home to one large family. In one corner stood a flimsy shower stall. Running exposed along the wall were the water lines, copper only because the state building code mandated its use.

Joe showered, then rejoined his friend. "Any more of that shirt left?" he asked.

Steve ravaged the tattered remnants of the T-shirt and produced several more strips.

"So what's the news?" Joe queried as he re-bandaged himself.

"Nobody called."

"You don't have a TV?" Joe asked in disbelief as he scanned the room and sighted only the computer.

"Have you watched television lately? Within two pages in the dictionary are the perfect words to describe the current programming: dreck, drivel, and dross. I'll stick with my other screened friend."

"How about a radio?"

"I had a clock radio, but I threw it out about five months ago when it failed to wake me up three days running."

Spotting its replacement next to the computer, a simple Westclox, he muttered, "Big help."

"Look, yesterday I hadn't the slightest notion this place would be turned into a safe house and I would need to have immediate access to information concerning infamous crimes. I'm willing to help, but let's figure something out without fighting each other."

"You're right," Joe said, instantly chastised. "Sorry. Any ideas?"

"I'll just do what comes naturally. I'm hungry, so I'll go out to get a little breakfast. While I'm out, I think I might pick up the Sunday paper, just like anyone else would do. I might even bump into someone I know and we could have a friendly chat."

"Sounds like a plan," Joe said.

"You must be hungry, too. Help yourself to my meager fare."

"Thanks."

"Remember, while I'm out no water, no noise."

Joe watched clandestinely from the window as Steve walked calmly down the stairs, got into his car, and drove off to the north.

After a two-Pop Tart breakfast, Joe lay down and contemplated his agonies for what seemed like forever, finally being torn from his thoughts by low steady thumps indicating someone was ascending the wooden stairway that led to one door. He tensed, awaiting whatever the Fates had in store for him. The door was unlocked and opened, however, not torn off its hinges, and Steve entered, one bag and one thick newspaper in hand.

Steve laid the *Times Herald-Record* on the table. "I had to go to three places before I found it; this is humongous news around here." The bag was from a McDonald's, signifying he had driven quite a distance, as there were no fast food franchises within the borders of the town of Marlborough. "Here, got you some coffee," he said as he removed a foam cup from the bag.

Joe sipped the liquid, then forced himself to face the newspaper. After staring briefly at the photograph of the flaming remains of the proud house he had visited just two days before, he turned the page. On page three, they were together once again, Kenneth DeLuca in a photo on the top and Joe in another on the bottom. DeLuca stared at him from a time before they had met, but he recognized the picture of himself. It was full-face identification photo taken just after he joined the Sunnyside force. Although he was in uniform, it looked uncomfortably like a mug shot.

They began reading—there were three articles. The first, a play-

by-play of the fire together with some background on the revered doctor, did not make mention of the dog and begged the question of the
cause of death. The doctor's son and daughter were also at the scene, it
related. The bottom story, "Policeman Sought in Slaying of Westchester Woman," was far more specific, damning, and disturbing.
Elizabeth Brooks, according to the article, had been shot in the head,
probably as she was attempting to phone for help, by a distraught Hanlon, dismissed from the Sunnyside Police just one day before. Moments
later, it went on, the suspect fled the scene, pursued by two FBI agents.

"God DAMN it," Joe said, much too loud, compounding his slip
by banging the table with his fist. Though the story confirmed many of
his suspicions, seeing the lies in print caught him off guard. And shot!
That was something he wasn't expecting. The article laid it out for all
to see, shouting guilty, Guilty, GUILTY, though the words "alleged"
and "suspected" were dutifully used. It was a perfect example of a
"smoking gun" case, except in this instance the gun was not found.
There had been no gun except in the hand of his almost-killer, the one
now marshaling all available forces of the law against him.

Steve put his hands on his friend's shoulders.

"That was stupid," Joe said. "Let's see the rest of it."

Off to one side and between the two others, the third, shortest
story linked the Brooks and DeLuca deaths—through Hanlon. Building
upon the long association between Joe and the doctor, the key point of
the article was that Joe had probably seen DeLuca the night before the
fire.

That's a surprise, Joe thought, wondering how the reporter had
learned of the visit. He dropped the paper to the floor. "Anything
new?"

"On my way to the store, I passed two police cars parked at the
town line. One was from the Ulster County Sheriff's office, the other
was a Marlborough cruiser. It wasn't a roadblock, but they were eye-
balling every passing car with interest."

"Meet anyone?"

"I talked to a couple of clerks, and overheard a conversation while
waiting in line at McDonald's. You apparently made the TV news last
night about what happened in Sunnyside, and these things are the top
stories on all the local radio stations, but I didn't hear anything substantial that wasn't in the paper, just a lot of rehash and conjecture. They're
all finding it quite exciting."

"They would," Joe agreed, well aware that the biggest local news
was usually something like the opening of a new hardware store.

"One thing that's for certain is that everybody wants you, bad. I don't think it'll be long before they start questioning everyone you ever worked for, bought a doughnut from, or hung around with in high school."

"I need more information. Would that thing help?" Joe asked, gesturing toward the computer.

"Sorry, cable's out; not an unusual occurrence in these parts. Even if it were working, the Internet would be n.g. for our current situation. We might access advertising, communication, and information, but info places a poor third and is at least a day old. And 'communication' is really stretching the meaning of the word; I'm sure the transcripts of a typical chat session could be used as proof that the world has gone completely mad."

"Maybe it has."

"Any ideas?" Steve asked.

"I have something of a plan," Joe said, turning to his confidant. He explained it to him.

"Bad idea," Steve said strongly, as if he was saying "bad dog" to a puppy that had just crapped on the living room rug.

"I need her help," Joe said, deeply reluctant.

"Okay, I'll try to set something up, but I don't like it. When was the last time you saw her?"

"Ten years ago, this June."

"Shit," uttered a surprised Steve. "You've been back here plenty and so has she. All those vacations and holidays? You must have been consciously avoiding her."

Joe had been.

———

It had been an idyllic Saturday in the suburbs for the entire family, and Richard Tobin was pissed about it. While he was mowing the yard for the first time that spring, a woman had been murdered cross-county. While he was playing with his kids on the freshly mown lawn, the biggest manhunt in a year had been taking place a few miles from his house. While he was making love to his wife after the kids were asleep, another tragedy was unfolding in Ulster County. In all three cases, his friend Joe Hanlon had been involved in some way, yet no one had called him, though almost everyone from his office had been informed. No, he was more than pissed, Tobin considered: he was shitting mad.

His rage began the previous night when, lying in bed and thoroughly relaxed, he turned on the eleven o'clock news. Nearly asleep, he had been startled into abrupt consciousness by a full-screen picture of

Joseph Hanlon, fugitive wanted for murder. As homicide was not, in and of itself, a federal crime, he was not surprised that he had not been called, but the newscaster concluded the segment by stating, "State and local officials are assisting the FBI in the case."

Immediately, he was on the phone to Oscar Ottoway. Already on thin ice with his boss, he was also aware that Ottoway did not appreciate calls made to his home after ten o'clock, but he didn't care. Predictably, he was told—again—to butt out. Because of his personal interest, Ottoway told him, there was no way that he was going to allow Tobin to work on the Hanlon case, and that responsibility for the investigation had been given to Thomas Harvarnik.

Having endured a fitful night's sleep, Tobin entered the White Plains Federal Building and went to his office. At his desk, he read the papers again, the ones from Westchester, New York City, and Middletown. Everything indicated Joe had stumbled into a quagmire even worse than the incident the year before, something Tobin had not thought possible.

The agent needed more information and for that he would have to talk with Harvarnik, but Harvarnik was an asshole, and had been for a very long time. Tobin would have liked to see him repent his assholiness, join Assholes Anonymous, and there, before God and his fellow assholes declare, "I'm Thomas Harvarnik, and I'm an asshole," but that was a forlorn hope. Some fifty or so years hence, Harvarnik would die, a chronic asshole to the end. As he had seen the car of his nemesis in the parking lot, he knew Harvarnik was probably in the building somewhere, on a binge.

As Tobin walked down the hall, he passed the office of Carol Kowalesky that had so recently been occupied by the Unknowns. Finally, they were gone, he thought. Thank God. In his few dealings with Philip Roberts, Tobin had thought him a prime candidate for AA.

Farther down the hall, he heard Harvarnik talking on the phone. He walked toward the sound and stopped just short of the open door. Although eavesdropping had been part of his training, he knew it was forbidden inside his own facility. Well, here it starts, Tobin thought as he turned perpendicular to the hallway. His peripheral vision established, he leaned over and feigned tying his shoe to placate anyone stumbling onto the scene.

". . . case is open and shut. I talked with Agent Roberts a few minutes ago. He has the body and all of the evidence and is just waiting for Hanlon to be delivered to him. Per his request, we're staying out of the Sunnyside end of the case."

The agent's deprecating reference to Joe Hanlon caused blood to rush to Tobin's face. Harvarnik compared to Joe made the former look like an—well, ten times the jerk he already was.

Harvarnik's rant continued. "Yeah. Getting him into custody is our top priority. We have the local cops working for us, but I'm going to have to kick them in the ass to get them to toe the line. We're concentrating in Ulster County, a backwoods hole called Marlborough, where the crazy bastard apparently killed somebody else last night. Torched the place, too."

Though his prepared disposition for the upcoming confrontation had dissipated, Tobin forced himself to continue listening.

"So he calls you in the middle of the night because he's upset? Well, boo-hoo; I'll take care of him as well as his psycho friend."

Mercifully, the conversation ended. Tobin walked to the men's room to readjust his clothing and his mood. After splashing water on his face, he smiled at the mirror a few times to remove his involuntary scowl, then walked back down the hall. "Tom," he greeted as he entered Harvarnik's office.

"Out," came the gruff reply. "I don't give a shit what kind of murderers you make friends with, but I want you to take it out of my sight."

"That's kind of harsh, Tom. Hanlon and I worked together on a case last year and we've talked a few times since then, but I would hardly call him a friend. I want to catch the asshole as much as you do."

"No way can you work on this case," Harvarnik responded, softened by the a-word, but still wary.

"I have a caseload of my own," Tobin said truthfully. "I didn't come in this morning to play an active part in this one," he lied. "I just wanted to tell you some things that might be helpful in finding the guy."

"Like what?"

"You said it yourself, Tom. I knew the asshole, back before he was a renegade cop. I've met some of the people he worked with; I've been to his apartment."

Harvarnik relaxed slightly. "Well he isn't going back there. Nobody was around when I went there last night. There was plenty of blood, though."

"You might want to pull the guys out of Sunnyside and focus on Marlborough, up in Ulster. That's where his family is."

"And that's where he plugged another guy and torched his house after finishing off his girlfriend down here. That's old news. Besides, we never had anyone at Sunnyside; that was taken care of by Roberts and his men."

Tobin was pleased, having picked up two new bits of information from one statement. "Hanlon's parents have a big place up there; are you watching it?" As he talked, he noticed a telephone report on the desk. Although he couldn't see it clearly, Tobin did notice that one number was circled. Next to it, written in red, he made out the upside-down word "DeLuca."

Harvarnik frowned. "Buddy, again, that's yesterday's news. If you don't have anything except a rehash of stuff we already know, take it someplace else." He returned to his work.

Following the abrupt dismissal, Tobin returned to his office. So DeLuca had been shot, he thought, and had been contacted by Hanlon recently, assuming that it was Joe's telephone report lying on Harvarnik's desk. That was something, but it was the Sunnyside investigation that concerned him. He was mildly surprised Harvarnik had missed it. Roberts' people had been a notable presence in the Federal Building on Wednesday and Thursday, but they were mostly gone by Friday. Now, all members of the group had vacated the area. It begged a big question: who had completed—in less than one day—the Sunnyside murder investigation? Even if Roberts had been psychic enough to pack the extensive equipment needed for a proper investigation, there was no way he had the number of personnel necessary for the work. And that was just the number, not the type; highly specialized, acutely trained experts were essential for that type of job. Maybe another group had flown in from somewhere, but Harvarnik stated that the apartment was empty just hours after the killing. Maybe this new team was on site right now, but Roberts told Harvarnik he already had all the evidence. Maybe Roberts had worked with the local cops after all. Not likely. Maybe Roberts was a superagent with five degrees and training in eight specialties. No way.

"Time to go to work," Tobin expressed to the office walls. He leaned forward and opened the bottom left drawer of his desk and removed a small plastic case. Although he had not received additional training on lifting latent fingerprints after his initial Bureau schooling at Quantico, he had become quite adept at the craft.

Like everyone else in his office, he heavily relied on the fingerprint technicians in his investigations, but the resources of these specialists were finite, the opportunities often fleeting. Once he had conclusively identified a suspect by lifting his prints off a urinal handle at a busy bar. The technicians wouldn't have been happy about going into that hellhole anyway, even if there had been enough time.

The experts would not have been pleased about the next places he was going either, though for different reasons. He seized the plastic case and walked through the door. Down the hall, he could hear Harvarnik, shouting at one of the men unlucky enough to be assigned to his care.

Tobin began his field work in Carol Kowalesky's office.

CHAPTER 14

L ying on their bed down the hall, his wife was crying. His in-laws, just down the road, were traumatized more than they had ever been. Almost the whole county was in a kind of worried mourning. The man lounging on the living room couch, however, was as happy as a pig in shit. Though he made a conscious effort not to show it, he could not have been in a better mood had he been in the midst of disassembling a big buck with one of his semiautomatic rifles.

Michael Fleming was a deer hunter, and because of this, he owned a large collection of pistols, shotguns, bows, rifles, and dead deer parts. Taxidermied hoofs upheld many of his weapons, and most of the walls in the house featured mounted heads and antlers. In one of the few times his wife had put her foot down to him, he relented on fully mounting a particularly large twelve-pointer he had butchered one profitable weekend, finally agreeing their modest bi-level home was a little small for such a display. The glass eyeballs of that particular beast, now only a head, looked down on him from across the room.

So it became a necessary side passion to acquire a larger house, a place big enough to properly display the evidence of his prowess over deer. The mounted heads were forced into too dense an array throughout the residence, and that did not include the trophies of his lesser conquests that had been relegated to the basement. A large home with an oversized entry was needed, a foyer large enough to comfortably display a huge buck with all of its parts intact that would stand in silent greeting to all who came in the front door, providing mute witness to the character of the master of the house.

The man smiled and glanced again at the newspaper on the coffee table, thinking about his next house. He had a specific one in mind, and now it seemed closer than ever to his grasp.

Fleming had disliked Joseph Hanlon from the first time they met.

Joe had been a returning war hero, while Fleming had been six months wedded to a wife that had just given birth, struggling to improve his position in his father-in-law's construction company. He recognized Hanlon as a threat then, and his feelings had never diminished.

That asshole, his main rival, had done everything to jeopardize his own position over the years, recalled Fleming. He could have gone to college after high school, all expanses paid, but he joined the Army instead. He did go to school after he came back, but he studied law enforcement instead of engineering or architecture. To top it off, he then went to work for some hole-in-the-wall police force. All of that had been against his father's wishes, and still the bond between Albert Paul and Joseph Charles remained strong. He could have squeezed his way back and stopped me from taking over the company at any time, Fleming fumed. Could have until now, that is.

"More than I ever wished for," Fleming said to himself as he opened the *Times Herald-Record*. He never imagined his brother-in-law as a murderer, but there it was in black and white. He even looked guilty in the photo. Maybe his war experiences had finally driven him crazy like all of those Vietnam vets. He might even be crazy enough to come to his sister's house, but if he did, he was in for a surprise, Fleming considered, glancing at the .30 caliber rifle leaning against the couch, fully loaded, safety off. There was also, with his full knowledge and unhesitating consent, an unmarked police car on the cul-de-sac in front of the house, but he didn't dwell on that.

He picked up his rifle, and walked onto his back deck. The house was located at the end of a small, one-road development. Of the twenty houses planned, only half had been built, and there were vacant lots to either side of Fleming's home. As there was only undeveloped acreage beyond the tiny subdivision, the house was almost entirely surrounded by woodland. He loved the location, as the deck was a perfect place to sit back, relax, and kill deer, in-season or out, as they vainly attempted to pass him by. He wondered if deer ever ventured into the large lawn at Idlewild.

Maybe he would ask about it, offhandedly, when he dragged his weeping wife and gun-shy six-year old over to see his in-laws that afternoon. He had big plans for that visit, intent on calming, consoling, mollifying, but mainly cementing—his position. And watching, too, for the errant brother-in-law he knew could not stay away forever.

If he was going over for a friendly visit, he would need another gun, a suitable substitute for the large rifle. Maybe his .45, a good, steady semiautomatic pistol that could stop a—well, a deer in its tracks. He had actually done that once, emptying the seven-round magazine into the animal. It had been a thoroughly satisfying experience.

———————

"It's still being cleaned, so it's not ready to be rented yet. You can see it tomorrow."

Richard Tobin was flabbergasted beyond all conception, rendered immobile and speechless. It was not that the large woman in front of him was exhibiting callousness; in his years as an agent, he had seen worse. What bewildered him was that a murder had taken place in Joe Hanlon's apartment less than twenty-four hours previously, yet it was nearly ready for its next occupant, having been released to the woman by one Philip Roberts.

He recovered and took out his badge. "FBI, ma'am. I'm here to take one last look. Can you tell me when you received custody of the apartment?"

"Well, I came up to clear out Mr. Hanlon's things this morning. I'm having them moved to the storage room in the basement. That other agent said it was okay. I asked him as he was leaving yesterday."

"What time was that?"

"I guess it was about four."

"Has anyone been back since?"

"Only a couple of Sunnyside policemen. I let one in, and he left right away because of the—mess. The other just asked a few questions and went away without going in."

"Thank you. I'll try not to be long," Tobin said, forcing politeness. He watched as the woman descended the stairs. Four o'clock, he thought. Less than six hours. Jesus.

There was an odd assortment of boxes in Hanlon's living room, obviously brought up by the building manager to transport the former occupant's possessions, but it was the evidence of violence that most interested the agent. As well as the irregular puddle of nearly dry blood on the carpet, he saw blood on every surface, in pinpoint specks, in drops, in dollops. It was irregularly dispersed on the ceiling, walls, and floor, but some attempt had been made to clean it, as most of the drops were now smears.

Tobin went to work, collecting samples of blood and clipping fibers from the carpet, chairs, and drapes, putting each into a plastic evidence bag. He found some hairs on an end table, a pencil in one corner, and, almost hidden by a window latch, a triangular shard of plastic the size of a zipper pull. He then lifted a few fingerprints and examined all rooms of the apartment. He saw no indication any investigation had taken place.

He went into the hall and knocked on the door of the adjacent apartment. No answer. Descending, he scrutinized all aspects of the stairwell. Nothing. Finally, he had success at Apartment 2B, and Josephine Gavin opened the door.

Tobin smiled encouragingly. "I'm here for one final check, ma'am. Could you please relate what happened here yesterday one more time?" *Yesterday,* he repeated to himself, still unable to comprehend the rapidity of the so-called investigation.

As Gavin recalled the events, Tobin listened intently, scribbling furiously as she went into details and several sidetracks, ending at the point when she called the police.

"When did they arrive?"

"The first person here was not a policeman, it was that FBI man, Mr. Roberts. I heard him coming and saw him go up the stairs through my peephole. He was involved in quite a scuffle up there. Then he came back after a few minutes and talked to me."

"Tell me about the fight."

"I didn't see it, but I could hear bangs and pounding. Then one person ran down the stairs, and the other ran down a few seconds later."

"By bangs, do you mean gunshots?"

"No, I don't think they were. There were two popping sounds, but they were not nearly as loud as the shot I heard earlier, and this hallway has a much worse echo than the apartments."

"Who did you see next?" Tobin pressed.

"Well, there was a young policeman, then another man who was dressed like Mr. Roberts. He stayed the longest and went up and down the stairs several times. Then two men came and carried away the—body."

There goes the "team of investigators" theory, Tobin thought. After concluding the conversation, he returned to the third floor, to the scene of the second personal meeting between Joe Hanlon and Philip Roberts. He dropped to one knee, carefully examining the floor and walls. Any scuffmarks from the fight were indistinguishable from the dozens of scrapes the floor had received since its last cleaning.

He almost missed it, something barely perceptible on the wall near the base of the doorframe. He dropped down and examined it. It was a wall patch of some sort, filling an indentation about three-quarters of an inch in diameter. He poked it, and his finger sank into the material that blended almost perfectly with the beige wall. He sniffed at the substance, then ventured a taste. It was toothpaste, but colored to match the wall with—what, mustard? He tasted it again. Yes, it was a mixture of mustard and toothpaste, an ingenious way to hide a bullet hole.

The agent cleared the inch-deep pit, first with his finger, then with his pen, and found nothing. Damn, he cursed to himself, then placed a sample of the mixture into a plastic bag. But the woman said she heard two pops. After three painstaking minutes, he found the second hole about two feet above the landing just below Joe's apartment. This time, his finger poked straight through the paste.

Seized with possibility, Tobin retrieved a small toolbox from his car. He grabbed a keyhole saw and enlarged the hole, cutting and searching until there was an ugly three-inch wide vertical gash in the wall that ended less than an inch from the tiles of the landing. In the midst of the broken plaster, savaged lath, and bits of mortar lay the bullet.

With the chunk of lead safely deposited in an evidence bag, he returned to the Hanlon apartment, this time to search for two specific items. Though he did not find the toothpaste, he was rewarded by the sight of a jar of dark mustard on the kitchen counter. He pocketed it and left the flat, locking the door behind him.

"What's going on here?" It was the large form of the landlady, angry, looking down at the results of Tobin's wall exploration.

The agent braced for another round of politeness. "I'm sorry ma'am. It was a necessary part of the investigation, but we do pay for damages." He retrieved his wallet. "I'd also like to hold the Hanlon apartment, rent it if you will, for three days. Would a hundred for the damage and fifty a day for the apartment be acceptable?" He held out the money.

"Okay," she said, grabbing eagerly for the tax-free bills.

Although the loss of two hundred fifty dollars left Tobin with less than a sawbuck, he parted with it without the slightest regret, knowing with sun-will-rise-in-the-morning certainty it was the right thing to do.

———————

A monument to shortsightedness, the ancient rural strip of asphalt was called New Road. Like many such thoroughfares in Milton, it was flanked by woodland for most of its distance, and it was through a patch of these woods Joe now walked, traveling perpendicular to the country lane. His journey was not an escape from the road as part of a quickly conceived plan to evade the authorities, but as he traveled toward his rendezvous with Susan DeLuca he could not have been filled with more dread had the police been right behind him.

One day long past but not so dim, he and Susan had strolled

through those same woods together, seeking the solitude of nature to escape an unpleasant discussion between Kenneth and Christopher De-Luca at the house on Milton Turnpike, where they all had gathered for dinner. During their walk, they discovered a large beech tree and Joe carved their names into its smooth bark. He now saw this tree through the other, lesser trees, and Susan was standing by it.

She saw him approach and spoke first, upset and angry. "I don't know what I'm doing here, but good old Steve talked me into it. First my father dies, and now *you* appear."

Joe spoke gently, but firmly. "Susan, I am sorry for your loss; I loved your father too. In many ways, he was a mentor, even a second father to me. I visited him on Friday, and he was the same warm, helping friend he always was. I spoke with him yesterday, just before the fire, and he was just as happy and helpful as ever. Like you, I will mourn his death for the rest of my life."

"What's going on? Why this meeting?" she asked, softening slightly.

"I know Steve told you I was in trouble, but he didn't tell you how—huge, how life-and-death these troubles are. I've been accused of a murder I didn't commit, the murder of my fiancée, and the police are after me."

"But—but why did you want to see me?"

Joe slowly withdrew the folded newspaper pages from his pocket. "I'm almost certain the same men who killed my fiancée, Elizabeth Brooks, also murdered your father."

"*You* are involved in my father's death—murder?" she asked, dumbfounded.

"You haven't read this morning's paper, have you?"

"No. I had it in my hands, but I only saw the headlines before Christopher snatched it away. I thought I saw your picture in it."

"You did," he stated grimly, handing her the front page and page three torn from the *Times Herald-Record*.

She read every one of the harsh words within the three articles, her hands shaking slightly, her eyes glistening. The accounts were something, but not everything, and experience had taught her never to take something as fact based upon its appearance in print. That there was some truth within the pages was certain, as she had stood numbly before the smoldering ruins of her home and witnessed much of what was now related. When the article by Joe's picture stated as clearly as it could that Joe was guilty of murder, however, she felt nothing but disbelief. Joe could be difficult, she knew, but the events described were against his nature. She continued her examination, attempting to pierce the clouds of emotion swirling like an all-encompassing cyclone through her mind.

Standing by, Joe glanced at the venerable, vandalized beech and noticed that the testimony to their former visit was still in evidence. Though aged, "Joe" and "Sue," still linked by the two short marks of a plus sign were still discernable. It would perhaps be another fifty years before they were completely extinguished.

"How are you involved in my father's death?" she finally asked.

"He called me yesterday, just hours before the fire and was extremely excited about something I gave him on Friday. I believe that some very bad people overheard that conversation."

"But people aren't killed over a phone call."

Joe ignored the painfully false statement. "Steve talked to Cheryl Clarke last night. She was at the fire and overheard some things that were not made public. A definite determination of arson was made at the scene. She didn't know the exact nature of your father's death, but she said that the dog had been recovered in the ruins, and that it had been shot to death."

Susan staggered at the knowledge that her beloved Edson was also dead and that a gun had been used. She dropped unsteadily to the ground and found herself sitting against the beech tree.

Joe knelt beside her, and they sat for a few minutes in the hushed woods. He ventured a calming hand to her shoulder, and she accepted it, trusting her instincts that in the past decade he had not changed from a gentle and sensitive person into a murdering lunatic.

"Who was it?" Susan asked, breaking the silence.

"I don't know. A small group of men appeared in Sunnyside on Wednesday, claiming to be FBI agents, but they probably weren't. Although they had tremendous authority over the FBI and the local police, they actually proved themselves to be a bunch of homicidal thugs."

She glanced at the damning article on Joe visible in her hand. "What happened down there?"

For several minutes, Joe related what had occurred from Thursday morning's stop at the Bonnelli house to Elizabeth's murder. "It was a bomb, Susan, a bomb in the phone, detonated over the telephone lines by these—people who now hold all the evidence. It was my apartment, and I was supposed to get that call, but by some tragic twist of fate, Elizabeth answered it instead. When they realized their mistake, they tried to rectify it in person, but I managed to escape. Barely," he added, rubbing his left thigh.

Susan shook her head, trying to make sense of the bizarre story, then turned and looked straight at Joe. "I still don't understand what this has to do with my father."

"It has something to do with what he discovered during an autopsy of a dead squirrel."

"What?" If there had been a world record for confusion, someone else would have had to take second place.

As succinctly as he could, Joe explained his discovery of the animal, his visit to her father, and the doctor's excited call to Sunnyside.

"It might have been nothing," she replied to her stone-faced companion. "He did say he had to verify his discovery before he told anyone else."

"I think he did tell someone else, inadvertently. I'm sure the people who altered my telephone heard our exchange, and that they considered his findings to be anything but nothing. They thought it was something enough to murder two people and to destroy all evidence of your father's examination."

Susan sat in silent contemplation over what her ex-lover had told her. To think that her father could have been killed over a dead rodent was painfully bizarre. Although she did not believe it, she finally accepted the possibility. "What are you going to do now?"

"I have to get out of here. The police are all over the place looking for me. I'd turn myself in if I didn't know I would quickly end up in the hands of the men who tried to kill me, and succeeded in killing your father and Elizabeth. Before I go, I need your help; I need some information."

"What do you want?"

It was so flimsy, this one captivating clue, that it did not stand up of its own weight. It had fallen to the ground in a misshapen heap. He had kicked at it and poked at it, but he was still unsure about how to utilize it. He outlined his thoughts to Susan.

"Those things were all burned in the fire," she stated as a multiplicity of visions surrounding the blaze engulfed her. "I know where we can get some answers, though."

He immediately focused on the critical word. "Susan, there hasn't been a 'we' for some time; you don't have to do anything except go back to your brother's house. Maybe I'll see you again before another ten years have gone by. I'd just appreciate it if you wouldn't mention this meeting to anyone."

Susan stood quickly and asserted herself for the first time since leaving Boston, exhibiting the pugnacity that had served her so well in her dealings within the male-dominated corporate world. "So it's 'Poor Susan' from you too, is it? Since coming here yesterday, I've had enough of that shit to last me a lifetime."

"It might be dangerous for you to help me," Joe replied as he got up.

"No, *you* are going to help *me*," she said decisively. "You come to me with this outrageous story, expecting a little information to guide you on your merry way? That's not the way it's going to work. I want to know what is going on, and I'm sure not going to get anything out of that bunch of idiots on Milton Turnpike. You be there at one o'clock; I'll be waiting."

"Okay," Joe capitulated.

"Besides, I'm the only one who knows where the key is," she said as a parting warning. She walked away from the beech tree in the direction of the house, headed to her brother's guest room to have a good cry, then to prepare for another rendezvous.

Joe picked up the pages of the newspaper Susan had dropped and stuffed them into his pocket in preparation for his walk back to Steve, cruising somewhere along New Road. As he glanced one last time at the words on the tree, he had a fleeting, involuntary thought that perhaps some types of love never completely died.

CHAPTER 15

O nly because of his prominence as a local author, the Marlborough Free Library had obtained one copy each of three
of Dr. Kenneth DeLuca's seven books. Still in pristine condition after years on the shelves, the thick medical volumes were Greek
to the average citizen, and at least Icelandic to the average doctor.
Susan and Joe, standing close together in one of the aisles of the otherwise deserted library, were examining the last of the three tomes, *Electromagnetic Effects of Cardiovascular Neural Impulses.*

"Nothing in this one either," Joe commented. "Nothing at all on
enzymes, to say nothing about the specific enzyme 'photofructease,' or
whatever it was. Your father was talking so fast."

"He worked on so many projects, it's going to be difficult to identify the one we're after, especially if it's one of the obscure ones; his
career spanned thirty-five years." Susan was calmer, having gained
both a little more information about the tragedy on Ridge Road and a
mission to accomplish, aligning her more closely with the professional
life to which she was accustomed. "When did he say his research on
enzymes took place?"

"His exact words were 'years ago.'"

"Big help. Let's assume it was before he retired."

"What's next?"

"Let's try something a little more basic," Susan suggested as she
walked toward the reference section.

Located on Route 9W near the center of town, the library was a
rectangular building of decorative block and aluminum. Closed on
Sundays, Susan had arrived a few minutes before one o'clock and
parked near the town square, which in Marlborough was a triangle,
leaving the small library parking lot deserted. As she was sure she
would, she found the key to the front door under a particular reddish

rock near the entrance. Although the librarian had her own key, the hidden one was necessary to allow occasional access to a select few. Susan learned about it when she worked part time in the library in high school. She had used the key only once during her employment, to let Joe in late one Friday night for a passionate session of forbidden love-making amidst the knowledge.

"Damn, he's not even in here, the bastards," Susan said as she perused the large directory *Who's Who in Medicine.*

Removing the book gently from her hands, Joe returned it to the shelf. "He still maintained his medical license, didn't he?"

"Yes. His career would be outlined in detail on his application, but probably the only copy—now—would be in the state records in Albany."

Joe's eyes widened at the last word, one of his obscure clues, but he set it aside for the moment. "State offices are definitely closed on Sunday." He glanced over at a computer by the checkout desk. "I'm not a hacker, are you?"

"Forget it. I've done a little unauthorized poking around in my company's files, but what you're asking about is at least a quantum leap away from my experience."

"Well, maybe while we're here in the reference section we can at least find the word we're looking for."

After several minutes, Susan found a list of mammalian enzymes. "Take a look at these," she directed.

Joe scanned the pages, thinking that if he didn't know better, he might have been looking at pages out of an English-Goroto dictionary. "Got it," he finally said, pointing. He walked to the front desk to retrieve a pen and scratch pad to record his triumph as Susan read the entry.

"It says this 'phosphofructokinase' is an integral part of the chemical reactions that assist neural impulses to transmit messages to the circulatory system. Not much to go on."

"At least it's something."

"Let's try the newspapers," Susan ventured as she walked toward a side room. She opened one of the slim metal drawers that held the library's microfilm files. "A few months after we moved here, I remember a long fluff piece about my father," she recalled, removing two small boxes from the drawer. With Joe looking over her shoulder, she threaded one spool into a reader and began to scan the white-on-black pages of the local weekly.

Having little in the way of real news, the *Marlborough Gazette* was a treasure trove of bits of information on its citizens that would quickly find their way into the circular file at almost any other paper. Articles detailing fishing trips, farmers' purchases of new equipment, and scout camping trips were often featured. At last, Susan came upon the story "Prominent Doctor Now Marlborough Resident" and sat back.

The testimonial went on for two detailed pages. Obviously the product of copious research, the article mentioned many other doctors that Kenneth DeLuca had worked with over his long career. Among these was Dr. Salvatore Monnell, a research chemist who had worked with DeLuca on enzymes relating to the heart in the late sixties.

"Now *that's* getting us somewhere," Joe said.

Susan walked over to the microfilm drawer and took out another box. "I think this Monnell was at my mother's funeral ten years ago."

Joe did not need to be reminded of the number of years; they both knew the exact date. He reached out and grasped Susan's hand. "There must be more on this guy somewhere else," he said. "We don't have to go there today."

Susan jerked her hand away. "We're traveling wherever the road takes us," she said angrily. "And if that means going here," she continued, twisting the box in his face, "then tough shit on you."

"Okay," Joe said, recalling the rainy night a decade before. The two of them had been out on a late date, dinner followed by a movie at the town of Newburgh Cinema Complex. While driving back on Route 9W, one of the tires on Joe's car went flat a few miles short of the Marlborough line. As the spare was also flat, a call for assistance went out over a nearby pay phone. It was answered by her mother, who told Susan she would be down directly. After an hour's wait and the passing of two police cars, lights flashing, they had walked a sodden mile to the site of the head-on collision. Susan's mother, having not worn a seat belt for such a short trip, was dead. The other driver, alone and grossly intoxicated after visiting several Newburgh bars, escaped the wreck of the fused cars with only slight bruises, saved by his air bag. The accident, funeral, and ensuing trial had been Marlborough's biggest news that year, but one small piece of the story remained known only to Joe, who carried the agony of that unwritten footnote with him constantly.

Visibly upset at having to relive the time when her mother was lost so unnecessarily, Susan scanned the article. "I think that's him," she said, pointing to a figure, one of a group of eight mourners in the largest of the three photographs on the page.

"Let's see if he's mentioned," Joe said. He was.

Susan found the reference and read aloud, "'Dr. Salvatore Monnell, one of Kenneth's longtime associates, drove up from Washington and Lee University to attend the services.'"

Joe wrote down the pertinent information.

Susan switched off the machine and began to roll up the film reels. "I don't remember meeting him."

"Let's check the books," Joe suggested.

"He might be in *Who's Who in Chemistry,* or whatever, but he's not in here," Susan commented as she closed the medical directory that had slighted her father.

"Where is Washington and Lee University?" Joe inquired.

"In Virginia, the Shenandoah valley."

"Well unless he commutes from Richmond, he's not listed in any phone directory belonging to this library," Joe commented after examining a five-foot shelf of thick yellow books.

"Maybe you're wrong," Susan said, inspired. Behind the front desk, she found what she was looking for, the U.S. Telephone Directory on a computer CD. As Joe continued to search elsewhere, she turned on the computer.

They both met with success at the same moment. "Here he is," Joe said as he held up a year-old college catalog from Washington and Lee. "Professor of chemistry and head of the medical research facility. No picture, though."

"And here's where he lives and his home phone number," Susan said, gesturing at the computer screen. "Let's call him."

"NO!" It was loudest thing Joe had said all day. "Susan, in dealing with the guys who are after me, phone calls are at best chancy and at worst—fatal. What took us an hour to find would take the thugs after me about a minute; I'm sure no state licensing bureau is closed to them. Besides, what am I going to say to him, 'tell me all you know about'"—he checked his notes—"'"phosphofructokinase," it's a matter of life and death?' No, I have to get out of here anyway, and now I have a direction. I'm going to see him."

"I'm going with you."

Though outraged and terrified, Joe spoke calmly. "Susan, you can't. There are people out to kill me. You need to be at your father's funeral. I know you want to help, but you're in a fragile emotional state and . . ."

"'Fragile emotional state'?" she threw back acridly. "Listen, asshole, one thing I'm not in the mood to hear today is menkus. You need help, I can supply it, and maybe I can find out what happened to my father at the same time. If there's any trouble, I'll say you kidnapped me. My brother can take care of the funeral; I have my own plans to deal with this." Her voice quivered only slightly as she laid out a course of action.

"Okay, but before *we* leave I have to go somewhere."

She thought it was insane, but assented.

———————

There's a big-ass buck out there right now, he mused, out there somewhere without a care in the world, just munching away and growing bigger, not having the slightest notion that its destiny is going to bring it right to the foyer of this house, Michael Fleming thought, almost smiling.

"Okay, everybody in," he said to his wife and son as they approached Idlewild's front entry. "It's cold outside." Cold enough to keep my jacket on, he reasoned, feeling the heft of the .45 in the holster against his back. After his mother-in-law answered the door, he started to follow his wife and son straight into the living room.

"Al is in the den," Rose Hanlon said.

Although he knew commiserating with his father-in-law wasn't going to be any fun, Fleming forced a look of concern and walked down the front hall. Outside of the study, he knocked and upon receiving a melancholy response entered.

"Oh, Mike, it's you," Albert said, even more sorrowfully. He was sitting in the chair behind his desk, but was not working.

Fleming hated the room, detested the sight of the framed mementos of Hanlon martial glory dating back to the Civil War. When I move in, those things are going in the basement, he thought, or maybe I'll sell them. Some of these medals can bring in a good buck, probably enough for a few more mountings that can be hung right where the frames are now.

As he sat down, Fleming addressed his inheritance. "Listen, Al, no matter what Joe's done, we can get through this."

"Nobody knows exactly what Joe did."

"The papers were pretty clear."

"If you came here to throw around a lot of accusations that you know about just from the papers, you can leave."

Fleming backpedaled quickly. "What I mean is that first he has to be brought into custody, unhurt if possible, then there will be bail, maybe, and formal charges, and he'll need a good lawyer. I'm here to help out that's all."

"Okay," was the unconvinced reply.

"Maybe you and Rose can put out an appeal to him to turn himself in."

"The police suggested that; we're thinking about it."

"You talked to the cops?"

"They've been around several times. I'll admit, from what they told me, it looks pretty goddamned bad, but I just can't believe it."

"We passed a parked car at the end of the driveway on the way in."

"It's an unmarked police car, or maybe it's from the FBI. I told them if they wanted to watch the house they could, but from outside the boundaries of my property."

Although Albert mentioned the property first, Fleming resisted asking about the deer population on the estate. "How about that De-Luca killing?" he asked in the same tone he asked others "How about those Mets?"

"Tragic, horrible; we could see the fire clearly from here. I've read the papers, and just can't figure out how Joe could possibly be involved, except . . ."

"What?" asked Fleming, leaning forward in his chair, desperately trying to elicit information while sounding sympathetic.

"You keep this to yourself; I haven't told the police, and I haven't even told Rose. Joe visited here with his friend Elizabeth Friday night. While they were here, Joe slipped out for a while. He told me he was going to visit DeLuca. First time in he'd done that in months."

"So what the paper said was true."

"I don't know where they got that, but it wasn't from me. Maybe he told Elizabeth, but . . ."

"Yeah." *Blam.* Just like a deer.

"Damnedest mess," Albert muttered. "This is all just the damnedest screwed-up mess."

"Tomorrow is Monday. Are you going to take off from work for a few days?"

Albert sat up, his attention finally focused. "Maybe, but I'll be here by the phone for most of the day. I want you to go down to New City to check out the progress of that strip mall foundation. Come here with a status report as soon as you get back."

Fleming said "Okay," but he thought, "Shit." It would take him all day to travel down to Rockland County and back. He got the distinct feeling that Albert did not want him around.

"Matter of fact, I have a few calls to make right now."

"I better go check on the kid; never know what the little bastard's going to get into next," Fleming said, deluding himself into thinking he had not been summarily dismissed. He walked through the foyer and into the living room. His son was playing quietly on the large Persian rug. Playing with a small dump truck and a cement mixer, he saw, when he should be shooting up the place with one of his many toy guns. Fleming recalled his vain attempt to introduce him to a real gun. It was just a small rifle, a .22, but he still shied away from its insignificant noise and puny recoil. They both had been holding on to it, of course; to expect the youngster to handle a gun by himself at his age was—optimistic. Maybe next year.

"I'm sure everything will be all right," Rose said to Charlotte Fleming. They were both seated on the couch at the far end of the room, consoling each other. Charlotte was crying again.

Damn it, turn off the water works already, Fleming thought. He escaped the living room without a word and entered the kitchen. Upon opening the large refrigerator, he discovered it contained only five cans of beer. Disheartened at finding less than a two-hour supply of the precious liquid, he grabbed two containers and walked out of the house and onto the wide back patio overlooking the Hudson.

The view of the woods, where there might be deer, had a calming effect. "Yes, Rose, I think you're right," he said to the expanse before him. "I think everything is going to be all right." He felt almost content, but there was something in the air. He could sense it as he could sometimes sense a buck clear over a ridge, treading silently on rain-soaked leaves, walking slowly to its fate as a delightful home decoration. But this time it wasn't a deer. Maybe he was just feeling the past presence of his rival, Fleming considered, but if Joseph Hanlon was crazy enough to kill his girlfriend and murder DeLuca, he just might be somewhere nearby. He'd be a hero, Fleming convinced himself, if he killed the mass murderer as he was making his way back to the old homestead to off his entire family. He'd probably even be awarded medals from groups all over, which would hang within a thick oak frame on the wall of the DeLuca den. It might be dangerous, though. He resolved to consider the matter further after a few more beers.

"Forget what I said about the 'how ya doing' police wave-bys I saw up on 9W this morning," Steve told Joe, reclined below window level in the Dodge. "Something's happened; the entire town is locked down tight."

"Give me the details."

"After I dropped you off at the library, I decided to see what was going on at the Orange County line. It was a balls-to-the-wall full-fledged roadblock. About eight cops were checking every vehicle, coming and going. I had to open the trunk, and they were even underneath the vehicles like they were looking for that guy from *Cape Fear*. I didn't want to go through that again, so I swung around and came back by way of Dawesville, but right where you got into the trunk last night—*wham*—another roadblock. Maybe you better leave that way; there were only four cops."

"I'll find a way out somehow."

"The library do you any good?"

"Well, I have a destination, but I don't know if anything's there."

"You won't tell me where you're going?"

"Steve, honestly, it's better you don't know."

"Or who you're going with?" Steve looked over at Joe, and was rewarded with a decidedly pensive glance. "I knew it! Susan talked herself into going with you, didn't she?"

"More like ordered me."

"9W coming up, buddy. Keep low." Steve maneuvered the car down a steep incline, stopped at the main road, then crossed over. "I still think this next move of yours is crazy, but I guess you have to do it."

"It's all set; Susan is meeting me on the other side."

The car passed the town's sewage treatment plant and descended toward the Hudson. Near the river, Steve turned around and headed back up the deserted road, stopping after traveling a hundred yards. Thick woods extended to the north on the passenger's side. "End of the line, if you really want it to be. You can still change your mind."

"I'm all set. You know what to do?"

"Yeah, get out of Dodge. I'm going to the Poughkeepsie Galleria all afternoon to get away from anyone who might want answers to a few pointed questions. Maybe I'll come back and find that you've been picked up, or maybe I'll find you in the bushes near my front steps, but I hope I won't be able to find anything and you'll be long gone, out of this immediate mess."

"Thanks, Steve. I'll never forget this."

"One more thing. During your little tryst with Susan, I visited my ATM in the square and got you a little going away present." He shoved what looked like two hundred dollars in twenties into the pocket of Joe's shirt.

As Steve drove away, Joe plunged into the woods, considering that maybe he had never been broke after all, but he didn't go so far as to think he had a wonderful life.

Now on Hanlon property, the son of the owner made his way north through rocks and trees, keeping the guiding tracks of the railroad along the river just in sight to his right. The lands of Albert Hanlon stretched in front of him for another half mile, extending down to, but not quite touching, the Hudson, separated from the waterway by the thin strip of land on which the rails were laid. Typical of former river-front lands on both sides of the Hudson from New York City to Albany, the railroad rights-of-way were seized by eminent domain during the days of the great capitalist robber barons. Remarkable in their foresight, the entrepreneurs entered into a lease extending property rights to their venture for four hundred years, with an option to renew for an additional four hundred.

Joe thought of the large, relatively slow freight trains that now infrequently rolled down the rails. If trouble arose, he might avail himself of one of those trains as contingency transportation, but he didn't know if he could make it on board with his leg, painfully pulsating after a nearly level walk of only two miles. Finally, he saw it in the distance, a reference point amidst the monotonous backdrop of trees and rocks and rails. It was a building about eight feet square, or at least what was left of a building after having been ravaged by over fifty years of disuse. The roof had long been eaten away and the three stone walls that remained were crumbling, but it was still a welcome sight. At one time it had been a pump house, conveying irrigation water from the Hudson to fields now shaded by plants with dozens of annual rings. Now it served as a rallying point for a one-man rally.

He sat on a horizontal chunk of fallen building and rested his back against a wall. He had discovered the place in the earliest days of his youth, and had camped here often. He glanced over and noticed the stone ring that once encircled his campfires was still there, but leaves from the surrounding oak and ash trees covered any evidence it had ever been used.

He forced himself to rest before his two planned journeys, one round trip and one from which he would not soon return. It was peaceful, so quiet that he could hear the small waves of the Hudson lapping against the railroad ballast sixty feet away. He closed his eyes.

He thought he heard something as if through a fog. He opened his eyes to the sight of his brother-in-law standing over him ten feet away. Joe had never cared much for Michael Fleming, and cared for him even less now because he was holding a large black pistol pointed straight at his chest.

"Get up, asshole, you're coming with me," slurred Fleming. "You're damn lucky I didn't shoot you when you were asleep."

"I'm not armed." Joe stated, extending his arms straight out until they pressed against the side of the ruin.

"Just get up and let's go. Don't try anything, because I know how to use this thing." Fleming waved the gun in short, unsteady jerks.

Joe got up slowly, favoring his uninjured leg. "Actually, I'm glad you found me. The cops shot me in the leg; I need a doctor."

"Maybe you can get a prison doctor after they put you away."

"I'm serious. I don't know if I can make it up the hill." Joe took two limping steps toward Fleming as if testing the leg's fitness.

"I don't care if you crawl, I'm taking you in."

"Okay, I'll try," Joe said, then lowered his hands and placed them loosely on his injured thigh, feigning an examination of the wound.

"Let's go."

Joe looked straight past Fleming's left shoulder at an angle of about twenty degrees. "Wait," he said in a whisper. "Jesus Christ, don't make a sound. That's the biggest buck I've ever seen."

When Fleming was halfway through his turn, Joe lunged for the gun, grabbing the barrel and twisting it down and away. Fleming tried to fire, but the extra safety feature of the .45 that required a firm grip on the pistol to depress the hammer prevented the discharge. The gun flew out of their struggling hands and landed in the campfire circle five feet away. Fleming went for the weapon, but Joe went for the balls, kneeing his adversary in the groin. Fleming crumpled at the victor's feet.

While his brother-in-law writhed in agony, Joe walked three steps to the .45 and picked it up. He sat back down on his seat of walls and waited for Fleming to recover, at least a little.

Insuring the safety was engaged, Joe pointed the gun at the wretched refuse in front of him. "I'm sure you wanted to be a big hero by bringing me in. After all, I'm a wanted murderer."

"What are you going to do with me?" Fleming asked, his trembling voice mimicking the involuntary motions of his body.

"Sit up and take off your jacket and shirt and undershirt." Joe waited for the tasks to be completed. "Now put on your jacket; it's cold out here." He waited again. "Now tear that T-shirt into nice long strips about four inches wide." Another wait. "Now tie your feet together with the first strip."

The nearly petrified Fleming eagerly complied with the whims of the man pointing a gun at him. At least it was something to do rather than lie around the forest dead all day. After all tasks were completed, Joe directed him to put his arms around an adjacent tree, a small one about six inches in diameter, then he gathered the remaining strips. With the gun in his mouth for ready use, he tied the first two pieces of cloth around his captive's hands, then put the .45 down and tied four others. He considered a gag, but vetoed it in favor of a stern warning.

"You're not going to leave me out here, are you?" Fleming quavered.

"I'll be nearby. In fact, I'll probably be the closest person around here for some time, so keep your mouth shut. If I hear you, I might get angry."

Joe received only a vigorous nod in reply.

CHAPTER 16

Very carefully, the man sized up the job before him. Weekdays were for work and Saturdays were for the wife, he always said, but Sundays were for the house and grounds. Although this Sunday was far from ordinary, Albert Hanlon decided, after an unhealthy few hours brooding in his den, to do the ordinary thing and attend to his lawn. He stepped onto the wide expanse of grass at the rear of his house and headed in the direction of the river. His wife and daughter were on the back porch, somewhat calmer now, talking quietly while taking in the view of the Hudson. His grandson was near them, engaged in some excavation work with a miniature backhoe at the edge of the brick. His son-in-law was pleasantly absent.

Albert reached the far edge of the lawn. Although professional landscapers cared for the grass, he still personally attended to many of the other details of the yard work, and that included the edges of the lawn. Beyond the lush grass, there were no neighbors to pacify, only brush and trees, but he still liked clean, well-defined edges. This year, his plan was to edge the yard with a uniform two-foot strip of mulch and therein plant hundreds of multi-colored geraniums.

He entered the small shed at the northeast corner of the lawn, then put on a pair of gardening gloves and grabbed a stiff rake. Properly outfitted, he began to attack the bags of mulch that had been placed every twenty feet around the property by his landscapers the previous Thursday.

As Albert broke open a plastic bag with the rake, his mind began to wander back to the disturbing questions he thought he had left in the den. What happened in Sunnyside? Why did Joe run from his own police? How was Joe involved in the DeLuca tragedy? Something had happened, and two people were dead: the bright-faced girl who had been to the house on Friday, and Kenneth DeLuca, whom Joe had seen that same night, and from whose home the police had discovered some very damning evidence. Why did Joe join the Army and then become a cop? Such things didn't happen in the construction business. If he had only followed his wishes and . . .

As he always did at that point, he stopped himself, and dwelled once again on his own coming-of-age and the disputes with his own father that had both enraged the old man and saved him from poverty in his declining years.

Captain Sheldon Hanlon, USN (Rtd.) had, after World War II, built his entire life on the past, specifically his four war patrols as commander of the fleet submarine USS *Squalus*, during one of which he earned the Medal of Honor. Four months out of a lifetime. For a great many years, he was outstandingly successful in centering his life on those brief months. He wrote books about them, lectured about them, went to Hollywood to consult on movies about them, and talked about them constantly. His favorite private audience was his only son, Albert Paul, the child learning at an early age that it was his destiny to attend the Naval Academy and then to enter the "Silent Service," the nickname of the Navy's submarine branch.

No matter how exciting they seemed at first, however, countless retellings of incidents long past tend to wear thin. By the time Albert was a high school senior he had experienced the same stories for eighteen years and wanted absolutely nothing to do with naval vessels, submerged or otherwise. Arguments inevitably followed, and upon graduation Albert joined the Marine Corps as an escape. The outlet of military service actually brought him closer to his father in two ways. First, through his exposure to the outside world, he gained respect for the value of a good education, perhaps like that offered at the Naval Academy. Secondly, he experienced the terror of war in a then-unknown place called Vietnam, not far from where his father had fought the Japanese in the Pacific. In the year the Gulf of Tonkin became a household name, Albert returned to Marlborough with an honorable discharge and a few medals for his service. Immediately, Sheldon again attempted to convince his son to attend Annapolis, or perhaps, he reluctantly conceded, West Point or the Air Force Academy in Colorado. As the son of a winner of the Medal of Honor, Albert would have bypassed the grueling competition for admission to any of the service academies and was almost guaranteed acceptance, the rule stemming from the belief that heroes begot heroes. Albert had not found military service to his liking, however, so the young ex-marine used his military education benefits and entered nearby Marist College instead.

Although arguments inevitably followed they were not so intense, as Sheldon was experiencing problems of his own. He was slowly finding out that the war experiences on which he had based his life were no longer held in such high regard. His books went out of print, he was asked to lecture only when no fee was charged, and movies about World War II were no longer in style. Even the Navy came to consider the once-proud fleet boats that had won the Pacific War to be ancient relics. Finding themselves overextended in their large home, Sheldon and his wife were forced to pinch pennies for the first time since he was a newlywed ensign in the early days of the Great Depression.

When Sheldon began to sell off chunks of his estate, Albert proposed that he be permitted to develop the land, to sell off lots with completed houses instead of less profitable bare acreage. A rough partnership was formed, with Albert shouldering all of the responsibilities, including continuing his classes at Marist. Three grueling years later, during which time he occasionally gazed down the Hudson and imagined the relative life of ease of a West Point cadet, Albert had his degree, but did not have to proffer it to any potential employers because he also had a small but successful business. That was also the last year that any part of the original estate had been parceled off, and Hanlon holdings elsewhere had been growing ever since.

Because of his experiences, Albert attempted to raise his own son, Joseph, differently, to guide instead of command him. Only infrequently did he relate to him the martial exploits of his ancestors or his own lucrative experiences in the construction business. Still, when it was approaching the time for Joe to decide what to do with his life, Albert, being both a father and human, allowed his guiding to become more insistent. He made it known that he considered a bachelors degree in engineering or architecture followed by a position in the family business to be the best career path for Joe.

But nothing was agreed upon. There were some discussions, but Joe's mind was more on romance than continued education. Then he broke up with the girl, DeLuca's daughter, and did not go to college at all, but joined the Army instead. After Joe returned, with an honorable discharge and a few medals for his service, he did decide to attend college, but again he infuriated Albert by setting his sights on a career in law enforcement. Discussions followed, but no more arguments as the father had resigned himself to letting his son follow his own path.

Joe seemed to be doing well in the life he had chosen, and Albert had almost convinced himself that the decisions he could not understand were perfectly fine. It's okay, he told himself a thousand times. But it was not okay now.

"Dad," the low voice said.

Albert turned around and looked for his daughter. He could see her clearly, but she was still sitting on the porch two hundred feet distant.

"Over here."

It was Joe, Albert saw with his next glance, just behind the shed, thirty feet away. He resisted the impulse to rush to his son and embrace him, immediately recognizing the clandestine nature of the visit. He moved closer to the shed along the edge of the lawn, then knelt down, pretending to work the mulch with his hands.

"I didn't do it, Dad."

"Son . . . what . . . what is going on?" The father asked, imitating Joe's hushed tone.

"I was set up by some people who tried to kill me, but murdered Elizabeth instead. By mistake. I barely escaped."

Though comforted by Joe's presence and his explanation, Albert still had one overriding concern. "Do you know about DeLuca?"

"I'm sure the same people who killed Elizabeth also murdered Dr. DeLuca, then burned his house to eliminate all traces of something I gave him on Friday."

"Son, just before I came out here, I got a call from the police chief. I asked him to keep me informed. This morning they found a bottle of gasoline at DeLuca's place with your fingerprints on it."

"What kind of bottle?"

"It was a large plastic soda bottle. Dr. Pepper, he said."

"That's positive proof of who killed DeLuca, all right. That bottle was in the refrigerator at my apartment. The killers obviously brought it up here after they finished in Sunnyside."

"Isn't there any way you can turn yourself in? We can get lawyers, hire investigators to prove your innocence."

"Dad, it's so much more complicated than that. I can't go into the details. Please just trust me; I have to get out of here."

"It's not going to be easy. The chief also told me police from all over are putting roadblocks around the whole town. He said he's never seen anything like it."

"I know, but I still think I know a way out."

"And watch out for your brother-in-law; I think he's poking around here somewhere." Although maybe he just went out for more beer, Albert thought, disconcertingly recalling the empty cans that Michael Fleming had strewn about his patio.

"We met. I got this from him," Joe stated, briefly exposing the .45 to his father's view. He went into the details of the encounter.

"That is it for him; this is the last straw." The thought of the drunken Fleming hunting Joe as if to add his son's head to the obscene number of dead deer hung on every wall of his daughter's house was far too much. "If your sister still wants to stay married to the moron, I'll keep her comfortable, but if that idiot ever wants to work for me again it will be as a junior assistant to a laborer's helper."

"You can tell him that when you release him in about three hours. He's sure to shoot his mouth off, but by then I'll be long gone."

"Where will you go?"

"I can't tell you, Dad. Then you'd have to lie, and you know how you hate that. I do have to go now, though."

"Do you need anything?"

"All I want here is for everyone not to worry so much. I'm no murderer, and I'll get out of this somehow. Tell Mom and Charlotte about our talk about the same time you go down and release Michael."

"Love you, son."

"Damn it, Dad, I love you too. Now more than ever."

Joe retreated and in moments was lost amidst the trees. Albert turned back to his work at the edge of the lawn, calculating how much mulching he could finish in three hours.

"That wasn't done by the fire," Richard Tobin said to the air. After half an hour poking around the ruins of the DeLuca house, he finally found something of interest, a broken aluminum door handle. Although the first floor of the house was built close to ground level on all sides, the basement had an exterior sliding glass door, accessed by a ramp cut into the ground and shored up on either side by landscaping ties. Tobin had come upon his find after he ventured down the debris-filled incline and moved away a twisted piece of blackened fascia that trimmed the edge of the roof, when there had been a roof. It was obvious he was the first to discover the clue.

The heat of the fire and the falling, flaming remains of the house had shattered the slider's glass, but its frame and latch, though scorched, were still intact. The handle was bent back and broken at the top, attached to the frame at an odd angle by one screw. After taking three photographs of the latch, Tobin examined the area around the door. Amidst charred timbers lay more scorched fascia, shattered glass from windows that had hung as high as twenty feet overhead, and electric wires, their insulation melted away, their outlet boxes no longer confined within walls. Underneath it all, about five feet up the incline, Tobin found a soot-blackened but intact two-by-four.

Carefully removing the debris from around it, Tobin discovered that it was a perfectly normal piece of lumber, about three feet long, somewhat weathered, its ends squared off. As it had no nails in it, was not burnt, and lay directly against the dirt of the ramp, it had obviously been in the location before the fire. It looked like a perfect lever to pry open a sliding glass door.

He took another picture, but was reluctant to touch anything. This was not like the abandoned murder scene at the apartment in Sunnyside; here there was an active investigation underway, over which he certainly held no jurisdiction. Even if the FBI was involved, it was still not his case.

"Who are you?" A young police officer stood at the edge of the incline, gazing down at Tobin.

Surprised, Tobin forced a calm expression, then walked up the ramp. "FBI, Officer . . . Bachman," he replied, reading her nameplate. He revealed his badge without revealing his name.

"Oh," she exclaimed. "I know the FBI took over the investigation, but I haven't seen any of you—agents since we discovered the bottle this morning. Actually, I'm the one who found it, over there by that shed." Tina Bachman pointed toward the back of the property.

"I'm here to do a final check," Tobin said. "So you're the one! Please tell me what happened; I haven't heard the details," he elicited, not having any idea what she was talking about.

"Well, I knew when I saw it that it was important, a bottle with gasoline in it in this type of case, so I carefully took it back to our station. We normally don't get fast action on fingerprints, but with this being a murder investigation, and with all of the police and FBI agents around, and a possible suspect, they were identified almost immediately. There was one set of prints, belonging to Joe Hanlon. He grew up around here and he's a police officer and now he's killed two people!"

"Yes, Joe Hanlon. We know all about him, but I didn't see the bottle. Exactly what kind was it?" Tobin asked, desperately hoping the agents assigned to the case did not suddenly appear in the DeLuca driveway.

"It was a two-liter soda bottle of Dr. Pepper."

"Thanks. What brings you out here now?" Tobin asked with forced gaiety. "Looking for more case-breaking clues?"

She blushed. "No. I've been here several times. My chief asked me to keep an eye on the place, but I can't stay here all day because we're so understaffed. All the other officers from our station are out on the roadblocks."

Tobin was aware of the police inspections, having been looked over in detail by two officers on his way into Marlborough. "It was great work finding that bottle."

"Thank you. I better be getting back now. Things are very busy. This is the biggest thing we've had to deal with—ever!" she said, clearly excited.

After he watched Bachman's car disappear down Ridge Road, Tobin considered the too-large possibility that the officer would tell "everyone else" at the Marlborough Police Station about the nice FBI agent she had talked to, and that a car would be headed his way soon.

"Screw it," he said. Carefully, he picked up the two-by-four and carried it to his car. Returning with a screwdriver and a large evidence bag, he delicately removed the broken handle from the basement door and placed it into the container. After taking off the handle, he noticed the soot marks on the door indicated the handle was in its odd position before the fire. He hastily snapped a photo of his new discovery, walked to his car, and was soon driving on Ridge Road in the direction opposite that of Officer Bachman.

"Get in the trunk."

"Susan, Steve and I were on the back roads all day. If I keep low, I'm certain we'll be fine."

"Your extended game of chicken with the police is of no concern to me," Susan DeLuca relayed to Joe Hanlon as she stood by the rear end of her new acquisition, an old Toyota. "It's going to be tough enough to get out of here without me being seen in this car. I want you as far out of sight as possible."

"Are you sure you know where to go?"

"Yes; I'll let you out after we pass the last house. Now get in." She was in a foul mood and not in any state of mind to conceal it.

Joe entered the Toyota's trunk. Although they both noticed the spare tire at the bottom of the hiding place, neither made mention of it. Susan started the car and drove up the narrow dirt track to Route 9W. On the way, she passed the barest trace of a path, at the end of which, unseen over a small rise, was her Ford Taurus.

She crossed the main thoroughfare and began her planned, circuitous route along the back country roads to Marlborough Mountain. Having made a quick purchase of the Toyota from a trusted friend, she was not sure the car switch was necessary, but wanted to reduce the pair's exposure as much as possible. It couldn't have helped if the exact description of the car in which she and Joe were traveling, complete with the plate number, was available to the police or the FBI, or those others Joe insisted had killed her father and his girlfriend.

Her brother had been uneasy when she told him of her plan to leave the area for a couple of days, "just to get away," but reluctantly let her go, not being in a mood to argue with her concerning the strange way of mourning she had obviously picked up in Boston. Although she vowed to return for the funeral, she did not know if she would make it back in time. She knew that would be tough to miss, but she viewed her current mission as far more important.

No one took note of the Toyota as it negotiated the rolling country byways. After several more miles, the car passed Burma Road, although the short, level farm lane was nothing like the famous winding passage in Southeast Asia during World War II. If anything, the road on which the car was traveling deserved the name, although the reason was not apparent for another mile.

Susan drove past the last farm, a large enterprise whose western boundary lines ran slightly up into the slopes of Marlborough Mountain. Three fiberglass water tanks in a field were the last structures she passed before the car nosed up a steep upgrade. After climbing another hundred yards, she stopped and freed Joe from his uncomfortable berth.

"Since you say you know this so-called road, you drive," Susan ordered, handing Joe the keys. "What's with the gun?" she asked pointedly after noticing the object in his belt.

"A little something I picked up from my brother-in-law. We may need it." He went into the details as they entered the car and began to move slowly up the unmaintained mountain road.

"You just had to go see your father, didn't you? You almost blew it. Big time."

"It was important," Joe said as he maneuvered the Toyota up a washed-out switchback, the tires climbing over stones up to eight inches across.

"Just try not to screw up again." Susan warned as the front right tire bounced over a large branch. Shortly after, the edge of the deeply rutted road dropped away precipitously from the left side of the car. After another hairpin turn, the steep slope down was to the right. Stopping only twice, to push a group of large rocks and a hefty tree branch out of the way, they finally reached the top of the ridge. With the ground sloping away through the trees to both sides of the road, they bumped along for nearly half a mile before Joe stopped the car. The ragged lane descended a steep incline to the left; ahead of the car ran an unused road, nothing much more than a trail.

Joe and Susan got out of the car and stood near one another among the newly budding trees. The rutted road down was a dead end, leading to a curious colony of fourteen summer cottages. The place was invitingly secluded and devoid of people, but hiding out was not on the couple's agenda.

"We have to go that way," Joe stated, pointing straight ahead.

"You're expecting the car to go down *that?*" Susan said with disgust. "When was the last time you drove this—*path?*"

"I've never driven it. I hiked it about twelve years ago."

"I can't believe I listened to you when you said you knew a road out of Marlborough. This isn't a road," she said vehemently, "it . . . it's a cruel joke. How do you know that it hasn't been hopelessly washed away in places, or that trees haven't blocked it?"

"I don't know, but I think it's worth a try. It's a better option than attempting to run the roadblocks."

"This isn't an option, it's nothing. It's shit."

Joe grabbed her by the shoulders and looked straight into her eyes. "Susan, I never wanted you along on this. This would be a perfect opportunity for you to leave. You don't understand, you truly have no conception of the deadly nature of the situation that motivates me to take a risk on this road. Yesterday, I asked the girl I loved to marry me, and saw her face beaming like never before. Within minutes, bits of that same face were blown on me and she was dead. I came within two seconds of being killed in that explosion and shortly after came within two inches of having my head blown off by a bullet. While on the run, I learned the man I had spoken with that morning, a man I loved as a friend and mentor, had been murdered and his house had been burned, probably because of something I gave him on Friday. The men who did these things are ruthless, Susan, and they are powerful and they want me. Dead. Let me go on alone; I don't want you to end up dead, too." He let go of her and turned away, shaking.

They stood silently for a long while, lost in their own thoughts of the situation and the many facets of their relationship, past and present. Finally, Susan placed a gentle hand on Joe's shoulder. "I understand your loss; I've lost too. I haven't been in danger much in my life, but I want to find out what happened to my father. Let's give this road a try."

Joe, his back still to her, reluctantly nodded his assent.

The road traversing Marlborough Mountain was over a hundred years old, but had not been used regularly in decades. It had been temporarily improved about ten years before, however, just enough to allow the passage of logging trucks. As tree harvesting went, the operation had been a small one, as only one in a hundred trees had been deemed suitable for milling into lumber, so the improvements were far from elaborate. A decade of disuse resulted in other problems as well.

At times Joe drove, coaxing the car over the rough terrain as if he was driving one of the Humvees he had operated in the Army, but more gently, ever mindful of the limitations of his current vehicle. On other stretches, Susan took the wheel and followed her partner as he removed rocks from the road, or used stones to fill ruts up to two feet deep. Three times, they both were called upon to move away small trees that obliquely blocked the path. Portions of the road consisted of bare bedrock, others were water-filled hollows, one of which the car negotiated driverless, as both Susan and Joe were at the rear bumper, pushing it through.

After descending two rocky switchbacks, they faced a steep incline. This time, Susan pushed away the rocks while Joe chanced the grade. No longer much of a road, or even a trail, it was more than anything a streambed, carrying water straight down the mountain during heavy rainstorms. Nervous, Joe heard the grating of rocks and too-loud bumps at his feet, but realized he was committed. He shouted to his companion to move aside and gritted his teeth as the car jostled down the last two hundred feet of the slope. At its base, he turned off the ignition and exited the car, breathless. When Susan caught up with him, he was examining the underside of the vehicle, looking for fatal damage.

"How is it?" she asked, also out of breath.

"Lots of dents and scratches, but no apparent mechanical wounds. I don't know why, but it appears to be okay. We'll have to drive it a bit to make sure. I'm not looking forward to doing that again."

"You won't have to. Look."

Joe saw it, too, and smiled at the sight. It was trash: several piles of wonderful plastic bags, beer cans, and old tires dumped haphazardly in the woods by people too cheap to properly dispose of the items and too lazy to venture far from their vehicles. They were at the base of Marlborough Mountain, in Plattekill. Ahead of them was a decent dirt road.

"We made it," Joe said as he got up and moved over to Susan. "We made it. There is no way I could have done it alone." He hugged her, the first time he had done so since she aborted his child.

"We still have a long way to go," she said. "Let's get at it."

After a mile and a half, the dirt lane became a narrow paved road and the travelers once again found themselves in farmland. A few miles farther, the car was skirting the tiny village of Plattekill, where they encountered evidence of a road crew in the midst of tearing up the asphalt to prepare it for repaving, though no one was working on Sunday. Among the flashing warning lights was a temporary marker, an orange diamond with black lettering.

"Look at that," Joe commented grimly.

"Is that a sign?"

"Rough Road Ahead," it cautioned.

Philip Roberts knew it was dark outside, but could not see the night from his windowless office. Things were finally calming down, getting back to normal. Having reasserted his professionalism, he was not angry anymore, but was tired. Ignoring the papers piled on the desk next to his computer, he settled back in his chair and gazed purposelessly at the walls of the room. Even if there had been a window, he mused, he still would not have been able to tell that the Sun had gone down.

Among the piles on his desk were the papers of an administrative nature that were necessary to his position as the supervisor of the six-person group known as Team One, and as the manager of both his crew and the equally sized Team Two, together comprising the entire security force of the project. He never counted the four-man Team Three at the project's remote site near Albany, as the men did little but sit around on their collective asses. When he first assumed command of the teams, he had been astonished at the pitifully small size of the groups in relation to the tasks required of them, but had since grown accustomed to his tight-knit squads. Supported by unknowing legions of others, they had performed flawlessly in providing facility security for years, and had executed many offsite missions without a major problem.

Until this week, he thought, staring at two file folders. Filled with notes, telephone numbers, photographs, and diagrams, they bore a resemblance to tens of thousands of other case files on the desks of law enforcement officers across the country. These folders, however, contained only items of a private nature. Nothing within them was meant for a court of law, public record, or even the eyes of his superiors.

The top file, consisting of information related to the demise of Victor Bonnelli, was a case closed upon the delivery of the much-examined body of the mobster to the funeral home in New York. The other folder was an enigma, as he had never before had to open two files relating to one mission. The bastard Hanlon was still loose, he fumed inwardly before forcing himself to regain his objectivity. It would mean only a little more work each day, a few phone calls to a few people, guiding them in a few possible directions. If Joseph Hanlon were to be caught, the file would be closed quickly; if he somehow managed to stay on the run as a desperate fugitive, the case would fade away, leaving the project as secure as ever.

"Phil, got minute?" The head of Eric Kauffman appeared at the doorway to Roberts' office.

"Sure, Eric, come in. What are you doing here this late?"

"I was just leaving, but I wanted to see you first."

"What's on your mind?"

"It's about our last mission; it still bugs me," Kauffman said. "We've had minor glitches before, but this was something else."

"You're right, it was a good job gone bad. Although I anticipated more problems as these missions expand to more exposed positions, I didn't think that one asshole cop could screw things up so much."

"Yeah. I guess I regret the girl the most. She was just a bystander; she didn't know anything."

"Don't be so sure. We didn't hear their conversation over break-fast. He could have told her everything. Setting off the device on her was an error, but it might have been for the best. You know what we stopped, don't you?"

"Hell, yes," Kauffman said. "The entire project might have been jeopardized."

"Exactly. There is such a thing as a greater good and sometimes we have to make unpleasant choices to serve it. When you were a young U.S. Marshal, you must have had to make one of those choices, didn't you?" The question was leading; as a good supervisor, Roberts knew the backgrounds of each of his charges intimately.

"Once, with a serial killer. He had already killed at least twenty girls by the time we cornered him with his last victim. He wired a shot-gun against the back of her neck and had three lines extending from the trigger to both hands and a belt loop. Bringing him down was tough; the girl was killed as his body fell."

"I had similar experiences in the CIA. Sometimes innocent people die, sometimes you don't know if someone is innocent, and they still have to die."

"Well, I think we picked up a few pointers in the last few days," Kauffman said. "Now we know about things like the damn dead squir-rel."

"And the damn dead cat. I think I'll have an in-depth talk with our techs. They might have warned us."

"Yeah. Thanks for the talk; I'm headed out."

As Kauffman left, Roberts checked to see which two members of Team Two had guard duty that evening. It would be their last shift for a while, Roberts knew, as Team One was due to assume responsibility for facilities security the next day while the other group prepared for a field mission. A mission that had better go more smoothly than the one just finished.

Or not quite finished, Roberts thought as he stared at the annoying open file on his desk. Where are you, Joseph Hanlon? I can hardly wait until we meet again.

———

Dinner didn't look much like its picture, but it would be naïve to think that it would, being typical of all nationally franchised fast food chains. Joe knew if those places were forced to display photographs of what they actually stuffed into those paper bags, they would go the way of the Pony Express, and just as quickly. Still, he greedily wolfed down the burger concoction and the dry fries Susan handed him, the late repast temporarily sating his appetite. He threw the garbage from his meal into the back seat and started the car. Soon, the Toyota was once again on Interstate 81, headed ever south.

"It's less than thirty miles now," Joe said in a fatigued voice as the lights of Staunton grew dimmer in the rear-view mirror.

Finally free from the back roads of New York, Susan had driven into Pennsylvania and joined the interstate just outside Scranton. Joe then took the wheel, and they alternated the chore for three hundred fifty miles, through Maryland, West Virginia, and into Virginia. Gas was always obtained at the farthest pump of a large station, with Susan paying—in cash. There had been no tollbooths to confront.

As they closed on their destination, they relaxed slightly. Surrounded by dark farmlands and hills between widely spaced small cities, they felt somewhat protected, slightly distanced from the horrors of the past. The feeling did not last long. At the point where they traveled out of the Shenandoah-Potomac watershed and into the valley of the James, they passed a semi bearing a small blue sticker on one of its large rear doors proclaiming, "It is not a choice, it is a child." Both Joe and Susan saw it, and both knew the other had seen it, but they drove on in silence, it being neither the proper place nor time to bring up what had been the most crucial turning point in both of their lives.

It had been shortly after the death of Susan's mother on rain-soaked Route 9W, Joe recalled. Though grief-stricken and riddled with guilt, he had done his best to comfort Susan through that horrendously difficult time. He stood next to her at the funeral, in the same prolonged rain that had inundated Marlborough since the night of the crash. Afterward, he stayed with her, coaxing her to eat, to talk, and to finish the final few hours of her high school studies. Nothing he did helped. She was in shock, pale, even physically sick at times. At the end of a long month, her father took her to a hospital in Poughkeepsie, where she was told she was pregnant, due to deliver in five and a half months.

When Susan told Joe the news, he felt as if he had been jolted out of a deep sleep into full consciousness, and through the telescopic vision provided by that moment, he looked past the constant pain he felt over the death of her mother and saw with crystal clarity the path over which he would travel for the rest of his life. Over the hours that followed, his joy was absolute. It had been only hours; when he returned to the hospital the next morning, the child had been aborted, and Susan rejected him as well.

In the few short conversations afterward, both Joe and Susan acted like drugged medieval history majors attempting to discuss the finer points of particle physics: there just wasn't anything there. A few weeks later, Joe drifted from the chasm that had replaced his joyous vision and joined the Army as an escape. The last time he saw Susan was during a farewell visit to her father, still a friend and mentor, before he traveled to Fort Dix for boot camp. She had been two rooms away, barely visible, and did not speak to him or even look in his direction.

Joe glanced over at Susan and rejoined the present. After nearly a decade, he was with her once again, at another turning point, and just as confused over both the situation and his feelings. One thing he did know was that he wanted her protected. "Susan," he said at last, "tomorrow when I try to see this guy, I think I better go alone. I'll give you the details afterward."

"So you can have a man-to-man chat without being distracted by any inane female questions? Not likely; I don't give in so easily to that kind of menkus."

"No, that's not what I mean . . . what *is* that, anyway?"

"Menkus? It's nothing but shit—the shit that keeps women servile to the whims of men. It's chauvinism, sexism, and plain outrageous injustice all rolled up into an odious concept so dense it almost has physical mass. The laws, customs, social mores, and attitudes of men—and women, too—that promote the misconception that women are inferior to men, less worthy than men, and are mere objects for men to manipulate are all examples of menkus."

"Never heard of it."

"It was originated a few years ago by a columnist for a tiny paper in Missouri. She became frustrated attempting to find adjectives emphatic enough to express her outrage over the abuses women face every day, so she coined the word. 'No longer will I write of a "blatant, atrocious, contemptible example of sexual discrimination,"' she wrote in her now-famous column. 'From now on, it's just menkus.'"

"And it caught on?"

"Too slowly. It's a word that's been long overdue."

"But there have been great strides made in women's rights over the past few years."

"Just because the river has silted in a little doesn't make it any less treacherous. Menkus flows thickly through our lives almost as deep as it ever has, and will continue until women are judged equally. When someone—far in the future—addresses a large group, referring in their speech to 'a famous female ship captain,' or 'the renowned lady senator.' or 'that well-known woman basketball player,' and everyone in the audience turns to one another genuinely puzzled as to why the sex of the person was mentioned, then the millennia of menkus might be at an end."

"That's a tall order."

"Well, it's a goal, but we have a more urgent mission, one that does not involve leaving the little woman at home while the man goes to parlay with the big boys."

"Uncle," Joe replied, holding his hands spread above the steering wheel momentarily in a gesture of surrender. "But we have to be careful. The guys after me have big ears and wide eyes." And guns and bombs in phones and gasoline to burn you to a dead, charred mess, he added silently.

"Understood," she replied as she gazed out the window. A sign indicated that Lexington could be accessed from the next four exits. "Looks like we better find a place for the night."

As a precaution, Joe drove past the most convenient exit to Washington and Lee University and continued south.

"Damn, I didn't know that place was here too," Susan commented acridly as she read the directional sign to both of Lexington's schools of higher learning, the other being the Virginia Military Institute."

"V.M.I.? How about that. My chief went there, and I knew a couple of officers in the Army who got their commissions from V.M.I. It's referred to as West Point of the South. Why so disturbed?"

"If a map of the United States were overlaid with isobaric lines indicating density of menkus, V.M.I. would be Mount Everest."

Joe nodded, having some knowledge of the eight-year court battle in which Institute officials fought to keep the cadet enrollment entirely male, finally losing in a landmark Supreme Court decision. "Hey, other things to worry about, remember?" he gently chided.

After eight more miles, Joe exited Interstate 81 and turned north on U.S. Route 11. "That looks like a likely candidate for tonight," he said after a few miles, indicating a weather-beaten frame structure with a neon sign that proclaimed it to be nothing more than a "Motel." He pulled into the unpaved parking lot.

"Wait here," Susan said, then walked toward the neon sign identifying the office."

It was quiet, Joe noted as he surveyed his surroundings. Cars passed on the route at a frequency of less than one a minute, and there was no activity around the string of units. The adjacent strip mall was dark, as was the bank across the street, except for its sign that informed passersby of the time and temperature every few seconds. Forty-six degrees, it flashed. Chilly.

Susan returned with a key. "Around the back," she said. There they located the crude cardboard marker on the door with their room number, 12A, between the doors with stamped aluminum numbers indicating "12" and "14."

Inside the small room, they found a full-size bed with a faded, dirty spread, one folding chair, and a chipped dresser, on which was a black-and-white television.

"Any ship in a storm," Joe commented, examining their small confines.

"That's 'any port in a storm.'"

"If you want to be so optimistic."

Susan took the bed. Joe grabbed one of the two pillows and the soiled spread and threw them on the floor. He fell asleep the moment his head hit the pillow, the same moment that the sixty-two white bulbs on the bank sign across the street changed from 11:59 to 12:00.

**MONDAY
13 APRIL**

CHAPTER 17

In an instant, Susan DeLuca gained a surprising new perspective on her traveling companion. She was looking at Joe, who stood in the doorway to the motel bathroom. Having just finished showering, he was clad only in a bath towel, the scars on one arm and both legs evident "What the hell," she uttered. "What happened to you?"

"What, these old things? Just a few souvenirs I picked up in government service."

"I had no idea," Susan said. Although she knew Joe had seen action overseas, the local publicity on his homecoming had been subdued, primarily because the newspaper had not been able to elicit any details from him concerning his experiences. "*That* injury is not years old," she observed, looking down at the almost-healed wounds on his left leg.

Joe sat down at the foot of the bed. "No, but these days, police officers sometimes take more hits than soldiers, even policemen from sleepy villages like Sunnyside. Speaking of that, did you bring any bandages with you?"

Susan retrieved the medical tape and gauze pads from her overnight bag but did not understand their necessity, as the injuries she had seen were not in need of first aid.

"Looks like you're going to see a little more of me than you figured on," Joe said as he hiked up the left side of the towel.

"Damn!" she exclaimed as she caught sight of not only the ugly red line of his new wound, but the old buttocks lacerations as well.

"This," Joe said as Susan helped him dress the partially scabbed, oozing furrow, "was done to me by the same man who killed your father. Ouch!"

"Sorry," she said in apology for her involuntary jerk that slightly abraded the wound. "You say it was the same—man? Not just the same group?"

"His name is Roberts, at least that's what he told everyone. After Elizabeth was killed, he came after me with a gun. I escaped, but not before he gave me this going-away present. In my refrigerator at the apartment was a soda bottle, and that was found yesterday, with gasoline in it and my fingerprints on it, behind the Ridge Road house. Although its presence at the murder scene makes it crystal clear to me that Roberts is the killer, the same object seems to be guiding everyone else toward a different suspect."

"I think we should be concerned about publicity," Susan said.

"I'm not worried. There are thousands of murders in New York City every year that only get a mention in the back pages of the tabloids, if that. It's big news in Marlborough and Sunnyside, but we're hundreds of miles away."

"Think about it. You're a police officer accused of two murders and on the run. And in some way connected to Bonnelli's death, which did make the Boston papers."

"Maybe you're right," Joe said. "Even Bonnelli's supposedly innocent passing made the New York news in a big way, but nobody knows I was there, nobody that would talk, anyway."

"I'm just advising caution; we have to avoid anyone who might recognize you from a publicized photo," Susan said as she finished packing. "What should we do first?"

"I think we should try the doctor's house. We have his address, but we have little idea of where his office might be at the University. This early in the morning he should still be home. We'll find his street and I'll go in and do a little reconnaissance on foot."

Susan shot him a decidedly dirty look.

"I know, no more menkus, but I've been on recon missions before; I know what to look for. We can't just rush in. He might be away on vacation or at some kind of conference or he might be sitting at his kitchen table having coffee with two or three federal agents. If everything is okay, I'll come back and we can go in together."

"Okay. I think we're ready."

"Susan, it's a hell of a time to bring it up, but I have to," Joe said in a firm voice that was curiously overlaid with hesitancy.

The odd tone stopped Susan, and she turned to face him.

"It's about your mother; I feel responsible for her being killed."

"I know; I've always known. Do you think women are so stupid that they don't know tires don't go flat lying in the trunk of a car?"

"It was about a week before the—accident. I was driving alone on Western Avenue and hit a bent nail. I just didn't bother to get the tire fixed, but I could have. Nobody knew, and no one ever asked."

"So you didn't get a flat fixed, and the world ended," she said calmly. "And I called Mom because she was slightly more convenient, even though any of my friends would have gladly picked us up. And I used an unnecessarily urgent tone in our last conversation that motivated her to hasten to meet us, so she was a hundred yards ahead of where she otherwise would have been when that drunk crossed the centerline. And I knew she didn't wear her seat belt on short trips; I could have urged her to, just that once. And there are a hundred other things that have occurred to me repeatedly during the past ten years. Some wounds aren't caused by bombs and bullets, Joe. In this case, we both have similar scars. They have faded somewhat over the years, but they never will completely disappear. I can't help you."

"I'm sorry, Susan, truly sorry." All four eyes glistening, they hugged. "Is that what happened between us?"

"No," she replied with dread decisiveness, catching Joe completely off guard. "That was something else, but it will have to wait."

He was smoking again. On Sunday afternoon, he had purchased his first pack of Marlboros in nearly a year and, to his wife's chagrin, had lit up on their dark back deck. Now he was puffing away in his office in the White Plains Federal Building, which was not allowed, but it was a rule often overlooked in the offices of the FBI due to the pressure under which agents sometimes worked, and Richard Tobin was pressured more than he had been for a long time.

He extinguished the butt of his cigarette in a foam cup containing an ounce of gritty coffee and opened the bottom drawer of his file cabinet. Stored there was the bulk of the evidence he had gleaned from two cases that were not his: odds and ends from the Hanlon apartment, including a jar of mustard and a bullet, and a broken sliding door handle from the DeLuca house in Marlborough. Together with the two-by-four carefully leaned against the cabinet, his notes, and a roll of film being developed at a one-hour photo place a few miles away, it was all he had, except for an overpowering feeling that Joseph Hanlon, fugitive murderer, was a good guy and that some of the people who until recently worked next door to him were very, very bad.

There were no latent print cards from Carol Kowalesky's office because Tobin had found no fingerprints. Someone from Roberts' gang had cleaned everything in the room, from the desk to the phone to the keys on the computer keyboard, the pictures that hung on the walls, and the thermostat switch. What kind of agents do that? Tobin asked himself for the tenth time.

He perused his notes. After fleeing the Ridge Road site, he paid a respectful call on Albert Hanlon, and the two of them engaged in a long conversation as the older man leisurely mulched the edge of his lawn. Tobin picked up a few names to check from the elder Hanlon, and picked up a few more from a convenience store clerk named Cheryl Clarke on his way out of Marlborough. He compared the lists. Several of the names matched, but one in particular stood out: Stephen White. Albert Hanlon told him Joe and Steve and two others had been the best of friends in their teens, but that of the four only White still lived in Marlborough. Clarke mentioned she had called Steve after the excitement of the fire was over, but he seemed to take the news calmly.

Tobin turned to his computer terminal and began to access the databases so crucial to his normal work. Now, he hoped they would serve him equally well in his abnormal activities. Though court orders were necessary to use the information to prosecute a case, such legal niceties were often overlooked when quick action was essential and judges and lawyers were far removed. Tobin turned to the vast database of the local telephone company and pulled up the records on Steven White, discovering that White made no calls from his apartment over the weekend, but received several. The call from Clarke was noted, along with four others, all short. Two, Tobin gathered from the company names, were from telemarketers peddling their wares. The other two were—not. He looked up the numbers and found them to be pay phones, one in Peekskill, the other in Beacon. I believe I'll pay a visit on Mr. White, he planned.

After making a few calls pertaining to his assigned cases, none of them crucial, Tobin selected three items from his trove of ill-gotten evidence and walked down two flights of stairs to the enclave of Janine Wolf, the overseer of the division's small crime laboratory. Tiny by FBI and even most police department standards, it was Wolf's passion to insure that the taxpayer dollars expended on it were justified.

"Morning, dear," Tobin called as he entered the room.

"It's not enough you verbally abuse me, now you have to take a stick to me?" the woman replied, eyeing the two-by-four in Tobin's cloth-covered hand.

"Just a few things for you to take a look at. I'm interested in any prints on the lumber and the jar, and I'd like to know if there's anything of interest about this." He held up the plastic bag containing the triangular shard he had recovered from Joe's apartment.

"I suppose you need it now, as always?" Wolf asked.

"I'd love it if you could tell me something by this afternoon," Tobin requested.

"Do these things have anything to do with Joe Hanlon?"

Visibly shocked, Tobin made an attempt at recovery, but could tell that she could see right through him. "That's Harvarnik's case. Just label these items 'Mamaroneck.'"

"If you say so. You seem to forget that, unlike most people in this office, I was here last year. While you and Hanlon were out in the field, I was in this room, examining a few disturbing items, and catching the drift of some amazing speculations. I don't know the details, but I know you and he saved a bunch of people, with him being shot in the process. To think that you would be working on anything else this morning, authorized or not, would be quite incredulous."

"You won't let on to Harvarnik?"

"That asshole? He was down here this morning screaming about the latest developments."

"I haven't heard."

"Hanlon slipped right through their fingers yesterday," Wolf explained. "He tied up his brother-in-law in the woods near his old home, probably had a chat with his father, then disappeared."

"That's some news. Thanks."

"Okay, I'll keep your secret and see if I can come up with anything."

"I know you will. You women make the best lab techs," he said as a parting compliment, but as he was leaving, he thought he heard her utter a curse. He didn't understand it, though; it sounded something like "mucous."

———————

Joe was in an older residential development near the outskirts of Lexington on a quiet, affluent street boasting mature maples and dogwoods, clipped hedges of holly and box, and planting beds by picket fences. Not bad for cover and concealment, he judged. He had left Susan with the car in the parking lot of a convenience store four blocks away and was walking alone on the flagstone sidewalk in the sumptuous neighborhood. He looked like a typical citizen out for an early morning stroll, just his eyes betraying the fact that he was once again on a reconnaissance mission, a mission every bit as serious and potentially deadly as those he had performed in his overseas hell.

Half a block away, he saw them both simultaneously. One was his objective, number sixteen Cherry Street, a large brick colonial whose foundation was obviously built on the bedrock of more-than-moderate wealth, though it was no fancier than a dozen other mini-mansions on the street. The other was the one aberrant vehicle in this world of Volvos, Mercedes, and BMWs. Now *that* is an FBI car, Joe thought, gazing at the dark gray Ford sedan parked across the street from the home of Dr. Salvatore Monnell.

He ventured a few more steps. There were two men in the car, their backs to him, and two cars in the driveway. Both were good signs. He made a one-eighty and beat an anxious retreat back to Susan, still parked at the Kwik-E-Mart on the commercial strip.

"We have a problem," he told her. "I found the house, but the FBI, or some similar group, has it under surveillance."

"Oh, God . . . no!" Susan said in horror.

"Now listen," Joe said firmly, calmly. He took her hands in his and looked her straight in the eyes. "I'm almost certain these are just standard agents, not the people who murdered Elizabeth and your father. I don't want to be caught by these guys, but they are probably not the enemy."

"What makes you so sure?"

"To have murderous agents here, among numerous other possible locations, would involve a huge conspiracy, and I don't believe in huge conspiracies; they're too easily compromised. Roberts and his small clan have to be extremely secretive; I think the two agents are here on an assignment they don't understand, just like a dozen or a hundred others across the country, each staking out an acquaintance of your father's or a friend of mine."

"So this is a good thing?"

"Roberts has to have limitations. His gang may be some kind of renegade federal agency, or a militant group with extremely strong governmental ties, but these guys do not wield so much power that they can enlist the entire FBI in plots of assassination." Joe did not add that it was possible the phantom group did have enough power to have custody of certain individuals transferred to it by the FBI, no questions asked. That, he thought, would not be good.

"So what's next?" Susan asked, slightly calmed.

"I surveyed the neighborhood, and I think I can evade the surveillance car by approaching the house from the back. Unfortunately, that means going through the yard of the neighbor on the next street over, and it's the type of area where people seem to be keenly protective of their property lines. I'm likely to get the local police called on me."

Susan was silent for a moment. "Get this straight one more time," she finally said, "this is a 'we' situation. We are both going to this house. This guy knew my father and I want to meet him. Besides, the two of us have a better chance of going through someone's backyard than a lone, furtive male. And to top it off, I have an idea."

"Look, maybe we're not going to get shot in the street, but the situation is still dangerous. I need to go in alone."

"The one thing I don't need to hear right now is menkus; just shut up and wait here." She walked into the convenience store.

Joe waited, properly chastised with a word he was quickly beginning to hate. Susan emerged a few minutes later with a small paper bag.

"What's that?" he queried.

"A prop. Let's go over my plan."

This was it, Brenda Stone thought as she pulled away from the roadblock on Route 9W and headed into the town of Marlborough, this was her man-cuts-off-own-dick story, the news item that would finally garner her widespread attention. After reluctantly accepting an assignment from her newspaper to try to dredge up something more on Victor "Last Week's News" Bonnelli, Brenda had traveled to Sunnyside. After being rebuffed by house sitter Marc Grunner, she struck gold at the home of Kathleen Jackson, the neighbor to the north, who told her Joe Hanlon had been at the house on the morning of the mobster's death. Linking the dead mob boss and the double murderer was just the kind of story that could launch her onto the national scene.

Years before, when she was new to the reporting game, she began to think about various news items that might have ended up as a sensational tidbit in some local rag, but which had instead been placed squarely in front of the American public by mainstream news media. To attain such exposure, she realized, a story had to be unique, suspenseful, and full of human interest, so to train herself to be cognizant of these desired facets, and to just fantasize about the Big Time, she had mentally created her own perfect scoop.

He is a hunter, alone in the woods and miles from civilization, perched on his deer stand, a rude wood platform with steel supports bolted to an oak tree fifteen feet above the forest floor. While waiting for his prey, the platform collapses under his weight, The boards break, the jagged supports bend and tear into his pants, and he finds himself clinging to the oak, his penis painfully and inextricably caught in the twisted steel, still secured to the tree. With only a penknife at his disposal to free himself, he works feverishly at the tree to attempt to dislodge the lag bolts screwed deeply into the wood. After hours of work, he realizes his efforts are useless. With a cold night coming on and his jacket lying on the ground below next to his rifle, he faces up to the only option available to save himself from a death by exposure. Without anesthesia of any kind, he saws his own penis off with the now-dull penknife and drops exhausted to the ground.

But the drama is just beginning. Tying off his stump of remaining manhood, he walks miles to his home and summons a rescue team. Temporarily bandaged, he leads the group back over the rugged miles to the site of his misfortune, arriving just in time to warn off a raccoon about to ingest a tasty morsel. One man attends to the severed member with an ice pack, while another attacks the steel with a portable oxy-acetylene torch. Battery-powered spotlights illuminate the work. The victim's loyal, horny wife is also on the scene. Having never even dreamed of Bobbitizing her husband, she pleads with the others to save the part of her spouse she had grown to love so much.

At last freed, the organ is transferred to an improvised, ice-filled penis caddy, and the group trudges back. A dramatic operation follows, and the man is reunited with his wife after he is reunited with himself. And they live happily ever after, as does the exclusive reporter of the story.

"This is just as good," Brenda said as she turned onto Old Indian Road. She had verified with the Sunnyside Police that Hanlon had been fired because of his unauthorized activities at the Bonnelli residence on the morning of the death, but beyond that, none of the cops would talk. Just like the good, tight-knit group that they were, none of the policemen had said anything to any other reporter, she knew, until she aggressively burst into the station demanding to know why the Sunnyside Police Force had hired a Bonnelli henchman. Although the outrageous statement was invented just to incite the police into giving her a little information, on the ride up the Hudson Valley she had begun to think that it might actually be true. Why was he there at the house? she asked herself. The police didn't want him there, neither did the FBI. It was possible that Bonnelli had hired Hanlon to be his eyes in the community, to warn him of any impending actions. Perhaps Hanlon had actually been a hit man for the Mafia who had temporarily been given a different assignment.

But things had gone wrong, Brenda reasoned, and with his boss dead Hanlon went berserk, bumping off his girlfriend in his rage, then bringing his madness to his old homestead, where he killed a family friend. After that he went on, capturing and threatening his brother-in-law, then kidnapping or killing his old girlfriend, the daughter of the man he murdered on Saturday. Now he was at large, a threat to all newspaper readers in the country. "This thing just gets better and better," Brenda said with a smile.

She turned into a small subdivision and wound around to a cul-de-sac. At the house that matched the address she was given, a man with a rifle stood in the front yard. At first stunned, she quickly recognized that the man bore no resemblance to Hanlon's photo, and was probably the person she had spoken with on the phone.

The man walked eagerly toward her as she got out of her car. "Are you the reporter from New York?" he asked.

"Mr. Fleming? I'm Brenda Stone. I'm here about your run-in with Joseph Hanlon yesterday."

"Of course. I already talked to other reporters, but they were from local papers."

"Tell me what happened."

"Well, I was over at my in-laws house, trying to calm everyone down concerning what Joe did down in Sunnyside and up here with DeLuca. With Joe loose and all, I didn't think the police were covering the house properly, so I took a walk to check things out. I was in the woods when Joe jumped me. He had a gun, but I didn't; the Hanlons don't like guns at their house. I edged closer to him, then lunged. We fought, but he had training in hand-to-hand combat in the Army. He overpowered me and tied me to a tree. I thought for sure he was going to kill me. I think the only reason he didn't shoot me was that the noise would have alerted the police in the area."

"Did he say anything to you about the killings?"

"He told me he had killed those people and many others before that."

Yeah, working for the Mafia, Brenda thought.

"After I was untied, the police searched the area and found Susan DeLuca's car in the woods. They're still searching the area for her body, but I think he killed her somewhere else and drove her car to that spot before he found me."

Brenda already knew the facts, and had come to the same conclusion. "Maybe you can give me a little background on Hanlon."

Fleming shouldered his rifle. "Sure. Let's go up to the house. I need a beer."

She walked beside him to his front door, then followed him inside.

Although initially awestruck by the copious number of dead deer exhibited in Fleming's living room, Brenda recovered quickly. "So you're a deer hunter?"

"I've been known to bag a buck or two."

"Let me give you my number for future reference. If anything—

unusual happens to you during one of your hunting trips, please call me first."

Emily Bloom was, according to all who knew her, an elegant woman. A stately forty-five, tall, thin, and brunette, she was also alone and preparing to consume her first vodka martini of the day, but was interrupted by the lilting chimes of her five-tone doorbell. She opened the door and found a young couple standing on her front porch. They seemed out of breath and the woman had the sparkle of tears in her eyes.

"I'm sorry to bother you, ma'am," the man said in a light Southern accent. "I'm Jack Ryan and this is my wife Cathy, from South End Apartments." He made a slight gesture toward a group of low-rise buildings just visible through the maples across the street. "We're chasing our dog, a little black cocker spaniel."

"His name is Zeus," said the woman. "I was just about to take him for a walk, but he ran off before I could get the lead on him."

Emily saw the braided leash in her hand, tragically unattached. Snapped out of her melancholy, she suddenly had great concern for the little lost dog. "No, I didn't see, uh, Zeus."

"Please," the woman pleaded with the man, "the longer we stand here, the farther away he's getting." She clutched the leash even tighter.

"Could we look in your yard, ma'am?"

Touched by the plight of the pair, Emily readily consented and led them to the spacious rear yard, bracketed on three sides by mature hemlocks. In the direction of the next block to the rear, a dog barked.

"That's him! Please, Jack, let's catch him." The woman took off in a fast walk toward the rear row of trees.

Hastily, the man thanked Emily for her help, then followed his companion through the hedge.

"Nice going," Joe complemented Susan as they made their way across the backyard of number sixteen Cherry Street. "Keep that leash handy and be prepared to do it again if we meet with anything unexpected at this house."

"Lucky break with the dog barking when it did. I just hope the guy is here."

There was no rear bell button. A plump woman dressed in a maid's uniform answered their knocks.

"Good morning," Joe said in his cheeriest voice, flashing his warmest smile. "We're a little early, but we were so anxious to see Dr.

Monnell again that we couldn't help but be a little hasty."

Susan joined in the mock reverie and did her best happy face impression.

Somewhat suspicious but warming slightly to the cheery couple, the woman asked their names, then disappeared through an inner doorway. Shortly after, an older man, bald with gray sidewalls and wearing nearly circular glasses came out to greet them.

"Joseph Hanlon, Susan DeLuca?" Salvatore Monnell queried.

"Dr. Monnell, years ago you worked with my father, Kenneth DeLuca, on an enzyme research project," Susan said.

The effect of the name was electric. "Of course!" he exclaimed. "One of the finest doctors and one of the most thorough scientists I ever had the pleasure of working with." He beckoned them into the house and went on joyously. "We were absolute fiends on that project for the entire time it lasted, one year, or was it two? We became close friends, our wives, too. I haven't seen Kenneth since . . ." He stopped abruptly, remembering.

"It was ten years ago," Susan said. "We might have met then, but I don't recall."

"It was a tremendous tragedy, the loss of your mother," Monnell said as they entered the kitchen, a large room with white cabinetry illuminated by a platoon of recessed ceiling lights. A woman sat at an oblong table. "Claire, this is the daughter of Ken and Terri DeLuca," he introduced.

The woman beamed. "Terri and I were the best of friends for almost two years. Our Jason was almost ten at the time, about the same age as your brother. Those boys managed to get themselves into all fashion of mischief. In the final months before Ken left to take another position, Terri was pregnant with—well, that must have been you." Her smile turned into a frown as she continued the chronology. "I was deeply upset by the horrible accident. Please sit," she said, motioning Susan toward a chair.

"Dad also died in an accident, more recently," Susan stated flatly.

"Dear girl!" the woman sympathized. "I am so sorry to hear that."

Joe looked through an open archway and saw that, although the ruffled curtains on the large front windows were tied back, the shades were drawn. "We came here to talk to you about some of the late doctor's research," he said.

"Let's go into the library," Monnell offered.

"I'd like to stay here and talk with Mrs. Monnell," Susan said. "It's been a long time since I talked to a friend of Mother's."

With Susan guarding his rear, Joe followed Monnell into the large library and they sat down. "Dr. Monnell, two days ago, Dr. DeLuca was murdered and an attempt was made on my life that resulted in the death of my fiancée," Joe began. "I believe these murders have something to do with the federal government and the enzyme research you and Dr. DeLuca worked on almost thirty years ago. This notion was reinforced this morning when I noticed that the FBI is staking out your house. That's why Susan and I came through your rear yard and used your back door."

Monnell was silent for a moment, then reflectively rubbed his chin. "Young man, while you may believe what you have just told me, you will have to do some hard convincing before I will even start to give your bizarre story any credibility."

Starting with the events of the previous Thursday, Joe explained the situation to the doctor, telling him about the cat and the squirrel, the excited call from the doctor, and the grisly deaths of Elizabeth and DeLuca.

As he listened, Monnell rose from his chair and peered out the front window through the small space between the drawn shade and the window casing. Seated again, he stared at Joe. "What exactly did DeLuca tell you in that phone call?"

"He told me the squirrel died due to an absence of the enzyme phosphofrucinate."

Monnell sat up. "Chemically, that makes no sense. Could he have said 'phosphofructokinase'?"

"Wait, I wrote it down." Joe reached into his pocket and took out a page from a Marlborough Free Library scratch pad. He handed the crumpled paper to his examiner.

"Yes, that's it," Monnell said. "Go on."

"Dr. DeLuca told me there had never been a death like this. Very excited, he told me he was going to spend all weekend verifying his findings, then on Monday—today—he was going to announce his discovery to the scientific community. Within two hours of telling me this, over a phone I know now was bugged, he was dead, probably by a gunshot, and his lab and house were burned."

After a few moments of reflection, the doctor sighed. "What DeLuca told you would have indeed been a remarkable find if it could be verified, and it appears it might not be a coincidence that he was killed just after his conversation with you. Those men in the car outside don't seem to be Jehovah's Witnesses, either."

"You can trust that they are not."

"Well, Mr. Hanlon, you did it; I am convinced enough to look into this matter further and to be careful. We will have to go to my office; it has been over twenty-five years since I did that enzyme research, and my notes are stored in some very old file boxes. Do you have a car?'"

"It's parked about two blocks from here."

Monnell gave Joe directions to his office at Washington and Lee University, telling him to use an obscure parking lot at the rear of his building. He was catching onto the game fast.

Joe and Susan hastily bid farewell to Monnell and his wife at the back door. Susan returned to her thespian routine as they passed through the rear hedge, looking dismayed and clutching her barren leash. From her back porch, Emily Bloom noticed the couple and descended to meet them.

Joe put his arm sympathetically around Susan and addressed the homeowner as she approached. "I'm sorry to bother you again; we didn't find him, so we're going to search for Zeus in a wider area with our car."

"I feel terrible about this. Maybe Zeus will come back this way later. Please give me your number in case I see him."

Joe racked his brain for Monnell's three-digit exchange. It did not come. "We won't be home for awhile. After we finish our search by car, I'd like to stop back by here if we don't find him. Would that be okay, ma'am?"

Touched that she could be of help, she agreed and bid them good luck. Her subsequent vigil for the nonexistent Zeus would keep her out of her liquor cabinet until early afternoon.

CHAPTER 18

"**N**ow this is something new. You do know who this is, don't you?" a disturbed Jeffery Slusher asked as he reviewed the details regarding the week's mission.

"The others don't have to be informed," replied Philip Roberts to his Team Two leader. "I'm not thrilled about it, but I understand it originated with Badger, and Hightower agreed—reluctantly, if I read him right. Seems there's been a little trouble with the man over some financial matters, and he knows way too much." The men grimly faced each other across Roberts' tight, windowless office.

"Okay, but the woman, too?"

"That decision was made by the techs weeks ago, before he was chosen. They want data on any differences between males and females."

"I don't like it, not one bit, but we'll pack another bag."

"Better take two. You never know what else you might find lying around."

"Knock knock," said a voice at the open door.

"Perfect timing, Dr. Pedrozo," Roberts said, waving the new arrival toward one of the four empty chairs in the room, "We were just talking about last week's unexpected developments."

"Ah, you mean the cat," Ernest Pedrozo said.

"And the squirrel. That furry beast almost cost us a bundle."

"Amazing, that one," the doctor said. "It was a one in a million shot. To think that it was found and taken to one of only a handful of men in the country who could discover the actual cause of death—it's astounding."

"Astounding or not, we need some guidance to avoid another one in a million shot."

"You both know that we started our experiments with animals—

mammals. Birds, reptiles, fish, and lesser creatures are not affected. I would suggest that, in the future, an examination of the area be made for ten meters in all directions, including attics, basements, roofs, and trees."

"Would you please assign a tech—technician to that task on every mission, Doctor? We'll help when we can, but our side is becoming more taxed as we expand the scope of these taskings."

"I'll do that, Phil. You may be interested to know that the effects on any body are completely dissipated within four days after death. After that, not even the most knowledgeable specialists could determine the cause of death."

"Could you get me a list of people who have the knowledge you just spoke of? You said there were only a handful."

"Yes, I think I could compile one by the end of the week. You might want to monitor their activities in relation to our experiments, but I would hate to have them end up like that doctor in New York."

"That guy was killed by a local cop."

"Of course," Pedrozo said coolly as he left the office.

Roberts turned back to Slusher, "You all set?"

"So far we're on schedule. We'll be working our asses off all day, then we'll leave tonight. The body—bodies—will be here on Thursday, and you'll see my smiling face again Friday, *if* we don't run into anything unexpected."

"Don't. It's not fun."

After Slusher's departure, Roberts gazed at the file folder containing his one open case: Hanlon. He had closed the week's primary file; after scanning its contents into a secure computer storage program, he had shredded the papers. It was routine, but there would be nothing routine about the eagerly anticipated shredding of the Hanlon file. He would relish the occasion as if it was one of the high points of his career.

For the moment, however, the monument to his failure would have to remain on his desk. Surrounded in his hometown, Hanlon had somehow eluded the roadblocks and escaped once again. Roberts opened the file and picked up the sheet of information from Washington concerning his nemesis. War hero overseas while in the Army, it stated, no further details provided. College graduate, then highly rated policeman with the tiny Sunnyside force. Something to do with the FBI the previous year, no narrative available.

Under different circumstances, Hanlon might have made a valued member of his team, Roberts realized, as the young man appeared to be as qualified as any of the superb people he had recruited from various federal agencies five years before. He would probably do well filling a position on one of the teams, except he wanted Hanlon in only one position now, and that was on the ground, dead.

He sat back, contemplating the time when the odious file would be shredded. Maybe when he finally had Hanlon transferred to his custody he could even shred Hanlon himself, perhaps utilizing some kind of farm equipment. Roberts made a mental note to look into it.

The back door to Wallace Hall, the medical research facility at Washington and Lee University, could not have been more nondescript. White like the concrete walls of the building, the flush steel door was mounted flush to the wall. Inconspicuous and unlocked, Joe and Susan found it to be the ideal entrance.

Inside, they moved slowly up the stairs, keeping a watchful eye for the occupants of the car Joe had seen on Cherry Street, now parked in front of the research facility. Joe stopped at the second floor landing and peered through the wired window within the fire door, then moved into the hallway. The couple turned left and walked to the office of Dr. Salvatore Monnell, Professor of Medical Research. Monnell ushered his guests in without a word.

"I keep all my old papers in here," Monnell said, gesturing toward a narrow door. At eight feet square, the room was large for a storage closet. A coat rack adorned the left-hand wall, facing three file cabinets on the right. The rear wall was over half concealed with more than three dozen banker's storage boxes of various sizes and states of repair. Scrawls in heavy black marker identified the contents. "I believe this is it," the doctor stated, putting his hand on a box labeled "Enzyme 9-O" halfway down the stack.

Joe freed the box and placed it on a nearby worktable. As he was perusing the files for the first time in many years, Monnell began to explain the basics to his untrained colleagues. "An enzyme is a catalyst, a substance that greatly improves the efficiency of a chemical reaction. There are hundreds of enzymes in the human body, carefully regulating the reactions necessary for life from thought processes to digestion, respiration, and motor skills. Without enzymes, all higher life forms would cease to exist."

He pulled a well-worn file from the box. "Here is the project overview. There were four of us: Riley, Parker, DeLuca and Monnell. We examined dozens of enzymes, plotting, cross-referencing, and comparing. The research was unremarkable. Nothing much was expected, as enzymes do not cause health problems. They just plod along, reliably doing their varied jobs. Though we clarified some minor points and uncovered some areas in need of additional research, we found nothing to give the medical community even a minor tremor. Even our discovery of the peculiar properties of the enzyme phosphofructokinase was generally considered unremarkable," he said as he studied page after page.

"Yes," Monnell said after finding a crucial page. "Phosphofructo-kinase catalyzes a chemical reaction that helps regulate heart rhythm in mammals; without it, the heart could not function. The odd thing we discovered about this particular enzyme was its tremendous rate of regeneration. All enzymes are depleted and regenerated at a steady rate. While there are various causes for the depletion, the overwhelming reason is that a small percentage of an enzyme breaks down as it catalyzes a chemical reaction. To use an analogy, visualize the existing supply of an enzyme as a pond, with a small stream of enzyme entering the pond from a regeneration mechanism, and a stream going out as the enzyme is slightly depleted as a result of its acting as a catalyst. A steady state exists, and the amount of enzyme in the pond remains constant."

Joe and Susan nodded that they were still with him.

"As with all enzymes, we can measure the separate components of the phosphofructokinase pond. The level of the pond remains steady, and the exiting small stream is consistent with the depletion expected from the enzyme's function as a catalyst. We found the incoming stream, however," Monnell stated, extending an index finger into the air for emphasis, "to be a torrent, and we were unable to explain why the bulk of the enzyme dissipated so quickly. We measured evaporation, ground seepage, looked for hidden streams, pipelines and pump trucks, but we were unable to come up with an explanation," he went on, continuing the analogy. "We knew the enzyme was being broken down by something, but we had no idea what."

Monnell turned toward Susan as he pulled out another thick file. "Your father was the main sleuth among us, extensively investigating theories to explain this mystery, always coming up empty."

Susan saw that the pages in Monnell's hand were filled with her father's deliberate handwriting and imagined his excitement as he discovered, just two days ago, a clue that might solve the decades-old mystery.

"Did Kenneth tell you anything else, anything at all?" Monnell asked.

Joe thought for a moment. "He said something to the effect that the replacement was okay."

"That is important. It means he verified that the regeneration system was intact, indicating that the mysterious depletion of the enzyme was the cause of death. As far as we know, that has never happened before, in nature or in the laboratory, and we tried."

"He also said I was as lucky as a lottery winner to have given the dead squirrel to him for examination."

Monnell chuckled. "That's true enough. Outside of the four doctors who worked on this project, and Dr. Parker died some ten years ago, there are probably less than a dozen others who would have discovered the cause of death in time, had they been inclined to look. Standardized tests have never been developed, and the enzyme dissipates naturally within seventy-two hours after death, making any subsequent measurements worthless."

"So can you think of anything that would kill this squirrel, a cat, and a Mafia mob boss in this manner?" queried Joe.

"I have no clue," replied Monnell. "The only possible explanation I could give right now is that Kenneth was wrong, that the observations were in error, possibly due to contamination. He did tell you he needed to recheck his findings. On the other hand, though unusual and unexpected, his conclusions are not inconsistent with the mysterious nature of this enzyme."

Joe knew he was running out of ideas and began to play his last few clues. "Have you ever heard of a Dr. 'Z'?"

"No; one of my old professors was named Zeigler, but he died when I was a mere intern, over half a lifetime ago."

"How about Pope, possibly Dr. Pope?" Joe persisted.

"Besides the religious leader, the only Pope I know of was a major general at the head of a federal army that invaded this fair state in 1862. Unsuccessfully, I might add."

"I seem to be having the same success at finding out what's going on," Joe said. "Albany?" he blurted.

"Capital of New York, never been there," Monnell said as he returned the files to the battered cardboard box. As he replaced the De-Luca file, he removed the adjacent folder quizzically. Compared with the others, it was newer and thinner, containing just three sheets of paper. "Of course!" he exclaimed.

"What is it?" Susan asked.

"I completely forgot about this final, strange chapter to our unsolved mystery. Eight years ago, I received a request from a Dr. Gabriel Burke, a professor at Caltech, for a copy of the phosphofructokinase research data. He read a blurb in some obscure journal about our dilemma and became intrigued. He was a physicist, of all things, and had a theory that the unexplained enzyme depletion was somehow caused by subatomic particles. I forwarded copies of several files to him. This last sheet, dated some eight months later, is a letter from Burke thanking me for the information, but stating he had found nothing conclusive and was moving on to other issues."

"It might not be a bad idea to talk to him, if we can," Susan said. "We don't have much else to go on."

"Perhaps we could contact him," Monnell offered.

"No, we can't call him, not from here, anyway," Joe stated firmly. "Remember our friends outside and their penchant for telephones."

"I was thinking of something a bit different," replied Monnell. "Follow me."

D-O-W-N, he wrote in bold letters, then underlined it. Twice.

"Steve, someone to see you," called the secretary of the firm of Brent Parmenter and Associates, Architects. Stephen White stood up from his drafting table and walked into the adjacent room where he met a serious man in a suit and tie.

"Mr. White, I'm Richard Tobin. I need a few minutes of your time."

Guessing that the purpose of the man's visit had nothing to do with building design, Steve led Tobin to the firm's small conference room and closed the door. "What's up?" he asked.

"I'm from the FBI," Tobin stated, holding up his identification, "I need some questions answered, truthfully."

"I talked with two of you guys yesterday; they seemed to go away satisfied."

"Tell me about Joe Hanlon and those two pay phone calls you received on Saturday."

"Look, I already told the other agents that I haven't seen Joe in months. Those calls were from some drunk trying to get ahold of his wife. Said he was from Rhinebeck or Rhinecliff. I never heard from him again."

"That's a pretty good story. Do you want to know why those other agents went away satisfied?"

"Why?" Steve asked nervously, sensing Tobin was not buying it.

"Because they are already convinced that Joe killed DeLuca, and if those calls came from him, it would be proof that he wasn't anywhere near Marlborough at the time of DeLuca's death."

"Maybe," Steve replied, suspicious. "It still doesn't clear Joe of what happened in Sunnyside, and it still doesn't prove I saw him."

"Maybe a thorough investigation of your apartment will indicate otherwise. I can have experts up there within the hour," Tobin bluffed.

Although he had thoroughly cleaned his room and car, Steve did not trust his skills against the wily investigator. "If I wasn't there, and Joe Hanlon snuck into my apartment . . ." Realizing the ridiculousness of the hasty concoction, he relaxed his shoulders in defeat. "Okay, you got me."

"Steve, I'm here because I want to help Joe. I know he didn't murder anyone. I think he was set up by some people working way outside the law."

"Yeah, FBI, like you."

"No, not FBI, although they went around claiming they were Bureau agents, and, no, nothing like me."

"I don't know where he went."

"I'm sure you don't; most likely he didn't tell anyone, not even his father, who he probably paid a visit to yesterday afternoon."

Steve relaxed in his chair. "That was after I dropped him off; I haven't seen him since about one o'clock yesterday."

"He stayed at your place on Saturday?"

"Yes."

"Then you had time to talk. There are a number of things that bother me about this case, but the biggest concerns what happened in Sunnyside. From all I've learned, he was the only one with Elizabeth when she was killed."

"That's true. Joe told me an explosive device in his telephone killed her when she answered a call. He said the call was meant for him."

Tobin scribbled furiously in his notebook, pleased he was getting somewhere at last. They talked for several more enlightening minutes.

"One last thing," Tobin inquired. "Where is Joe's car? It could contain some evidence of value."

"He said he left it in the Newburgh slums, place called Lander Street, locally known as 'Crack Alley,' but it's probably long gone by now."

It was obvious Tobin was not going to accept the statement without a search.

The laboratory on the second floor of Wallace Hall was an open affair, close to fifty feet long and thirty wide, brightly lit by numerous ceiling lights and large windows. Eight men and women stood in the room, clustered into three groups.

"Good morning, Dr. Monnell," said the three members of the closest group, more or less in unison.

"Morning," Monnell replied curtly as he led Joe and Susan along the wall away from the windows to a door at the far end of the room. "Curry," the doctor called in the direction of a group near the door, "Please join us."

A lanky, pale man slightly younger than Joe and Susan responded with a smile.

The foursome entered the adjacent room and Monnell closed the door. "This is one of our newest toys," he explained, waving in the direction of an elaborate array of equipment. "I have found it to be somewhat valuable, but I leave it up to the younger generation to operate it. Mr. Curry here has proved to be quite adept at mastering the intricacies of the system."

"Don Curry," the man introduced himself as he sat in a chair in front of the console. Joe reached out to shake, but Curry's hands were busily occupied turning on half a dozen switches and making adjustments to a rectangular screen only slightly smaller than the windshield from Joe's long-lost Nissan. Though it was still blank, it emanated a faint, gray light that betrayed the fact that it was indeed on. Around the screen, three computer monitors, a video camera, several speakers, and two telephones sat on several computer cases. "I take it that this is not another demonstration, that you really want to use it. These people don't look like they have much money."

"I would suggest that you curb your impertinence if you expect to be awarded a doctorate within the next six months," Monnell said.

"Just one question," Susan said. "What is it?"

"Ha! We really are not very good tour guides today, are we?" Curry asked rhetorically. "This is the Avintcom Communications System, an integration of the Internet with digital satellite technology. This big screen has over six times the resolution of television, and the audio is also superb. The system was designed to transmit very detailed scientific and technical information."

"And it's secure," added Monnell.

"You've never been concerned with that aspect before," commented Curry.

"It has never been important before. Please explain the safeguards."

"The system was designed for both academic and business users. With scholastic piracy and corporate theft on the rise, the security features were considered essential. This box," he said, slapping a gray plastic case the size of a loaf of bread, "is the scrambler that makes interception impossible."

A short beep emitted from a panel next to the keyboard. "Ready to rock and roll," stated Curry, turning to Monnell. "Who are we calling? And do they have one of these things?"

"Donald, please listen, because I am absolutely serious about this. Everything that transpires here is to remain confidential; you are not to tell anyone anything about what goes on here. Understood?"

"Noted and agreed, Doctor," Curry replied.

"We are looking for Dr. Gabriel Burke, hopefully still in the Physics Department at Caltech, and, no, I don't know if they have this equipment."

"Caltech? Sure, they should." He spoke as he typed. Within seconds, an initial connection was completed, and an image of the campus of the California Institute of Technology flashed onto a monitor. "Okay," Curry announced. "We're in, and we're in. Gabriel C. Burke, associate professor of physics, works in the Wattendorf Physics building." He hit a function key. "And their Avintcom systems, three of them. The closest to the physics building is in Coyle Hall, a chemistry building. Their system is currently not in use, which is not surprising considering it's only 7:10 out there."

"What are the options?" Monnell asked.

"This device is not a telephone, so we can't just ring up this Caltech Avintcom. Normally, we would E-mail a request to the good doctor to coordinate the details of a link. The process usually takes a couple of days, a marvelous example of the wonders of modern technology."

"That is not acceptable. We got on quickly enough, and they have the equipment, what else is needed?" Monnell asked.

"We need an Avintcom operator at the other end and Burke. I assume, of course, that these people will not be one and the same; I don't know anyone with more than a master's degree than can operate one of these systems."

"That condition might continue indefinitely if you do not curb your impolitic attitude," Monnell chided mildly. "We don't want to use the phones, and E-mail is too unreliable for an immediate response. Do you think we could safely use the fax lines?" he asked, turning to Joe.

"Well, we only saw one sedan watching the building. While those men might be monitoring voice communications, It's my guess that deciphering faxes is beyond their capability."

"Who is watching the building? Spies?" Curry now showed intense interest in the situation.

Monnell ignored his assistant. "Maybe it's okay, but it still might be slow. No." Canceling one possibility, he seized on another. "Donald, listen up."

"Yes?" Curry replied. "What spies?" he added.

"I'll give you the details later. Right now, I want you to take a printout of the Caltech numbers across the street to the office of the student union. You know what we want; make some calls to establish a link and persuade someone to get in touch with Burke, ideally by walking to the physics building, by telephone as a last resort."

"Spies at Caltech, too?" Curry asked as he set up the system for the satellite link and turned on the video transmission camera.

"Donald, we're counting on you."

"Then I shall return, if I am not captured, tortured, and shot by spies."

Nobody smiled, and the doctoral student beat a sheepish retreat.

The remaining trio looked over the apparatus. One computer monitor indicated sender, receiver, and other parameters of the link. The last line blinked "Ready."

"You really are extending yourself for something that will probably lead nowhere," Susan commented to Monnell.

"I'm glad to help. I wouldn't want to do something like this every day, but it certainly breaks up the routine."

"This technology is amazing," Joe said with some awe.

"Technology itself is amazing, unpredictable, even baffling," Monnell said. "In some areas, we have made amazing advances, in others we have remained stagnant. I'm old enough to remember the late 1950s, when everyone knew that technology was sure to advance geometrically well past the turn of the century. By this time, hovercraft skimming gaily over pristine elevated highways was to have been the norm. Anyone back then who would have dared to predict that such a simple thing as videophones would not be in universal use forty years later would have been considered insane."

The trio waited nervously, staring at their not-so-universal videophone. A short time afterward, a new line appeared on the status monitor. "Ready to Receive" blinked in unison with the "Ready" line above it.

"Ho!" exclaimed Monnell as he sat down at the console. "Looks like Mr. Curry met with some success. I believe it's all set up. I think we just hit the 'enter' key on the keyboard," he said, simultaneously doing just that.

The big screen snapped on, revealing an amazingly sharp image of an ordinary-looking man. "A happy good morning to you," he greeted with a broad smile.

"Good morning. I am Dr. Salvatore Monnell from Washington and Lee University. Are you Dr. Burke?"

"Yes, indeed, Dr. Monnell. It's a pleasure to finally meet you face to face, as it were. And do I see others with you?"

Monnell noticed by the video feedback monitor that the transmission view was too tight, as only portions of Susan and Joe were visible. He adjusted the camera until the monitor showed a good image of all three of them. "Meet Joseph Hanlon and Susan DeLuca. We would like to ask you some questions concerning the files I sent you several years ago."

"I'm happy to meet you both. Susan, aren't you the daughter of Dr. Kenneth DeLuca?"

"How could you possibly know that?" she asked.

"Much of the work Dr. Monnell sent me was compiled by your father. In one of the files, I noticed that one day, perhaps after a telephone conversation with your mother, he took a few moments from his work and, doodling on the back of one of his laboratory data sheets, listed twelve girls names. All were crossed off except 'Susan,' which was circled."

Touched by the story and flabbergasted that the man would remember such an insignificant detail after eight years, Susan was silent.

"Doctor, could you please tell us about the work you did involving our files?" Monnell asked. "Please remember that there is a big difference between 'physicist' and 'physician.'"

"I was working on solar neutrino theory. Neutrinos are illusive byproducts of nuclear fusion at the center of the Sun. Both photons and neutrinos are created by this conversion of hydrogen into helium. Both are very small, essentially massless subatomic particles that travel at the speed of light. Apart from that, though, photons and neutrinos are vastly different. Photons account for visible light and reflect easily off objects, allowing us to see. Neutrinos, however, essentially do not interact with matter; all matter, no matter how dense, is almost transparent to these particles."

"Transparent like glass?" Joe asked.

"Your analogy is essentially correct; neutrinos pass through matter much like visible light passes through a pane of glass, even more easily, as neutrinos are not refracted or diverted in any way. We surmise that millions of neutrinos pass through any given cubic centimeter on Earth in any given second, a constant flow not impeded even by the entire 7,926-mile diameter of our world. As far as we know, neutrinos travel endlessly, passing through stars, planets, and infinite space un-hindered."

Burke went on in his easy manner. "Because it is thought that we have an almost complete knowledge of the physics of solar fusion, we believe we can accurately calculate the exact number of neutrinos which will pass through a given point at a given time. The trick is to verify that number by scientific experimentation and observation."

"But how can you measure something that passes straight through any and all matter?" Susan asked.

Burke grinned. "Your question indicates you have grasped every-thing to this point and brings up that character that occasionally occurs in physics: the Exception. It was surmised that, once in a great while, a neutrino will interact with an atom of chlorine and change it into an atom of argon. To verify this prediction, an experiment was set up deep in an abandoned gold mine in South Dakota, so situated to shield the test from unwanted cosmic interference. There, a large tank was con-structed and filled with a hundred thousand gallons of industrial clean-ing fluid—essentially chlorine. The odds of a neutrino-chlorine encoun-ter resulting in an atom of argon were predicted at one over ten to the power forty-five—one followed by forty-five zeros—which for this particular experiment would have resulted in less than one argon atom per day. Every few days, the tank was swept for the expected neutrino-created argon atoms."

"Individual atoms can be counted with precision?" Joe asked.

"Yes, by utilizing several chemical processes and some extremely sensitive instruments," Burke informed his audience. "And the experi-ment was a success! Atoms of argon were found, and the existence of neutrinos was experimentally proved. There was one problem, how-ever: the numbers were off; only about one third of the expected neu-trinos were observed—two thirds of the countless particles were miss-ing. The discrepancy, known as the Solar Neutrino Problem, has never been solved."

"The experiment might have been contaminated somehow," com-mented Monnell.

"That is always a possibility with a single experiment, but the Homestake observations have been verified by similar underground work by a European team in Italy and a joint Russian/U.S. effort in the Caucasus Mountains. The Solar Neutrino Problem is based on fact and arises from either an incomplete knowledge of the Sun or from errors made in the assumptions concerning neutrino physics, and I believe it is the latter."

Donald Curry finally rejoined the group. "I stayed on the phone until I knew everything was set," he said. "Looks like the transmission was completed without a hitch."

Monnell ignored the cast for a compliment. "Dr. Burke, this is Mr. Curry, who helped us get in touch with you this morning."

Curry bent down and appeared in the transmission frame for a moment. "Hi, Dr. Burke."

"Don, good to talk with you again," Burke greeted.

Curry said, with obvious admiration, "I had to call Dr. Burke at home, and he rushed right over to the Avintcom, which he knew how to operate, unlike the several people I spoke with in the chemistry building."

"I recall it was the neutrino problem that brought you to me," Monnell commented to the physicist, returning to the subject.

"Yes. In the late eighties, a new theory to solve the Solar Neutrino Problem was advanced; neutrinos were categorized as 'low energy neutrinos,' such as those discovered at Homestake, and 'high energy neutrinos,' whose existence was inferred. In an attempt to experimentally prove the theory, a testing facility was set up in the Kamoika Mine in Japan. In the early days of this experiment, I was asked to visit the site and write a short article on the facility. I believe I was chosen because I speak Japanese. To prepare for the trip, I reviewed all available data on neutrino theory, and was drawn into the fascinating world of these tiny particles. By the time I left for Japan, I had completed mathematical modeling that indicated that the new theory was fundamentally flawed."

"I'll bet they didn't like that," Joe said.

"It was not so much a like or dislike, they just didn't pay any attention to me, which is understandable since I was there merely as a reporter and the scientists were very involved in their venture. The article I wrote on the operations in Japan was superceded for publication, and I returned to my routine." Relating the double disappointment, the barest hint of sadness crossed Burke's face.

"A few months later, I found myself with some time on my hands, so I decided to return to the study of neutrino theory. Using the available data, my knowledge of physics, and a great deal of supposition, I came up with a theory of what I called 'phased energy neutrinos' to solve the Solar Neutrino Problem. After this came the difficult part: devising a method to experimentally verify the theory. I worked for several months on potential experiments involving elements, compounds, subatomic particles, electrochemical bombardment, mercerization, valence transfers and just plain hydroxylation without success. Then I delved into the world of organic molecules and after two weeks,

I finally came upon a possible answer. My calculations concerning the potential properties of a pentagonal ring of specific organic compounds, oriented in a certain direction relative to a neutrino flow, indicated that not only would neutrinos break down the organic molecule, but the encounters would deflect the neutrinos themselves."

"I sense we are getting close to our involvement," Monnell commented.

Burke paused and showed all his teeth. "Very close, Doctor. You see, using mathematics and chemical laws, I had deduced the necessary organic ring. I knew it could exist, but did not know if it did. My search began, and thanks to some exceptional groups within the medical community, ended quickly. The unique ring was found in a portion of the organic molecule forming the mammalian enzyme phosphofructokinase, and the best research ever done on the enzyme was done by you, Dr. Monnell, with Drs. Parker, Riley and DeLuca."

"Then what happened?" Susan asked.

"After I reviewed the file Dr. Monnell was so kind to ship to me, I was beside myself. This enzyme naturally depletes, but no one had ever discovered the reason. Of course you know this, Doctor; I do not know the extent of knowledge of you others."

"Joe and I are aware of the findings," explained Susan.

"The figures on the enzyme depletion matched my neutrino bombardment calculations precisely. Interestingly, my mathematics indicated neutrino encounters with the enzyme to be enormous; if interactions were taking place at this same rate as at Homestake, over four cubic meters of argon would be created each day instead of one atom. Although pleased and encouraged, this discovery did not prove my theory, as there might be many other causes for the mysterious phenomenon. Because of the fascinating, annoying property of neutrinos that allows them to pass through everything, the best solution seemed to lie in the creation of a 'mirror.' I predicted that if a large quantity of phosphofructokinase were refined, then crystallized on a flat surface, salted with a specific mix of subatomic particles, and maintained within an electromagnetic field, the resulting plate would serve as a neutrino reflector. This mirror, acting as an umbrella to protect a test sample from the rain of neutrinos, would have allowed us to prove without a doubt the existence of phased energy neutrinos, in all probability solving the Solar Neutrino Problem."

"You speak as though this never came about," Monnell observed.

"Due to some sad economic realities, it didn't. Although we put together some detailed designs, construction of a neutrino mirror would have employed vastly expensive and sophisticated manufacturing techniques, involving several technologies that have yet to be developed."

"I noticed you used 'we' and 'us' in your last few comments," Joe observed.

"You are very perceptive. Yes, during the last few months of my work I was assisted by a fellow physicist, Dr. Alfred Zeichner, and three students: Mark Robel, Kathleen . . ."

"This Dr. Zeichner," Joe interrupted. "Did he have a nickname?"

"I believe he was generally known to the students as Dr. 'Z.'"

The comment caused a stir between Susan and Monnell, but Joe's mind was reeling. "Please tell us more about Dr. Zeichner," he requested, his voice barely above a whisper.

"He was a hardworking young physicist here at the University, although somewhat ambitious and impetuous. I introduced him to my theory concerning neutrinos, and we worked together for three months. We might still be working together if he had been successful at NASA."

"NASA?"

"Dr. Zeichner was excited, even fanatical, about this project. When we reached an impasse concerning the funding necessary to construct the neutrino mirror, he approached several scientists at NASA with the phased neutrino theory and its potential effects on manned interplanetary travel. You see, the Earth travels around the Sun at a relatively constant distance, so humans have been exposed to the same concentration of neutrinos for millions of years. If my theory is correct, our bodies have adapted to this flow, as evidenced by the biological regeneration mechanism for phosphofructokinase. As we move further from or closer to the Sun, though, the neutrino concentration changes. Mars receives less than half the neutrino density we get here, while a person on Venus would be exposed to double the flow we consider normal. That is a cause for concern because a body's phosphofructokinase regeneration system might be overloaded; the enzyme might not be replaced at an adequate rate to compensate for the loss from the increased neutrino bombardment, and serious health problems could result."

Something was forming in Joe's mind, but it was as of yet nebulous and incomplete.

"Although the personnel at NASA were somewhat intrigued, they declined our proposal, stating that the phased neutrino theory was extremely speculative, that manned interplanetary travel had an extremely low priority, and that the technology needed to create the neutrino mirror and prove the theory was too expensive. The reflector we designed was a hexagon about one and a half meters on each side, and the various processes necessary to manufacture that small object would have cost several hundred million dollars."

"No wonder NASA did not want to take up the banner on this one," Joe commented. "Doctor, please humor me. Would it be possible to use one of these reflectors to apply a lethal dose of neutrinos to a person?"

"I see you have a predilection towards fantasy, young man. Sometimes great scientific discoveries are based upon such outrageous questions, but in this case you are somewhat off the mark. For scientific purposes, the number reflected would be astoundingly large, but as an addition to the natural neutrino flow it would be insignificant, not dangerous at all."

"How about a large concentration of these reflectors on a single point?" Joe persisted.

"Because of my love for theoretical calculations, you seem to have drawn me into your fantasy world." Burke sat in silence for a few moments. "Taking into account the properties of the enzyme and the neutrinos and the characteristics of the mirror design . . ."

Those in Virginia watched Burke mentally ponder the problem for twenty seconds.

"To deplete an individual's phosphofructokinase to a lethally low level would probably require a concentration apparatus the size of Aricebo. To function, the entire reflector array would have to be maintained within an electromagnetic environment from the time of manufacture. If power were to be interrupted for even one instant, the molecules of the crystallized enzyme would be randomized in a period of time measured in single-digit nanoseconds. The structure would be useless, and would not in fact reflect either neutrinos or photons, as it would be instantaneously transparent, at least if built according to my specifications, utilizing two panes of specially manufactured glass."

"But it would be possible to build such a structure?" Joe pressed.

Burke frowned. "Even if the technology to build it were available—and it isn't—the cost would be well into the billions of dollars."

A vexed Monnell decided to wind down the conversation. "Dr. Burke, we appreciate you taking the time to talk to us today—"

"—but I have just one more question," Joe finished. "Is Dr. 'Z,' Zeichner, still at Caltech?"

"No, he left us nearly seven years ago, quite abruptly. It was just after I closed down the project; as a matter of fact, it was two days before the fire."

"Fire?"

"It was a heartbreaking day for me. A freak gas leak destroyed my office and laboratory. Twenty years of records, including all of my neutrino files, were completely consumed. Arson was suspected, but never proved."

"Was Zeichner a suspect?" Joe felt compelled to ask.

"Of course not. He was a dedicated assistant and we parted on the best of terms. He was three thousand miles away in Washington at the time of the tragedy."

"Continuing with my one more question, Dr. Burke, do you know where Dr. Zeichner is now?" Joe smiled, attempting to be pleasant.

"No, and it's baffling," Burke said. "He just dropped out of sight. From my perusal of the rosters of applicable scientific associations, I take it he is no longer a physicist. The last communication of any type I had with him came in the form of a Christmas card his wife sent me over five years ago. There was no return address, but the postmark indicated it was sent from Manchester, North Carolina."

"Thank you, Dr. Burke," concluded Monnell. "You have been very enlightening—and indulgent."

"Any time, Dr. Monnell."

As Curry was shutting down the various components of the Avintcom, Monnell turned to him. "Thank you, Mr. Curry. Did you happen to catch sight of our friends outside?"

"You mean the spies? As a matter of fact, there are two men in a car across the street, watching everyone who enters and leaves this building. I really would like to know what gives here."

"I promise I will give you the sordid details later. Right now, I believe you are somewhat behind in your thesis."

Acknowledging the unpleasant fact with a nod, Curry returned to his work.

Monnell turned to Joe and Susan. "Quite a conversation, wasn't it? Did you make anything of it?"

Joe spoke first. "I might be wrong, but I think this Zeichner is the Dr. 'Z' we're looking for, and that he's somehow mixed up with the government. I think he stole Burke's ideas, if not his actual files, and has come up with some poison or weapon that uses neutrinos."

Susan was skeptical. "Maybe there's something there, but my father and your friend weren't killed by any concentration of subatomic particles. Speaking of that, what is Arecibo?"

"I believe it's an astronomical observatory," Monnell ventured. "Follow me and we'll find out."

They descended to the entry level of the building and Joe and Susan followed Monnell to a back office. The plastic plate next to the open door proclaimed the proprietor to be "Dr. Charles Johnston, M.D.,

Head of Neural Research."

In the manner of an old friend, Monnell addressed the burly figure behind the desk. "Chuck, what is Aricebo?"

It did not have to be explained that Eck's avocation was astronomy. A small brass telescope stood on a tripod by the rear window, and large framed photographs of Saturn, the galaxy in Andromeda, and an unidentified comet hung on the walls. On top of a credenza was a globe, not of the Earth, but of the Moon.

"As a hack astronomer, that's a little out of my league," he replied gaily. "It's the world's largest single-dish radio telescope, in Puerto Rico. Wait, I have a picture."

From a walnut bookcase containing medical references and several stacks of journals, he pulled out a well-read copy of Carl Sagan's *Cosmos*. Referring to the index, he turned to his target page. Two photographs pictured a giant silver bowl set into a valley, dwarfing several peripheral buildings. "It's a thousand feet in diameter and covers about twenty acres. Multiple dish arrays are more in style now, and to be honest their capabilities and accuracy are better, but Aricebo is much more impressive."

"What is it made of? Is it a secret installation?" Joe was desperate, and sounded so.

Eck frowned. "The surface consists of aluminum panels, and, no, there is nothing secret about it. The dish has served as a set for several feature movies, and guided tours are available."

"Please excuse my young friend," Monnell said as he put a hand on Joe's shoulder. "He's a little agitated today." After ushering Joe and Susan out of the room, he led them back to his office.

"Just one more thing to check," Susan said.

"What?" Joe had about two dozen things on his mind, but no single one stood out.

"Manchester, North Carolina, of course. We must try and locate the illusive Dr. Z."

"Just a moment," Monnell requested as he slipped out the door. He returned less than a minute later with a travel atlas.

Utilizing coordinates provided by the North Carolina index, they quickly found Manchester, a small circle located less than an inch northwest of the somewhat larger circle of Fayetteville.

"I believe we have located your Holy Father," Monnell said.

Seconds later, Joe and Susan found it too. The feature immediately to the south of Manchester was a tiny airplane symbol, identified as Pope Air Force Base.

CHAPTER 19

G iving the policeman outside his window a nod, Richard Tobin lit up another Marlboro as he was passed through the southern 9W roadblock on his way out of Marlborough. He had talked to two people in the town after his visit to Stephen White; one had been grim, the other far too happy.

The Hanlons of Idlewild, including the recent additional residents, Charlotte Hanlon Fleming and her young son, were somewhat put at ease by Joe's visit to his father the previous day, but were still extremely worried. In his conversation with Albert, Tobin had verified much of the information that Steve White told him, and picked up a few new bits of knowledge that provided him with a little more insight as to just what the hell was going on. So Joe was armed now, with his soon-to-be-ex-brother-in-law's .45 automatic, Tobin thought. Well, that was probably a good thing, with all of the shit flying around, but Joe's father was concerned that it might get him into more trouble than it was worth.

On the other side of town, the atmosphere had been entirely different. For a man who had lost his job, his wife, and a tussle with Joe Hanlon, all in less than twenty-four hours, Michael Fleming was in a surprisingly jovial mood. After Tobin demanded that Fleming engage the safety on his rifle, he listened to the fanciful story about the heroic engagement between the criminal and his rival, although Tobin had his own opinion on which of the two was the lawbreaker. Tobin left the deer-filled bi-level with nothing except contempt for the moron with whom he had spoken and, because Fleming proudly boasted about the reporters he had talked to, the sure knowledge that his lies would soon pollute the land, eagerly shoveled up by journalists near and far for ingestion by the general populace.

Neither Albert Hanlon nor his ex-employee had been able to give

Tobin any information concerning Joe's missing Nissan. Although he knew that the odds were against finding it, he drove on toward Newburgh—the city of Newburgh, he reminded himself; he was already in the town.

After checking his map, Tobin turned left and drove toward the Hudson River. Stately homes on lots as large as ten acres greeted him as he proceeded through the section of the town known as Balmville. This can't be right, he thought as the car passed one elegant house after another. Shortly after, he went straight through a traffic light and the change in scenery became immediately apparent. This is it, he knew: the city of Newburgh. As if to punctuate his realization, his car began to vibrate from wildly uneven pavement and unfilled potholes. Never had he experienced a wider variation in neighborhoods over the span of one mile on the same road.

Years previously, before temporary Newburgh residents—outsiders known as "urban pioneers"—had fled the area for somewhere more hospitable, a group of historic preservationists had prevented Liberty Street from being paved, arguing that the ancient brick street was an essential aesthetic component to the Historic District. Acquainting himself with his surroundings, Tobin saw that the heaving, broken road perfectly matched the streetscape, although in a book-length description of the place he would have never utilized the word "aesthetic."

Amidst the ruined buildings, trash-choked gutters, and shattered sidewalks littered with broken bottles of beer and other, cheaper, alcoholic beverages, were the residents. Those visible were for the most part men, standing on the corners, sitting along the chipped brick walls of the decayed buildings, and lying in the doorways of empty storefronts devoid of glass. Some stood in small groups, talking idly and some stood alone, gaunt stares on their faces, doing nothing in particular in a daily repetition of what they had done for years.

Tobin negotiated a maze of unmaintained one-way streets, each lined with buildings in various stages of disrepair, finally coming upon Lander Street. He drove the length of "Crack Alley" three times, searching in vain for a red Nissan Sentra. Following this expected disappointment, he searched the side streets, alleys, and driveways of several abandoned shells that looked as if they had been transported from Stalingrad after the battle, then had been left to deteriorate for another fifty years. Graffiti was everywhere, on buildings, signs, hydrants, and abandoned, mutilated automobiles, displaying a wide assortment of names, obscenities, and illegible scrawls.

Increasingly frustrated and depressed by his surroundings, Tobin widened his search area. He crossed over Broadway, the wide, once-proud main street of the city that had become just a broader, more visible version of Crack Alley. This is even worse, he thought, as the larger buildings along the main thoroughfare seemed to have fallen further into decay than their smaller, more numerous counterparts. Behind one such dilapidated structure, Tobin focused on another wreck. It was a Nissan Sentra, or at least what had been a Nissan before it had been converted into a pile of refuse. The former conveyance was sitting on its discs at the corner of a large, weed-choked municipal parking lot originally built as a convenience for long-departed patrons of long-departed shops along Broadway.

Tobin parked his car and rushed to what he hoped was his objective. The car had been thoroughly ravaged from its tires, which were gone, to its roof, which had been briefly used as a trampoline before it lost its resiliency. The front passenger's door had been kicked in and was hanging open; the driver's door was gone. Despite innumerable cracks and gaping holes, out of one of which protruded a brick, the windshield still clung to its frame; all other windows and mirrors were completely obliterated. Having failed in their efforts to understand the intricacies of the support bar, the vandals had completely bent back the hood over the shattered windshield before they raped and pillaged the engine compartment. The trunk was savagely ripped open, which, considering the other devastation, did not seem unusual to Tobin, unaware that the key to the car had been provided. Several empty beer cans had been added to the trunk; everything else had been removed.

What was not missing from the interior of the car was smashed. All of the seats had been removed, along with the steering wheel, radio, and the door to the empty glove compartment. If this had been Joe's car, Tobin thought, it was the most thoroughly compromised suspect vehicle he had ever seen.

Although the license plates, registration card, and all other means to immediately verify ownership were long gone, Tobin was nonplussed. After taking several photos of the vehicle, he examined its vehicle registration sticker, still attached to pieces of the lower left windshield. Insuring that the longer number on the tag matched the identification number riveted to the front of the dash, he separated the sticker from several shards of glass and pocketed it.

Now what? he thought. As he was in no mood to apprehend city of Newburgh car thieves, he vetoed taking fingerprints. He checked the floor, a task made easier due to the lack of seats, and found nothing except a copious amount of broken glass. Dutifully, he collected three samples, not believing for a moment that the evidence was worth the cost of the bags that contained it. He looked over the outside of the vehicle. What the hell was I expecting, anyway? he wondered just before he saw the red vinyl tape on the right side panel.

Carelessly, he peeled back one piece, and found a hole. A bullet hole, he realized, if twenty years of experience had taught him anything. Carefully, he removed the other piece of tape and bagged it. Tobin stared at the orifices and paused. If the car were native to Newburgh, it would not be unusual to pick up a couple of bullets, and the fix was also befitting the give-a-shit atmosphere. If it were Joe's car, however, and he picked up the speed holes somewhere else, applying the tape just to hide them during his flight north, that was something else altogether. Tobin took two photos, then went to his car and returned with his toolbox.

Inside the car, Tobin unscrewed the vinyl molding around the front seat belt door penetration, then pulled away a plastic panel, revealing the interior of the car's body. Taking out a small flashlight, he peered into the cavity. There they are, he rejoiced, spying two misshapen chunks of lead at the bottom of the space. He retrieved the bullets and placed them carefully into evidence bags.

He found nothing else, but what he had discovered satisfied him. He started his car and made his way to Broadway. Just past the decrepit city hall, he turned south and soon put the wretched city behind him. He would never know how fortuitous the location of the car had been, as the Nissan's last driver, originally bound for a location some miles distant, had taken his booty less than a thousand feet before it ran out of gas.

"What are we doing here?" Susan asked disgustedly.

"I though you might want to see the lair of these purveyors of evil menkus," Joe said. "My map shows that this street, Letcher Avenue, leads to the road out of town. After all, it's your tax dollars at work." As Lexington's two colleges were adjacent to one another, they traveled directly from the campus of Washington and Lee University to the grounds of the Virginia Military Institute. Academic buildings lined the street to their right; to the left lay a large parade field, beyond which was the cadet barracks, a four-story fortress that looked like a poor combination of castle and gothic cathedral, rendered by an architect who had previously designed nothing but prisons.

"First, menkus is a word that transcends adjectives; that's why the word came into being. Second, you are obviously ignorant of what went on here," Susan stated as she took in the surroundings. "Although everyone else knew what the correct course of action with regard to the admission of women to a public school, the male club here used every sleazy legal means they could to postpone the inevitable.

"Women were admitted, though," Joe stated, searching in vain for a girl among the several cadets he sighted strolling on the sidewalks on their way to or from class. Sighting an Institute seal instead, complete with founding date, he did a quick calculation. "It broke a tradition of over a hundred fifty years."

"Yes, after the geniuses here dredged up every stereotype in the book. Women couldn't possibly undergo the stress of their freshman hazing rituals, called the 'Rat Line,' they argued, but that was only the first item in a long list that included physical conditioning, sports, military training, and even living conditions in the barracks. Everything had to be changed, they bemoaned, with all things made easier for the delicate girls. I think the bastards actually believed that garbage; most probably still do."

"But women can't compete with men on an equal basis in most physical activities."

"Don't take that as fact. Given two bell curves on the physical prowess of men and women, the female curve might be somewhat lagging, but there would be a great deal of overlap."

Joe maneuvered the car down a hill, stopped at the intersection with the main road, then turned left. "Susan, maybe you won't believe this, with me being a man and all, but I think it's a good thing that women are finally being allowed to attend V.M.I., more so for the males. Nobody can deny that times have changed, and the fact that the Institute wanted to hold itself as the last bastion of outmoded ideals didn't make it the smart thing to do. Chauvinistic attitudes are no longer an asset in our society; some may get by without getting hurt by them, but they certainly don't help, and have led directly to many a man's downfall. Now these cadets can see that women are people too, capable of doing perhaps quite a bit more than they gave them credit for."

"But the things the administration did skewed the whole process."

"Give them a little time. Most will come around eventually, and the rest will die off. You might look to West Point as an example. Women still aren't totally accepted in the Corps of Cadets, but it's about a hundred times better today than it was at the beginning. From what I've heard, the guys back then, especially the bastards from that last all-male class of '79, made it unnecessarily tough."

"It still burns me."

"Okay, but we have our own unnecessarily tough, maybe impossible, problems to face," Joe stated, finally willing to discuss their next move. "I don't think this Zeichner is going to treat us anywhere near as well as Monnell."

"If we can even find him. I can't imagine his name being in the phone book if he's involved in some kind of secret project. Even if we could find him, what would we say?"

"How about 'Hi, Dr. Zeichner. We just learned you stole information on neutrino activity from Dr. Gabriel Burke, and we want to ask you a few questions concerning your current classified activities,'" Joe offered.

"Not likely. Besides, we have no proof that anything we've learned relates to what happened in New York."

"Susan, it relates big, I just don't know how yet. The references to 'Dr. Z' and 'Pope' might be taken as coincidences, but not when everything else is taken into account. Those people in New York went to incredible lengths to cover up what I stumbled upon, what your father analyzed. That brought us down here, where things have finally started to fall into place. There's something going on with these—neutrinos."

"I don't know. That thing Dr. Burke was talking about, that dish a thousand feet across and the billions of dollars it would take to build it. It's unbelievable."

"Even I have a tough time swallowing that. The government has done some strange things over the years, but the idea of a huge satellite dish built to kill one person at a time is beyond anything I imagined. Even if it were possible, it sure would be one big son of a bitch to hide. I guess it could be in space."

"You're in fantasy land again," Susan stated as Joe turned onto Interstate 81. "An object in space hundreds of times larger than anything out there would certainly have garnered some news. The Space Shuttle may have had its secret military missions, but putting up something like that wasn't one of them."

"Idea duly scratched," Joe conceded. "Perhaps it could be in the middle of nowhere, maybe in Nevada or Arizona."

"So why is Zeichner working at Pope Air Force Base, which is about as far from nowhere as you can get? Look at the map; there are roads and towns everywhere around there."

"I don't know; maybe it's his headquarters."

"There's also the money issue. A few billion dollars may be small potatoes compared with the entire Defense budget, but it still has to be accounted for."

"I don't know," Joe repeated, less sure of his ideas than ever. Still, he urged the car towards North Carolina, not having a clue as to where else he might go.

Half an hour later, they left Interstate 81 and headed for Richmond along Interstate 54. The pair traveled in silence. Sometimes in such taciturn circumstances, usually when alone, Joe reflected on the loss of his child and his wife—the never-married woman now beside him— and the life he briefly envisioned a decade before. It wasn't a daily agony anymore, but once in a great while, he would think about his dead baby that he never knew, who would now have been a playful nine-year-old boy—or girl.

"Susan," he began haltingly, painfully unsure. "I need to know what happened to us. I understand more about the abortion now; it's the way things are done, I guess. But why did you reject me?"

She did not answer immediately, as the thoughts and feelings of those years past, so long just under the surface, ascended at last. "I didn't reject you, or our child. I loved you, deeply, and I embraced the baby as the dazzling product of our love."

"Wha—what?" Joe stammered.

"I rejected myself. After you left the hospital the night I told you I was pregnant, I was still in shock over the news. It was a life-changing event, but the more I thought about it and you and our relationship, the more I came to celebrate it. I was gloriously happy imagining our life ahead in that last hour."

"Last hour? Before what?"

"Before my father paid me a visit. I told him the news, about my newfound joy, but in return he offered nothing but a scowl. For the next three hours, he stood over me as I lay in bed, offering me his vision of how my life should be, and it did not include a child, at least not for many years. It wasn't a question of morals to him, and it wasn't my relationship with you; he always liked you, before and after. He was obsessed with me going to school, then getting on a fast career track. He was mourning the loss of Mother as well as severely disappointed over my brother's recent career choice, but there was no excuse for what he did. While he continued his long talk, he administered several medications to me, then just before I passed out ordered me to sign a consent form for an abortion. Even though I was no longer a minor, he could have used his influence at the hospital to have the operation done without my consent, but he wanted to pull the idea from my mind as well as the child from my body."

"Damn it," was all Joe was capable of saying as he pictured the man he had known for so many years in a vastly different light.

"The last thing I remember was the sight of the clock as I was wheeled from my room by the healers who had turned into midnight abortionists. The next morning, I woke up alone, empty, without a mother to run to or a father who understood. And I absolutely could not face my would-be husband whose baby I had, by my drugged scrawl of a signature, just killed. I edged out of my depression and away from the medications after several months, but by then you were long gone. I proceeded to follow the plan of my life outlined by my father."

"Susan, I could have helped."

"I doubt it. If you recall, you were deep in guilt yourself because of my mother's accident."

He nodded.

"In that brief, happy time before the abrupt entry of my father, I had chosen two names, one for each sex. I don't remember where I picked up the information during the dark, drugged hours that followed, but I am sure our child was a boy. His name was Sheldon. Sheldon Hanlon."

Heedless of any police cars that might stop to offer assistance, Joe stopped the car on the shoulder. He reached over and hugged Susan, tightly, and together they wept over their lost child.

COL(P) David A. Powers, Jr., his title indicating he was a full colonel in the U.S. Army and on the list to be promoted to brigadier general, was a soldier's soldier, but not a whole man. His career spanned twenty-four years, starting at West Point, where he was the first in his class to elect to be an infantryman, those sixteen classmates with a higher academic standing generally choosing to join the Corps of Engineers. During his career, he had commanded troops in two wars, three uprisings, and one "incident" in a place he could not legally talk about. It was during this last command that, thanks to a particularly vicious piece of enemy ordnance, his left foot was almost blown off. Although his life and foot were saved, his first three toes were not. In their place, he was given a Purple Heart and was awarded, along with one other member of his group, the Distinguished Service Cross, the Army's second-highest decoration.

The Pentagon was Powers' current assignment, and in the rarified air of the office of the Army chief of staff, his rank and decorations didn't count for much. After completing an assignment as the commanding officer of an infantry brigade, he had been "promoted" from being in charge of almost two thousand battle-ready soldiers to heading a group of five, including himself and his civilian secretary. Instead of looking out of his office window at a vista of the Rocky Mountains, His small office in "C" Ring had an unobstructed view of the next ring over.

Life outside the world's largest pentagonal structure was pleasant enough, though. With a loving wife and a son doing well in his Yearling year at West Point, he was generally content with a little dinner each night, a little television to catch up on the day's events, and a little fishing on weekends. Anyone who had been watching him over the previous ten minutes, however, would have thought him anything but content. He was sitting in his study, remote in hand, frantically changing channels on his television in an attempt to coax more information out if the box concerning a particular news story, when the phone rang.

"Powers here," he blurted.

An electronic voice asked if he would accept a collect call from "Jubilation," a word he had not heard in years. Eagerly, he took the call.

"Colonel Powers, this is Joe Hanlon."

"Joe! Nice to hear from you," he forced. "What's new?"

"Sir, you told me once that if I ever needed anything, you would be glad to help."

"I remember that vividly. We were sharing the same room in an Army hospital. I meant it then, and it still goes. Let me see if I can help you out now. Are you in a public place?"

"Uh, not really. It's a phone booth, but it's fairly out of the way. Why?"

"Because your name and photo just made the national news."

"Shit!"

"An appropriate word, Sergeant. It was on a cable network; I don't think it has been reported on any of the broadcast stations yet, but I'll keep checking after our conversation. Have you ever been arrested?"

"No, sir. Why?"

"Because the photo they're using looks like a mug shot."

"It dates from my first days as a policeman," Joe explained.

"The report said you are a recently fired cop suspected of being a secret member of the of the Bonnelli crime family, and that you had a tussle with the FBI while trying to help your boss, the dead don. After that, it seems you went crazy, killed your girlfriend and another man in New York, then killed or captured yet another girlfriend, almost did away with your whole family, and are now an armed and dangerous fugitive, a threat to us decent Americans everywhere. So what is really going on?"

Joe went through a narration of his situation, attempting to avoid being characterized as a lunatic.

"So you decided to call for advice before you stormed the gates of Pope Air Force Base in your quest for the evil Dr. Z. I call that a smart move. I used to fly out of Pope quite a bit when I was at Fort Bragg, right next door. Those Air Force guards are very big and carry large guns, and don't take kindly to fugitive murderers. I haven't been there in several years, but I imagine that the guards are even bigger and carry larger guns now that it is also a B-2 base."

"B-2 bombers? Stealth bombers?" Joe asked.

"One and the same. The base has proven to be quite a boon to the area's economy. I hear the hanger housing the planes is quite impressive, too. As you might expect, security surrounding the most expensive airplanes ever built is somewhat tight."

"We're headed down there anyway; I don't know where else to go."

"Who else makes up 'we'?"

"Damn it, I wanted to keep her out of this. It's the girl I 'captured or killed.' She's the daughter of the man killed in New York—not Bonnelli, Dr. Kenneth DeLuca. She ordered me to take her with me to try and find out who killed her father."

"Okay. If you were thinking of turning yourself in, don't. The characters after you sound nasty, and don't doubt that they might just have the power to deliver you to them, wrapped nice and neat. That comes from me personally, not as an officer and defender of the Constitution. If you really think there might be something at Pope, maybe I can give you a contact."

"That would be nice, but it would have to be someone—understanding. Not like most West Pointers at all."

"That eliminates most of the people on my list, but you're right. Most of my classmates at Bragg are a touch anal retentive." The colonel paused while he searched his mind. "I dealt with quite a few civilians, too—government types, and a few businessman in Fayetteville, but—damn! I think I know just the guy, if he still lives in the area. Eugene Evans is his name, and, sorry, he is a West Pointer, from my father's class in the late forties. They were roommates and good friends. That was back in the days before the Air Force Academy opened, and he went into the brand-new Air Force while my father, like most of his classmates, went Army. He retired as at lieutenant colonel and moved to Fayetteville a few years later. I visited him several times when I was with the 82nd, but haven't seen him in almost five years."

"I don't know; do you think he could help us?"

"His history in the area points to it. He worked at Pope for a few years as a government civilian, then did some kind of service contracting there. He's in his mid-seventies, so I'm sure he's retired now."

"Can you put in a good word for us?" Joe asked.

"I'll find out if he's still living down there and attempt to advance a letter of reference if he is. Call me back in a couple of hours."

"I'll do that, sir. Thanks."

"Joe, I know you can take care of yourself, but I'm going to tell you to be careful anyway, and I also want you to take care of that girl traveling with you. Try not to get into any more trouble. I'm not going to play Richard Crenna to your Rambo; I might not be around to pull your ass out of the fire."

"Yes, sir."

"I'll talk to you in an hour or two." Powers concluded. He hung up the phone and began searching for a telephone number. His wife joined him after a few minutes. "Dear, I could hear you mumbling from the kitchen for quite a while. Were you on the phone?"

"Janice, you know I don't plan to take up talking to myself for at least another five years."

"Who was it?"

"Just someone I used to work with, now a noted television personality."

"Plastic."

"For that we need lab technicians?" Richard Tobin quipped. He and Janine Wolf were alone in the FBI laboratory in White Plains. Hands gloved, she was holding up the small triangular shard Tobin had given to her with a pair of tweezers. It was obviously a piece of plastic.

"That's not what I mean," Wolf retorted. "It's plastic explosive; there is definitely residue of expended C-4 plastic on this sliver of— plastic, which looks like it came from some kind of equipment casing."

"Like a telephone?"

"Possibly."

Tobin was pleased, as it confirmed what Stephen White had told him with physical evidence. It was also proof that the so-called investigation by Philip Roberts had been geared toward something other than solving a crime. "That came from the murder scene in Sunnyside."

Wolf quickly put the tweezers down on the counter before she dropped them. "That girl was shot," she said, drawing her information from the preliminary report that had been faxed to her by Roberts.

"This indicates differently, doesn't it Janine? I think we're dealing with some bad folks here, and I mean in this very building, at least they were here until a few days ago."

"Is Harvarnik involved?"

"I don't think so; he's just an asshole headed in the wrong direction." He related his conversation with White.

"So if Elizabeth Brooks was killed by an explosive device, and it can be shown that Hanlon was nowhere near the scene when DeLuca was killed, then he's in the clear."

"If you call being pursued by a group of murderous federal agents being in the clear. Besides, I'm sticking my neck way out on this one, and I want to be as prepared as I can when the axe starts to fall. I need more."

"I have more," Wolf said. "First, the mustard jar. There were prints of two individuals. I came up with one 'yes' and one 'no' when I ran them through Washington, the Big Program." By "Washington," she was referring to the vast computerized fingerprint database maintained at the FBI's Hoover Building, the "Big Program" of which compared requests to not only criminals, but to all prints on file, including those of individuals with past military service and federal employees. "The 'yes' was Joseph Charles Hanlon; the 'no' was possibly a grocery store stock boy or checkout clerk."

"Only if supermarket employees have a habit of mixing their wares with toothpaste to fill in bullet holes." Tobin explained the circumstances surrounding the discovery of the jar.

"You've been a busy boy."

"What else do you have?" asked Tobin tiredly. He could sense Wolf was also exhausted. It had been a long day for both of them.

"The two-by-four. Luckily, the wood was weathered, making it smooth in spots. Again, I found indications of two individuals, and the Washington program again found one 'yes' and one 'no ident.' The match was Kenneth Alphonse DeLuca. And, no, the unidentified prints from the jar and the board do not match."

"Let me show you where I picked that up," Tobin said as he pulled an envelope of snapshots from his pocket. He went into detail about his discovery of the lumber and his theory concerning its use to pry open DeLuca's basement door.

"You of course know the DeLuca murder is Harvarnik's case," Wolf said.

"I know. I hope to have enough evidence to make a presentation to Ottoway tomorrow. Hopefully, I can convince him to both help Hanlon and not chop my head clean off."

"That will take a heap of convincing."

"I have more that might help. I picked up a couple of things today that I need you to look at," he said, reaching into his jacket pocket.

"No way, my man," Wolf insisted before she caught sight of the items. "It will have to wait until tomorrow. I am totally beat, and any examinations I might make would be suspect anyway because my eyeballs don't function well after twelve hours on the job."

"Okay," Tobin conceded, drawing an empty hand out of his pocket. "I guess it's been a long day for both of us."

"In addition to my other large workload, I'm handling competing Hanlon cases. Try not to make a habit of this."

"I won't, believe me," the agent said as he opened the door, simultaneously removing pack of cigarettes from his shirt pocket.

"What's that? You don't smoke."

"I've been meaning to start and finally got around to it," Tobin replied through the closing door. It was the same line he gave to everyone regarding his reacquired, odious habit. Puffing eagerly away as his heels clacked down the empty hallway, he returned to his office.

At his desk, Tobin laid plans for the next day. An examination of the two bullets he had discovered in Joe's abandoned car might point somewhere, he thought, but what would really help would be some identification of the prints of Roberts and his crew. He thought long and hard on where the members of the covert group had gone, what they had touched. He briefly thought of his successful coup with the urinal handle, and just as quickly discarded it. Still, there had to be something. . . .

"Looks like we're getting somewhere at last," Thomas Harvarnik stated triumphantly. He was standing in the doorway to Tobin's office, smiling, a newspaper in hand. "Have you seen this?"

"What?"

"Hot off the press," Harvarnik stated, slapping the newspaper on the desk as if he were striking Tobin himself. "Looks like your buddy is more of a character than we thought." The paper was one of the New York tabloids. Directly beneath the banner, in letters all of three inches high, was the headline: "Mob Cop on Murder Spree." Directly under that was a large blowup of the photo of Joe Hanlon that Tobin had seen in the papers Upstate, the one that looked like a mug shot. Incredulous, he opened the paper. The article, by a reporter named Brenda Stone, explained Hanlon's nefarious deeds in great detail, with the added twist that the murderer was "allegedly" a Bonnelli family hit man who took an undercover job as a Sunnyside cop to help his boss. The article wound up with a grisly supposition on the fate of the missing Susan DeLuca, and a warning to readers everywhere to be on the lookout for the notorious criminal.

"What the hell!" Tobin exclaimed, quivering. "You believe this shit?"

"We're looking into it. It does provide a clear motive for his actions. Having his boss die under his watch, whatever the cause, would definitely have ended his career with the Mafia—permanently. Under the strain and none too stable to begin with, he goes crazy and kills a few more people. Makes perfect sense."

"If you say so," Tobin said, realizing there was no point in trying to reason with an utter moron.

"This also supports us in another way. With all this publicity, it shouldn't be too long before somebody spots him."

"Can I keep this?" Tobin requested, too tired to pay heed to his rule to never ask anything of the man standing before him.

"Hell no, get your own. This is going up on my wall." Harvarnik snatched the paper and disappeared down the hall.

"Asshole," Tobin said, but not loud enough for anyone else to hear.

CHAPTER 20

With increasing foreboding, the couple traveled through the night, straight south on Interstate 95. "You're not a spy are you?" Joe forced in an attempt to ease the tension within the car.

"Maybe," Susan replied. "Why?"

"This whole thing reminds me of that movie we rented once, *North by Northwest*. Remember Cary Grant is accused of murder and goes traipsing around the country with that blonde, trying to figure out what the hell is going on."

"Yes, but she turned out to be one of the good guys after all." She recalled the incident fondly. It was during the months when the two of them were dating, back before their lives fell apart.

"You were the one who noticed that barest glimpse of Bannerman's Island through the window of that train going up the Hudson. I hope you've retained your keen eye for detail; we'll probably need it."

The reference sparked another warm memory in Susan's mind. About a month before the accident, they had taken an illicit trip to the island and its huge ruin of a castle. Joe packed a small rubber boat and a picnic lunch and paddled the two of them across the narrow strait to a small, stony beach. Otherwise deserted, they walked, talked, explored the giant shell of the ornately decorated building, and made love in a secluded clearing on the far side of the tiny island.

Joe noticed the thin smile on her face. "Hey, you're looking too happy for someone I 'killed or kidnapped.'"

Her smile faded. "My brother is probably worried sick."

"We'll drop him a postcard or something tomorrow, after we figure out our next move. We had better think of something good, because I have a feeling your picture is going to appear next to mine in quite a few newspapers and broadcasts. That's going to put a crimp in obtaining supplies."

"I guess they found my car, even though they shouldn't have for at least a week. I had it hidden well, but then you had to tie your brother-in-law to a tree less than half a mile away."

"I guess I could have killed him and buried the body, or I could have brought him with us, but they still would have made a search, no matter how much he's disliked."

"Here's the North Carolina line," Susan said as the car crossed out of Virginia. "Let's start looking for another phone. It's been a little over an hour since we left Richmond. I'm still leery about calling someone who works in the Pentagon. Are you sure he's okay?"

"Believe it or not, Susan, the situation Colonel Powers and I were in was worse than our current predicament. I trust the man absolutely."

"There are a lot of people we may trust but can't call, though, because of phone taps and records traces."

"The details of the mission I was on with Powers are certainly still highly classified, and we weren't part of any regular military unit. It would take someone at the highest levels in Washington to connect us."

"Somehow, Joe, that doesn't put me much at ease."

They found a telephone about two miles south of Halifax, in front of a gas station closed for the evening. Although the phone was near the road, it was concealed by two scraggly pines. Susan waited in the car, engine running, while her partner made the call.

Susan considered where the couple might have been had the accident never taken place. With her wits about her and her mother's support, her father would have been held at bay and she would be a wife and mother now. Like Albert Hanlon, Joe would probably have gone to Marist and would now be working a steady job in the family business, perhaps squabbling with his brother-in-law, but certainly not running for his life, his body covered with scars from incidents he would not talk about. She would not have her brilliant career in Boston, but what had that gotten her? Plenty of work and money, stress and heartache. Perhaps, she thought, it was not too late for a change.

The passenger door opened, and Joe settled into his seat. "We have a place to go. His name is Eugene Evans, an old Air Force officer who worked as a civilian at Pope for over ten years. Colonel Powers says we can trust him. I don't know if he can help us, but the colonel assured me that meeting him won't hurt."

Susan pulled back onto the nearly deserted highway. "Where do we go?"

"He lives alone in a house a few miles from the Air Force base. I wrote the directions down."

"I just hope we aren't met by Lucifer's version of the welcome wagon when we get there."

"Colonel Powers told Evans a little about my military service, vouched for my character, and said we were in deep trouble, but that's it. We'll have to fill in the gaps when we get there."

"Some gaps," Susan sighed. "Still, I guess it's worth a shot; he ought to know something if he worked at the air base." She reached out and took Joe's hand in hers.

"What's this?" he asked, gently squeezing her hand.

"I've just been thinking," she said in a slightly melancholy tone. "About our situation, and about life in general."

"'Life in general,' huh? Sounds pretty deep."

"Well just don't let it go to your head. This isn't a fucking joy ride we're on."

"What kind of joy ride?"

"*Fuck-ing*," she pronounced without hesitation. "In this particular case the word may be considered a simile to 'merry,' 'happy,' 'amusing,' 'festive,' and 'revelrous.' Would you like further clarification?"

Joe looked at Susan, his face registering several battling emotions. Briefly, love reigned victorious.

———————

"You should have shot that bastard the first time you laid eyes on him." Ronald Hightower's normally calm demeanor and steady moral compass were both wavering a bit. He was standing alone in his library with a white-knuckle grip around the receiver of his secure phone. "What do you have?"

"The publicity will probably flush him out, but right now there's just too much static in the reports," Philip Roberts stated. "Dozens of possible sightings have been reported to FBI offices nationwide. Add to that a shitload of calls from people who are just plain scared and want more information, and the usual assortment of nuts claiming to be Hanlon and confessing to the murders. I've had the calls transferred to the Hoover Building, where a task force is being assembled. Eric Kauffman is in the air at this moment, headed in your direction to act as our liaison with the feds."

"That puts you a man short down there," Hightower said.

"You know we've had team members out on sick leave before, even take a short vacation or two. Remember, we've been down here for five years. The security situation at the project is well under control."

"How is the remote team doing?"

"The mission *teams* are on station," Roberts corrected. "Everything is set, although, as you might have expected, there was a bit of grousing about the target."

"Couldn't be helped. Badger convinced me that the man is as much a threat to the project as Hanlon is—or was."

"I'm still considering Hanlon to be a threat until I throw his twitching body headfirst into—"

"I don't need to know the details, I just want this over with. I don't like headlines like this," Hightower said as he stared at the front page of a New York tabloid.

"When we really get rolling on this thing, the headlines will be a lot bigger, although we won't be able to read most of them."

"That's true, but by then the remote teams will be well out of the way, if they are used at all." Calmed somewhat, Hightower sat down. "How's Zeichner?"

"Couldn't be happier. The way these tests have been going, we should be fully deployed for static targets within six months and moving targets within a year, eighteen months at the most. He's not upset with last week's mission, and does not consider Hanlon a threat, although he knows he could have been."

"Good. Philip, I think things are going moderately well, but I will sleep easier when this Hanlon situation is completely behind us."

"I'll do my best, sir," Roberts concluded.

Finally a "sir" out of the man, Hightower thought as he hung up the phone. First time in years. Maybe Roberts had been humbled a little by his recent mistakes. If so, it would be the only good thing to emerge from the mess.

———————

Joe squinted at his map in the dark and gave directions to Susan. "Looks like we want to take Exit 56 and make our way to Route 23, headed north out of Fayetteville."

"Joe, do you have any ideas about what we can do if we don't find anything down here? This trip may well prove to be a colossal nothing. This is the Air Force; we can hardly waltz in and start asking questions about some secret project, assuming there even is one."

"Beyond our safe arrival at Eugene Evans' place, I don't have any plans," Joe said. "Susan, as far as the cops and the FBI and the press and everyone else are concerned, you are not involved in my problems. I think you should consider going back to your life. I'll bet when you left you didn't tell anyone in your company you would be away for a few days, and as far as they're concerned you're AWOL."

"With all the publicity, I'm sure they think I'm dead. I might rectify that notion after we finish at our next destination, but until then I want to see what develops."

"And if nothing happens?"

"You said I should consider getting back to my life, but I can't because I'm already here. For better or worse, being here with you right now *is* my life. If nothing happens here, I'll make a decision on where to take my life, and only then."

"It would be crazy to come with me. I have absolutely no idea where I'll be going. I might be on the run for years. More probably, I'll be captured, perhaps tomorrow, maybe in a few months, but it's almost inevitable."

"Maybe it would be crazy," Susan agreed. She already considered herself more than a little bit insane for having come this far with Joe. Going farther, though it would have been unthinkable to her a few days before, now seemed within the realm of the possible. The decision whether to resume her normal life or remain with Joe should be a no-brainer, she knew, but it wasn't.

They drove on into a night illuminated only by the red and white lights of the traffic, finally leaving the interstate for a business route where the main lighting came from motel franchises, fast food outlets, and car dealerships. After a few miles, they crossed the Cape Fear River and drove through Fayetteville. A few miles outside of town, they traveled through an unguarded stretch of Fort Bragg's 148,000-acre military reservation, and the concept of dual police jurisdiction briefly passed in and out of Joe's thoughts.

"Where to now?" Susan asked as they left a small community with the pleasant but uninspiringly common name of Spring Lake.

"We want to take a left at the light in the next town, which should be in about two miles."

"Were you saving this as some kind of goddamn surprise?" Susan asked sharply as they approached the sign welcoming them to Manchester. "Next you'll be telling me that this Evans lives right next door to Zeichner."

"We should be so lucky," Joe said as Susan slowed for the turn. "From these directions, he lives in a small house on a large lot some distance outside of town. We need to head out about three miles."

After five miles over three roads, they saw the mailbox indicating 23 Rimrock Road. The headlights of the car flashed by the house as Susan made the turn into the driveway. It was a small ranch-style home with an integral one-car garage on its right side. There were two front windows, one to either side of the front door. The anemic lawn was liberally spotted with bare patches of sandy soil. Although they could not see the rear yard, it ended at some point at a stretch of tall pines, above which could be seen a dull glow, as if there was a city a few miles distant through the trees.

Susan parked next to an old Subaru. Nervous, they got out of the car and walked together to the door. It opened before they could knock.

"Joe and Susan, I presume," the old man wheezed as he ushered the pair into the house and closed the door. "I'm Eugene Evans." Although slightly taller than Joe, the man was thin, even gaunt, his bulk having deserted him along with most of his hair. He wore casual trousers and a simple shirt, both of which hung from his bony frame.

"Sir, I'm Joe Hanlon," he said as they shook hands. "This is Susan DeLuca."

"No titles are used within these walls," he stated as he took Susan's hand. "Please just call me Gene." He guided them into the small living room containing a worn love seat along the interior wall and a well-used leather easy chair in one corner. Two end tables held lamps that illuminated the somewhat dingy surroundings. "Please sit," he said, then settled into the soft leather of his chair. "So, young David tells me you are in some trouble."

"Sir—Gene—we, I mean I, am in a huge shitload of trouble," Joe began haltingly. "We appreciate you allowing us into your home, but I want you to consider my situation carefully before you decide whether to help us. I have been accused of two murders that were committed by others last Saturday in New York. Recent news stories have portrayed me not only as a ruthless killer, but also as a hit man for the Mafia and a psychopath. Right now, there's a nationwide manhunt underway to apprehend me."

"That certainly is more than I was expecting," Evans said as he stood up uneasily. "I think you better get into your car . . ."

"Yes?" Joe asked as the elderly man completed his exertions to assume an erect posture.

". . . and move it into my garage. This is a quiet road, but let's not take any chances, shall we?"

In minutes, the car was nestled in the small, cluttered space. After closing and locking the overhead door, the two men reentered the house and resumed their seats and the conversation.

Evans looked at Susan. "And what is *your* role in the alleged infamous deeds of this young man?"

"My father was one of the people murdered this past Saturday. I'm with Joe to try to uncover the real killers."

"Ha! So you're here on a mission, not just running away. That makes the situation much more exciting. Well, young lady, from what I heard from David, Jr., you couldn't have picked a better companion." Evans turned his eyes toward Joe. "Did you know David recommended you for the Medal of Honor after you saved the mission, and his life, over in—over there," he corrected himself after a quick glance at Susan. "He said it was finally vetoed for political reasons by more timid higher-ups at the Pentagon."

Although it was news to both occupants of the love seat, it was more of a shock to Susan, as Joe already could not respect his former commander more highly.

"Young David's father, David Senior, and I were roommates at the Academy," Evans reminisced. "He had a spectacular career and retired as a lieutenant general in the Army; I was not so fortunate in the Air Force. He died tragically about a year ago, of cancer." He coughed several times, deep, guttural coughs that reached to the bottom of his lungs.

Joe looked at Susan, and both wondered what they could possibly gain from the wreck of a man sitting before them.

"The Fates brought you here for some purpose. Please tell me what that might be and how I might be of assistance," Evans stated after he recovered somewhat.

"Last Thursday morning, I stumbled on some kind of government operation at the house of a mobster named Victor Bonnelli," Joe began. He continued the chronology, explaining his discovery of the squirrel, DeLuca's findings, the deaths of Elizabeth and the doctor, and his subsequent activities in Marlborough hiding from the law and meeting up with Susan.

Susan then picked up the thread, relating their meeting with Salvatore Monnell. Using the physician's analogy of the pond and the streams, she explained the unique and unsolved mystery of the massive rate of depletion of the mammalian cardiovascular enzyme phosphofructokinase. As she outlined the complex facts, Evans settled deep in his chair and closed his eyes.

"The depletion of phosphofructokinase was not explained by it possibly acting as a catalyst for two or more separate chemical processes, perhaps widely distinct from one another?" Evans asked, his eyes still closed. Although weary, he made it quite clear to his guests that he was not only listening, but understanding.

"Dr. Monnell did not mention that specifically," Susan replied, "but he did say his team had exhausted every possibility."

"So Monnell was stuck for an explanation." Evans said.

"He hadn't a clue, but we then had a long conversation with Dr. Gabriel Burke, a physicist," Joe said. "His theory is that the enzyme is depleted by tiny particles from the Sun called neutrinos."

Evans slowly opened his eyes. "Yes, I know about solar neutrinos, one of the byproducts of nuclear fusion."

"You do?" Susan asked in wonder.

"I began my career in the Air Force as what they call today a 'hot fighter jock.' After Korea, I was downed while testing a new fighter in Maryland. While I was one of the lucky few to survive such mishaps, my flying days were over, so I found another branch more suitable to my reduced physical capabilities. To prepare for a career in that field, I went back to school and in the late fifties received a doctorate in nuclear physics. I haven't used the degree in decades, but I still manage to keep up on some of the developments." Exhausted after the long explanation, his chin dropped slightly. "So what more did Burke tell you?"

"To test his theory, Dr. Burke designed a neutrino reflector made of crystallized enzyme to isolate test subjects and prove the existence of what he called 'phased energy neutrinos,'" Joe explained.

"Which he thought would solve the Solar Neutrino Problem?" Evans asked.

"Yes," answered an astonished Susan, realizing, like Joe, that there was an extremely sharp mind within the frail body before them.

"What were his results with the reflector?" Evans asked.

"He never built it," Susan stated. "He said the complex methods to create it were prohibitively expensive, and that some of the processes were yet to be devised."

"After that, I pressed Dr. Burke into telling us what it might take to kill a person, or a squirrel, using his reflectors," Joe said. "He stated that it would take an enormous array of his 'mirrors,' arranged like a gigantic satellite dish to apply a lethal concentration of neutrinos to any mammal."

Evans fixed his gaze on Joe, then Susan. "Did Burke mention any specifics with regard to the manufacture of his reflector?"

Susan filled in the details. "Besides telling us that its construction was beyond current technology, he said that his device would have been in the shape of a hexagon about a meter and a half on a side. He also said that it would be extremely sensitive, that if it were not constantly maintained in an electromagnetic field its surface would break down and turn transparent."

"I see." Although his body looked just as weary, his eyes seemed to burn with a renewed intensity. "How big was this fictional array supposed to be?"

"Hundreds of feet in diameter, probably utilizing tens of thousands of reflectors," Joe replied. "According to Dr. Burke, it would cost billions of dollars. I know it sounds crazy . . ."

"Wait," Evans cut him off. "What exactly brought you down here?"

"At Bonnelli's house, I heard one of the so-called FBI agents mention someone named Doctor 'Z.' We found out in Virginia that Dr. Burke's main assistant in his neutrino research, a man named Alfred Zeichner, had that nickname, and that he lives here in Manchester, at least he did four or five years ago. Have you heard of him?"

"No," Evans stated. "That's intriguing, but there has to be more."

"Also at Bonnelli's, one of the members of the mysterious team said something like 'we need to get these things to Pope.'"

Evans addressed the young couple calmly, the barest hint of a smile on his face. "So you came to the middle of North Carolina to search for some gigantic, excruciatingly expensive weapon that killed a mob boss, along with two furry bystanders, by a massive concentration of solar neutrinos. Further, the huge weapon is so secret that a murderous band of renegade government agents is hard at work to silence you. Have I got it right so far?"

"Well . . ." Joe and Susan began together, stumbling through a response.

"That's one crazy story, totally insane," Evans stated, as he rose slowly from his chair. "Probably wouldn't even make a decent novel; it's too bizarre. Follow me."

The pair stood and followed the old man as he ambled through his kitchen and opened the back door. Haltingly, he stepped outside and walked into the darkness. Matching their host's sluggish pace, Joe and Susan remained slightly behind him.

The lawn soon gave way to pine needles as Joe and Susan entered a pine forest, except it wasn't a forest, they soon discovered, but merely a strip of conifers about a hundred feet wide. They finally joined a nearly exhausted Evans at the other side. Twenty feet in front of the trio, paralleling the trees, was a chain link fence, fifteen feet tall and topped with triple helixes of razor wire. Uniformly posted every fifty feet were signs that warned "U.S. Government Property: No Trespassing."

Hunched over, hands on his knees, Evans explained their trip. "This is the boundary of Pope Air Force Base. That," he said, lifting a hand from his knee and pointing to an immense building in the distance, "is Pope's B-2 bomber facility. From what you told me, I now know it is also your neutrino weapon. I always wondered why they built the damned thing."

Joe and Susan stared across the two flat, open miles that separated them from the floodlit structure. Nearly eleven hundred feet in diameter, with exterior walls seventy feet high, the circular structure was completely covered with a dome whose peak rose two hundred feet above the surrounding terrain. It was the largest dome they had ever seen; it was the largest dome anyone had ever seen.

Amazed at the sight of the facility, but baffled at Evans' conclusion concerning it, Joe turned to the man. "We're looking for a dish of some kind," he stated. "That dome can't be it; if anything, it's upside down."

"Have you so quickly forgotten the unique property of solar neutrinos?" Evans asked. "Where is the Sun right now, this late at night?"

"It's on the other side of the world, nearly directly beneath us, but the flow of neutrinos is not impeded one bit," answered Susan excitedly.

Like a flash, the meaning dawned on Joe, and his mind was filled with a thousand questions. "But how does it work? Who else knows about this? When was it built?" he asked in quick succession.

"I don't know everything, but I can tell you a few things. It will have to wait, though," Evans said, his exhaustion painfully evident. "I hate to be a bother, but I must go to bed. I usually don't remain up past nine o'clock." He turned toward the house, then checked his wristwatch, the face of which was dimly illuminated by the distant glow of the Air Force base. "Damn, look at the time; it's midnight."

TUESDAY
14 APRIL

CHAPTER 21

In a daze, he looked around. He was in the center of a vast metal bowl, a giant wok at least a mile across, its distant edge distinct against the coal black sky that gave no hint as to what was illuminating his view. The surface he was sitting on was hot and quickly getting hotter as the entire receptacle fell slowly through space like a dead leaf, gently undulating in wide arcs as it descended. For some reason, he could not stand or roll or even move his hands to escape the heat that had increased to a temperature well past what he thought he could bear. As if struck by a powerful wind, the huge bowl abruptly inverted, giving the man certain hope that he would be free of the burning caldron, and he welcomed the precarious prospect of freefalling through the blackness as a more desirable fate to being fried alive. But the alternative was not to be, as he remained inexplicably affixed to the searing steel despite the pull of gravity and his intense efforts to extricate himself. It wasn't long before the entire conveyance became white hot and he briefly wondered why he was still alive.

It was a soft rustling that woke Joe Hanlon; there had been no noise at all in his dream. For the third time in as many days, he reacquainted himself with an unfamiliar room that served as his nightly refuge. His eyes briefly scanned the sparsely decorated room as it came back to him. He was in a small bedroom in the house of Eugene Evans. In North Carolina. A few miles from a large building shaped like an inverted bowl that might play a significant part in his immediate future.

Susan sat at the foot of the full-size bed putting on her blouse. "Good morning," he said to her back.

"Hi, Joe," she said as she stood. "How did you sleep?"

"I've had better nights, but it could have been worse," he replied, sitting up in the bed, certainly more comfortable than the floor. "Thanks for not kicking me out of bed."

"You were zonked when I came out of the shower. I figured you needed a good night's sleep, but it doesn't look like you got one; you're covered in sweat."

"Bad dream," he explained.

"Well, the bathroom's clear, at least it was five minutes ago. Colonel—Doctor—Evans is still asleep. Do you think he can help us? He seems so weak."

"He's very sick," Joe agreed as he stood up. "He certainly knows something, but the next step is going to require a lot more than that."

"Still, we have to try."

"*I* have to try," Joe countered in a low voice as he opened the bedroom door and headed for the shower.

"After you get dressed, I'll meet you in the living room," Susan said sternly, not missing Joe's attempt to exclude her.

Ten minutes later, showered, shaved, and dressed, Joe joined Susan on the small couch.

"So what do we do today?" Susan asked lightly, her attempt at gaiety failing to cover her apprehension.

"I don't know," replied Joe. "I'm not even sure we're in the right place, despite Colonel Evans' assurances. It's the dome. I surmised its existence, looked for it, and found it—maybe. Actually seeing that huge building only made the situation more surreal. I find it hard to believe that such an enormous structure is at the center of some super-secret government weapons project, capable of killing—what?—one person at a time."

"Believe it," Eugene Evans said as he haltingly made his way into the living room, a tattered bathrobe draped over his emaciated body. "The big dome is nicknamed the Beehive by those who work under it because its ceiling consists over sixty thousand electrified hexagonal panels exactly like the one you described." He seated himself in his leather chair. "That part of the story is no secret. As part of the construction of the building three years ago, the work on that ceiling was one of the largest electrical contracts ever awarded in this state."

"Good morning, Dr. Evans," Susan greeted.

"Remember, that's Gene," Evans corrected, wheezing. "I don't believe that just having a degree should change one's name forever. West Point was much harder to get through than attaining my Ph.D., but there's no eternal attachment to my name for that."

"Gene, you seem to know a lot about this project," Joe said. "Were you involved in it?"

"Not directly, but I'm aware of a great deal about . . ." Cut short by a bout of phlegmy coughs, Evans caught his breath. "Until I retired two years ago, I worked at Pope as a civilian contractor. The decision that brought the stealth bombers here was made in Washington a few years before that when the Air Force finally negotiated with Congress to increase the number of B-2s from twenty-one to thirty-three planes. Part of that decision involved a political plan to share the wealth by increasing the number of bomber squadrons from one to three, each based in a different state. Whiteman Air Force Base in Missouri, the original B-2 base, is presently at full strength with eleven planes. After several weeks of congressional infighting, Pope was chosen as the host for the East Coast squadron. The West Coast base has yet to be picked; rumor has it that it's going to be either March or Vandenberg in California."

Joe and Susan forced themselves into patient silence. With a calmness born of finally obtaining information and an excitement that came from anticipation as to what would come next, Susan took Joe's hand in hers.

"I've always been a big supporter of the Spirit Bomber," Evans continued. "It's by far the best airplane ever built, the finest weapon in the Air Force inventory. It disgusts me that it has become a universal sport to rail against its cost. The Pentagon officially puts the per-plane cost at 1.3 billion, and some analysts, using several convoluted techniques of mathematical manipulation, put it at 2.5 billion. Even if the higher number is to be believed, however, I think it's well worth it. What everyone forgets is that the B-2 was only an innocent bystander to the largest waste of tax dollars in American history. It stemmed from a political promise by presidential candidate Ronald Reagan, who savagely berated his opponent, Jimmy Carter, for canceling the production of the B-1. Upon assuming office, Reagan was informed of the secret development of the vastly superior B-2, so the infamous decision was made to build both. Decades of governmental assistance to needy individuals pale in comparison to the resultant corporate welfare. Without the B-1, we would now be well on our way into producing the original quota of over a hundred Spirits, at a cost of under $600 million per plane."

Another fit of coughing was met with respectful silence by the pair in the love seat.

"Forgive my digression," Evans pleaded. "I know you're here because of another outrageous, perhaps criminal, expenditure of tax money. The Beehive was built to house the full squadron of B-2 bombers under one mighty roof and as a classified experiment in itself. The official story, couched in vague terms, is that the building is a high-tech prototype, constructed as the ultimate deterrent to electronic and visual surveillance. Offering the best security possible to the ultimate in aviation technology, no type of sophisticated remote sensing is said to be able to penetrate the dome. It's a nice theory."

"But you don't buy it?" Susan asked.

"I had my doubts even before your revelations last night. For one thing, those panels use too much electricity, and are two damn sensitive. I've never seen the phenomenon myself, but from what I've heard, about a dozen panels blow out each year, just as you described: the electric flow is interrupted and they turn transparent, allowing five-foot hexagons of sunlight to filter down to the hanger floor. A simple electrified grid would probably work just as effectively at foiling attempts at surveillance."

"So you believe the dome is some huge weapon?" Joe queried.

"I do now," Evans said. "Your description is so accurate and the official explanation is so unsatisfactory that I find myself willing to accept the fantastically improbable."

"But how does it work?" Susan asked, edging forward in her seat.

"That's a question much more difficult to answer." The old man closed his eyes to ponder the problem. "If the purpose of the dome is to reflect neutrinos toward a central point, then somewhere, deep underground, a concentration of sorts is reached. Somehow, that agglomeration of particles was organized into a dense, parallel flow and directed at your mobster. What was his location?"

"He lived in Sunnyside, a small town about thirty miles north of New York City," Joe said.

"Were there any other fatalities besides the man and the two animals?"

"None that I'm aware of," replied Joe. "There were people all around him, outside a radius of perhaps a hundred feet, but no one else seemed to suffer any ill effects."

"That rules out the possibility that the flow was directed straight from here to there," Evans concluded. "The angle from here to New York is much too shallow; other people and animals would have been caught in the beam for hundreds of feet in either direction. The neutrinos concentrated here had to have been reflected from a location that increased the angle to a more perpendicular orientation. A satellite in the proper position might suffice, as would a more remote earthbound location."

"Maybe Albany?" Joe offered.

"Yes . . . that's it!" Evans exclaimed, abruptly opening his eyes. "Why did you say that?"

"It was the last clue I overheard at Bonnelli's house last Thursday.

'Looks like things went okay at Albany,' one of Roberts' people said. I thought about driving up there to investigate, but everything else led us down here."

"You can't get to Albany by car," Evans stated. "Not the one they were referring to. It's not well publicized, but a small Air Force facility was established at about the same time the Beehive was going up—near Albany, Australia, about as close to the other side of the world from here as you can get without swimming in the Indian Ocean. Officially, it was set up as a long-range flight test station for the B-2, but to me it has always been one of the many things in this project that didn't make sense—until now."

"So these deadly neutrinos . . ."

"Were created at the Sun, traveled at the speed of light to Earth when it was night here, then passed through the planet to the dome. Here, they were concentrated and deflected to Australia, then were instantaneously reflected through the Earth a third time, precisely aimed to pass straight up through a sleeping Mafia boss, killing him and, collaterally, a cat underneath his bed and a squirrel in a tree directly overhead." Excited by the revelation, Evans wheezed heavily.

Joe and Susan exchanged grim glances. To Joe, the path was clear, though the tangled terrain that closed upon it from all directions was thick with deadly perils.

Evans slowly rose to his feet. Standing quickly, Joe took a hesitant step toward the old man. "Colonel Evans—Gene—I don't comprehend all of this, but I do know that the men who killed Bonnelli, my fiancée, and Susan's father are almost certainly under that dome. I have to attempt to pay an unscheduled visit on those individuals. I know the odds against success are long, but at this point, I don't see any alternative. I hope you understand and won't try to stop me."

Though unsteady on his feet, Evans looked into Joe's eyes with an unwavering gaze. "I understand the situation more than you know, more than anyone knows. I'm not going to stop you, I'm going to help."

Stunned by the offer of assistance that he could only characterize as bizarre, Joe remained motionless as Evans slowly walked toward the kitchen.

"We'll talk more after we eat," the old man said. "I don't get to play host very often. It would be my pleasure to make you breakfast. I have a knack for cooking up marvelous concoctions in my wok."

It had been a thoroughly exhausting three days for Andrew Weiss.

The funeral on the previous day had been the highlight of the week, as expected, although it could not yet be said if it had been the pivotal event in his quest to gain the upper hand. It was a decidedly odd affair. No one with Bonnelli blood was present, yet only "family" members were there, others who might have attended having decided there was nothing to be gained from being seen at such a dangerously open ceremony. Something was to be said about non-attendance, everyone present thought at least several times during the three-hour extravaganza, as the press, police, and FBI were each well represented, though kept at a distance, fenced off from the proceedings. Though there was scattered reminiscing among the crowd of a hundred fifty or so, those present quickly turned their backs on the man being buried and the collective conversation became focused entirely on the future. Not a tear was shed.

Weiss was not totally accepted by those present, but he did command some respect from his close relationship with the deceased. Though he heard the absence of the son occasionally whispered about as he carefully made his way through the assemblage, no one indicated dissatisfaction with the current leadership, either denying or blissfully unaware of the fact that there was no current leadership to speak of. Nicky's nominal representative at the gathering was Joey Messina, who also quietly worked the crowd.

He had seen Messina three other times since their departure from Vito's Bar, and felt his presence at several other of the countless encounters with Bonnelli businessmen over the previous sixty hours. The meetings had gone fairly well under the circumstances, but had taken their toll; since Saturday, Weiss had slept a total of twelve hours.

It's almost over, he thought as he gazed in the direction of his television, using it as a meditation device as he let the sights and sounds of a mindless government conspiracy drama wash over him, hearing and seeing but not registering a single bit of the action.

"Mr. Weiss?"

"Yes?" the lawyer responded, somewhat unawares. "Oh, Karl, come in," he said to Karl Kastner, already six steps into the room.

"Television, sir?" Kastner observed, surprised to find his boss supine before an obviously mediocre teleplay.

"I was flipping around trying to find any new items on Bonnelli. I was not successful," he said with satisfaction. "Looks like that batch of stories last night on the funeral was the end of the line for the current media circus train."

"I did the same earlier. Except for that silly story about the policeman, I think it's dead," Kastner stated as his gaze turned toward the screen. An ominous figure, obviously an enemy of some breed by his expression, dress, and the sinister way he was lit, was pointing a pistol at the head of the light-haired, well-dressed, benignly lighted protagonist. "Sir, I don't know what this is you've settled on, but I can see *fauxfire* coming a mile off."

"Okay, Mr. Kastner, I'm game," Weiss said, seizing the opportunity to revel in a few more seconds of down time. "What is that?"

"It's standard fare in this type of show. The bad guy has a gun pointed at the helpless good guy. Bam! A shot rings out, but surprise, surprise, it's the bad guy who is shot by a third person: another good guy, a love interest, a reformed bad guy, et cetera."

"Amazing," Weiss said as a shot was heard and the dark, evil one fell to the bottom of the screen. The camera panned dramatically to the shooter, a woman whose seductively posed legs and stiletto heels had not thrown her aim off one bit.

Disgusted with the predictable melodrama, Weiss clicked off the television with a finger to the remote. "Time to get back to work."

"I have the figures on the transportation companies you asked for," Kastner said as they walked to the desk.

"Good, good," Weiss muttered as he perused the first three pages of the thick file. "I have meetings scheduled with four of these company heads this morning. I need to get a few things straight before I head up north this afternoon." The buzz of his telephone cut into his last syllable. "Yes?"

"Mr. Weiss, there are two detectives here to see you," the voice said.

"Send them in," Weiss stated, then addressed Kastner. "I've been dodging these guys since Saturday; maybe it's time we find out what they plan for our noble heir."

"Do you wish me to stay, sir?"

"Absolutely," Weiss replied. "You certainly will be involved when Nicky comes back to New York."

It was Mutt and Jeff who entered, a young, short man following a gentle soul of six-six. Both were dressed in nearly identical suits and ties similar in pattern and only slightly different in color.

"Good morning Detective Nash," Weiss said to the older, taller gentleman.

"Mr. Weiss, thank you for seeing us," New York City Police Detective Larry Nash said with the barest wisp of sarcasm. "This is Curtis Moler," he introduced.

"Karl Kastner," Weiss said, ending the introductions, though no hands were shaken. "Have a seat."

Nash began the interrogation. "Weiss, we need to have a sit-down with your client, Nicholas Bonnelli. We've been after him for days, as you certainly know. For some reason, he's been avoiding us; missing his father's funeral was certainly an indicator."

"What's he done?"

"He killed two people in broad daylight, for starters," Nash stated coolly.

"That was self-defense and you know it."

"That may be, but we'd like to hear the story from the sole survivor of the incident."

"I think you can tell what happened from the forensic evidence," Weiss said flatly.

"Still, Mr. Weiss, three men died," Moler piped in. "I think you can understand that we would like to talk to him, just to get the record straight."

"Is he charged with anything?" Kastner ventured.

"We have a warrant to bring him in on a weapons charge," Moler replied.

"That is crap!" Weiss bluffed. "You know Capizzi had a permit to carry, and had at least two pistols registered. Mr. Bonnelli just used one of them when he was savagely attacked with an automatic rifle."

"We have doubts about that," Nash said with a thin smile. "It would be a simple matter to clear up, though. All Mr. Bonnelli needs to do is bring us the gun so we can verify the serial number and perform a ballistics test."

"I don't know Mr. Bonnelli's exact location right now, but I'll see what I can do to satisfy you gentlemen," Weiss said.

"Please take my card," Nash offered.

"I'll try to get back to you in the next couple of days," Weiss said.

"They should have better things to occupy their time," Kastner said after the policemen's exit.

"Certainly no legitimate case is as important as a big headline-grabbing mob hit," Weiss said cynically. "We're just fortunate that it was the one thing in Nicky's life he was actually justified in doing."

"And the weapons charge?"

"If we can't get him off completely, he'll only have to pay a fine," Weiss predicted.

"What was that about not knowing Nicky's location?"

"What I said was *exact* location. He could be in the can, taking a long stroll around the grounds, or fishing in the Hudson for all I know."

Kastner soaked up the tip. "Of course, sir."

"Which reminds me, I have to get to those meetings if I'm going to make it to the Farm before nightfall."

"Hope you bring in a good crop," Kastner said.

———————

"I find it ironic that my work on the lowest level of the military food chain might provide you access to its apex," began Eugene Evans, once again seated in his recliner. Slightly recovered after a brief post-breakfast rest, his sallow features and ravaged frame still created doubt in the minds of the man and woman who sat before him that his ability to aid them would last long. "'Might' is the word I can't emphasize strongly enough," he went on slowly. "This is an extremely perilous undertaking you are considering, with possibly lethal consequences. I have my own reasons for wanting to see you succeed, but the decision to undertake this mission must be yours alone. I am immune from danger; you are not."

"Whatever happens, the outcome has to be better to a life on the run," Joe stated firmly. "I'm committed to going ahead."

Susan remained silent.

"When most people consider the Defense budget, large weapons systems acquisitions and funding of major unit deployments come immediately to mind," Evans said. "Behind these headline-touted expenditures, however, is a vast support structure. By far, more tax dollars are expended on salaries, routine operations, and maintenance than on new hardware and publicized deployments. At Pope, like all other military bases, the government pays for just about everything; even shopping, entertainment, and religion are subsidized. Running the show are military personnel, government civilians, and contractors. Until my final retirement two years ago, I was a member of the last group, employed as a project manager responsible for facilities maintenance."

"So you maintained the dome?" Joe asked.

"No, on two counts," replied Evans. "First, it wasn't completed until after I retired. Second, the facilities maintenance contract excluded the big building; repairs are made by government employees, not civilian contractors. Security is extremely tight, which is understandable considering the assets it protects, although it was unusual that this security was in place from the beginning. Two miles of double perimeter fence were put up months before the Beehive's official groundbreaking, and I think fully a quarter of the construction site workforce was comprised of security personnel. There was massive media coverage, of course, as the dome was not only an engineering marvel but was the premiere construction project in the state for three years, but the stories were benign."

"I don't understand, sir," Joe said. "How does your old job performing maintenance outside of the B-2 complex help me get inside the facility?"

"Because of three hours I spent with an engineer five years ago. One of the lesser functions of my contract was to maintain the public works technical library, a large repository of drawings of Pope's real property assets. The engineer was looking for as-built utility plats to assist his firm in designing the connections from the dome to the base's existing water, sewer, electric, and communications systems. To assist the youthful P.E. in locating the information he was seeking, he grudgingly revealed to me several of his own blueprints. They were only schematics, but they were revealing. The plans showed an extensive network of underground utilities, ranging from small buried cables to wide, long galleries."

"I can't believe I can just stroll right up to the building through one of those tunnels," Joe said.

"Make no mistake about it, you can't," Evans warned. Thick steel doors and electronic surveillance would stop or detect you before you were within four hundred feet. No, the value that might have come from that meeting involves something much more convoluted, a subtle cross-connection that probably lies outside the site's security perimeter.

"Please go on," Susan said, her attention keenly concentrated.

"Unless those plans were changed, I believe you can gain access to the main drainage tunnel from one of the electrical galleries. For simplicity, apparently, it was decided to divert all storm water on the site to one underground passage that runs several hundred feet from the complex to the Little River. Because it is the sole drain for the twenty-acre roof of the dome and the impermeable concrete and asphalt that surrounds it, the channel must be huge."

"Something as large as that can't be left unsecured," Joe commented.

"You are absolutely correct, but water is notoriously unkind to electronic devices, and you will be bypassing the foolproof passive security constructed at the end of the passage. The tunnel flares out where it empties into the Little River, and in this space was placed an array of hundreds of steel pipes, each perhaps twenty feet long and eight inches in diameter. With the spaces between the pipes filled with reinforced concrete, nothing larger than a miniature poodle can get into that tunnel, although the drainage water is not impeded. I expect some kind of steel mesh is welded to the interior end of the pipes to prevent the passage of even small animals."

"Surely all that detail wasn't on the schematic you mentioned," Susan observed.

"No, that bit of information comes from personal observation during several angling forays to the Little River while I was still working at the base. The fishing wasn't great, but the watercourse was a convenient distance from my office, and it lay outside the security fence of the dome complex. The curious thing I noted during those jaunts was the large amount of water emptying into the river from the pipes, even when it hadn't rained for weeks." The old man settled back slightly as his ubiquitous daily weariness crept up on him.

"Sounds like groundwater," Joe said.

"Has to be. I estimate the flow of groundwater from the facility to be somewhere between five and ten thousand gallons a minute, indicating the underground work went a good deal deeper than was reported. The fact that extensive excavation took place was never concealed. It couldn't be, with dozens of men working night and day for over a year with explosives and huge boring machines. I believe upwards of half a million cubic yards was excavated. At one time, rumor had it that the underground facilities were fallout shelters. Nowadays, I don't think much thought is given to it at all; out of sight, out of mind, you know, and there is enough to do on the surface. Those Spirit bombers are very demanding birds."

"I don't think my interests lie anywhere around the airplanes," Joe said.

"You're right. Your chance to get into the complex lies underground, and about a thousand feet down you will probably find your answers."

"A thousand?" Joe queried, surprised. "That deep?"

"That's my guess, based on simple mathematics. It's a fact that the dome is a section of a sphere with a radius of about a thousand feet. If the purpose of this inverted dish is to focus neutrinos, then the focal point of these rays—the center of the sphere—lies almost a thousand feet below the surface. There are problems with this hypothesis, though. For one thing, it is a section of a parabola, not a sphere, that concentrates parallel rays to a single point, and that occurs only when the parabola is facing directly toward the source of those rays. At our latitude, the Sun never shines directly overhead, and that offset of fifteen degrees or so does not change at night. I'm at a loss to explain the discrepancy."

"I'll try to figure it out for you while I'm down there looking for evidence that clears me of being a murderer," Joe offered. "What do you think of my chances?"

Evans frowned as he reflected on the problem. "Just getting inside the facility will be a flip of the coin, the first of perhaps four."

Fifty percent, twenty-five, twelve and a half, six and a quarter, Joe calculated. He knew he should be terrified, but his fear was diffused into a stark, nebulous fog encompassing the details of his situation.

"I'm going," Susan said abruptly.

"Susan . . . no," Joe almost whispered as he turned to his companion, wounded by the possible implications of her statement.

"This isn't a suggestion or a request," she stated firmly. "It's a fact."

Joe turned his head toward the old man. "Colonel Evans, please tell her it's impossible, that she can't do this."

"I'm not going to presume to tell either of you what to do. This is something you're going to have to decide for yourselves. Whoever goes has to enter the situation eyes wide open, though. This is not going to be safe, easy, or even sane. My knowledge is incomplete, to say the least. You might find yourself unable to continue or captured at any point."

"Susan, please listen; please reconsider. Why do you want to do this?"

"Why? How dare you ask me why?" Susan spat as shifted toward the far side of the couch. "'Why' is the pile of charred lumber on Ridge Road. 'Why' is being put into the ground at Cedar Hill Cemetery, maybe even at this moment. 'Why' is the silence that remains now, when there used to be a rush of paws and yelp of joy whenever I returned to a home that was destroyed in every possible way by these bastards." Shaking and exhausted by the outburst, she settled back in the sofa.

Gently, Joe brought a hand in contact with hers. "Susan, I don't think your father would have wanted you to do this for him. Infiltrating a high-security federal facility is a serious offense, and so far you haven't committed any crimes."

"Well that's going to change very shortly, isn't it?" she said without looking at him.

"Yes, I guess it is," Joe acknowledged, capitulating to her immutable will.

"You've already indicated you're not very computer savvy," Susan said. "We need information, and the key source of information is probably going to be their computer network." She turned toward Evans. "How do we get onto the base?"

"That's the easy part," the old man replied. "We just drive right in;

I have a sticker. I go there often to take advantage of my retirement benefits: shopping trips to the base exchange, movies at the theater, that kind of thing. I'm always alone when I go through the gate, though; I think it would be best if you two ride in the trunk."

"Ever been transported in that fashion, Susan?" Joe asked as they rose. "It's an experience, one of many I'm sure we'll have today."

Evans gestured to Joe to follow him. "Let's go out to the garage. I have a few things out there that might prove useful." Once there, he turned and faced his guest. "Joe, Susan is obviously a strong woman, and I think she'll carry more than her own weight. She might even allow you to pocket one or two of those coins we spoke of rather than toss them."

CHAPTER 22

Fighting the urge to lose his temper—not at the man who sat across his desk, but at the unreachable people and unseen forces that had taken his department's finest officer—Anthony Dempsey addressed his guest. "Damn it, Tobin, of course I know Joe Hanlon didn't go on a murderous rampage after learning that Bonnelli—his 'real' boss—was dead. The newspapers and TV reports are full of crap, as are the so-called investigators looking into the matter. Still, I don't know what I can do to help."

"Maybe something will come to mind while I bring you up to date," Richard Tobin said. "There are a number of things—" He stopped and looked furtively around the room. "But maybe we better discuss this outside."

"What, you think my office is bugged?"

"It's possible."

"That's goddamn ridiculous."

"Maybe so," Tobin said as he stood. "But how many other ridiculous things have happened around here over the past week?"

The chief led his guest outside the station. Though they found themselves on Main Street, Dempsey steered Tobin toward one of the level side streets to continue their conversation, avoiding the steep downgrade of the wider thoroughfare as it descended to the Hudson and the inevitable strenuous hike back up.

"I'd like to clear Joe's name, but I have no official channels that would do any good, and I've spoken to the reporters as much as I dare," Dempsey related when they were half a block from the municipal building. "They've dutifully noted my defense of him, but without exception my statements have been wrapped in allegations that some kind of cover-up is underway. Some say I'm protecting a fellow cop, others say I'm distancing the force from him to avoid embarrassment that I hired a man with mob connections. It's one extreme or the other, and both of them are wrong. It's starting to piss me off."

"I have a number of things that point to Joe's innocence," Tobin stated as he strolled at an easy pace to Dempsey's right. "I need more, though."

"You're going out on a limb for our young friend, aren't you?"

"I've been out with him farther and on a much thinner branch, and you know it," Tobin said. "Besides, the goal is to save Joe, not sacrifice myself in some bullshit heroic gesture, and for that I need more ammunition to counteract the damage done by these government thugs. I know those guys murdered the girl here in Sunnyside, I'm almost positive they killed the doctor in Marlborough, and I have an overriding suspicion they were responsible for the death of Victor Bonnelli as well. That makes them damn near serial killers in our book. Well, in my book, anyway; to almost everyone else in my office, they're the furshlugginer Untouchables."

"What can you tell me about the death of Elizabeth Brooks? I can't believe a murder took place right here, the first in a decade, yet I know next to nothing about it."

"You've been to the apartment?"

"Of course, but the only people I talked to were two men laying new carpet in the living room and a handyman repairing a nasty gash in the stairwell."

"That was my doing," Tobin explained after sidestepping a small pile of leaves and poplar husks. "I dug a bullet out of the wall, left there during Joe's escape from the building."

"Shot by Joe or the guy after him?"

"By the latter, I'm sure. My understanding is Joe didn't have a gun."

"He turned his service pistol over to me on Friday morning, and I'm almost certain he didn't own another, but . . ."

"But there's a lot that bothers you about the circumstances surrounding the death," Tobin finished.

"I have to admit, Tobin, it looks bad. I know Joe—well. He couldn't have killed that girl, not unless he went immediately and completely insane, and that's damned unlikely. Still, I keep trying to imagine what bizarre scenario took place that explains the facts, and I keep coming up empty."

"What bothers you the most?" Tobin asked as they turned right and headed up a slight upgrade.

"The one witness, the woman downstairs, was positive she heard Joe shoot the girl, that no one else went up or down those stairs during that time period. If someone had come up the fire escape to kill, why did he stop with just one shot, which is all that was heard? And the witness said Joe remained in the apartment for at least a couple of minutes before he made his escape, and that's a hell of a long time if there was a bad guy with a gun after him. I don't get it."

"The answer is that only Joe and Elizabeth Brooks were in the apartment; there wasn't anyone else, and there wasn't a gun," Tobin explained. "There was an explosive device in the telephone. Brooks answered it, and died because of it. Joe then stayed on to try to help her, or because he was in shock, or maybe both. Then the bad guys came and it was time to go."

"How do you know this?"

"It's what Joe told his friend while he was holed up in Marlborough. I also have physical evidence: a small piece of the telephone those murdering agents overlooked; it had explosives residue on it."

"That's good," Dempsey said, relieved, then immediately realized the hideousness of the words. They made another right turn and headed back toward the station. "There won't be any other evidence coming from that apartment. The place was completely cleaned out. New tenants are moving in this morning. That's pretty quick investigative work, even for the FBI."

"We both know it wasn't a proper investigation, and those fellows certainly weren't FBI," Tobin responded.

"Well, they're *federales* of some perverted color," Dempsey shot back.

"Yes, they are," Tobin admitted. "I have what I'm sure are some of their fingerprints, but they haven't been identified yet."

"You run them through your new supercomputer?"

"Of course, but results were negative. Either these guys have never had anything to do with government service, which I know is not the case, or they have the connections to have their fingerprints removed from the files, and something like that takes pretty powerful contacts."

"So what else is new? They also think they can get away with murder."

"Well it's up to us to prove to them wrong," Tobin said as they approached the station.

"You know, Tobin, speaking of fingerprints . . ."

"Yes?"

"I have a couple of things in my office, and a story to go with them. I think you'll be pleased."

As they precariously hung on to the narrow steel ladder, the two figures used their backs to move the cast iron manhole cover back into its seat. With a burst of exertion, the pair maneuvered the large disk the final three inches and it dropped into position, separating them from the light and sounds of the surface.

Susan descended seven rungs to the floor of the underground passage, followed by Joe, who noticed her jacket had been marred by rust from the manhole cover. Inadequately lit by the small flashlight, the ruddy swaths looked disconcertingly like dried blood.

They acclimated themselves to their surroundings. Although Susan stood with ease in the tunnel, Joe had to stoop slightly to travel the dank passage. The three-foot width would have been more than ample were it not for the numerous pipes that pressed in toward the center from both walls, making a traverse physically difficult and mentally claustrophobic.

Joe retrieved a rucksack from the floor, a present from Evans filled with gifts from the garage. Evans had also given them directions via an indistinct map drawn in pencil on an envelope.

"This way," Susan said as she turned on her flashlight and headed off. Joe ducked his head and followed.

The cool, humid air in the passageway hung heavy, smelling faintly of diesel and methane. It was difficult to judge distances in the alien environment. After they walked two hundred or five hundred, or a thousand feet, they encountered the first major intersection. Susan stopped and turned. "Where to?" she asked.

Joe held the map up to his light. "Go left." The first turn was clearly indicated; he silently hoped all decisions would be as easy.

They were not, of course. After four more turns, they entered a maze with one dead end after another, the pipes within the passages continuing their journey through solid concrete.

"We're lost," Joe finally said as they confronted yet another wall.

"Get out the map," Susan demanded, frustration competing with anxiety.

"Forget the map; it's brought us as far as it's going to. Let's try to read the pipes. Look for the bigger ones, the newer installations."

A large water line finally gave them access to what they were looking for. Susan spotted the new eight-inch lateral going into the wall through a pair of steel plates, one to either side of the pipe. Joe produced an adjustable wrench from his pack and unscrewed six lag bolts holding up the left-side panel. As he carefully lowered the heavy plate to the floor, he and Susan were greeted by new construction: a concrete passageway about three feet wide and two high, to one side of which ran the water line.

With Susan in the lead, they crawled through the tight tunnel, finally coming upon a pristine passageway of exquisitely finished concrete. Gone was the hodgepodge of styles and haphazard placements; all of the gleaming stainless steel piping ran straight along the right side of the gallery. Joe and Susan proceeded along the dark corridor for hundreds of feet, finally coming upon a gleaming metal door, very thick and very locked. There were no bolts, no knobs, not even a keyhole, indicating that it had to be opened from the other side, if it was not permanently sealed.

They retraced their steps, looking carefully for any other way out besides the one they had used coming in. About midway through their journey back to the older tunnels, they heard it: water, coming from somewhere. They soon discovered that the sound emanated from a grate at the base of the wall. Three feet long and less than a foot high, it was sized by an engineer to protect the passageway from catastrophic flood. There was no flood, however, or moisture of any description in the passageway. The sound of water was coming from somewhere beneath them.

Joe unbolted the grate and looked dubiously into the hole beyond. The drainage pipe was sloped down at a thirty-degree angle; its end could not be seen. The sound of running water was distinct, but whether it was ten or a hundred feet away could not be determined.

Susan dropped to her knees and examined the passage. "Let me have the pack."

"What do you need?"

"The whole thing," she answered, holding out her hand but not pulling her eyes away from the hole. After receiving the knapsack, she briefly considered its bulk, then placed it in the hole and gave it a shove. It disappeared.

"Susan!" Joe managed, before being immediately shushed. After a second and a half, they heard a gentle thud, then hollow reverberations, indicating that the pack had come to rest in something larger than the tiny drainage tube.

"This thing can't be more than ten or twelve feet long," Susan said. "There's obviously no grate at the end, and whatever it opens up onto is certainly big enough to hold us."

"Susan, we need that pack."

"We need it if we're going on, but not if we're going to turn tail, and I think you know that this is the only way forward."

"If we both can squeeze through that pipe—and I have serious doubts that we can—this might be the only way, but this is a point of no return. Look at the slope down, the small diameter. If we make it through, I doubt if we could get back up here."

"And we could end up in a room with no exit?"

"Exactly."

"Okay," Susan replied. "It's a risk, but one worth taking; don't even try to talk me out of it. I'd like you to come along; I'm sure you'll come in handy later. What do you say?"

"Who goes first?"

It was Susan, they decided. Joe watched as she contorted herself into the hole feet-first, then disappeared slowly around the bend, moving herself inches at a time by convulsing her body. "My legs are through," she stated breathlessly forty seconds after she moved out of Joe's view. "Oh!" she uttered a few seconds later.

"Susan, are you all right?" Joe called.

"I'm okay," she responded, her words resonating up the pipe. "It's about a six foot drop after you get through. Come on down."

Toes pointed, Joe forced his legs into the pipe, followed by his waist, torso, and head. Like Susan, he kept his arms extended. His buttocks filled the entire pipe, and the gash on his thigh hurt from the pressure. Where Susan traveled an inch or two at a time, Joe's progress was much slower: a quarter inch per exertion, a half inch tops. The anxious confinement he had felt while wandering the underground labyrinth was magnified tenfold in the tube. When he was surrounded by the rigid conduit, he briefly worried that his wound might swell up, pinning him inextricably. He knew of one man, probably close by, who would certainly love to remove the obstruction with a razor auger.

One strenuous thrust of his body was followed by a second, then a third, but after that he had to rest, exhausted, not knowing if he had made any progress at all. Once, twice, three times he violently moved, then rested again to contemplate the time in the very near future that he would be completely out of strength and still surrounded by metal and concrete and earth.

Finally, he felt someone at his feet. Something was being wrapped around his ankles, then he heard the muffled word "move." He did move, progressing an inch at a time thanks to his partner's steady pull. Fifteen seconds later he was through and sitting on a sloping concrete floor.

"I thought you might not make it," Susan said.

"It's a cinch I'm not going back that way," he replied. "If there's no other exit from here, you'll have to climb out and get help."

"Not this gal," she stated matter-of-factly. "As much as I hate to admit it, it was a tight squeeze for me, too. I probably could make it out if you were up top at the other end of a rope, but that isn't going to happen."

"Point of no return, as I said. Let's see what's beyond."

A quick perusal of their new environs revealed that the space was another tunnel, but much larger and completely bare. From wall to wall, it was fully twenty feet wide, capped with a flat ceiling eight feet above their heads. From the walls, the floor sloped down fifteen degrees to a central channel, filled with water to a width of six feet. Though the stream was moving swiftly from right to left, in their immediate vicinity it slipped past noiselessly; the sound of running water came from the distant darkness in both directions.

Joe turned off the flashlight and, far downstream, the barest hint of light reached their eyes.

"I have a feeling what we want is at the headwaters of this flow, so I think we should head toward the light," Joe said as he rose painfully to his feet. In the dim glow of his flashlight, he caught the baffled expression on his companion's face as she contemplated the incongruity. "I just want to examine any other options before we rush into things—I mean even further," he added, acknowledging the absurdity of the statement.

After they traveled fourteen hundred feet, they neared their objective. The sound of falling water was much louder, and the light, though still not bright, illuminated the scene enough to prevent Joe from walking off a ten-foot ledge. Barely.

"Damn," he uttered, stopping abruptly at the end of the tunnel. The water continued on, cascading onto the floor of a fifty-foot wide concrete box. On the opposite wall fifteen feet in front of the couple was the source of the light, a forty wide by ten high matrix of pipes, each eight inches in diameter and capped with steel mesh.

"Wonderful," Susan said. "We've managed to verify something we learned this morning from Evans, something that doesn't do us any good at all. He even had the animal-proof grates pegged down."

"We have to at least check for some kind of hidden maintenance manhole," Joe said, searching the featureless concrete in vain for something other than featureless concrete.

"Okay, nothing here," Susan said. "Keep your light on while we go back. We may just spot a tube a little larger than our one-way pipe."

They did spot several inlets as they walked, but they were uniformly smaller than their too-small egress. Every two hundred feet or so, two pipes, one on each wall, exited into the tunnel from a road or parking lot or some other exterior drainage. They finally passed a slightly larger pipe with no counterpart on the opposite wall and realized they had reached their starting point.

As they moved on, they noted an increase in the frequency of the drainage inlets. A square group of four appeared on one wall, followed by a four-by-four grid of sixteen a hundred feet further on. Two hundred feet after this were the legions: six ranks of twenty-four marching up the sides of both walls, almost three hundred openings, not one of which was accessible.

"We must be directly under the edge of the dome," Susan said. "The water from—what?—twenty acres of roof drains to this spot."

"We can't have much further to go," Joe said after a few more minutes of travel. "The damned thing is only twelve hundred feet across."

"I can see it," Susan said after catching the slight sparkle of falling water just at the limit of her flashlight beam, at once dubious of exactly what an observation of water exiting one or more eight-inch pipes would mean for them. Two minutes later that is precisely what they were observing: water gushing from four of twenty outlets on both sides of the tunnel.

"Big deal," Susan said and Joe realized simultaneously. "Let's move on."

Sixty feet farther on, thanks to a slight increase in the slope of the tunnel, the channel was clear of water. Twenty feet beyond that, the tunnel ended. For several seconds, despair reigned free as they both knew they would have to starve themselves into emaciated skeletons before making a weak attempt to cram their bodies up the pipe that brought them to the accursed place. Then Susan saw the ladder, half a dozen steel rungs set into the concrete. Training her beam upward, she caught sight of a silver door, flush with the concrete and nearly invisible in the dim light. It sported a lever handle. No lock was evident.

Joe ascended the ladder. Locked or alarmed, he knew it was the only way out. He pulled the handle, and it moved. He pushed the door, and it opened. No alarm pierced the gloom of the tunnel. "Wait here," he called down in a whisper.

This can't be to code, he thought as he struggled through the doorway and into the space beyond, a hallway scant inches wider than the door and no more than seven feet from floor to ceiling. And not longer than ten feet, he noticed as he scanned down the corridor and saw a dark, wider space beyond. That's not to code, either, he thought as he reached the end of the hallway, but it was "Son of a bitch" that he verbalized.

Directly in front of him, with nothing so prudent as a guardrail to arrest his forward motion, was a rectangular hole twenty feet across and twenty-five wide with a bottom that could not be seen. Taking the clue from Evans, he guessed the drop was a thousand feet.

Joe explored the rest of the space. The hallway did not end directly at the hole, but onto a four-foot wide concrete walkway, which went off to the left, then turned ninety degrees and skirted another of the dark pit's sides. Within the left wall was a set of double doors, each eight feet wide and twelve high, featureless matte silver surfaces as imposing as those of a bank vault. On the opposite wall were grouped the utility lines servicing whatever it was in the depths below, a series of ducts and pipes that came down from the ceiling and continued into nothingness. Joe also noticed the room could be illuminated by four large mercury halide lights mounted on the ceiling. Beyond the far light, pointed at an angle to encompass the whole area, was a surveillance camera.

Another "Son of a bitch" was immediately followed by a retreat down the hallway.

"I can tell you found something," Susan said after Joe rejoined her. "You look pale."

"I guess we'll find out in about two minutes if this is the end of the line. If it's not, we have quite a journey ahead of us. There's a room up there. For starters, it's covered by a camera. I couldn't tell if it was on or not, but if it was, we can expect visitors shortly. On the plus side, I can't think of a case where someone would be paid to watch an absolutely dark, perfectly secure room on a monitor, but this *is* a government facility."

"Let's assume you weren't observed. Is there a way out?"

"Normal people would get out using a set of steel doors, but they're locked."

"There's an alternative?"

"Well, for that Colonel Evans came through for us again," Joe said as he took off the pack. "When was the last time you went rappelling, Susan?"

"You know when."

With that answer, he did know, and recalled the unseasonably warm spring afternoon nearly ten years before, three weeks prior to the incidents that had so tragically and unnecessarily blasted their relationship apart. Susan had packed a lunch, Joe threw some rock climbing gear into the trunk of his car, and they drove down to Storm King Mountain. They hiked, ate, made love in a grassy cleft near the crest of the high hill, and engaged in some purely recreational absailing down a slope that hardly called for a rope. It had been easy and fun, a wonderful experience in a beautiful setting, the exact opposite of the hellish place and situation they were in now.

Joe picked up the kernmantle climbing rope so presciently packed by Evans. "The other way is down, Susan, maybe a quarter mile straight down to the focal point Evans was talking about. Most of the room up there is nothing but an open hole."

"And I assume something sane like an elevator or stairway or ladder is not to be found?"

"The shaft is straight down, featureless except for a few pipes and ducts bolted to the wall," Joe replied grimly as he removed the only other items of climbing equipment in the pack: six snaplink carabiners.

"How can we go down a hole a thousand feet deep with—what—two hundred feet of rope?"

"It's about two hundred now, but it'll be less shortly," Joe replied as he took a knife from the pack and cut one, then another fifteen foot length from the line. "We should have harnesses or nylon tape, but these will have to do," he said, his hands shaking slightly. "We should have gloves, decent shoes, belaying plates, even a little better light than these flashlights provide, but we don't have even that."

"Is it possible?" Susan asked softly, reflecting Joe's obvious worry.

"It is, but it's going to be very difficult," he said as he continued preparations. He wrapped one of the short ropes around his jacket at the waist, then brought the two ends through his legs and, pulling tightly, wrapped the lengths around themselves by his thighs. "This makeshift sling is going to tend to cut into you, and it's going to have to bear your weight the whole way down, so it needs to be tight." He finished the rope work by tying the ends of the rope together with a square knot on his right side. "Now you," he said.

After Susan was sporting an equally sturdy and uncomfortable rope around her waist and legs, Joe cut two more short lengths off the main rope.

"The one advantage we have is that this place is solidly built; nothing should give way under our efforts. One of the pipes going down the shaft, a round one about six inches across, is secured to the wall by brackets every ten feet or so. The hardware holds the pipe away from the wall about two inches, and the brackets are nice and solid and round. I'm going to sling this rope over one of them until it's a double rope, seventy-five feet long. Then I'm going to rappel down seven brackets and tie myself to the fixture with one of these five-foot pieces, releasing the rope. Then you can come down and join me, and secure yourself to the bracket as well. Then I'll pull on the main rope until it slips completely through the first bracket above us, and sling the rope over the bracket we'll be hanging from. Then I'll rappel down the next leg, and you'll join me after I'm secured. Then we do it again, and again and again, as many as fifteen times."

"Easier said than done," Susan said, stating the obvious at the same time she realized it was obvious there was no other way. "You'll have to teach me the details about these things," she said, fingering one of the carabiners."

After a few minutes of practice, they ascended the ladder. At the edge of the hole, Joe reached three feet into the abyss and threaded the long rope through the first bracket, waist-high in front of him. He hooked into the rope with a double twist around a carabiner, then pushed off the ledge and descended into the blackness. One, two, three, four pipe brackets, he counted as he slipped down a few feet at a time, hoping Susan was up to the task. . . . six, seven, he counted, then, gauging he had enough rope remaining, dropped to bracket number eight. After securing himself, he flashed his light, the signal for his partner to take the uncertain plunge.

Although it seemed longer, it was only three minutes until Susan slid smoothly to his side.

"Very nice," Joe complemented as he helped her tie off.

"This thing pinches my ass," she replied.

He pulled on the main rope. "Watch your head," he advised just before the rope cleared the bracket far above and sailed past them.

Joe dropped deeper into the pit. Susan's second descent was even better than her first, and his admiration for her grew as she roped herself next to him.

The third, fourth, and fifth legs were negotiated without incident. Then, as Joe's mind began to turn away from the current predicament to wonder what was next in store, he erred. As he prepared for the next leg, a carabiner slipped completely out of its sling as he was unhooking it and dropped into the darkness. Breathlessly, Joe and Susan waited several seconds before an almost inaudible clink of aluminum hitting concrete echoed up to them.

After the seventh set of rappels, when the rope sailed past the couple, it hit bottom with a healthy slap several dozen feet below, surprising them both. Their calculations indicated that they were but five or six hundred feet down and so had at least another five hundred feet to go—six or seven more legs.

Within minutes, Joe was on a concrete floor, stooping down to recover his lost snaplink. In less time, Susan was by his side and they faced another set of double doors. These did not present the formidable obstacle of the heavy, secured slabs hundreds of feet directly overhead, however, but had the same hardware as the door that led from the drainage channel: a handle with no apparent lock.

Shaking with equal portions of exhaustion and relief, Joe and Susan sat down next to one another on the cold, smooth concrete. "That was quite an accomplishment; Evans outfitted us well," Joe commented, whispering to guard against the possibility that a person or group or army was in hearing range beyond the big doors. "Smooth sailing from here on in," he said encouragingly.

"Nice try," returned Susan. "Security may not have been an insurmountable obstacle yet, but as we get into the more trafficked areas of this complex I have a feeling we'll find more cameras, and the won't be off, and more people, and they will be armed. Do you still have that souvenir from your encounter with your brother-in-law?"

"It's in the pack. We might use it to threaten, Susan, but using it is unthinkable, or damn near. We'd need a mountain of justification, and we'd still be branded as terrorists."

"Keep it close just the same," she said firmly.

They stood and walked slowly to the doors. With only slight trepidation, Joe pulled down the handle and with a grunt opened the door three inches.

Very subdued ceiling lighting illuminated the space beyond. No movement was seen, no sound heard except for the breeze rushing into the shaft, caused by a slight overpressure.

Joe forced the door open a few inches more. It was not a room that lay beyond, but a hallway. Of generous dimensions, its termination some yards ahead was visible but indistinct in the gloom cast by the dim lights. It looked deserted.

Upon entering, the first thing they noted were the twin cameras pointing down into the hall from the ceiling, labeled "LA-43" and "LA-44" in two-inch white characters.

"Wait," Susan said, focusing on the details of the two devices. "Relax—a little. These cameras are not activated. Look up there—that dark nub to the left of the lens is a red 'on' light. They're not active."

"Not to say that they might not snap on at any instant, activated by some sensor or curious observer," Joe said.

"Agreed," Susan replied as they moved down the corridor.

Fifty feet down the hall, inset into a small alcove, was an elevator. There were no call buttons or lights indicating the floor or level, however. In their place was a console that would have been mistaken for an ATM had it been anywhere else, with keypad, card slot, and small television screen.

Seconds later, they were at the end of the hallway, and what had seemed like a fairly substantial room by some trickery of the light finally revealed itself as what it was: an immense circular cavern, four hundred feet across with a domed ceiling that reached seventy feet over their heads. Suddenly, they felt very exposed.

Yet no one shouted an alarm from across the vast space, no spotlights came upon them, and none of the cameras that ringed the vast enclosure clicked to life. The cavern was illuminated by no less than fifty large bell-shaped lights that angled into the room from the top of the circular wall at even intervals, but although the combined wattage was impressive, the huge space diluted the light to such an extent that it was dimmer than in the hall. The floor was on two levels. Extending out from the wall on the same level as the hall was a walkway eight feet wide. The rest of the room was a huge, level circle recessed ten feet, big enough to encompass a football field, ample sidelines, and stands for several thousand spectators, but instead it contained a tight array of eight thousand shiny red hexagons, five feet across. Each was surrounded by a brushed metal border and attached to a framework that lifted the crimson plates to within two feet of the perimeter level.

"I almost didn't believe it," Joe said in wonder as the pair started to walk, keeping to the darkest area near the wall. "Here they are, though, exactly as Dr. Burke described them."

"Incredible," Susan said as she took in the panorama.

"This isn't the focal point, though. Where are we?"

"I think I get it," Susan said. "Look at that machinery underneath the panels, and the very slight differences in angle between the plates. We're at the bottom right now; the focal point is not below us, it's above us, probably hundreds of feet up given the small angle differences."

"So once again, following the path of these neutrinos . . ." Joe began hesitantly.

"They come up from below, hit the panels on the thousand-foot dome, which reflects them, concentrating them into a smaller space—here. Then they are reflected to a point of concentration above us, then in this state they are sent off to Australia where they are aimed at whoever the proprietors of this place want to do away with."

"So why the double reflection? They didn't want to dig deeper?"

"I don't think that's it; I think the answer is right here in front of us. The dome is huge and rigid, while this field is both smaller and adjustable. The exact orientation of the dome to the Sun changes slightly every day. I think this group of panels compensates for the change."

"You are good," Joe complemented. "One last question: this is a huge machine of enormous complexity. Where the hell is everybody?"

"They must be above us somewhere, controlling everything by computer. Somebody must come down here from time to time to check on things, though."

The soft voices were the first indicator that there were at least two others in the chamber. Moments later, Joe and Susan saw them: two men in white coats entering the cavern from the hall. Instantly, the pair crouched down in the shadows.

"I don't think they can see us," Joe said directly into his partner's ear.

Still talking, the men turned out of the hallway in the direction away from the couple and disappeared through an unseen opening in the wall. Moments later, fluorescent lighting beamed out of a portal, a standard-sized opening, but without a door.

"Well, shall we?" Joe whispered.

"I think it's the opportunity we need," agreed Susan.

"We're going to try this the easy way first," Joe said as they started back toward the hall, but he retrieved the .45 from the pack as he spoke. They heard the voices coming out of the illuminated room during the entire time they made their way to the hall, but they did not see either of the men again. After rounding the corner, they power-walked to the alcove, where the doors to the elevator stood joyfully open, held in that position by an identification card in the console. Joe grabbed the card and joined Susan in the conveyance. "Maybe those guys will be riveted to whatever they're doing for hours, but get ready to think on the run," he advised.

Susan pushed an arrow-shaped button pointed up, and the doors slid silently closed.

CHAPTER 23

"**E**ven though we've made it this far, I still have big doubts about this," Joe told Susan as they made their way at a quick walk down a concrete corridor, the third in as many minutes since leaving the elevator.

Susan nodded, but did not speak. Within a complex of many acres and numerous levels, within well-lighted hallways with cameras at every intersection, and now with two men far below who would shortly find something amiss, it was obvious they were running out of time.

As they came to a ninety-degree jog, Joe abruptly stopped and Susan collided into him. A half second later, she also heard the voices coming from the left and the footsteps that accompanied them, resolutely approaching. There were no alcoves in which to hide, no doors that might be open, and the intersection to the next hallway back was seventy feet away. Joe gripped his .45 in a wet palm in preparation for the upcoming confrontation.

The meeting did not take place, however. When the footsteps were mere seconds from the intruders, they abruptly stopped. Then the voices, still active, faded quickly until they were heard no more. Joe ventured a glimpse around the corner. The hallway was empty, but there were doors within the walls, the first he had seen since exiting the elevator. He wondered how a door could have opened and closed so soundlessly, then noticed that the doors sported flat push plates instead of knobs or levers.

"Okay, Susan, looks like we're going to run the gauntlet," Joe said. "We are certainly getting closer to the action. There are five doors around the corner and another corridor off to the right about forty feet up. Anyone could pop out without warning at any time."

"Let's go," Susan urged.

Using as much stealth as they could manage, the two moved down the hall, bypassing the first doors on either side, as behind one of them were the two or three people they had heard just a minute before. Joe opted to try the second door on the left, and was grateful for the advantages ball bearing hinges and a finely tuned door closer offered, as they entered the room with nary a squeak or click.

Fortunately, the room was empty; unfortunately, it was a tiny restroom. Aesthetically comparable with the rest of the complex, the four-foot-square space had concrete walls, floor, and ceiling, with a single light fixture that apparently stayed on constantly, as there was no switch, and privacy that was apparently provided by a foot against the door, as there was no latch.

"Let's try another," Susan suggested.

Slightly better success met the furtive pair in the room across the hall. It was twenty feet wide and thirty deep, filled with row upon row of identical metal cases, a phalanx of large computers.

"Anything here?" Joe asked, deferring to the expert.

"This has to be the mainframe of the entire complex, or at least the underground facilities," Susan replied. "All kinds of information must be here, but there are no work stations, no monitors or keyboards. If we had several hours, we could physically take the machines apart and remove some vital components, but I don't think we have even several minutes. We have to try elsewhere."

"No problem," Joe said, but realized immediately it might have been a big problem. As he opened the door to the hall, the restroom door closed its last two inches and he realized he missed an encounter by less than a second. Swiftly, he led Susan up the hall to the next door.

It was an office. The centerpiece was a large double pedestal desk, upon which sat a computer, a telephone, and a nearly full coffee cup, and behind which was an executive chair. Two other chairs flanked a small square table in one corner. Except for the cup, the place looked unoccupied; there were no pictures on the walls, no knickknacks on the desk, and no papers anywhere in the room.

Susan immediately moved behind the desk, her hand reaching for the coffee. "It's still warm," she observed, then turned toward the monitor. "Get on your guard; I'll see if I can pull up anything interesting."

"If this office belongs to the guy in the bathroom, we don't have long," Joe said as Susan's hands flew across the keyboard.

"First, where are we?" she asked the electronic box as she typed, finally finding a file of diagrams after two false starts. "Here it is," she said. "That's a good side view. There's the drainage tunnel, touching the shaft that leads down to that sea of hexagons below us, labeled here the 'Lower Array.' And there's the elevator; looks like we're about two hundred feet down, directly under the dome but more toward the edge than the center. At the center at our current depth is the long-lost focal point, called the 'Lens Array.' Damn, it's huge, too: a hundred feet across and at least a hundred fifty feet high. At the top of the lens is a 'Diverter' which sends the beam over three hundred feet parallel with the surface to the 'Final Diverter' which deflects the beam straight down, obviously to Australia."

"See if you can get a floor plan of our current level."

"Coming up next," Susan said as she clicked the mouse half a dozen more times "Here it is: a lot of hallways and a few rooms. We seem to be in the thick of it. The way out seems to be back the way we came, taking a right past the elevator."

"Any info on how this place is manned?"

After minimizing the graphic representation program, Susan brought up another file, then another, then another. "Here it is," she said at last. "Damn."

"Something wrong?"

"There has to be. Maybe this is only a partial list, but I don't think it is. This indicates about forty people—only forty!—regularly work down here, and that exactly fourteen are on site at this moment."

At that moment, one of the fourteen walked through the door, a man of moderate build and medium height wearing a white lab coat. Although he appeared to be in his mid-forties, his ample hair appeared a bit too full and too dark for his age.

"Who are you?" the man demanded. "If this is some kind of security test, I do not have the time." He walked into the room and around the desk, making it clear that he expected Susan to vacate the chair. "What are you doing there?" he asked her. "Those files are being accessed under my code. You can't do that."

"Hey buddy!" Joe said sharply. "Wake up and look around."

Somewhat taken aback, the man did just that, considering Susan, of mussed appearance with a somewhat desperate gleam in her eye, then turning to Joe he noticed the dirty clothes, the gun, and finally the face, which he recognized. He took a short, involuntary breath. "You're Joe Hanlon!" he said as years of absolute certainty concerning the perfect security of his working environment evaporated in an instant.

Joe stared grimly at the figure. "The very same, Mr. . . . ."

"Not 'Mister,' it's 'Doctor,'" Susan said, verifying her suspicion with a glance at the pictures in the personnel roster. "Joe, this is Dr. Alfred Zeichner."

"Dr. Z, it is a pleasure to finally meet you," Joe stated with the bitterest sarcasm he could muster. "Sit down."

Zeichner sat in one of the two chairs in the corner.

Joe looked down at his captive. "Dr. Z, we know all about your neutrino death ray and your goon squads, and we're here to insure their days of harming other people are over."

"You can't do that!"

"Susan, show him how wrong he is," Joe requested with a slightly arrogant air.

But Susan did not share her partner's confidence as she searched frantically for a way to end the heavy veil of secrecy that enveloped the project. "I can't," she said at last.

"What do you mean?" Joe asked, a little on edge. "Just get on the Internet and get the stuff out to the public like that girl did in the movie."

Susan gave him a look of disgust. "I understand the goal, but it's not going to happen, not on this machine. This computer is part of a large network within this complex, but it has no links whatsoever to any outside communications. Systems like this usually have a firewall to protect inside information from outside eyes, but this is like a PC without a modem. The security is perfect."

"But there has to be communication to the outside, to Albany at least," Joe insisted.

Goosed by the name of the Australian town, Zeichner's eyes widened at the knowledge of the interlopers.

"There must be another computer system or specialized interfaces constructed for that, probably involving strict computer-to-computer mathematics, difficult to decipher even for someone familiar with the project," she guessed. "Of course, Dr. Z, you can correct me if I'm wrong."

Zeichner remained silent.

"So what are the alternatives?"

"There's only one: we copy as many files as we can, and we carry them out of here." As she spoke, she looked at Zeichner, who remained calm.

"We can do that here?"

"Yes," Susan said. "The good doctor has a disk drive and a supply of disks right here in his drawer." She held up a shiny disk that looked like a standard floppy, though slightly larger and twice as thick. "These are probably used to transfer data to outside sources, perhaps higher-ups elsewhere. I've never seen disks like this—they even have serial numbers—but I think they'll work."

"Good," Joe said. He took off his pack and retrieved the four short lengths of rope that had been used in the couple's descent. "Do it and let's go; we're running out of time." He turned his attention to the captive. "As much as we might be tempted, Dr. Zeichner, it is not our intention to hurt you," he said as he tied the man's hands behind his back. "Susan, is Philip Roberts here?"

She did not hear him, as the open file before her held her attention completely. She hesitated, disturbed by the evil datum. "What was that?" she finally asked after tearing her eyes from the screen.

"Philip Roberts; is he on duty now?"

She pulled up the personnel files and shook her head. "There are two security personnel on duty; neither one is Roberts. Fortunately for him."

"Two for the whole complex," Joe said in amazement. "No wonder the cameras were turned off; they don't have the personnel to monitor them."

"Two is still enough to cause us plenty of problems."

"Okay, Dr. Z," Joe said after the man's hands were securely bound. "I don't trust this chair; please sit down on the floor by the desk."

"You are never going to get away with this," the doctor protested, but he complied with the order.

"Damn it, another roadblock," Susan said with frustration. "It's blocked. I need a password before I can copy any files."

Joe looked down at Zeichner. "I'm sure someone here can help out with that, can't he?"

Zeichner remained silent.

"Let me put it this way," Joe stated with firm resolve. "We want to leave here as quickly and as quietly as we can, but I am going to be very pissed if we leave empty handed. I guess I could take this," he went on, picking up one of the two chairs and gritting his teeth in rage. "I could take this and go next door and between this chair and my big feet, I'll bet I could damage every one of those computer cabinets in less than sixty seconds. If that isn't enough, I'll wager you one of these .45 rounds will go completely through the thin metal of three of those cabinets before coming to rest in the inner workings of a fourth."

"Joe, let me try a few things first," Susan said.

"To hell with that! I'm tired of this shit; it's time to take some real action." With the chair hooked under his gun arm, he grabbed the door handle with his free hand.

"'Demarcation,'" Zeichner said with extreme reluctance. "It's 'demarcation.'"

Susan entered the word and began to pull up files and copy them onto the disk. As the file labeled "SUB24" was being transferred, Susan called to her partner. "Look at this, Joe, just a week after Bonnelli, they're planning another one. Tomorrow night."

Joe took a quick glance at the screen. "That explains why practically no one is working now; for the next couple of days they're all on the graveyard shift—so to speak."

"That's enough files," Susan said. "We can't stay here all day. Now to find a way out."

"Don't tell him," Joe mouthed to Susan, gesturing toward the immobile figure on the floor.

Once again, Susan brought up the graphical representations of the complex. While electronically thumbing through the map files, she came upon a set filled with symbols, labeled with somewhat familiar designations. Her eyes lit up; she began clicking on them and was rewarded with insets that showed the view of each camera attendant to its symbol. Quickly, she moved from image to image, floor plan to floor plan.

In the few minutes that followed, Joe recognized that Susan seemed to be less and less intent on leaving. "Let's go," he finally urged.

She looked up, her countenance grimly determined. "Joe, we're going to give these guys a kick in the balls they won't forget and clear the way for us to get out of here with one swift strike."

"I just want to leave by the easiest, quickest means," Joe protested. "I was only half serious about smashing those computer consoles."

"Well I'm wholly serious about this," she said as she pulled the disk from its tray. "Put this in your pocket and let's go."

"I don't think I want to do this," Joe again resisted.

"I think you've forgotten who these people are," Susan hissed. She grasped the handle to the door. "Follow me," she commanded.

With one last glance at Zeichner to assure he was firmly bound and gagged, Joe followed. "This is wrong," he said as he followed the determined woman to the right and down a new hallway.

"I'm sorry, Joe, but this is exactly where we need to go," Susan replied as she opened the second door on the right.

It was an examination room of some sort. One wall was lined with instrument cabinets and a countertop ran along another. In the middle of the room was a stainless steel table, just large enough to hold a person. Or a body, Joe realized, as along a far wall were six large drawer fronts that instantly identified the room as a morgue.

"It was in one of the files, Joe. She's in there, bottom right."

Though his mind cried an agonizing "no" over and over, he found himself at the drawer, his hand on the handle. Totally against his conscious will, he pulled.

Not covered, still in the bloody clothes she became engaged in and minutes later died in was Elizabeth.

Head bowed, Joe kneeled next to the body of his fiancée as the agonies of her death once again immersed him. "I guess they didn't know what else to do with her," he said at last, his voice cracking as he stroked her hair.

Susan moved next to him. "I'm sorry," she repeated. "I felt I had to remind you what all this has resulted in. They did this to your girl, they did the same to my father. Now they have to pay."

After ten silent seconds, Joe stood up, slowly slid the drawer back into place, and turned to Susan. "Let's get the bastards."

"Anything yet?" Richard Tobin asked of Janine Wolf as he stepped over the threshold of the White Plains FBI lab.

"With all you've given me to work on, I shouldn't have, but I do," she replied, not looking up from her computer screen. "Hanlon's gun seems to have gone through a few hands since he last cleaned it. Most of the prints were readily identifiable as Hanlon's; about half of the remainder were Anthony Dempsey's."

"And the rest?"

"They came from two people, and both of those individuals do not have records in the National Data Base. That would normally not be considered good, but in your Bizzarro world where you get opposite conclusions from those legitimately assigned to investigate a case, it seems to be very good indeed."

"The others?" Tobin asked gleefully.

"Yes, the others. I managed to match the partial thumbprint on the two-by-four with a print on the pistol. As far as the other unknown fellow, three of the prints lifted from the mustard jar you found in Hanlon's apartment matched prints found on the gun."

"We are getting close," Tobin said. "It's fairly certain our two unidentified men are Eric Kauffman, who handed the pistol over to Dempsey last Thursday, and Philip Roberts, who was the one who disarmed Joe at the house earlier. Any way we can tell who was where?"

"Yes, if you can identify the person who planted a perfect right thumb print in the middle of Hanlon's badge. It belongs to Mr. Two-by-Four."

"Roberts," stated Tobin, having gained the knowledge from

Dempsey's recollection of Joe's irritation concerning the agent's lack of respect for the badge.

"That places Roberts at the scene of the DeLuca murder before the fire, probably engaged in some very unprofessional activities."

"Depends on what his job is," Tobin said. "As far as I can tell, he's a professional killer."

"That means Eric Kauffman was the clean-up man in Sunnyside, the inventive filler of bullet holes with mustard-colored toothpaste."

"That makes sense. According to the rookie Sunnyside cop, Roberts and Kauffman split up a few minutes after he arrived; Kauffman stayed while Roberts left for parts unknown. Good to have a little proof to back up the statement, though."

"As for the bullets, none of the four projectiles was in great shape. The one in DeLuca's dog was flattened when it impacted the skull, the two you recovered from the car were deformed by their journey through sheet metal, and the one you dug out of the wall in the stairway was worst of all."

"Still, there's something?" Tobin asked confidently.

"Yes, something," Wolf said. "With about an eighty percent probability, you're looking at two guns here. Both shot the car, and one of those fired both the Sunnyside wall and the DeLuca bullets."

"Another big step toward the truth," Tobin proclaimed. "It proves Joe didn't kill DeLuca's dog if the same gun was used to fire at his car as he was fleeing."

"There's one other thing. The three bullets from the same gun all had striations inconsistent with normal pistol barrel rifling. I think a silencer was used."

"I considered that possibility when the woman living in the apartment under Hanlon's told me she only heard the one 'shot'—the bomb blast—yet I found those two holes in the stairwell."

"Well, here's proof of it," Wolf stated with a slight smile. "That's about all I can offer you, Rich. I'm going to send a few things down to Washington for further study. A neutron activation analysis of those bullets should turn that eighty percent into a ninety-nine point nine, but nothing will be known for at least a few days."

"You've been great. I can't thank you enough, Janine," Tobin said.

"You're going up to see Ottoway now?"

"Yes, right away," he said with a tone of foreboding as he placed Wolf's notes into his unauthorized Hanlon file.

"You have a good case, but you're going to have to be damn persuasive to get him to listen to you after you tell him the subject of your visit."

"I'll do my best. I'll also keep your name out of it."

"Don't go out of your way," Wolf stated. "I mean it, Rich; what you are doing rights an important wrong, and I'm willing to back you up. This is something worth falling on your sword for."

"Beautiful metaphor," Tobin said morosely as he headed for the stairs.

———————

The smooth ride provided by the forklift as it made its way along the wide aisle allowed Joe Hanlon the opportunity to think. Unfortunately. Although he wanted revenge, he was not sure the course of action he had committed to was the right move. Susan's plan seemed like the quickest way to an almost certain death, with at least two backup means to a fast demise waiting in the wings. We each may go insane in our own way, he considered as he moved inexorably on, but this is completely nuts.

According to information gleaned from Alfred Zeichner's computer, he was two levels below the main floor of the dome, somewhere in the southeast region of those twenty round acres, headed for a particular gray metal box among scores of similar cases throughout the huge facility. Susan gave him specific directions: straight for three hundred feet from the point they had gone their separate ways, then left, then right after two hundred feet, then right again at the first opportunity. Then *Bam!*, and unass the AO, which was military slang for getting the hell out of the area of operations, quickly.

At least they had escaped the inner sanctum, the area where, with but forty souls authorized, everyone certainly knew each other. The pair had balked at the last, sturdy one-way revolving door exit with its cameras and sensors, but passed through without a problem.

Joe had never had a full-time job operating a forklift, but he did drive one occasionally while in high school. Grateful for the experience, he maneuvered the propane-powered vehicle deftly, missing walls and workers alike. Though he would have liked the corridors to be deserted, he expected to encounter more than the scant half dozen men he passed on the way to his goal. Obviously not security people, when Joe went by he received nary a glance. The hardhat that obscured his features helped him blend in, as did the yellow rain jacket he found in the compartment under the seat, but he placed most of his faith in his erect posture and confident attitude. Just like he belonged there, just like he knew what he was doing, though he knew the first statement was false and the second nearly so.

Susan's plan was to cut the facility's electricity, which would serve the double purpose of dealing a serious blow to the people responsible for the deaths of their loved ones while allowing the two of them to escape in the dark. According to Susan, the door to the last pipe gallery they had been in before squeezing down to the big drainage tunnel was on their present level and thanks to an electromagnetic catch would be accessible once the power went out.

Turning out the lights wasn't a matter of pulling a switch, though; several tens of millions of tax dollars were expended to prevent an electrical interruption of any sort. An entire power plant was built to prevent it, with a complex system of transfer switches designed to insure uninterruptible power. After a quick study of diagrams and video images in Zeichner's office, however, Susan devised a plan involving strikes on two widely separated points that might thwart the efforts of the electrical engineers.

As Joe rounded the last corner, his concentration was interrupted by multiple alarms. Initiated by the first person to enter Zeichner's office or perhaps by a security guard looking at the right camera at the wrong time, the peals were loud and distinctive enough to rouse everyone in the building.

Straight ahead, the corridor he was traveling ended at another, wider thoroughfare for people, vehicles, and large conduits. Two seconds later, against the far wall of the larger tunnel, he glimpsed his target box, a key junction of lines running from the auxiliary power plant.

Behind him, Joe heard a shout over the din of the alarms—a command to stop. He responded by fully depressing the small accelerator pedal, urging the forklift to its maximum speed. The relay box loomed larger. About six feet high and nearly five wide, it extended out from the wall almost four feet. At least eight six-inch silver pipes entered the right side of the case, within which were thick wires that carried enough high-voltage electricity to service a medium-sized city.

When he heard another shout over the alarm, the whirring engine of the forklift, and what he imagined to be the pounding of his own heart in his ears, Joe forced himself to tune out the aural and concentrate on the visual. He could now see that the box was set on a concrete foundation about eighteen inches high; the tines of his machine, set three feet off the ground, would miss it easily. He cleared the last tunnel wall and jerked the wheel to the left to align the vehicle to the center of mass of his target, then tensed against the inevitable collision.

The forklift hit at a fifty-degree angle to the box, the right tine, five feet long, striking it first. The metal, much thicker than that of a standard junction box, dented, buckled, and was finally pierced by the enormous pressure exerted by a two-ton forklift on a two-square-inch point. After penetrating a foot and a few inches, the steel spear was joined by its twin, paralleling it three and a half feet to the left. The tines cut and smashed several other sturdy pieces of hardware unseen behind the newly contoured face of the box until their motion was arrested by the front frame of the forklift meeting the unyielding concrete pedestal. Though Joe was restrained, the lap belt did not protect his upper body, which lurched forward and slammed his forearms painfully against the steering wheel. Abruptly, the engine of the forklift ceased.

For all the grating, grinding sounds that emanated from the metal case during the collision, the main function of the junction box did not appear to be impaired. In a frantic effort to coax life out of the machine, Joe rotated the ignition key, then again, then again. Finally, the vehicle sputtered to life and he jerked the lift handle, hoping the twisted frame could perform one last job. The silver tines strained and screeched against the metal of its adversary. Firmly secured to its base and further held in place by a dozen thick conduits, the metal box fought its attacker for every millimeter of movement.

Joe frantically thrust the controls forward, then back, then forward again in an effort to jar something loose. The tines had dropped from their uppermost position for the fourth time when it seemed like the sun rose inside the box, so bright was the light. For a moment, the noise accompanying the display was deafening, as wires interacted violently with other wires that were designed never to touch. The sun glare subsided—to the painfully bright but intermittent illumination of an arc welder, complete with showers of sparks exiting from the two penetrations and several seams opened in the battle with the forklift. Then came acrid smoke, the byproduct of burning insulation.

Four feet away from the conflagration, Joe was singed and choked by the black smoke, but was otherwise unharmed. It seemed like a prudent time to leave. As he was climbing off the wrecked vehicle, a chip of concrete spalled off the wall behind him. Though the destruction emanating from the box was impressive, Joe knew immediately that the latest damage was not caused by errant sparks. He was being shot at.

Joe returned to the plan—Susan's plan—one last time. It called for Joe to go back the way he came, feeling his way through unlit passages, but the corridors were still illuminated, and an armed guard was coming straight at him down his route of retreat. Susan had promised that her set of electric conduits would be pulled apart with an electric hoist and be out of commission at least a full minute before Joe hit the box. As he grabbed his pack, he vowed to chastise her concerning the miscalculation when next they met.

With the noise from the box reduced to a moderate crackle, Joe heard the next shot, but thanks to the dim lighting, the smoke, and the distance from his pursuer, it struck one of the steel uprights of the fork-lift instead of his head.

He grabbed his pack and sprinted away from the wreckage. After clearing the smoke, he saw three onlookers thirty feet ahead, civilian workers in hard hats and coveralls mesmerized by the fireworks. "Get out, get out!" he shouted as he closed on the trio, frantically waving his arms. "It's gonna blow!"

Joe didn't know what might blow, of course, but the effect of his exhortations was immediate and gratifying: the onlookers headed for the nearest exit. With an advantage in momentum, Joe caught up with the group, then intermingled with the men as they ran toward a metal door fifty feet away. He heard no more shots in the corridor.

The door opened on a wide concrete pan stairway. Joe leapt past his temporary companions and onto the stairs. He was at the bottom of the stairwell, which saved him the decision on which way to go.

Heedless of wounds new and old, Joe ascended the steps at a run, quickly distancing himself from his pursuer. There would be others ahead, he knew, as cameras pointed toward him at every landing. Even if they had not been activated before, they would certainly have been manned since the sounding of the alarm, the cacophony of which ech-oed even louder in the stairwell.

Losing strength, he forced himself to maintain a swift pace as he climbed another four runs and forty-eight stairs to the end of the line, the top of the run. Again he escaped a decision, as he faced a single door.

He opened the door and stepped into the space beyond. No one was waiting for him. There was only one way to travel—to the left—as all other directions were blocked by gray metal shelving stocked with cardboard boxes. He moved down the passage at a power walk and was quickly in the midst of more than a dozen workers, except they were not working, having been distracted by the alarm, which echoed hol-lowly in the large room.

Joe slowed his pace and adjusted his hard hat with grimy hands. "Everything's all right," he assured the pensive employees around him. "Nothing but a little fire down below. It's being taken care of." He walked on swiftly. The corridors widened, and the shelving was joined by a panoply of other gray furniture: chairs, utility tables, metal cabi-nets, small carts on stubby wheels.

Then he looked up and realized where he was. What at first glance appeared to be a ceiling twenty feet overhead was actually ten times higher and spread out for hundreds of feet in every direction. He could not see the entire circular side wall, but his vision encompassed enough of the vast space of the main dome to astound him. Just above the mercury vapor lamps that illuminated the immense enclosure, he could make out countless crimson hexagons that covered the curved ceiling.

Now what? he asked himself. Having lost his orientation, he only knew he could not stay in one location for long. He heard a door bang open somewhere to his left, and to his right heard running and shouting. Despite his verbal soothings, the people around him began to realize Joe did not fit in, no matter what the emergency. He moved left then right then left through the storage racks, trying to keep to one general direction. He turned another corner and the way was blocked by two uniformed personnel with boots polished to a mirror shine and smart berets and pistols pointed right at him. He swiveled ninety degrees and came face to face with another man, a civilian guard with a soiled white shirt, wrinkled pants, and a bigger gun, which made up for his lack of military bearing.

Joe was halfway through raising his hands when the lights went out, the annoying alarms ceased, and twenty acres of opaque hexagons became windows, exposing the interior of the dome to the brightness of a magnificent spring afternoon. It was a glorious message, a grand gift from Susan, he knew instantly. All eyes immediately looked skyward.

It was a sight to draw anyone's attention from whatever they were doing, but Joe, somewhat more motivated, recovered quicker than those in his immediate vicinity and within half a second was diving through an array of metal shelving, displacing boxes containing items that were much heavier than their small size indicated. He made it through with his pack, but lost his hat and picked up several bruises in the process.

After separating himself from his pursuers by three aisles and perhaps ten seconds, Joe boldly chose the high road, climbing up one of the sturdy shelving units and running its length, then jumping to another and doing the same. He gained sixty feet and some perspective of the floor arrangement, then dropped between two rows of cabinets.

Having temporarily lost the trio that had detained him, Joe moved quickly. There were people everywhere, some frightened by the abrupt change of their workplace, some confused at the alien appearance of their surroundings, illuminated by natural light for the first time, but most were merely awestruck by the dazzling blue sky that contrasted dramatically with the quixotic shadows within their thousand-foot fishbowl. No one in sight looked threatening, but he did not see the man who shot at him through the open shelving from two aisles away.

The gunman was the civilian member of the let's-corner-Joe-again group. Fortunately, his marksmanship was nearly as bad as his appearance, and he missed. A woman screamed as the bullet continued past Joe, penetrated a sheet metal cabinet, and lodged in a stack of technical manuals on a desk.

"Hey!" yelled the man behind the desk, sharply admonishing the shooter.

Joe leapt past people, shelving, and machinery and found himself in a wide passageway. A hundred feet up the lane, he sighted an open car, slightly larger than a golf cart and towing a small trailer. As he jumped aboard, he punched the silver pedal to the floor and was rewarded with a satisfying forward acceleration. One man out of a group of three ran cursing after the vehicle, but was quickly outdistanced.

Joe looked for an exit at the same instant he realized he was abandoning Susan. Not having any idea of the direction she might be, to even think of linking up with her was impossible, he realized, the knowledge searing itself into his soul with all the pain and permanence of a branding iron. Fight or flight: openly exposed and with the world on his tail, the decision was again made for him, but the situation was too close to his running retreat after the death of Elizabeth. The lack of knowledge concerning Susan, whether she was killed, wounded, or captured, only made it worse.

It was also worse because instead of one, there were six men after him, and those were only the ones Joe could see in the wide alley, running, shouting, waving guns. A different path was obviously needed, and he found one in the narrow space between a concrete wall and a large stack of pallets. Fifty feet later, the wall jogged in front of him and he made a quick right turn into an uncomfortably open bay.

"Halt!" he heard off to his right, a sharp command. A quick glance showed four impeccably attired airmen carrying M-16s. They would have made a fine honor guard at a military funeral, except their rifles were not pointed skyward in salute, but were aimed at the driver of the closest vehicle.

"Now this really *is* it," Joe hissed. Gritting his teeth in defiance, he hunkered down a few miserable inches and kept on trucking.

"Hold fire!" was the next crisp command, and was so totally off, so precisely opposite of the only possible order to the riflemen, that Joe ventured a look around. To his right were the military guards, guns at the ready but not yet filling him full of nasty 5.56mm holes. The answer to why not loomed large to the left.

Though he had never seen one and the closeness of the huge black object made it impossible to view it all at once, he realized he was driving behind a B-2 bomber, and it was his proximity to it that was saving his life. Although the bulk of airplane rose above the direct line of fire, it was close enough that the commander of the armed foursome had obviously deemed it unwise to risk hitting the plane with errant shots or ricochets. At best, damage to the worth-more-than-its-weight-in-gold plane might be calculated at a million dollars a round; at worst, an unlucky bullet would puncture a fuel tank, resulting in a conflagration that would consume the plane, its sisters in adjacent bays, and the entire facility, tens of billions of tax dollars up in flames.

Reluctant to leave the object that was keeping him at least temporarily free from a bloody death, Joe made a sharp left turn and aimed for a spot between the landing gear. Within seconds he was directly under the plane, his head missing the nadir of the bomber's dark undercarriage by inches. Beyond the B-2, he caught sight of a possible exit, seventy feet ahead. It was a huge hanger door, thirty feet high and just short of two hundred feet wide. A roll-up door, it had been in the process of opening or closing when the blackout occurred, resulting in the presence of a narrow gap between the concrete floor and the bottom of the door. It was difficult to tell whether the space was two or four feet high—he needed three and a half to make it through with the vehicle—but he went for it anyway. Twenty feet from the door, he knelt down on the floor of the small car to assure that he would be conscious if he crashed and would not be decapitated if he went through.

He went through, though the hard weather stripping bolted to the bottom of the door marred the cart's paint and clipped off a rear-view mirror. Quickly recovering to the drivers seat, Joe punched the pedal, then looked around. As expected, he was on wide-open concrete. To his right, beyond the slight curve of the dome, was Pope's main runway. Two hundred yards to the front was a fence, beyond which was an open, empty field. Twice that distance to his left, beyond the same fence, was a forest. He turned left.

The way seemed clear. There was no one outside in the vicinity and none of the three other hanger doors he saw was even partially open. Several figures emerged from the dome through the same exit he had used, including the M-16 quartet, but they hadn't the slightest chance of catching up to him.

The same was not true of the pair of black Humvees that popped into view five seconds later. Probably summoned by a radio call, they closed fast on the intruder.

Joe looked ahead, gauging his next move as he approached the fence, or rather the double fence, the parallel barriers being separated by twenty feet of weedy gravel. The first was topped with razor concertina, the second with three strands of barbed wire, angled away from the complex. Between the far fence and before the woods was a wide, open depression. It was the Little River, Joe realized, though he could not yet see any water. It also didn't look little; the space appeared to be almost two hundred feet wide, not good at all for cover or concealment.

As he reached the fence, Joe braced for impact. The heavy chain link of the barrier held, but stretched as it brought the vehicle to an abrupt halt in three short feet. He struggled through the narrow gap that opened up between the wire and the ground, ripping his yellow jacket on the jagged twists at the bottom of the fencing as he went.

Between fences, Joe looked back and saw the Humvees, side-by-side, less than a hundred yards away and closing fast. He hit the second fence running; with a painful pounce, his hands achieved a hold two thirds up its height. More agony followed as he awkwardly clambered up the obstacle. For a moment, he regretted the weight of the pack, but then had an inspiration as the steep riverbank came into view. He incurred only one puncture in one hand as he cleared the barbed wire, then dropped to the ledge beyond. The tactical vehicles stopped and several guards were out of the vehicles' doors within seconds.

Joe dropped down the bank, out of sight of his pursuers. Figuring he had but fifteen seconds before the armed men would get through the first fence and have a clear shot at him through the second, he pulled off his rain jacket, tied it onto his pack with a sloppy overhand knot, then heaved the items into the river. Then he moved upstream into the folds of the bank.

He was a hundred yards away when he heard the first shots, signifying the destruction of the jacket and pack with its rope, flashlight, carabiners, and pistol, which might, for a few precious minutes, be mistaken for a fleeing suspect.

After the first barrage, he heard more shots, sporadic and farther away. A half mile after passing a familiar array of eight-inch pipes protruding out of a concrete wall, he waded across the river and entered the woods beyond. The shade under the trees looked inviting, but he did not stop to rest.

CHAPTER 24

Maneuvering the car onto a steel truss bridge, Andrew Weiss finally caught sight of his destination. The Farm, as it was known by all connected with the Bonnelli organization, was purchased by one of Victor's lieutenants after the don expressed a desire to obtain the kind of bucolic retreat that so enthralled the visitors to Appalacin decades before. Consisting of a hundred sixty acres of open fields and wooded hills upon which stood a dozen buildings ranging from a stately clapboard house to a brick schoolhouse, the place had been all but abandoned when Bonnelli took over.

Seventy yards beyond the bridge, Weiss turned left onto the property. For the most part, the buildings lay in a line along the half mile of Hudson River frontage. The river at this spot, forty miles north of Albany, was narrow, no more than a stone's throw across for those with a minor-league arm.

After he passed four buildings, Weiss stopped in front of the main residence, a wide frame structure two and a half stories high. Although he managed to work in a nap before starting the long trek, he was still very tired. Even with Victor Bonnelli dead, he obeyed the old rule regarding visitors to the Farm: only those close to the family were allowed, drivers included. The two other times Weiss had visited, a man from Nicky's crew had chauffeured him; this time, a driver had not been available.

Weiss grabbed his briefcase, exited the car, and was admitted into the house by one of Nicky's henchmen. The five men inside were doing exactly what they had done in lower Manhattan, confining themselves within a single dingy room. A card game was underway with three participants, one of whom was the man who admitted him. Nicky, facing away, was watching an *I Dream of Jeannie* rerun on a television in the corner. By a window, Joey Messina was reading a novel entitled *Elbow*

Room.

Weiss walked over to Nicky. Only on a few other occasions had he encountered such a disheveled man, and most of those had involved Nicky himself in the midst of past binges. Immediately, he determined his long trip had been wasted, that the stinking, sweating man before him was in no condition to aid him in any way and would not be for at least another three days.

"Nicky, how are you?" the lawyer greeted his client.

"Weiss, you fucker!" Nicky slurred after unevenly jerking his head to the side and sighting the man through narrow, bloodshot eyes. "What the fuck are you doing here?"

"Just came to see how you are getting on," Weiss replied, surprised that Nicky was coherent.

"I'm just fucking great, stuck in this fucking hole for . . . for . . . for as long as I fucking have."

"Looks like you're doing fine, Nicky," Weiss encouraged. It was the biggest lie he had told all week.

"That's *Mr. Bonnelli* to you, fucker! *I'm* the fucking head of the— thing now. You're just here to fucking help, to tell me what the fuck is going on."

Weiss quickly grasped at any innocuous tidbit of information that might pass as business news. "All the tax returns were submitted on time. The IRS is still scrutinizing a few of our past submissions, though."

"They're fucking screwing with us; the fuckers are fucking with the fucking operation. Fuck!"

Adverb, noun, verb, adjective, interjection, Weiss mentally ticked off. All in one breath. Even for Nicky, it must have been a record. It was apparent the man was quickly losing any remaining threads of control.

The mention of taxes was also unfortunate in that it reminded Nicky of the man who used to sign the forms. "The fucking funeral was—is over, isn't it? I can still fucking hear things."

"You were in no condition to attend, Mr. Bonnelli," Weiss stated, then thought quickly and added, "The police are looking for you, too, for what happened last Saturday."

"You're fucking lying to me," Nicky concluded. "Where the fuck are the things, the fucking things from the house?"

"Everything was moved to secure storage."

"The fuck it was! Where's the fucking money?"

"It's being held for you; you can have it anytime you say."

"I'm saying, I'm fucking saying, but it's not fucking here, is it?

You fucking have it, don't you?"

"It's in the safe in my office, all of it."

"I'll bet it's fucking all there, in your fucking safe! Where's my mother's fucking jewelry?"

"In my safe with the money."

Nicky rose to his feet, involuntarily kicking an empty vodka bottle across the floor. From somewhere—his belt, an unseen holster—he produced a pistol. "You're fucking robbing me!"

"Nicky—Mr. Bonnelli—please sit down," Weiss urged, a shadow of panic edging his voice.

"You can't fucking do this to me, you bastard!" Nicky yelled, raising the quavering gun and pointing it as well as he could right between Weiss's eyes. At a range of three feet, it would be tough for even a drunk psychotic to miss. "This is what we do to fuckers like you!"

Bam! A body fell to the floor, dead. Even though his eyes had been wide open the whole time, it took Weiss a moment to realize it was not him. He looked down and saw Nicky, blood oozing from his head onto the dusty oak flooring. He then looked up and saw Joey Messina, smoking gun in hand. Like an epiphany, he instantly acquired an intense appreciation for the term *fauxfire*.

"Mess—" was all Weiss could manage before another crisis arose. Immediately, the three card players were on their feet, guns drawn.

"John! Eddie! Carlo!" Messina called out in quick succession. "Put 'em down! Put 'em down! It had to be done. You know we were going nowhere with Nicky; now we're free to get out there and kick some ass."

John, Eddie, and Carlo did not fire, and after a few interminable seconds slowly lowered their pistols. All four guns of the living were then re-holstered simultaneously. The three men took a few steps toward Messina, then the closest one spoke for all. "We're behind you, Joey. Always have been. Everybody else'll feel the same. Shit, that piece of crap never did anything for us like you have. Just give us a little warning before you open up next time."

"Okay, guys," Messina replied. "We have a lot to talk about, but privately. Let me get Weiss here to his room. Clean up the mess while I'm gone."

"You saved my life," Weiss managed, his feet momentarily refusing to move.

"I didn't really want to do that to Nicky, not yet anyway, but I couldn't let the little shit kill my favorite attorney; I need your legal mind working for me, not splattered all over the wall. Come on, Mr. Weiss," Messina said as he walked toward the foyer.

Weiss followed the nation's newest crime boss out the door, confident the Bonnelli organization would survive for some years to come. Though he knew there would be no great upheaval and his practice would continue to flourish, his abrupt discovery that he had no stomach for death up close led him once again to thoughts of another, safer career.

———————

With every breath a labored gasp and every step aggravating the multitude of sharp pains and dull aches that saturated his being, Joe forced himself to move back toward the Air Force base and its accursed, though now impotent, dome of death. He didn't want to go right up to the huge, round hanger, but he needed to see it to get the bearings to his sanctuary.

They had been after him all afternoon: helicopters of all description and vehicles of the Air Force, the Army, and at least two local police forces patrolling the intermittent two-lane blacktop roads and rutted trails of the sparsely populated area. There were also patrols on foot, from two-man teams to squads of paratroopers from Fort Bragg. Utilizing almost-forgotten training, Joe eluded them all, though the fact that he knew so many details about the extensive search effort was an indication that it had been a close thing at times.

The terrain helped. Varying from rocky, wooded hills to meandering brooks and more than one stretch of swampland, the landscape had provided concealment for him while it denied easy access to his pursuers. The setting of the Sun within three hours after his escape aided him too, but that was a decidedly mixed blessing. Though many searchers had called it a night while others moved closer to the roads, the almost total absence of illumination made it extremely difficult to walk without stumbling, bumping into rocks or logs, or getting whacked by low-hanging branches, all of which Joe did with increasing frequency as weariness entrenched itself in his bones.

He struggled on, hoping Susan was waiting for him at Evans' house. It was possible, if the magnetic security door opened after the electricity was cut and if she had not waited for him and if she remembered the way back to the manhole where they had first gained entry to the tunnels and if she linked up with Evans, who had promised to drive by the opening at 4:00 and again at 8:00 in case they needed a lift. It was a great number of "ifs." He was forced to consider that she might be dead, shot down in the passageway as she was ripping the cables from the wall, completing her task with her dying breath. Then both loves of his life would be there, in the same building, in the same state.

As he breeched the crest of a low ridge, he saw the dome at last, two or three miles distant. The electricity had been restored, though the reflecting panels would never work again. The interior lights now reached toward the night sky through the transparent roof. Evans' house, according to his muddled calculations, should be off to his front right—no, left—about forty-five degrees. Struggling to recall the intricacies of a forty-five degree angle, he pointed his body in the approximate direction he thought might possibly be correct and started off again. Within fifty yards, he dropped to a lower elevation and lost sight of the dome.

After traveling five hundred yards, during which he fell twice and was hit in the upper body half a dozen times by low-hanging branches, he came upon a welcome obstacle. It was the fence, the boundary of Pope Air Force Base. It was easy going, relatively, trudging along the fence line, as it was clear of trees and brush, almost a path. That was good, because he didn't know if he had the strength to travel another fifty yards through the woods. There might be patrols in the area, he knew, but he did not alter his plan to use the fence as a guide. Physically, he was running out of strength, and his diminished mental capabilities precluded coming up with anything better.

Gradually, the vegetation thinned; after half a mile, the trees were noticeably dispersed on Joe's side of the fence and were gone completely from the other. The dome again came into view in the distance, looking almost like it had the evening before from Eugene Evans' backyard.

Judging he was close to the house, he walked away from the fence through the strip of woods he and Susan and Evans had traversed the previous evening, hopefully at the right spot. It was not, though; the house in front of him, though similar in size and shape to his goal, had its garage on the right, not the left.

Going once again back to the fence, down the line, and once more through the narrow forest, Joe dropped to his knees three times. He was nearing the end. The house before him was dark and unadorned but to Joe it was a beautiful sight. It was his destination; every detail he could muster from his exhausted brain fit.

Quietly, he moved to the front of the dwelling and tapped on Evans' bedroom window with a pebble. The front door opened, and he walked six agonizing steps to the stoop.

"Come in," was the whispered command, followed by a muffled cough.

"Susan?" Joe managed to get out after being hit by the dizzying warmth and enveloping scents and sounds of a safe haven.

"No," came the simple, dreaded response, the last word Joe heard before he collapsed, half unconscious and half just plain asleep.

———————

Philip Roberts' day had begun fine, but quickly degenerated into the worst day he had experienced in ten years, so miserable that he could not conceive it could go any further downhill. After sleeping late, which he routinely did when night operations were underway, he ate a leisurely lunch, then went to work. He entered Pope and passed the outer gate to the B-2 complex without a problem, but as he pulled into his parking space, he heard the distinctive honks of an alarm coming from the big building three hundred feet away. He ran to the inner security post, slammed his identity card into its slot, then headed toward his workplace, deep underground.

He didn't make it. Just as he reached the elevator inside the main dome, the unthinkable happened; the electricity went out, and he watched the active surfaces of the object it had been his duty to protect disappear. Cut off from his work area, he made a beeline to the main security offices, where he overheard that a saboteur had just escaped the building. Roberts joined eight others who slipped into two Humvees and less than two minutes later they were closing on an armament supply cart. When they stopped, the fugitive was already over the top of the outer perimeter fence, and Roberts saw the yellow-jacketed intruder for less than a second before he dropped out of sight. In that brief moment, he thought the man's face looked familiar, but immediately dismissed the notion as a product of job-related dementia.

The security personnel snipped a wider opening in the bottom of the first chain link fence, then tossed a barrage of shots through the second at the yellow jacket receding quickly downriver. Seconds later, the outer fence was breeched and, stupidly, Roberts let himself be caught up in the thrill of the hunt. He traveled with the group a half mile down the Little River to the fallen log that finally entangled the pack and jacket. Immediately, the military policemen fanned out in all directions, as if the pack was the point from which the suspect fled; only Roberts realized they had been duped.

He aided in the subsequent search, but his attention quickly turned back to his duties underground. With one of the most sophisticated UPS systems in the world, he knew the electric service should have lived up to its acronym, should have been an uninterruptible power supply. Eventually, he commandeered one of the circus train of generators coming from Pope's less electrically protected main post area. It took over an hour to wire the generator into the elevator panel box, but finally he was afforded the opportunity to find out what had happened underground. He personally led out twelve of the fourteen people present within the darkened passages, the last of the dozen being Dr. Alfred Zeichner, who had been discovered tied up in his office after the facility lost power. It was another hour before the other two were brought up. Caught by the blackout in the Lower Array, they were hoisted up the shaft used for deliveries of construction materials, major pieces of equipment, and hexagonal panels. Not pleased with their mode of travel, six hundred feet straight up in an improvised sling, they were nonetheless happy to be free from their deep, dark prison.

Considering the magnitude of the outage and the damage done, five hours was not an exorbitant amount of time to restore power, but to Roberts it was damn near an eternity. Twice, he looked over the shoulders of the tradesmen working on the big, burnt-out distribution box; three times, he visited the corridor where thick, twisted conduit had carried commercial power to the complex. The latter was repaired first; estimates to bring the auxiliary power back on line varied from twelve hours to two days.

It didn't matter, though, Roberts reflected from his office, as the reason for a reliable electrical backup was gone. Even after working with the project for years, Roberts did not completely understand the complex combination of physics and chemistry that made the panels function, he only knew that when the electricity was cut from one, it was irreparably altered and could not be turned back on like a neon sign. And when 60,700 of them lost electric power, every one was just plain busted.

He had done what was necessary with his own people, calling those nearby in to discuss how their operations would change now that it looked like their primary reason for employment was gone, and calling back those in the field because their mission could not be fulfilled. Their target had been called out of the area anyway, he learned from Jeffery Slusher.

It was Zeichner who told him who had done the deed. A portion of Roberts swung in admiration of Joe Hanlon, the fugitive who had not only evaded him but had bested him right on his home turf. It was only a small portion, however; ninety-nine percent of his being still wanted Hanlon dead, his body chopped up into tiny pieces before being fed to farm animals, then to be shit out into some North Carolina field.

Hanlon had not done it alone, though. Having followed the reports of his adversary closely, he knew of Susan DeLuca. The papers said

Hanlon had kidnapped or killed her after murdering her father. He knew that wasn't true, but never in his wildest conjectures would he have imagined he could convince her to join him in his quest for insanely risky revenge. A hell of a guy, Roberts thought, returning for an instant to the one percent.

He was fingering Hanlon's folder, when he heard a rap on his doorframe.

"Phil, got a minute?" asked Dr. Alfred Zeichner.

"It seems I have a lot of minutes—now," Roberts replied, his voice dripping with self-loathing.

"Don't count on taking a vacation," Zeichner replied lightly. "We're going to be busier than ever."

"How can you possibly be so cheerful?" Roberts asked, waving his arm at a nearby chair.

Zeichner sat casually, bringing an ankle up to a knee. "Make no mistake about it, Philip, what happened today was bad, a disaster of monumental proportions. I wouldn't have wished for it for anything, but within the year things are going to be better than ever."

"That doesn't make sense," Roberts protested. "At the least we're going to be behind schedule."

"First, the schedule was an arbitrary goal; it can be changed, although there will be some grousing among the higher-ups. Second, it will give us an opportunity to make some real improvements. About four months ago, for instance, as a direct result of the testing you have been so intimately involved with, we developed an alteration in the chemical composition of the panel coatings that will lead to a thirty percent increase in efficiency. Such a discovery was nice on paper, but we certainly weren't going to stop everything and retool. Now we don't have to wait until the next dome is built in five years; we can make the changes here and now."

"Security certainly won't ever be an issue again," Roberts stated, the enthusiasm of his visitor slightly rubbing off. "I'll be surprised if they don't double the topside force. I'll probably recruit a few more as well when we're ready for field tests again."

"Did you find out how they got in here?"

"We've poked around a few places, but we haven't found their path yet. Because they used Vaught's card getting out, they obviously made their way into the Lower Array, but we don't know if they took the elevator shaft or the pipe shaft."

"Maybe they rappelled down," Zeichner offered. "That was climbing rope they tied me up with."

"They obviously split up after leaving you, probably where Hanlon took the forklift." Roberts made a mental note to strongly address vehicle security and key control among the topside personnel. "After that, he pulled up a big electrical box like it was a pallet of parts while this Susan DeLuca made spaghetti out of some substantial electrical conduit seven hundred feet away. I don't know if they planned to link up afterward, but they didn't, not anywhere around here anyway. Hanlon hightailed it over the fence and made it into the woods north of here. I saw that myself. The woman, from all indications, escaped through the utility gallery leading back to the main post. Search parties are out, and will be until we find them."

"It was actually quite brilliant, this turning off the power. Somehow, they had pieced together what we had here, what would be most damaging. It was the woman who pushed for the sabotage; Hanlon just wanted to get away."

"*Her* idea?" Roberts asked, dismayed by the fact that, in dealing with her father, it was he who had put the venom in her to commit such an act.

"Seems to have thought it up as she was sitting at my desk, going through the maps and security programs."

"And Hanlon just wanted to leave, without doing anything."

"He felt having the disk was enough to expose our little operation to the world."

"Disk?" the question sounded with alarm.

"Yes. The woman copied files to a disk, I don't know which ones." Zeichner paused and noticed the dismay in Roberts' eyes. He held up an easy hand. "Not to worry, my friend. It was a Celltella, 'the disk with an acid core,'" he said as if he were reading an advertisement. "To read information off of one of those, they would first need the proper disk drive, which means they would have to break into another secure government installation, then they would need someone properly trained in the special handling of the disk, then they would need the proper passwords. One error, and the device's unique feature would be activated, and all information thereon would be destroyed to a much safer degree than just erasing it. But you know all this, of course."

"It has been a few months since I used a Celltella drive," Roberts said. "I don't have one on my machine."

"No, I'm not concerned about the disk, but I am somewhat worried about what our intruders might say. They learned a great deal about our operations over the past few days, and not just from their foray here. They know about Albany, for instance."

"How the hell . . ." Roberts started, then collected himself. "There's a slight danger someone might hear something they shouldn't, but I don't think it will amount to much. If they're not killed, they're going to be in somebody's custody soon, and when that happens, they're going to quickly be under our exclusive control. Then . . ." Abruptly curtailed, Roberts exhaled quickly and leaned up against the back of his chair to catch his breath.

"Something wrong, Phil?"

After a couple of short coughs, Roberts sat back up. "Not a thing, Dr. Z; probably something I ate at breakfast coming back to get me."

"Well, I want you to get a full examination in the next couple of days. You know what special conditions we work under. Doesn't hurt to be a little cautious."

"Okay, Doc, but I might have to push it back to next week. I have a feeling things will be extremely busy around here until then. Funding won't be a problem, will it?"

"Perish the thought," Zeichner scolded. "We're the top Air Force priority, although only a handful of people know it. No, we'll do a little of this, and a little of that, and a little of the other thing, and the money will be there. The B-2 project has always provided the perfect umbrella under which to hide: vastly expensive, shrouded in secrecy, and providing top security."

"Once we replace the panels, I suppose we'll have to run many of the initial tests again," Roberts said.

"Not to nearly the extent we did two years ago. Perhaps one or two fields of rabbits, then two or three human tests will bring us right back where we were."

Roberts chuckled at the mention of the rabbits. To calibrate the precise positioning of the neutrino beam, Roberts and his teams had placed caged rabbits two meters apart in a grid surrounding a point determined by Global Positioning System satellites. The center of the area where the five to ten rabbits died indicated where the beam had hit relative to the GPS point, allowing for directional calibration. A dozen tests had been conducted in remote fields. At first, the grids consisted of twenty-one by twenty-one cages—441 total rabbits—but as the aim of the reflecting device in Albany improved, the number was reduced to eighty-one, then twenty-five rabbits. When that phase of testing was over, the weapon was aimed perfectly: the nine rabbits in the center of a five-by-five grid died, and the sixteen around the perimeter did not.

"We'll be going back to death row?" Roberts inquired, referring to their earliest tests on human subjects. Controlled, immobile, easy to pinpoint with GPS, and expendable, the twelve inmates who cheated the hangman by mysteriously dying in their cells proved to be excellent subjects.

"I don't see why not," Zeichner said. "Two or three by the end of this year, then on to field testing and, within a year, to full stationary application."

Roberts nodded, relaxed. "Good news." The telephone on the desk rang, and before it completed its first set of pulses, the agent had the receiver in his hand. "What is it?" he asked. "Yes. . . . Yes. . . . That's something, anyway. . . . Okay, I'll be right over."

"What's up, Phil?"

"They found the girl, here on base. She's . . . ugh!" Roberts said, pounding his right hand flat against his chest, simultaneously attempting to stand. "She's . . . oh godDAMN!" he shouted, then pitched forward, his head hitting hard on the desk. He remained immobile for the rest of his life, all four seconds, when the last weak flutters of his heart ceased forever. The clock on the wall read three hands straight up: exactly midnight.

WEDNESDAY
15 APRIL

CHAPTER 25

A beam from the Sun awoke Joe Hanlon from a dreamless sleep. The neutrino emanating Sun, he reflected, except on this day, for the first time in years, those neutrinos could not harm anyone, anywhere. The cost of that happy circumstance, however, drove him into an agonizing despair he had not felt for—days.

At least he was free and fit enough to do something about it, he learned as he sat up on the bed and flexed his limbs. His entire body ached and his head throbbed, but no bones were broken, no open wounds gushed forth. He stood up and sat back down again immediately, dizzy and slightly nauseous. Maybe he wasn't so fit after all, he considered, but he still had to do something. He had no idea what, though.

Where was Susan? Dead or captured, probably. Still, he knew he should not count her out. She had proven incredibly resourceful for a— not a woman, not primarily, but for a desk-bound executive from a whitebread Boston company.

The door was open an inch and a knock opened the gap to four. "Awake Joe?" Eugene Evans inquired.

"Yes. What time is it?"

"About eight. You got a good nine hours sleep, but I still didn't think I'd be seeing you before noon."

"Things to do," Joe said flatly.

"In that you are absolutely correct," Evans said. "Take a shower, then come down to the kitchen for breakfast."

Joe did as he was told. It was good to get out of the damp, gritty underwear and under the warm water. Gradually, the stiffness lessened and the headache abated. His palm hurt from the barbed wire puncture and the gash in his leg still needed at least a week to completely close up, but otherwise he was fine. Involuntarily, his spirits began to rise, but the image of Elizabeth and the possibility that Susan might be close by to her and in the same condition tempered them from rising much.

"You caused quite a stir at the base yesterday," Evans began after Joe joined him in the kitchen. "It's the biggest news around here since—well, since the 'worlds biggest dome' was dedicated. There's a great deal of talk about the ongoing search, but so far, there has been no word of anyone killed or captured. You two didn't recruit anyone after you went underground, did you?" Evans asked.

"No, why?"

"According to the media, the facility was struck by a 'group' of terrorists, perhaps four or five strong. It's total fabrication of course, thought up by whatever breed of PR men they have over there. I'm sure they thought no one would believe just two infiltrators could cause such destruction. I had a hard time believing it myself."

"You knew we might take down the project when you dropped us off yesterday."

"Ha!" the interjection shot out of Evans' mouth like a bullet. "I knew you might *try*. A million to one shot, and you pulled it off."

"But still you helped us, in every possible way. I've gone over it and over it, but all I come up with is some nebulous concept of justice. I still don't understand why you assisted us."

"It involves a lesson I learned many years ago, one that changed my life in many ways. I suppose it's about time someone else knew the whole, sordid story. You know those fishing trips I was talking about yesterday? Well, the only fishing I've been involved with lately has been with a bunch of doctors who have been fishing for a way to keep me alive, and they haven't been getting any nibbles. I certainly don't have six months left and I probably don't have three. Since the tale isn't written down anywhere, I guess I'll pass it along as an oral history."

Evans shifted uneasily in the kitchen chair. "I love this country, but sometimes the damn fools that run it have to be put in their place, and other times they just need to be plain stopped. In the early sixties, I was a young light colonel assigned to ballistic missiles. My last duty was as the commander of three missile installations in North Dakota. These were ICBM bases: missiles in silos, six per facility, every one topped with a twenty-megaton nuke. As part of my assignment, I learned the ins and outs of dozens of systems, from the intricacies of the warheads to the function of the blast doors. During one particularly rigorous inspection of a relay subsystem that transferred launch commands to the missiles, I discovered a potential problem. Everything worked perfectly, but I noted that under extreme conditions an electrical short circuit could result in a positive launch code being issued by mistake—at least that was my theory. Not being a design engineer, I was somewhat scoffed at when I voiced my concern, but it was dutifully looked into. Tests were performed, but after the expenditure of two weeks and twenty thousand dollars, the determination by the experts was that my worries were groundless." Evans paused, out of breath.

"It happened one night in a storm, and a thunderstorm rolling across the plains of North Dakota is something nearly on a par with a hurricane or a tornado. There were six men on duty at site Baker, tired men at 0220. They knew of the weather through a dispatch but paid little heed to it, as they were scheduled to remain underground for another three days. Lightning can act funny at times, not 'ha ha' funny, but 'Earth reduced to a lifeless cinder where clouds of radiation waft over its dead surface' funny. The bolt entered the facility through the main antenna, frying the communications while simultaneously creating the short circuit I feared. Instantly, the verification codes for the launch of the six missiles were reflected back through the system, showing up as a launch command on the consoles. When authentication procedures were conducted, they matched, of course, and the officers began to follow the procedures leading up to the launch."

Joe frowned as he visualized the scene.

"The men were alert and the atmosphere was tense, but, no, they did not believe the world had gone to war. We conducted drills all the time, some of which were frightening in their realism. In this case, though, there were no test protocols in place; all entries were made to active and fully functional equipment, and it responded accordingly. In short order, the ICBMs were just a push of a button away from being launched at Russia."

"But the missiles did not fire," Joe stated with some confidence.

"No, because two weeks before, the officer in charge had personally removed an electric pulse manifold from every one of his eighteen missiles while he made further efforts to correct what he still considered to be a problem. The missiles did not move when those buttons were pressed. In the days following, it was discovered that the twenty-thousand-dollar tests came close to finding the problem, but the engineers failed to apply enough current, such as that generated by a bolt of lightning, to the crucial circuit board."

"Then what happened?"

"The episode ended with several 'official' versions. To the personnel at the complex, the incident was officially part of a special drill. To a handful of us who knew all the facts, perhaps five in all, it was officially damn near the end of the world. To those Air Force officers in between, it was officially sabotage of the facility by its commanding officer, due to stress or ignorance or a latent, sick pacifism. It was all handled quietly, without court martial. I was allowed to resign and received an honorable discharge."

"*Allowed* to resign?" Joe choked. "But without your intervention—"

"Then those young men deep within Baker Site would have been very surprised when, in the middle of the 'drill,' the walls rumbled and all of a sudden they found themselves short six items of military hardware worth several million dollars."

"Didn't they know you saved the world?"

"I think the handful of people privy to the facts realized it, then they sat down and second-guessed themselves. After several days of self-delusion, they finally concluded I had made several mistakes that culminated in an unauthorized drill, which, while unorthodox, would never have resulted in a launch because other safeguards would have been activated."

"That's crap, isn't it?"

"Pure and unadulterated, but at least they replaced the defective hardware along with me."

"Well, Colonel Evans, you've managed to scare the hell out of me, but I still don't fully understand how that incident motivated you to help wreck a top secret Air Force installation."

"That experience taught me that going outside the lines can be patriotic, even if no one else knows it. The same kind of ignorance and stupidity I faced exists at Pope. Although millions were not saved, a dozen or so people is still a respectable number."

Joe stared at him quizzically. "I still don't get it."

"About a year after the dome became operational, it became apparent there was a problem. Statistics were played with and skewed every which way by the media, the government, and the grapevine, but it became clear that serious heart-related health problems among those who worked under the Beehive were up to two and a half times more prevalent than those working elsewhere at Pope, which is at least significant, if not outrageous."

"I'd wager the problem was not solved."

"Various possibilities for the higher incident rate were discussed, including the fact that a portion of the site had at one time been used as a dump, that the fuel for the B-2s is toxic, that nuclear weapons are stored at the facility, and that the dome itself, being electrified, acted like high-tension wires and emitted a harmful electromagnetic field.

OSHA investigators were invited in to help uncover potential problems, but no deficiencies were found that could be related to an overall health hazard. None of this was a secret, but neither was it big news; the few stories that appeared in the local paper were buried on page five and beyond, even one about a slightly overweight government civilian who dropped dead on the main floor of the dome one night. I haven't been privy to everything, but I do know of at least three other workers who have died prematurely, all of heart problems."

"I don't see a direct connection," Joe said.

"Medical science is not black and white; there are plenty of gray areas. Your physicist friend Dr. Burke said that death by neutrinos was inevitable at thousands of times normal intensity, but it seems long-term exposure to lesser concentrations was messing with everyone's cardiovascular enzymes over there to some degree. For those under the dome at night, the concentrations were at least double, and the lack of neutrino flow during the daytime might also have had an effect on the delicate human chemistry of the workers. For the most susceptible, I believe the change in neutrino rate was eventually fatal. One at work, three at home, and that's just the ones I know about."

"Well, you'll be happy to learn that you saved at least one other life, and with more certainty. There was another test planned for to-night."

"That lifts my spirits a little," Evans said. "How did you find out?"

"It was on one of the files Susan copied from Zeichner's computer. Did you see the disk?"

"Yes, it's in the bottom drawer of my dresser, stuck inside an old issue of the *Air Force Times*. I wanted to take some precaution against the bad guys busting down the door and making off with it as well as you."

"Thanks. Any chance of you opening those files, maybe making some copies?"

"No chance at all, even if I had the proper equipment. I've never seen that type of disk, but it appears to be one of the latest generation of high security government data storage devices. Assuming it's like its predecessors, the information will be erased if any attempt is made by an unauthorized user to open or copy the information."

"It's hopeless, isn't it?" Joe asked, depressed over the loss of Susan and the seeming futility of what they tried to accomplish.

"It depends on your next move," Evans replied.

The two sat in silence, looking toward but not at each other for a long minute.

"I have to turn myself in, don't I?"

"If you don't, you'll probably never see Susan again and it will be business as usual over there within the year."

"Damn it," Joe swore. "I told her it was a huge risk to take down that place, but we gave it a shot anyway. I didn't realize that even it if we succeeded it would be all but useless."

"They have the knowledge and money to rebuild. I don't know where their funding is coming from, but it's a drop in the big black bucket compared to the immense B-2 program."

"I can't just turn myself over to the nearest authorities."

"If you do, you'll be throwing your life away. You need to get out of here and go to Washington. I think I know who you should see. From everything I've heard, he's a man to trust. I don't know if he is aware of the project at Pope or not, but I'm sure he doesn't know the details; he would never condone the murderous tactics of the men after you."

"Okay," Joe said with forced enthusiasm.

"Getting an audience with him is another matter altogether. It might take someone with good political connections to accomplish that."

"I know someone who might help," Joe said, fingering a soiled card in his pocket.

"I suggest you contact him as soon as possible," Evans urged.

"If I'm going to help Susan, I need to get out of here fast. I'm guessing that's not going to be easy."

"It's going to be nearly impossible. From what I've heard, a massive search is underway for thirty miles in all directions. Roadblocks everywhere, with Army and Air Force patrols in the woods and fields; aerial coverage is active as well. Travel by car is out, as are taking the bus or train. Stowing away might be possible, on a truck or . . ."

Joe looked at him, and saw a mischievous gleam in his eyes.

"Let me make a phone call," Evans said as he pulled himself up uneasily from his seat.

"What is it?" Joe asked. "It looks like you have something outrageous in mind."

"Joe, of all the conveyances in the vicinity that could transport you out of here, which specific one would you dismiss as being the most fantastically improbable?"

Joe looked at the man and wondered. He started to open his mouth, then thought the better of it and shut it. Again he thought, and again his mouth opened and closed. It was the magnified impishness in Evans' eyes that finally gave Joe the impossible answer. "You are shitting me," he finally managed.

Andrew Weiss was happy to be away from the Farm and en-sconced once again in his New York office. Still shaken by his near-death experience the day before—the word *fauxfire* kept bouncing around in his brain—he was nevertheless relieved that neither Nicky nor he was in charge of the mob family. With the promisingly firm grip of Joey Messina on the wheel, he had confidence that things would re-turn to what they were when Victor Bonnelli was at the helm. His dreams of great fortune evaporated with Messina's assumption of power, of course, but it was better to be worth millions alive than tens of millions dead.

Still, Messina was largely an unknown, a potentially volatile quan-tity. Both murderer and lifesaver, he had immediately become both a powerful ally and a potentially lethal threat. Weiss did not think that the new mob boss would have anything to gain from killing him, but there was no doubt that Messina could summon the will to execute him if he thought something was awry.

Perhaps it is time for a change of pace, Weiss thought. His experi-ence the evening before was something he fervently wished never to be repeated. Something that distanced him from the overt violence of the mob yet required the same expertise he enjoyed exercising on a daily basis would probably provide a welcome change. Washington politics came to mind. It wasn't unheard of for lawyers with reputations such as his to become involved in the political process on the national level, if not in an elective office than as high-ranking appointee. Perhaps it was time to work some connections.

Abruptly, the lawyer was beeped out of his musings by his tele-phone. He swiveled away from the window and answered the page, knowing from the instructions he had given to his secretary that it con-cerned something important.

The voice of the office manager crisply relayed the message. "Sir, I'm not sure if this qualifies as an emergency or not, but there is a very insistent man by the name of Marc Grunner calling on your private line. He says it is extremely important that he speak with you, and states that he is somewhere where it is impossible to call him back."

Grunner, the nearly forgotten house sitter at the empty residence in Sunnyside, Weiss recalled. "Thank you, I'll take it," he said. "Yes?" he greeted the caller.

"Sir, I'm sorry about the deception, but I felt that the less people that know I'm calling, the better."

"Mr. Hanlon, how are you?" Weiss asked, recognizing the voice. "No matter how busy I get, I can't seem to avoid you. Over the past few days, I've read about your nefarious exploits in the newspaper, heard about your dubious deeds over the radio, and seen two reports concerning your rather remarkable travels and accomplishments on television."

"Mr. Weiss, as you might expect, I am not doing well. The reports you mention are almost wholly off the mark."

"According to the media, you have graduated from murderer to saboteur over the last few days."

"I was framed for those murders, which took place because of what was discovered during an examination of that dead squirrel we found at Bonnelli's. I was at the Air Force base in North Carolina yesterday, but my involvement in that incident is—complicated. I am not a terrorist."

"Mr. Hanlon, I tend to believe you, more than those chronicling your actions, anyway. I certainly know that your reported close relationship with Victor Bonnelli is total crap. What is it you need?"

"Mr. Weiss, for reasons I don't have time to explain, I have to turn myself in to someone in authority as soon as possible, today, tonight, tomorrow morning at the latest."

"And you are in search of a legal representative and called me because I represent well-known alleged criminals, of which you have suddenly become one?"

"No, sir, I do not want a lawyer, though I probably should. Because of my peculiar situation, I have to surrender myself in public, to someone high in the government."

"Have anyone specific in mind?"

"Yes, the secretary of Defense."

"That *is* pretty high up the ladder."

"And even then, it's a gamble," Joe lamented. "But I have to do it, fast. Sir, I'm calling you because I heard you have political ties. I'm hoping that some of these contacts are in the Washington area and have the clout that would allow me to place myself directly into the hands of Secretary McGrath."

"Interesting . . . interesting you should mention that," Weiss said, chalking up his thoughts along those lines less than five minutes before as coincidence, but sprinkled with a little bit of prescience. "Let me make a call. I think I can help you," and help my contact which might help me, he thought. "You're not in Washington now, are you?"

"No, but I'm going there by the quickest possible means. If all goes well, I could be there by tonight."

"Call me between one and two hours from now; I should have some information for you then."

"Thank you, Mr. Weiss."

———————

"It all makes a perverted kind of sense, but it's incredible, just incredible. To think I've been working there over a year and didn't know a thing about it! Of course I'll help, Gene," the man stated. "How about you, Ben, you in on this?" Max Wilkins asked the man seated next to him in Eugene Evans' small living room.

"The bastards, the goddamned bastards," Ben Slade answered, red-faced with anger at the information imparted by Evans and Joe Hanlon.

"Then let's hop to it. Go get the bag out of the car," Wilkins ordered.

"Yes, sir," Slade said lightly as he bounced to his feet, eager for an adventure. Five long strides later, he was out the front door.

"I'm not quite getting this," Joe said hesitantly, having no idea why two strangers would help him after a mere thirty-minute explanation of the secret project under the dome at Pope Air Force Base, and having but the barest knowledge of what he was supposed to do next.

"Everything will be clear soon. It's really quite a slick maneuver. Exciting, too," Wilkins answered.

"These men will take care of you," Evans added in a tone that exuded both pride and confidence.

The front door opened. "Here you go," Slade said as he tossed a black overnight bag at Joe's feet. "Put those on."

Minutes after retreating into the back bedroom, Joe reappeared. "Ready for inspection, I think," he said uneasily.

"Not bad, really not too bad," Wilkins said with encouragement. "Let's check any minor details," he went on as he scrutinized Joe, now dressed in an Air Force gray-green flight suit pullover identical to the ones worn by Wilkins and Slade. "Well, Hanlon, you have the build and the haircut to pass as a pilot, if nothing else. The two-inch difference in height between you and Captain Slade isn't noticeable, either."

"That particular suit was always a tad too big for me," Slade commented.

"So I pass?" Joe asked.

"Let's check the salute," Slade said. "Saluting inside isn't proper etiquette, even in that cavernous dome, but we might meet someone going in."

Joe snapped off a quick hand salute.

"Pretty good," Wilkins said. "You were in the service?"

"The Army, but it's been a few years."

"Joe was a staff sergeant; he holds the DSC and the Purple Heart," Evans explained.

"Holy shit," Wilkins said in surprise as Slade let loose with a low whistle of admiration at a fellow serviceman who had actually been there and done that. "I think we're there. Put on the sunglasses and the hat and we're off. So how do we look?" he asked Evans.

"Like three identical peas soon to be nestled in a very pricey pod."

"Colonel Evans—Gene—there is no way I can adequately express my thanks to you," Joe said. "You've been incredibly helpful, and I'll try to justify your trust."

Evans extended his hands and grabbed Joe's shoulders as firmly as he could in an effort to physically impart his feelings concerning what lay ahead. "You get out here, save that girl, and rescue the other poor slobs being victimized by this thing while you're at it," he urged.

"Gene, we poor slobs will take care of your boy," Wilkins said.

"I know you will Max—Major," Evans returned. "Everything in your career has been damn near perfect, and I hope you know this is the right thing to do."

"One thing I know is that this maneuver will be highly frowned upon if just about anyone else in the country finds out about it."

"But we'll make sure that doesn't happen," Slade said. "It'll be even easier than last time."

"That couldn't have gone better," Evans managed before being cut off by a long bought of deep coughs. "Now get out of here and do some good," he finally managed.

"Sir, I hope to see you again," Wilkins said as he clasped one of Evans' hands in both of his.

"I hope so too, but we both know that might not happen," Evans said. "In any case, I'm considering my last request fulfilled."

Less than a minute after final farewells, the three men were backing out of the gravel driveway in a Chrysler convertible, open to the moderate morning air, with Wilkins driving, Slade at shotgun, and Joe in the back.

Ten minutes later, they were at the main intersection in Henderson, held up at a roadblock. Although the vehicles headed north received the most scrutiny, all were stopped. A man of about forty in a khaki shirt sporting an oversized seven-pointed star attended to the Chrysler and its occupants.

"Get any of 'em yet?" Wilkins asked the policeman.

"Not yet, but they won't get far," the man answered after glancing at the two passengers, instantly recognizing the shoulder patch of the 525th Bomb Wing, Pope Air Force Base. "You men flying out today?"

"Now, officer, you know we can't answer that," Wilkins chided.

"Yeah, I guess so, but it's no big secret. Everybody says three Spirits flew out during the night, and I saw one myself in the distance about two hours ago. Rumor has it you're headed out for good."

"That's something I'll deny right now," the major said. "If anything, we're temporarily relocating just to reassess and tighten up security. We'll be back—soon."

"That's good to hear," the cop stated. "That facility has been the best thing to happen to the economy around here in years."

"Very cool," Joe exhaled when the car was again on the move.

"Comes with the territory," Wilkins tossed back.

"Why are you doing this?" Joe finally asked.

"Eugene Evans has been more of a father to me than my own flesh and blood ever was," Wilkins explained. "Eighteen years ago, I lived just a few miles from here. My father, a sergeant assigned to Pope, was an abusive alcoholic, my mother was a cowering mess, and I was a screwed-up kid ready to drop out of high school. One night, Colonel Evans showed up with my father, drunk as usual. I don't know what he saw in me, but Gene took me under his wing. I was an obnoxious brat at first, but after a few months, I was tolerating life and excelling at school, well enough that two years later, to my amazement and largely due to the colonel's proddings, I received an appointment to the Air Force Academy. I think I'd do just about anything for him if he asked, but there's much more in this particular case."

"Damn right there is," Slade said, taking up the thread. "I love the Air Force, and I'd do just about anything for an honest-to-God double jet ace like Gene Evans. This thing, though, the dome being used as a giant weapon—I can still hardly believe it—is very goddamn personal. A few months after I was assigned to the Five-Two-Five, I was grounded by the flight surgeon, which of course is about as big a kick in the balls as a B-2 pilot can get. He said I had something called 'idiopathic atrial fibrillation,' meaning that my heart wasn't ticking quite right. Cause unknown, that's what 'idiopathic' means, I unfortunately came to know."

"We were surprised they made such a big deal over it," said Wilkins. "It's actually a very minor anomaly."

"Maybe physically, but when it takes you out of the sky, it's like having your heart ripped clean out," Slade said. "Anyway, I take a three-week leave at the good doctor's suggestion, and when I get back I go through the tests again, and there's no more problem; I'm put back on limited flight status pending further evaluation. Two months later, the fibrillation crap pops up again, but after a week's worth of tests, away from the work site, there's nothing to be found. Ever since, I've felt like my whole future is hanging by a thread."

"Sounds similar to the problems other people have had over there," Joe said.

"The kicker, the proof that it's these assholes who are behind my current problem is this: for some reason unknown until this morning, the powers that be figured the best thing for my continued career was a transfer to the 509th at Whiteman. Same planes, same rank, same work, just no Beehive."

"So there you go," Wilkins concluded. "These assholes think they can ruin the health and careers of good officers and funnel money away from a great air unit because they like beams over bombers? Not without us having some say in the matter. But enough talk of theory, action time is coming up. We're less than a mile from the main gate." Wilkins turned and handed Joe a card.

"How is this going to work?" Joe asked as he examined the plastic rectangle with a frown. It was a magnetic card, bearing the picture and signature of the car's driver, Major Max A. Wilkins.

"That's my extra," Wilkins said. "I was issued an ID at wing level when I got to Pope, then another when I was assigned to my squadron a few months later. It was a mistake, a good old military SNAFU, one that I've had a couple of occasions to take advantage of."

"The computer won't catch the discrepancy?"

"Apparently the programming isn't set up to flag the error," Wilkins explained. "I suppose if security perused a printout of the daily ebb and flow of hundreds of personnel they might catch it, but that's unlikely."

"Main gate dead ahead," Slade interrupted, his eyes fixed forward.

"Gut it out," Wilkins urged as the Chrysler crept toward a small building in the median, next to which stood an intense young man in uniform.

"Good morning, sirs," the guard greeted, snapping off a salute. "May I see your identification, please?"

The airman verified Wilkins card, gave a cursory glance to the cards of his two passengers, took a step back, and waved them through.

"What's next?" Joe asked uneasily.

"We're going to play the old shell game," Wilkins explained, "but the trick in our version is to make people think there are two peas instead of three. First, we're going to go through the checkpoint to the parking lot at the dome, something like we just went through. Then we'll be electronically carded at the perimeter fence, and again at the entrance to the building. Then we'll walk to the bay of our aircraft where they'll be another checkpoint, but since we're in uniform we won't be stopped."

"I hope," Joe muttered.

"Then it gets interesting. Ben is going to peel off and go to the can while we walk directly to the plane, 'just to do a preliminary check.' We climb into the bomber, then a short time later I get out and meet up with Ben. We'll then don the rest of our flight gear, receive a short pre-flight briefing, and join you in the cockpit. After that, it's 'away we go!'"

"That's crazy; it'll never work!" Joe protested.

"Look who's talking about crazy," Slade said. "We pulled it off when we took Gene Evans up for a short hop around the area for his birthday a few months ago; we'll do it again."

"Besides the uniform and the card, it's ninety percent attitude," Wilkins said. "If we act like we know where we're going and what we're doing, odds are no one will question us. It's generally chaos in there, especially before a flight. Everyone is busy attending to their specialized duties and no one is tasked with tracking the movements of the pilots to make sure they don't sneak another man aboard. After you're tucked away, we'll have some face-to-face with our higher-ups, to be sure, but that will take place away from the plane."

Despite Joe's gut-wrenching, bile-inducing, teeth-grinding reservations, the plan unfolded nicely. Walking in unison, dressed alike, and carrying identical black overnight bags, no one even tried to distinguish pilot from saboteur. They breezed through checkpoints and greeted those they passed with smiles and nods as they made their way quickly toward their goal.

When they stepped into the vast open space of the dome, the trio instantly became aware of a change caused by Joe's activities the day before that worked to their advantage. The morning Sun shining on the thousands of panes of glass in the building's huge, curved roof caused an annoying glare throughout the interior of the structure. Used to working under somber lighting, the majority of the workers they saw squinted their way through their various tasks, eyes turned down.

"It's a good thing the wing is temporarily relocating to White-man," Slade commented. "Something is definitely going to have to be done about this."

As he marched with a purpose down the center of the main thoroughfare, Joe knew he would not see Susan standing on the sidelines, but he could not help himself from looking.

Two turns and eight hundred feet later, they arrived at what was identified as "Bay 6" by a large blue sign. Wilkins deftly maneuvered himself in front of his two companions, was immediately recognized by the airman guarding the entrance, and the three men entered the area without a pause. After twenty feet, Joe glanced to his left and noticed Slade had disappeared.

"Almost there; keep it up," Wilkins said in a low tone after noticing that Joe was beginning to lose his fight to keep his limp concealed.

Overcoming pain, stiffness, and fatigue, Joe redoubled his efforts to achieve a passable pace. Finally, the corridor ended and the floor opened up into an expanse of concrete, in the middle of which was the huge black form of the Spirit of North Dakota. As they walked under the front edge of the left wing and headed toward the nose, they received hardly a glance from the two dozen men and women engrossed at various tasks.

"This bird ready to go up, Sergeant Ellis?" Wilkins greeted a man working near the huge wheels of the forward landing gear.

"Major Wilkins, is that you, sir?" the man asked as he put his right hand over his eyes to mitigate the glare.

"None other," he said with forced gaiety. "Any problems?"

"Nothing we didn't take care of an hour ago, sir. This baby's ready to fly."

"Good. All done in the cockpit?"

"Finished up fifteen minutes ago."

"Fine. We're going up to stow these bags."

Joe followed the pilot up a short exterior ladder and entered the belly of the bomber. After twelve more rungs, he found himself in the cockpit. He looked around in amazement. On all surfaces surrounding the four large windows were a bewildering panoply of controls, including eight computer display screens and a galaxy of indicator lights in all colors of the rainbow. Most astoundingly, there was a third seat, six feet behind the co-pilot's position. "That the stowaway seat?" he asked.

"That's the navigator's position, except B-2s don't have navigators," Wilkins explained. "When the bomber was being developed, it was thought that a third man would be essential, but advancements in avionics made the position unnecessary. Hell, this plane could complete combat missions with just one guy, but it's nice to have company."

"What now?"

"Just stow the bags in the cabinet in back and have a seat. I'll be back with Ben in less than an hour. Nobody else should be up here in the meantime, but should the improbable happen, crouch behind the seat; any technician will undoubtedly focus on the instruments forward."

"Okay," Joe responded without a bit of enthusiasm.

"One more thing . . ." Wilkins started as he was halfway down the hatch.

"I know," Joe acknowledged with absolute confidence in what the pilot was about to say. "Don't touch anything."

The almost unbearable wait was mercifully short. "Come on up." Joe heard twenty minutes later, and when he glanced over the top of the seat from his cramped hiding place, he was greeted with the sight of Wilkins and Slade getting down to serious business.

Joe watched in amazement as the professionals made ready the supremely complicated machine. For fifteen minutes, systems were activated, checklists were verified, and Wilkins kept up a running banter with several people by radio.

"I trust I don't need a helmet," Joe asked during a pause in the frantic activity.

"This isn't a fighter. We don't do loops, rolls, or even travel supersonic. I think you'll be pleasantly surprised by the ride," Slade said.

Finally, the huge hanger door beyond the nose of the bomber opened and Wilkins eased the hundred sixty-five-ton behemoth forward. After the airplane cleared the dome, he eased the nose gear to the right and headed toward the runway.

The takeoff was as smooth as any commercial airliner's.

CHAPTER 26

Rain again, was the certain prediction of William J. McGrath as he gazed out of his office window. The distant clouds beyond the Washington skyline looked innocuous, but he knew with practiced confidence that once more, probably by sometime that evening, drops of moisture would descend on his environment, inevitably bringing to the fore images of events over three decades in the past, images he would have liked to forget yet forced himself to remember.

It was in a dreary drizzle that they had come, NVA regulars in at least regimental strength, deployed in response to an encroachment into what they considered their sovereign territory by a tired company of ninety-six men commanded by young Captain McGrath, who considered himself a career officer though he was not a Military Academy graduate. Any thoughts of career on that particular afternoon, however, were immediately drowned by the hundred considerations that violently jockeyed for position in his head once he heard the chatter of a machine gun with an alarmingly different tempo than that of his own M-60s.

Like many similar baptisms-by-fire experienced by humans since the first skull was crushed by a rock in a hand, the battle was a pivotal one for McGrath. From the nightmarishly varied encounters with death he experienced on that sodden day, he had gained an intense appreciation of life, a desire to make the most of whatever time was left to him. He realized from the start that the notion somehow involved service to others, both like and unlike the service he had given to the members of his command. The dichotomy kept him ever alert: the sure knowledge that he had saved the bulk of his personnel from death constantly grating against the hideous fact that in the week following the battle, the families of twenty-eight of his men found at their front doors grim-faced lieutenants dressed in solemn attire, each bearing the same message.

Thirty days after the battle, McGrath traveled to Washington to receive the country's highest decoration from the president and since then had never been far removed from the nation's capital. Due to a combination of his sudden fame and the retirement of his home-district congressman, he was serving the citizens of four counties as a member of the House of Representatives within the year. Four years later, he began a four-term stint representing the population of Indiana in the Senate, then duty called him to serve the nation as a whole as head of the Defense Department.

McGrath disliked life in the Washington area, but never showed it, stoically accepting the endless hours of work as penance for leading his men into a situation that resulted in so much carnage, for not being among those who died. He never felt like a hero, he felt like a debtor, and the principal he owed seemed to increase every year as he was accorded more honors while the men he lost faded in the memories of all save one over each succeeding year.

Though relief was nowhere in sight, he could keep making payments, he knew as he concentrated on the latest scene of crisis, an Air Force base in North Carolina where terrorists had been plying their trade, at least that is what the initial reports said.

A knock on one of the double doors of his office pulled McGrath away from his thoughts. Seconds later, a figure as serious as he was sartorially resplendent stepped into the room and approached the desk. With the title of special assistant to the secretary of Defense, Rockwell Kajor's job encompassed a nebulous mass of duties that continued to evolve even after three years. "Sir, I have the latest on the Pope affair," he stated without inflection.

"Let's have it."

"The relocation of the bomber wing is proceeding without major problems. The bulk of the senior staff and about half of the maintenance personnel moved to Whiteman Air Force Base early this morning with the three operational B-2 bombers. Delayed slightly, the fourth bomber left Pope about ten minutes ago and will be at Whiteman within two hours. The two remaining Spirits are in the midst of major maintenance; the best estimate is that they will join the transports carrying the command elements and fly out between nine and midnight tonight."

"I still don't know if I agree with this move," McGrath said. "A small group of infiltrators chasing an Air Force unit out of its base—it's not promoting an image of strength."

"The Air Force says the move is the best way to keep the wing fully deployable while repairs are made to the facility. Excessive glare within the building has degraded operational capabilities. Also, keeping the planes in berths open to the sky makes them vulnerable to satellite surveillance."

"Hell of a design," McGrath commented. "Build a glass roof, then go crazy when the Sun shines in. So what's the lowdown regarding the repairs?"

Kajor pursed his lips, then reasserted his professionalism and unemotionally relayed the facts. "Preliminary estimates are that the dome will take between six and nine months to repair. Bringing it back up to design specs could cost $650 million."

"Hell's bells!" exploded McGrath. "Just because the electric was cut? The whole D.C. area could be blacked out for a week and less damage would be sustained. Who made these assessments?"

"Most of this information came from General Hightower. He's the chief Air Force contact regarding this matter, at least until General Van Valkenburgh's return sometime late this evening. The estimates were relayed from General Joshua Irwin, commander of Pope Air Force Base, and General Benjamin Wainwright, commander of the 525th Bomb Wing."

"Before we dump over half a billion tax dollars into this repair, I want to have a face-to-face with the key players on the effectiveness of that fancy electrified security envelope. It was built as an experimental prototype, after all; I think it's time to consider whether we really need it." McGrath swiveled in his chair and faced his desk squarely. "Besides the loss of the devices in the roof, what other damage was done?"

"The abrupt termination of the electric caused numerous computer problems, mostly data and other software losses. There is also damage underground where the bombs went off, at least we're fairly certain they were bombs. No one seems to have heard an explosion, and one report relates that the outage was due to a forklift crashing into power lines."

"That's not possible, is it?" the secretary asked.

"No, sir, not unless there was a similar crash at the same time all the way on the other side of the building. The dual transmission systems made it all but impossible that there would be a blackout. This was definitely sabotage, and by people who knew what they were doing."

"Have any casualties been identified since this morning's briefing?"

"None, sir," Kajor informed him. "No one killed, no injuries."

"I'm gratified to hear it, but puzzled at the same time. What do we have on the infiltrators?"

"Except for the one, almost nothing, not even a good number. Although reports indicate a group of four or five, I can't find anything to verify it. In the aftermath of the power outage, there were many sightings of suspicious people reported, but so far, no one from the group has been captured or killed. The only positive ID made was on Joseph Hanlon. Three people recognized him from a television report about two murders in New York, and nearly twenty others followed suit when his photo was passed around."

"Run his recent history past me one more time," McGrath urged. "I found the story you told this morning to be quite—strange."

"Strange it is, sir, and baffling, even bizarre. Up to last Thursday, Hanlon was a small-town policeman with an exemplary record. On that day, he interfered in an FBI investigation into the death of a mobster by the name of Bonnelli, and because of that, he was dismissed from his position on Friday. On Saturday, he killed his girlfriend and another acquaintance, then stayed in the area until at least Sunday, long enough to kidnap another girlfriend. There are FBI agents investigating a report that he may have stopped in Lexington, Virginia, on Monday, and on Tuesday, of course, he somehow managed to get inside one of our most secure installations, where he did a copious amount of damage."

"Busy week," McGrath commented. "That he did it all in such a short time is one thing, but what was his motivation? I can't think of a scenario that can explain both the New York killings and the Pope sabotage."

"Much of the media is now reporting he was secretly a member of the Mafia, and that he went insane after his boss died."

"That was no stunt bred of insanity he pulled yesterday. Both the plan and the execution were damn near flawless. As for his being involved with the mob, it makes no sense. Let's stick to what we can verify and not rely on dubious journalism. Anything else?"

"Hanlon has a military record, sir. He was in the Army for three years, reached the rank of staff sergeant, and received an honorable discharge."

"Come on, Rock," prodded McGrath. "What was his training? What units did he serve with? It seems like you're holding back."

"I am, sir, but not voluntarily. What I just related was all readily available information. His full record is classified beyond a level I am permitted to access."

McGrath raised his eyebrows and fixed his gaze on the aide. "That speaks volumes, or has the Department of the Army adopted oddly paranoid procedures concerning records of *all* former soldiers?"

"It is strange indeed, sir," Kajor answered. "There are not many things my clearance cannot do. If you would place a call to DOA, I will retrieve the records and we can clear up this mystery."

"Go on down; you'll have the authorization when you arrive. And bring me the written files on the Pope incident. I want this thing wrapped up as soon as possible."

Used to dealing with projects requiring years to develop, procedures that necessitated months to implement, and priorities that took days to attend to, McGrath would have been flabbergasted to learn that the answers were just hours away.

Cloudless blue sky was all Joe Hanlon could see out of the large cockpit windows from the back seat of the Spirit of North Dakota. In the front, Max Wilkins and his co-pilot were completing the myriad tasks involved in bringing the B-2 to cruising altitude, their frenetic activity slowly easing off.

"Okay," Wilkins said. "We're just entering Tennessee and level at 54,000 feet, high enough to protect us from the casual gaze of any taxpayers below."

"Wish we could show you what this baby could do, but we're locked into our current, mundane flight path, no deviations allowed," Ben Slade said, addressing Joe. "Any aerial antics would be picked up by both military systems and civilian air traffic controllers."

"I really don't need any more excitement, but I don't understand," Joe said. "This is a stealth bomber, immune from detection."

"Not quite right, on two counts," Slade informed him. "First, we're not invisible, even to radar, we just have to be a lot closer to the equipment trying to detect us. Some have used this lack of perfection to criticize the B-2, but reducing enemy radar to less than one percent effectiveness provides a tremendous advantage. Second, we're not in combat, so our onboard transponder is active, letting everybody know we're up here. The civilians don't know what we are, just that we're a military flight, headed west."

"So what's the plan after we land?"

"It's going to be even easier than at Pope," Wilkins predicted. "With the sudden increase in planes and personnel at Whiteman, they must be going nuts; we'll just slip out through the chaos."

"Any suggestions on how I can get to Washington?"

"That's going to be tougher. I'd be happy to rent a private plane and fly you there this afternoon, but we're going to be tied up at

Whiteman until the remaining bombers arrive tonight. I'm sure one of us can sneak away for an hour or so to get you off base and rent you a car, but I'm afraid it's ground transportation from there on out. You're just too well known to chance a commercial flight."

"Damn," Joe cursed at the news that his goal lay at least a full day in the future. Agonized images of Susan eclipsed all other thoughts. "I'll have to make a phone call as soon as we land; I'm already overdue now."

"Well, hell, at least that we can help you with. You can make a call right now," Slade said.

"What?"

"We have one of the most varied and sophisticated communications systems in the world within this contraption, and that includes a good ol' telephone link. It's even better than a land line because a unidirectional antenna fires the transmission directly to a communications satellite; can't be traced."

Wilkins expounded on the feature. "On occasion we use it to ring up girlfriends, make dinner reservations, and—my favorite—call up Academy classmates, especially those currently flying a desk, just to say, 'Guess what I'm doing right now?' Really bugs the crap out of them."

"I'll pipe the call over the speaker system so you can talk from back there," Slade said. "What's the number?"

Joe retrieved Andrew Weiss's card and read off ten digits, which Slade entered on a touch screen. Moments later, the sound of a telephone ringing through to its party filled the cockpit.

"Weiss," cut off the tone halfway through the second ring.

"Mr. Weiss, Joe Hanlon," he greeted over the drone of the airplane.

"Mr. Hanlon, I've received a rather enthusiastic response from my contact. Apparently, you are a person in high demand. How go your travel plans to Washington?"

"Things could be worse, but they are far from ideal. I'm afraid the only ride available was headed to Missouri. I'll be there in about an hour, then I'll have to drive. I don't expect to be in the Washington area before tomorrow afternoon."

"That's not good news, but I suppose we'll have to live with it. I'll apprise my associate of the situation; call me back sometime tonight."

A "yes, sir" from Joe was followed by a click over the speaker signifying the termination of the call.

Twenty minutes went by, down time during which nothing but innocuous banter passed between the trio in the plane. "Start descent in ten minutes," Wilkins finally said, ending the forced period of relaxation.

"November Delta One," resonated a voice from the radio.

"This is November Delta One, over," Slade answered.

"Priority traffic on Channel 'D.' Acknowledge."

"Roger; opening Channel 'D.' November Delta One, out."

"Strange," muttered Wilkins.

"It's been a long time since we used this commo system," Slade said as he attended to a touch screen and pulled up the controls for one of the secondary communications arrays.

"I think you're confusing simulator time with actual flights," Wilkins stated. "I've never used that system in the air."

"You're right. Well, I guess we'll find out what kind of traffic it's designed for," Slade responded before addressing Joe. "This system operates like the gadget we just used, like a telephone on a speaker, continuous back and forth throughout the cockpit."

"I'll be quiet," acknowledged the stowaway.

Slade touched five displayed numerals. "November Delta One, ready for priority transmission, over."

"Just face this speaker and talk in a normal tone, sir," was the initial response from the radio.

Another voice was then heard. "Boys, I'm Senator Alexander Thayer. How you doin' up there?"

"Holy shit," Wilkins blurted.

"Well, I imagine you're surprised to hear from me; I don't get to talk to you pilots nearly as much as I want."

"Yes, sir," Wilkins replied, mildly flustered.

"I've been monitoring the situation at Pope closely since yesterday afternoon. I've been informed that yours is the only plane from the air base in the air at this time, that there were a few flown out early this morning and a few more will be traveling tonight, but right now you're it."

"As I understand it, that is correct, sir," Wilkins replied.

"Might you be carrying a special package with you? One I might want to see here in Washington today, not tomorrow?"

Wilkins turned back toward Joe with a doleful expression, then after a long pause gave the answer he knew he must. "Yes, sir. We have something like that right here."

"Really, really, really," Thayer said, surprise overlaying his even tone. "I believe you need to come on over then."

"Sir, our orders are to proceed directly to Whiteman. We anticipate landing there in about forty minutes."

"Give me three shakes of a pig's tail and I think you'll find your orders changed."

The three men in the bomber soon discovered that a pig shook its tail three times in six minutes. Transmitted over their standard frequency, the new order was to proceed to Andrews Air Force Base.

"A whole new ball game," Wilkins said as he banked the bomber into a wide turn. "Had to have been the phone call."

"Senator Thayer must be Weiss's contact," Joe said. "He knew I was in a plane headed from the Pope area to Missouri, and Thayer, for some reason, knew that the only plane that fit the bill was this one. Who is this guy, anyway? I can't imagine all senators are tracking the movements of individual planes out of Pope."

"Senator Alexander Thayer is chairman of the Armed Services Committee," Slade said. "He's obviously following the situation closely because there's big money at stake regarding the relocation of the wing and the repair of the Beehive."

"Looks like I'm flying you to Washington after all," Wilkins said wryly.

"You guys are in big doo-doo, aren't you?"

"No sneaking around now," a dejected Slade said.

Wilkins turned to his partner. "Wait a minute, Ben. We're in the right here. As far as dirty deeds go, we won't even be on the screen if our friend here can expose that secret weapon project to someone with enough clout—"

"—who is not involved in the conspiracy himself." Slade interjected.

"Okay, yeah," Wilkins said, deflated. "Still, we could survive this thing."

Slade turned sharply and made eye contact with Joe. "I don't hold out much hope, but Major Wilkins is right—you are our only chance. Expose this thing and prove yourself innocent to the world, or we'll be joining you in Leavenworth."

"What's the Washington area weather like?" Wilkins asked.

Slade pulled up an information access screen on a multipurpose display unit. "Slightly cloudy; looks like rain tonight, but that'll be after we land."

————————

"This is professional; this is professional," the man whispered to himself over and over, alternately ending each iteration with a period, an exclamation point, and a question mark.

What would a fellow professional, like a surgeon, do? he asked himself. The case was like coming upon an accident victim on the open road, in dire need of immediate attention, but without adequate aid even remotely available, nothing but a highly skilled physician equipped with whatever was immediately on hand, which wasn't much. Does the doctor refuse to deal with the situation and back away because he doesn't have preparation time or proper instruments or supporting personnel? Of course not. He does whatever he can, even if the results might be inferior to what he was used to. To do anything else would be—unprofessional.

The man was comforted by the analogy. Unlike the hypothetical doctor, he did have the proper equipment, and for the particular job at hand, support personnel were not needed. It was the circumstances that made him uneasy. Used to having several weeks to prepare for most operations, he had never before had less than three day's notice. Two hours from order to execution was just too damned short.

There were reasons for the pitifully brief period, he knew, reasons that could not be changed by the people in need of his services, whoever they were. So when presented with an extremely difficult task with an impossibly short deadline, they had hired him, he considered with some pride. Surely, it was a sign that his professionalism was respected. With practiced skill, he snapped the bipod onto the front of his sniper rifle, an XM21 with Redfield scope and silencer. He then inserted a magazine into the well of the rifle and chambered a 7.62mm round. He missed Vietnam by five years, but his instructors at the Marine Corps Sniper School had gained their education and experience there, and had sworn by the battle-tested rifle. Their enthusiasm had been contagious, and from that point he had sworn by the venerable weapon, choosing it over all other so-called modern gadgets that didn't last a decade. Safety on, he focused on an intersection of support beams several hundred feet away and adjusted his scope.

He had never been an inside-the-Beltway man and still wasn't, he pondered, chuckling to himself as he examined the target area. He was satisfied with his perch on the edge of the roof of a ten-story apartment building in Virginia overlooking the Potomac River. The position was nearly ideal, just downstream from the Woodrow Wilson Memorial Bridge, which carried the Capital Beltway east and west over the river at the highway's extreme southerly point. Giant beams supported the roadway from beneath, so no superstructure obscured the travel lanes. Easily avoided were four towers that rose thirty feet above the guardrails toward the Virginia end of the mile and a half-long bridge. The monolithic structures housed machinery to operate the drawbridge section of the span, but it was too much to hope that the bascules would be raised at the optimal time to give him a stationary target, as it practically took a national emergency to stop the incessant interstate traffic.

Pleased with the firing position, the man carefully laid out an olive drab blanket on the flat roof, then placed two filled magazines side by side next to the rifle. The blanket served both to comfort him, thus aiding accuracy, and to catch expelled casings. He made the forty rounds in the extra magazines available as a contingency, in case the first twenty bullets failed to do the job. Finally, he placed a photo of his intended victim on the blanket, weighed down at the edges by the emergency ammunition. Torn from a newspaper just half an hour before, it wasn't a very good likeness; it looked like a mug shot.

From a telephone conversation that lasted all of three minutes, he had learned the name of his target, the suddenly well-known Joseph Hanlon; his mode of transport, a government sedan with particular plate numbers; the time, plus or minus twenty minutes—an outrageously large window—that he would start traveling a particular route to the Pentagon; and the mission, which of course was termination.

Very briefly, the man had wondered why Hanlon, obviously already in custody, needed to be killed, and why an independent contractor was called to do the job. He kept his thoughts to himself, however. Besides the operational information, it was only necessary to know that his instructions came from the proper level of authority; he didn't need to know why and to ask would have been considered highly unprofessional.

After receiving the instructions, the man had hastily packed the tools of his trade, drove nearly half an hour to the vicinity of the route he was given, then frantically searched for an adequate position, resuming his calm disposition only after reaching the roof of the architecturally unappealing structure on which he now crouched.

Scope fully adjusted to focus on westbound bridge traffic, which traveled toward him at an angle of about thirty degrees, he practiced identifying individual cars and reading license plates. It was not yet rush hour, which was both good and bad. The moderate traffic made the identification of a single vehicle much more likely, but the cars were averaging sixty miles per hour, which was a bit too fast for his taste. Still, he was confident that he could bring a round to within three inches of his aiming point on any vehicle he chose.

The man relaxed slightly, knowing that so far he had done the best that any man could do given the situation. There wasn't nearly enough time to set up a barricade that would stop or even slow down a major traffic artery; hitting a moving target had been the only course of action remaining.

He was also concerned because he would not be able to see his man before the first shot was fired. He did not like the idea of inflicting collateral damage—the killing of anyone else besides Hanlon—but grimly accepted the possibility. Aware that the interior of the government sedan headed his way was almost certainly obscured by heavy window tinting, he visualized the ideal: shattering the left rear window with one round, then recognizing his target within the car and dispatching him within half a second with a head shot, resulting in no one else being harmed beyond receiving a little blood, bone, and brain on their suits. The ideal was seldom realized, though, especially in a moving target situation. If necessary, the others in the car, probably one driver and one guard—unknown soldiers in the vast government bureaucracy—would have to be sacrificed.

He sighted up and down the bridge. The weather was nearly perfect, not dark, not raining, just slightly overcast. Alert but not anxious, he assumed his best professional stance and waited.

CHAPTER 27

"I couldn't believe it, just could not believe it. Andy Weiss had absolutely no idea he was giving me truly fantastic information regarding your whereabouts. It all fit, though. He told me you were on a plane headed from the vicinity of Pope Air Force Base to Missouri, relayed it just as a mildly interesting secondary piece of information. I checked the nearby airports, but all commercial flights were under a microscope and none were headed for the Show Me State; all private planes within a hundred miles were grounded. Still, it took twenty minutes of hard effort to convince myself to make that call to your plane, and I was still astounded to find that you were aboard."

"Senator Thayer, those pilots were not just helping me, they were acting in the best interests of the country," Joe Hanlon told the short, plump man sitting beside him.

"I'm afraid I can't take your word on that," Alexander Thayer said as the sedan they were riding in passed the brick guardhouse of Andrews Air Force Base.

"Sir, I think that almost everything you have heard about my activities over the past few days has either been grossly distorted or is completely false."

"Which is why I'm here, young man. I usually don't have intimate audiences with murdering terrorists, but in your case, I believe all is not as it appears. Weiss told me with absolute certainty that you have no connections with the New York mob as everyone is saying, and he also has big reservations concerning your guilt on those two murders. And you certainly convinced Major Wilkins and Captain Slade you were not one of the bad guys."

"They don't deserve to be treated like criminals," Joe said. Upon landing, the three of them were frisked, then handcuffed, although at the senator's insistence the restraining devices were removed ten minutes later. Following this, the two pilots were led away while Joe removed his Air Force coveralls and joined Thayer in his car.

"Procedures have to be followed when security is penetrated, and that flight of yours was quite a breech," Thayer said, retaining his easy tone. "As I understand it, they won't be jailed, but will be under close scrutiny while the incident is investigated. Giving unauthorized rides to buddies has been around since Army Air Corps days; even I bent the rules a few times as a transport pilot forty years ago. But this—the plane, the passenger—is something else."

"I'm sure the men will be vindicated," Joe said with forced optimism.

"Maybe, but you are definitely going to jail unless something drastic occurs, despite any leeway I'm granting you right now."

"Given what a few people have in mind for me, sir, I'll gladly accept that at this point." Joe said as the government car turned onto the Capital Beltway.

"Everybody wanted you in custody; nobody is gunning for you, or am I missing something?"

"Sir, I can tell you with absolute certainty that there is a government agent of some sort by the name of Philip Roberts who would kill me without hesitation, in custody or not. He heads up a group at least five strong, and I'm sure that my elimination tops their list of priorities."

"You obviously believe that," said Thayer, an expert in the identification of prevarication and duplicity thanks to his years in Congress. "So why did you surrender yourself if you think that these people will kill you, no matter what?"

"I'm here for one reason, sir, to save the life of Susan DeLuca. If I can," Joe added, a gloominess encroaching on his tone.

"The girl you kidnapped?"

"It didn't exactly happen that way, sir. For whatever reason, she was with me yesterday in the tunnels under the dome at Pope. We were separated and I escaped; I don't know what happened to her. She may have been captured, and to be taken by the people I just described is about the worst thing that could have happened. I'm sure Philip Roberts and his gang of thugs would not hesitate to torture or kill her to get what they want. I'm here to try to prevent that."

"And you think Secretary McGrath can help. Still, I'm missing something," Thayer said, slightly agitated. "Why do these men want you dead?"

"Because over the past few days, by investigating odd goings-on and talking with people and sneaking into places where I shouldn't be, I discovered the dark and dirty secret of the domed B-2 bomber facility at Pope Air Force Base."

"And that is?"

Joe looked uneasily at the two men in the front seat of the vehicle, the stern-faced and muscular armed guard directly to his front and what looked at first glance to be his twin behind the wheel. "Sir, the answer to that is complex, to say the least. I would like you to hear the whole story when I explain it to Secretary McGrath."

"Fair enough; I can wait twenty minutes," Thayer said with a thin smile. Outside, the greenery on either side of the interstate dropped away as the car clicked over an expansion joint and moved onto the Woodrow Wilson Bridge.

"How do you know Mr. Weiss?" Joe asked, shifting his gaze from his host to the Washington skyline, visible up the Potomac out of his darkly tinted window.

"A few years back, I was in the construction business in New Jersey. Though successful in my own backyard, I lacked expertise when it came to working in New York City. Pressured by politicians, unions, an oppressive bureaucracy, and 'others,' it was Andy Weiss who successfully dealt with those staunchly self-interested groups. His ability to call me up and ask a favor from time to time is a byproduct of that association."

"He's helped me a great deal, too, although I'm not sure why."

"Well, Andy is that way. He—"

Even had it been spoken, the next word would not have been heard over the earsplitting crack that accompanied the disintegration of the window less than three inches from the senator's left shoulder. Acting before he could think, Joe pulled the man toward him just as a bullet put a hole in the leather upholstery at the exact spot where Thayer's head had rested a half second before. This was immediately followed by a loud *plonk* that indicated to Joe's experienced ear that a round had impacted the rear door.

Trained for such a situation, the driver floored the sedan. The car lurched forward to the only cover immediately available, a large tractor-trailer. The barrier blocked the bullets for scant seconds, however, as two tires of the eighteen-wheeler were blown out in a quick fusillade and the truck's driver braked sharply. The government sedan cleared the front of the big-rig going seventy-seven, missing by inches several vehicles in the three travel lanes as it strived to slalom itself out of danger. The target car, an ancient VW Bug, and a slow-moving SUV experienced lead-on-sheet metal impacts in the ensuing five seconds of peril.

As the car cleared the end of the bridge, the firing ceased, but the chaos within the sedan did not. The driver was urging the speedometer toward ninety as the man next to him shouted instructions into a radio in his left hand while he waved around a 9mm pistol in his right. For a moment, Joe thought that the man might shoot him, as he was the closest thing to a bad guy in sight. Shrugging off the notion, he turned his attention to the senator, whose head now lay in his lap.

"Wha— what happened?" Thayer asked in a voice that, though shaky, was encouragingly strong. Then Joe saw the blood on his pants, and within seconds determined that it was not he who was wounded in the groin, but the senator who had sustained an injury to his face.

"Keep him down!" shouted the man with the gun as Joe gingerly lifted Thayer to ascertain the extent of his injuries. Joe unbuckled his seat belt, then pivoted his body a hundred eighty degrees, ending up crouched with his back against the front seat.

"Oh . . . oh, I'm hit," the senator said, spitting out drops of blood as he spoke. "Damn that hurts."

"Sir, please remain calm," Joe urged as he removed the man's tie and unbuttoned his collar. "You're going to be fine," he went on after he discovered it was not a bullet that had hit the politician, but a piece of glass and plastic about an inch long that had spalled off of the window into the man's left cheek. Carefully, Joe plucked the projectile out of Thayer's flesh, then used the man's tie as a compress to staunch the moderate flow of blood.

"Senator Thayer, are you conscious?" asked the driver.

"Yes, yes, yes," the injured man replied, each repeated word exuding more confidence.

"Sir, you were hit by this," Joe said, holding up the sharp shard for his patient to see. "You sustained a laceration a little over an inch long. We're going to get you to a hospital as soon as possible."

"Alexandria Hospital is just three miles away," the driver said over his shoulder.

"No," Thayer said, exerting his authority in a voice nearly recovered. "Go on to the hospital in the Pentagon. I can wait five minutes, and we have to get this boy to safety."

"But sir—"

"Look, maybe I got it wrong, but I heard you U.S. Marshals know how to take orders."

The comment served to silence the driver and launch the man beside him into making a bevy of radio calls.

"Sir, this is a brave thing you're doing. I really appreciate it," Joe said as the quaint streetscape of Old Town Alexandria zipped past.

"Brave? Appreciate? Don't BS me, son. You can see the gash on the outside is no worse than a bad shaving cut and my tongue says it's not much bigger than a pinhole inside."

"Well, it's a little worse than—"

"On the other hand, I believe that's a bullet hole up there where my gray head was at rest, just before you pulled it out of the way. Who should be thanking whom?"

"I can't hear you, sir," Joe kidded. "There's too much wind coming in from that busted window."

"I also expect to be treated very well indeed at the place I exert a moderate amount of influence over. They'll probably want to keep me awhile, though, so I think you should be the one to give this to Bill McGrath." Thayer reached into his jacket and retrieved the thick computer disk taken from Joe during the frisking he endured at Andrews.

"Thank you, sir."

"Hope it helps," he added. "Here's one vote against you going to jail."

The car exited the interstate going sixty-five, and slowed even further as it negotiated the curving roads leading up to the Pentagon. The guards at the gate made a security check in record time. After negotiating two more curves and a ramp down, the sedan screeched to a halt in front of a crowd of twenty.

Thayer sat up uneasily and Joe unbuckled the man's seatbelt. Three men helped the VIP onto a stretcher and he was whisked away.

The two marshals then addressed the nearest man wearing a Pentagon Police uniform. "We're delivering this—well, he's not exactly a prisoner, not unless you make him one, I guess," said one of them.

"I'll take him," boomed a voice to the right. When the men turned, they saw headed toward them in a confident stride a barrel-chested full colonel, his uniform resplendent with a cornucopia of ribbons. "I have his visitor's badge right here," the soldier told the two Justice Department men.

"Okay, sir, he's all yours."

"Colonel Powers, it's great to see you again," Joe greeted his old commander.

"You too, Rambo."

———

"Sir, I strongly advise against this," Rockwell Kajor urged his boss.

"Rock, I appreciate the dissenting opinion; I know it has kept me out of trouble on more than one occasion, but this time I'm going to follow my instincts," William McGrath said.

"There are established procedures that address this kind of thing, sir," Kajor said, not yet admitting defeat. "There are legal considerations, security issues. At least wait until he has been interrogated by our experts."

"No. He's headed up here right now, and I'm going to see him."

"For God's sake, sir," Kajor nearly shouted, uncharacteristically upset.

"Calm down, Rock," McGrath urged. "I didn't make this decision lightly, but given the circumstances it wasn't a tough call. For one thing, there's Hanlon's military record. What's your opinion of that classified file?"

"He seems to have had a successful week a few years back," Kajor admitted. "Still, a few days in combat do not define a man's entire life."

"Perhaps not, but the manner in which he handled himself tells a great deal about his character. He dealt with that situation in such a manner that he was awarded the Distinguished Service Cross. Most people are not familiar with the DSC, but its connection to the Medal of Honor is very close. Many, if not most awards of the DSC could have easily been upgraded to the Medal of Honor, but because of witnesses or documentation or circumstances removed from the battle including just plain politics, one was awarded instead of the other. The lesser medal does open some doors, though, this one included."

"But he's a killer. He murdered at least two people in New York a few days ago."

"I'm interested in hearing his story regarding those deaths."

"He'll just lie."

"I don't believe he's the type; if he tries, I think I'll pick up on it. I also want to know how he snuck into one of our most secure facilities and how he knew just what to do to cause the maximum amount of damage and how he then convinced two top-of-the-pyramid pilots to fly him to safety, except it really wasn't safety because for some reason his goal was to surrender himself, but in so doing he nearly gets himself and the chairman of the Armed Services Committee killed, and I want to know about that, too. Don't you?"

"Yes, sir, but I think it's better to find those things out from a proper interrogation report, not from a face-to-face interview. As for the incident on the Beltway, we still don't know what happened other than the fact that shots were fired and Senator Thayer was wounded, though not seriously."

"Perhaps I should wait, but something about this man compels me to bring him in here. It might turn out to be a very short interview."

A buzz from a telephone was followed immediately by a female voice. "Sir, Colonel Powers is here with Mr. Hanlon."

"Thank you, Loraine; please send them in," McGrath responded.

A door opened, two men entered, and the door closed. Powers saluted, recognizing both the man in charge of the armed forces and a Medal of Honor recipient. McGrath returned the salute but did not proffer his hand. "Gentlemen, have a seat. My special assistant, Mr. Kajor, will be sitting in on our meeting today. Colonel Powers, let me start with you. What can you tell me about the man next to you?"

"Secretary McGrath, I'm sure you have read the files concerning Operation Jubilation, in which we both participated."

"Certainly; that's why I allowed this meeting."

"More than anyone else, it was Sergeant Hanlon who was responsible for the success of that mission. He also saved my skin, more than once, and I would without hesitation place my life in his hands again."

"Do you have anything to say about the reports concerning Mr. Hanlon's activities over the past few days?"

"I don't know the details, sir. I only know that Joe Hanlon is not a criminal and if there are reports claiming he is, then those reports are wrong."

McGrath shifted his gaze to the anxious, unkempt man to Powers' right and sighted the blood on his clothes. "Do you need medical aid?" he asked.

"No, sir, I got this while giving Senator Thayer first aid."

"Very well; what brings you here?"

"Secretary McGrath, please forgive me for being blunt, but I am here on a matter of life and death. With me yesterday at Pope Air Force Base was a woman by the name of Susan DeLuca. I suspect she was taken into custody after the incident at the dome, but the fact was not released because she was captured by people who would torture her or kill her to support their ends. Do you have any knowledge of this?"

"Wait just a damn minute!" Kajor shouted. "You're here to answer questions, not ask them!"

"Mr. Kajor, please," McGrath said in a low voice, then turned and made eye contact with Joe. "It's obvious you feel strongly about this, so I'll answer that. Mr. Hanlon, except for yourself, no one has been taken into custody in conjunction with the incident yesterday at Pope. I have been following the situation closely and would have been informed."

Joe sensed and instantly admired the sincerity exuded by the man behind the desk, but the high stakes necessitated a further test to determine whether the Defense Department head was a practiced liar or merely ignorant of the nefarious activities of those operating under his purview. He took a deep breath. "Sir, are you aware that the domed B-2 bomber hanger at Pope Air Force Base—the building itself—was constructed as a gigantic weapon of individual assassination that can target any location on Earth?"

In the second that followed, the answer became clear. The look of total perplexity that formed on McGrath's face indicated to Joe that he might yet live out the day.

"Jesus CHRIST!" came the piercing wail from Kajor. "Rude behavior from this idiot we might be able to put up with, but we don't have to listen to the fantasies of a raving lunatic!"

"Mr. Hanlon, I have to agree with my assistant on this one. I have no idea what you are talking about, but you are certainly far afield of reality."

Even Powers gave his protégée a look that said, "If brains were taxed, you'd get a rebate."

Joe focused on McGrath. "Crazy or not, sir, I want to tell you the story of my adventures over the past week. Before I start, though, I would like to give you this." He reached into his pocket and withdrew a small plastic disk. Kajor was immediately on his feet in response to the movement, but McGrath motioned him back into his seat, well aware that his guest had been through at least three security checkpoints on the way to his office.

Joe put the computer disk on the desk. "I don't know exactly what is on this, sir, but I'm fairly certain that it contains files that will support what I am about to tell you."

McGrath gave the object a cursory examination. "Where did you get this?"

"From a computer in a large facility several hundred feet beneath the floor of the dome."

"All right, Mr. Hanlon, we shall see," a slightly intrigued McGrath said as he punched a button on his telephone.

"Yes, sir?"

"Loraine, please have Clifford Owens come up here right away."

"Sir, I could take that down to CCC&I for you," Kajor volunteered, his eyes on the disk.

"Thank you, but I have a few questions for our computer expert before he starts to work on this thing."

Less than a minute later, a man dressed in a white lab coat and wearing a security badge around his neck entered and skittishly made his way across the carpet.

"Gentlemen, this is Dr. Clifford Owens, the best computer man in the building," McGrath introduced. "Cliff, meet Colonel Powers and Joseph Hanlon."

"The colonel and I have met once before," the man stated as he exchanged nods with the Army officer. "Mr. Hanlon looks familiar, but I can't place him."

"Seen the news lately?"

"Oh my, yes," Owens said, jerking his head up and intently examining Joe.

"Mr. Hanlon brought me this," McGrath said, handing the computer expert the disk. "What is it?"

"*This* is something that is not supposed to be handled by a person who does not have a Top Secret clearance," Owens said. "*This* is a Celltella, a CJW-18 high security disk, the latest thing in tamper-proof technology. We've been using them about eight months."

"Who are 'we'?"

"This technology is the exclusive domain of the U.S. military. The devices and the hardware that goes with them are currently being phased into our systems at DOD level; so far, that's limited to about a dozen agencies here in the Pentagon. The Air Force was selected as the first service to receive them, and the disks and attendant equipment can be found at thirty or so bases worldwide. The other services will be introduced to the system later this year."

"Has this disk been tampered with?" McGrath asked.

"Obviously not, since you can still tell what it is," Owens said with a grin. "This may look like a simple device, but within every piece of plastic are microchips, extremely fine electric wires, and pipettes of a caustic chemical. Any tampering, any attempt to emplace or retrieve information utilizing unauthorized equipment or codes, triggers the release of the acid, and within seconds all that remains is a pungent, smoking pile of goo."

"Can you retrieve the data from this disk?"

"Without help from its owner, I assume you mean," Owens guessed. "These markings indicate this is an Air Force disk."

"I'd like to see what you can recover on your own," McGrath stated.

" I think we can manage to get something for you. Give me two hours."

"Thank you, Dr. Owens," McGrath said as the man retreated from the room. He then turned his attention to the youngest man in the office. "Mr. Hanlon, the floor is yours."

Joe swallowed nervously. "Sir, to understand what I am going to tell you, I have to acquaint you with the peculiar properties of tiny particles called solar neutrinos. . . ."

In a building where over twenty thousand people worked, it was unusual for two visitors to be vying for the title of most miserable person in the Pentagon.

Joe Hanlon was not a happy person as he sat brooding his fate with David Powers in a small waiting room across the hall from the outer office of the secretary of Defense. Though he had spent nearly an hour and a half relating his story, it was obvious McGrath was extremely dubious about its veracity. Joe didn't blame him; the existence of an apparatus that could direct a lethal beam straight through the planet still seemed fantastic to Joe, and his association with the facts had been tragically personal. He knew the files on the computer disk could help his credibility if they were both incriminating and retrievable, but doubts loomed large that they were either. Joe worried that McGrath would delay any investigation for days at least, if he felt the matter should be looked into at all. This did not bode well for Susan, whose survival might depend on quicker action. Fatalism crept in on his thoughts as he realized the most probable course of action of his enemies: they would use her, murder her, then blame it on him, in accordance with their standard, well-exercised MO.

Bernardo Marquez was not a happy person as he sat alone in a waiting room near the offices of the Department of the Air Force. The owner of a chemical supply firm, Marquez had grown rich from manufacturing large amounts of an extremely pricey synthetic enzyme for a B-2 bomber upgrade project, except those making modifications to the airplanes received shipments of an inexpensive carbon allotrope instead. Pallets of the two powders, which looked alike and were stored in identical aluminum urns, were switched by Marquez with a forklift as they sat on the loading dock of his factory. The result of his nocturnal activities was that pallets of carbon that normally sold for sixty-four hundred dollars were billed at a hundred seventy-five thousand, while the expensive enzyme became a bargain, being sold for less than a tenth of what it was worth. As the quantities were equal, it was a financial wash to Marquez. To those who initiated the deception, however, the switch was vital, as a mere eight million dollars was charged to the project that used the enzyme to manufacture hexagonal panels installed in what was known as the Beehive, while two hundred forty million was charged against the B-2 project. Applied to a single plane, the amount might have been challenged by someone involved in the debate on whether the per-bomber cost was one or two or three billion, but spread out over the entire thirty-three-plane project, the sum was not noticed at all, even by the lowballers.

Marquez noticed the money, though; the obscenely large and easy profits that flowed into his personal accounts transformed his life. At first overjoyed for himself and his wife Carmen, the euphoria over sudden wealth did not last. Too soon, he found himself embarking on a long voyage of self-discovery, during which he found out he had a gambling problem, sexual predilections few others could afford, and an obsessive affinity for expensive objects that offered little joy. All of this contributed to his overriding ability to create money problems no matter what the situation. Everybody knew he was worth ten million; only Marquez himself was aware if he were to shoot himself, nothing would be found but debts. Whether a person had a hundred dollars to his name, or ten million, or a billion, it's easy to go broke, he now knew: simply borrow four times your net worth and blow twenty-five percent of it. He had passed that point over a year before, and the situation had deteriorated steadily since then, but he really didn't give a damn. The only thing that surprised him was that his wife had not yet left him.

Having been summoned to the Pentagon to meet with the person who had put him on the road to riches and ruin, he was not looking forward to either a closer relationship with people he had grown to detest or the large amount of money sure to come his way as a result of the imminent replacement of over sixty thousand panels within the dome at Pope Air Force Base.

He had come to hate those trips to North Carolina, to that huge building he regarded as a place of death. To some extent, his too-close relationship with men high up in the project was his own fault. The formula and manufacturing processes for the synthetic enzyme were provided to him at the inception of his contract, but in filling his orders, he became an expert in all aspects of the substance. Soon, he was employed as a consultant, making frequent trips to the government-run panel assembly plant on a large, all-but-abandoned Army base in Tennessee and to the dome itself. Eventually, his education was complete and he had a working knowledge of the entire weapons system. Thereafter, he displayed another talent, the ability to conceal his dismay over the whole business.

But that was mostly in the past. Marquez's visits to the dome had become fewer since construction was completed. While still operating his forklift to qualify for his paycheck, he considered the distance between himself and the project to be an acceptable one. All had changed overnight, however. In just twenty-four hours, he was neck deep in taskings that would consume him for at least a year and a half. The intolerable situation, he knew, was due to one person, the murderer and saboteur Joseph Hanlon.

As Marquez thought of the hated name, he heard it spoken. Momentarily doubting his senses, he heard it again distinctly through the open door of the waiting room. He walked out the door and came upon two women talking at their desks. They were secretaries to a secretary, or perhaps a deputy secretary or an assistant secretary or an under secretary or a deputy under secretary or a principal deputy under secretary; Marquez didn't care which, but he was very interested in the subject of their conversation.

". . . and they pulled up to the hospital entrance and Senator Thayer was taken out, bleeding. They say the car was all shot up. Hanlon was arrested, but they didn't lock him up, they took him directly upstairs."

"Excuse me, ladies," Marquez interrupted, barely able to control his rage-laced curiosity. "Did I hear you say Joseph Hanlon has been captured?"

"Yes," the younger of the two answered excitedly. "The news is all over the building."

"Are they keeping him in North Carolina or will they be transferring him up here?" Marquez queried.

"He's here already, in this building," answered the other, giving Marquez a you're-not-getting-it look. "He came in through the basement and was taken straight up to see Secretary McGrath."

"Thank you," Marquez said over his shoulder as he moved at a rapid pace down the hall. Minutes later, he was standing at the security checkpoint at the end of the SECDEF's corridor.

"I was sent up by General Van Valkenburgh's office," he lied. "We need to schedule some time to see this Joseph Hanlon."

"Yes, sir, we've been expecting you; I imagine you want to have a long talk with him after what he did at Pope," the guard said as he checked Marquez's badge. "The secretary's people are just down the hall to the right. Hanlon himself is right across the hall in the waiting room, under guard."

"Thank you," Marquez said as he walked through the barrier.

He found the windowless room nicely appointed, featuring several pieces of Georgian furniture including four chairs, two of which were occupied. A powerfully built Army colonel was sitting by an oval table against the wall, on the other side of which reclined a much younger man in soiled clothing.

"You Hanlon?" Marquez spat at the man on the far side of the room.

"I am. Who are you?"

"I'm just one of the people whose life you wrecked," Marquez began, shaking with hate. "I don't know why or how you did it, but you destroyed the work of hundreds of dedicated men."

"I had my reasons," Joe said.

"Now I'm going to have to spend untold hours, weeks and months, restoring what you destroyed in an instant," Marquez said, his hands balled up into reddened, quaking weapons.

"That's just what you're *not* going to do," Joe shot back, jumping to his feet.

"What the good goddamn do you know about it?" Marquez yelled, advancing two steps toward his enemy.

"Whoa," Powers warned, rising quickly and putting up a strong hand in front of Marquez's chest. "This confrontation is *not* going to get physical."

"Sir," stated a young Pentagon policeman who appeared at the door and addressed the senior person present.

Powers turned toward the guard. "What is it?"

"We just received an urgent call at the security checkpoint from someone at Air Force. He requested that Mr. Marquez return there immediately."

"Thank you," Powers acknowledged. "I think we're done here; he'll be down directly."

"I'll let them know, sir."

"Marquez?" Joe asked in stunned surprise. "Bernardo Marquez?"

"How did you know that? We've never met."

"No, and if things had gone a little differently, we never would have," Joe said. "You're not supposed to be here; you should be at home. Covina, isn't it?"

"West Covina, there's a difference," Marquez mumbled, caught off guard. "I'm here because of you, asshole, not that's it any of your business."

Joe looked at Marquez dead-on. "I assume you know what that thing at Pope was built for. What it did to Victor Bonnelli last week and more than twenty others over the past year or so."

The further demonstration of knowing that which was impossible to know served to keep Marquez in a dazed silence.

"You were next. Tonight—or, more accurately, at two o'clock to-morrow morning—it would have been directed at you."

"I don't believe you!"

"It was right there on Zeichner's computer, the whole agenda. Do you think I would make something like this up?"

"No . . . no," a defeated Marquez stated, accepting the truth as he sank into one of the unoccupied chairs, eyes down. It all made sense, he knew. He had been long aware that the unnamed disease at the root of his physical and mental and moral decline was probably a terminal one. The way in which he was to be put out of his misery was almost too ironic, even poetic, he thought. Then he thought again, and true horror infected every neuron of his brain as he recalled who would have been close beside him in his bed at two o'clock in the morning. Though he knew his treatment of her had been increasingly shoddy as the years on the government's substantial dole ground on, Carmen stayed with him, and Marquez remained protective of his wife even as his capacity to love her diminished. That the life of someone so long suffering and innocent and loving should end at the same time and in the same man-ner as one whose punishment was well deserved was too much for the man, and he collapsed into a paroxysm of weeping. "Those bastards, those goddamned murdering bastards," he finally managed through his tears.

The witnesses to the contractor's epiphany let the man's life un-dergo a sharp turn uninterrupted. Finally, Marquez's shaking lessened and his body regained a semblance of structure.

It was Powers who broke the silence. "Have you ever met the sec-retary of Defense?"

"No."

"He's right next door. I think we can get you in to see him. Per-haps you'd like to tell him a few things."

Marquez looked up, eyes wide. "He doesn't know?"

"Everything Secretary McGrath has learned about the project has come from Joe here over the past two hours. He doesn't quite believe it."

"I think I can verify a few things and fill in the gaps on a few oth-ers," Marquez offered as he stood. He smiled and extended a warm hand toward Joe. "Thank you for saving my wife; I love her, you know," he said. It was both his first sincere smile and first declaration of emotion in over three years.

CHAPTER 28

"**E**nter," a tired, agitated William McGrath urged in response to a knock at his office door. "Rock, good," he said, glad to see a familiar face. "I just had a meeting with a man named Marquez, and . . . damn! It fits, it all fits, but I still don't know whether to believe it. It's just too fantastic."

Rockwell Kajor walked quickly to McGrath's side, a look of nervous concern saturating his face. "Sir, what is it?"

"No . . . no. Sorry, I can't get into it right now, not without more information, not without verification. Any word on Dr. Owens' progress with the disk?"

"I just came from his lab, sir. He told me a preliminary evaluation of the data will be available within the hour."

"There's a man standing outside in the hall, Bernardo Marquez. I need you to stick him in an empty room somewhere close by. I don't want him talking to anyone. I'll be here . . . thinking."

"Yes, sir."

Twenty seconds later, McGrath was alone, but the buzz of his telephone pervaded the office before he had any time to think. "Yes, Lorraine?" he answered.

"Sir, there's are two FBI agents out here."

"Tell him they can't have him, not yet, anyway. Maybe later on this afternoon, maybe tomorrow."

"Sir, to whom are you referring? The gentlemen did not ask to see anyone except you; they say it's a matter of some urgency."

"Sorry, Lorainne. I suppose we don't have the luxury of just having one thing to deal with today. Send them in."

Two men, intense and serious, strolled onto the carpet.

"Close the door and have a seat," McGrath said without inflection. "It's Mr. Moore, isn't it?" he said to the taller of the men.

"Yes, sir, Alan Moore," stated the FBI deputy assistant director, the Bureau's chief liaison with the U.S. military. "We last met at a lunch with Senator Thayer, just before Thanksgiving last year."

"Yes, it has been too long," McGrath replied. "How goes the investigation into the attempt on Thayer's life?"

"The Bureau is doing all it can. Agents have located the sniper's firing position on the roof of a riverfront apartment building and are canvassing the area. The Washington Metropolitan Field Office has lead authority in the investigation."

"Then you're not here about that," McGrath observed, recalling that the D.C. field office was a separate entity, located blocks away from the Hoover Building. "You must be here about the Pope investigation."

"Only indirectly, sir. Agents from the Charlotte Field Office are handling that matter, but their activities have been confined to areas surrounding the base, as Pope itself is apparently off limits to FBI investigators."

"And this has caused some friction?" McGrath asked, noting a slight strain in Moore's voice.

"Frankly, they're a bit miffed at the unprecedented secrecy, sir. Even the SAC himself was escorted off base after one short meeting with General Irwin."

"That sounds highly irregular."

"In my experience it is, sir," Moore stated.

"And yet that still isn't the reason for you being here. There is another matter of some urgency?"

"It was not our intent to make an unscheduled appearance here. We had an appointment to see the secretary of the Air Force, but before our arrival, Secretary Cordova left the building. Then we caught the rampant rumor that Joseph Hanlon had seen you earlier, and that brought us up to your office." Moore gestured to his right. "This is Special Agent Richard Tobin. He works out of a resident agency attached to the New York Field Office and he has uncovered evidence that indicates rather conclusively that there is a group of Defense Department employees engaged in illegal activity."

Tell me about it, McGrath thought sarcastically before mentally changing his tone and saying, "Tell me about it."

"Yes, sir," Richard Tobin said. After a loud but victorious confrontation with his boss in White Plains, Tobin took his evidence to the Hoover Building, where after two meetings learned that Philip Roberts operated under the purview of the office of the chief of staff of the Air Force. "Let me start by saying that I have never met a finer person than

Joe Hanlon. You don't know about his past service, the debt owed to him by the entire country. . . ."

"Agent Tobin, I am familiar with Hanlon's military record, but his activities in the Pacific are highly classified. How is it that you are aware of them?" McGrath asked.

"Sir, I don't know anything about that. The incident I am referring to took place last summer in New York, where he was instrumental in foiling a terrorist operation."

"I was just made aware of the classified FBI file on Hanlon this morning, sir," Moore added. "His actions last July were truly . . . amazing."

"Very well," McGrath said, gaining even more respect for the young man. "What can you tell me of his more recent activities?"

Tobin performed an abbreviated throat clearing. "Before he went to North Carolina, Joe Hanlon was wanted for two murders. Although the evidence looked bad, we now know he was framed, set up by personnel who operate out of Pope Air Force Base."

"I have Mr. Hanlon's story on those murders. Right now, I'm halfway to believing his account. Do you have evidence indicating that a bomb was detonated in his apartment?"

"Yes, a sliver of plastic from his telephone with explosives residue on it."

"And the doctor in his hometown?"

"We have proof Hanlon wasn't in the vicinity at the time of that murder."

"And the evidence that the men from Pope were involved?"

For fifteen minutes, Tobin explained his case in detail, ending with his most recent finding. Rushed by the Washington FBI lab, the neutron activation analysis tests on the four recovered bullets were conclusive, but not in the way anyone had anticipated. Normally used to match bullets to a small batch of projectiles and thus to a single gun, the test precisely measured proportions of minute impurities in the lead that changed minute by minute during manufacture. Tobin's tests did not differentiate which bullets came from which gun, however, as they showed that all four, shot from at least two different pistols, came from the same batch. Bewilderment at the incongruity was transformed into warm satisfaction, as Tobin realized it was proof that all guns used, including the one used at the DeLuca house, belonged to Roberts' gang. Obviously, they used the same box of ammunition when they loaded their weapons.

"Agent Tobin, Assistant Director Moore, thank you," McGrath said at the end of the discussion. "You have both cleared up a few things and given me a few disturbing problems in return. Please keep what you have related to me confidential."

After three more minutes, McGrath was again alone in his office, where he again attempted to retreat to his thoughts and was again interrupted by the buzz of his telephone. "Yes, Lorraine?"

"Dr. Owens is here, sir."

"Please send him in."

McGrath's door opened almost immediately. "You're not going to believe this," Clifford Owens said, holding up a sheaf of papers.

"I'd like to make you a large wager you're wrong, Cliff. Right about now, I'm liable to believe just about anything."

———

William McGrath gazed out of one of his office windows at the encroaching dusk, made darker by the rain clouds that were sure to unleash their moisture within the next few hours, certainly by midnight. The heavy atmosphere reflected his own mood of nervous apprehension, the worst he remembered feeling since his days as a combat commander in the jungles of Vietnam.

General Ronald Louis Hightower, deputy chief of staff of the Air Force, strode purposefully into the office at 5:59 P.M. Four silver stars gleamed from each shoulder of an impeccably tailored Air Force uniform that accentuated his muscular frame. Precisely placed insignia, pocket badges, and six rows of ribbons covered an impressive percentage of his jacket. He smiled briefly as he walked toward the desk, an expression of easy confidence that served to remind McGrath that the confrontation upon him would be neither smooth nor pleasant.

"Please have a seat, General," McGrath commanded.

Hightower sat and assumed a rigid, authoritarian stance. "I understand you have our saboteur in custody, sir," he said. "I would like him transferred to Air Force CID as soon as possible. They are anxious to interrogate him."

"Yes, we have him. He's under guard across the hall."

"I would like to call our people immediately; they can be up here in minutes."

"That will not be necessary, General," McGrath said, extending an arresting hand. "Mr. Hanlon will remain here for the time being."

"As you wish, Mr. Secretary," Hightower said reluctantly.

"I called you here to talk about what's been going on down at Pope."

"It has been hectic down there. The 525th Bomb Wing will complete its relocation to Whiteman within the next eight hours, and there is a massive search underway for the terrorists. Since I received no official word Hanlon was brought in, he is still being looked for; I would like to get that information out immediately to the search teams so they can concentrate on the others. Again, sir, I think it would greatly benefit everyone if Hanlon could be questioned at once."

"I don't think we need to bother about that, General," McGrath said. "I intend to cancel all search operations in the Fayetteville area as soon as we are finished here."

"I beg your pardon, Mr. Secretary?" Hightower said. "I don't understand. Surely you don't believe Hanlon acted alone."

"Perhaps you can tell me how many people were involved."

"Reports compiled from various witnesses estimate that between four and six people infiltrated the facility," Hightower said, calm but a bit stiff.

"Was a woman involved?"

Hairline cracks in the general's cool demeanor appeared. "I've seen one report stating that, but it has not been verified."

"Please tell me about the development of the facility at Pope," McGrath pressed.

Hightower's unease was first evident in the tiny beads of perspiration that appeared at his temples, then carried to his voice. "Sir, I don't mean to be rude, but we are in the middle of a crisis, and the information you are asking about is irrelevant to the current problem. I believe you should wait for General Van Valkenburgh to return. Although it's a grueling flight from Manila, I know he'll come directly to his office. He will be here in less than six hours."

"What I want to talk to you about does not primarily concern your acting in the stead of the Air Force chief of staff or your current position in the Pentagon. It concerns additional activities that have occupied much of your time over the past five years."

Hightower shifted in his seat. "I have been involved in a great many things over the course of my career, sir. The past few years have been particularly busy."

"Over the last few hours, I spoke with several people concerning a special project at Pope Air Force Base, one I believe you were involved with from the beginning," McGrath stated, his voice raised ever so slightly in irritation.

Hightower shrugged. "I did play a part in the establishment of the 525th at Pope, including the construction of its buildings."

"Are there any underground facilities beneath the dome?"

"There were some excavations made. Most of the material removed was used as a base for the surface improvements," Hightower deflected.

"Is there any truth to the reports I have received claiming the dome was built as a giant weapon that kills people by concentrating and reflecting particles called solar neutrinos straight through the Earth?" McGrath asked, disgusted with the charade.

"Sir . . . that is . . . that is . . . bizarre."

"Yes, it is. Do I need to repeat the question?"

"No, sir," Hightower answered, reestablishing himself slightly. "I am . . . I'm not comfortable talking about such a sensitive subject. This is highly classified; this room might be bugged. I should speak to the chief of staff about this."

"General Hightower, there are no listening devices in this room, there's only you and me and I am not going to wait for General Van Valkenburgh's arrival to discuss this."

"Very well, sir," Hightower acceded.

"Tell," McGrath prodded after ten seconds of silence. "And I want nothing but the truth."

Hightower sighed, but it was a gesture of accommodation, not defeat. "We have been developing such a weapon for several years. It started as the brainchild of a Caltech physics professor who turned to the military in search of funding for solar neutrino research. I met him seven years ago, and he started working for us immediately. At first, the whole scheme seemed like so much science fiction. I hardly paid any attention to the project during those first two years, and I don't think more than a million or two was expended. Slowly, the idea gained credibility, but when construction was started on the dome we were still confronted with many questions."

"Most of which you have answered by now, I assume," McGrath said, pleased that he was finally getting somewhere. "How does it work?" he asked, anxious to compare the answer with the description of the device given by Joe Hanlon.

"The panels installed in and beneath the dome act as neutrino reflectors. During the day, they disperse the particles harmlessly back into space. In the middle of the night, however, the big dome concentrates the neutrinos onto a smaller array of panels deep underground. From there, they are focused into an array of lenses, resulting in a parallel beam ten feet in diameter with a neutrino concentration three thousand to six thousand times greater than normal."

"The beam is lethal and can be directed anywhere on Earth, through the Earth" McGrath finished.

"Yes, Mr. Secretary," Hightower stated, wary but pleased that he still had his head. "The neutrinos break down an obscure enzyme found in mammals and the animal suffers a fatal heart attack."

"What does the facility at Albany have to do with the operation?" the SECDEF asked, not-so-subtly letting on that he knew more than a little about the subject at hand.

If Hightower was shaken by the question, he didn't show it. "We have a small reflecting station in Albany, Australia that serves to divert the neutrino beam to any location in the Northern Hemisphere."

"Exactly what locations have you illuminated with this beam?"

"The beam does not light up anything, sir. It is completely invisible, and cannot in fact be detected by any means," Hightower vacillated.

"So what locations have you *not* illuminated with this beam?" McGrath asked, irritation tingeing his voice.

"Various locations, all within the United States. We are still in the preliminary stages of development, but the results of the experiments are promising. The plan was to inform you of the status of the weapon after the completion of the experimental phase for potential deployment."

McGrath did not confront the obvious lie directly. "I've been here six years, and you were in on this thing from the beginning. In all this time, you didn't think I might like to be made aware of this wonder weapon?"

"Yes, sir, that certainly was given a great deal of consideration, but you were not informed for various reasons, the main one being that we had no idea if the device would work."

McGrath did not pursue the answer further, as he realized that more elucidation would be made up on the spot. "How was this project funded?" he asked, taking a different path to the same objective.

"A combination of the chief of staff's contingency fund and the authorized appropriations for the dome."

"Including its anti-surveillance features, which were a sham," McGrath stated.

"Although the dome offers a great deal of protection against electronic eavesdropping and overhead observation, you are essentially correct, sir. To protect the secrecy of the weapon, that project was both a front and a conduit that fed the development of the neutrino beam."

"That was highly irregular," McGrath said.

"Sir, there are various national security provisions under which we operate that do not necessitate informing Congress."

Oh, so we're going along the "perfectly legal" tack, McGrath thought. "Have your experiments involved human subjects?"

"Our testing program has been a rigorous one," Hightower began tentatively. "We have experimented on a wide variety of mammals."

"And it does not concern you that those were people you killed?" McGrath asked, pointedly ignoring the dodge.

"There are certain discretionary powers granted to the military," Hightower began hollowly. "As for 'people,' those few vermin we exterminated didn't meet the definition."

"I can see where you might think that," McGrath said as he referred to his notes and slowly showed his hand. "Death row inmates in eight states who cheated the chair or chamber or needle by a few days, a convicted child molester in Indiana, and a notorious mobster might be considered cockroaches deserving your foot, but I have two problems with your statement. First, I do not consider twenty-three victims to be a few, I consider it an obscene number. Second, please tell me about subject twenty-four. I understand you know Mr. Marquez well."

"That . . . that was just remotely contemplated . . . never seriously considered," Hightower stumbled.

"I thought I made it clear that this was not a good time to be lying to me. And speaking of people killed, how about the outlandish health record among those working under the dome, including several fatal heart attacks."

Head hung slightly lower, Hightower attempted an answer. "Isolated cases . . . we did a study, but we weren't sure. . . ."

"Bullshit! You *knew!*"

"Maybe," the general said softly.

"And yet, unbelievably, that is not all. There were two more deaths, in New York, not done by your infernal device but because of it, and they are just as dead. I imagine there are others I don't know about."

"*No,* sir," Hightower managed. "Those killings were completely unauthorized, and I had no knowledge of them until after the fact. The man responsible for them was our chief of security, Philip Roberts. He died last night."

"How?"

"You'll love it," Hightower said without a trace of humor. "He had an office underground directly beneath the dome since before the building was finished. He had a heart attack and died there, almost certainly due to the cumulative effect of a slightly increased neutrino flow over the last two years."

"Would you also like to tell me about several hundred million dollars illegally transferred from the B-2 bomber program to your energy ray weapon?"

Hightower's eyes met McGrath's. "Sir, please, you don't understand what we have here in our device."

"Please enlighten me."

"I seized upon the idea of the neutrino ray because of those enemy headquarters bunkers made from reinforced concrete and steel and located hundreds of feet underground. It is the job of the Air Force to destroy these fortifications, but we couldn't, not without using tactical nuclear weapons. Given the political climate, this meant there was no way to eliminate them. With the particle weapon, though, there is a way. With our beam, hundreds of feet of concrete and steel is nothing; hell, in most cases those neutrinos will travel through the planet three times to reach their objective—over twenty thousand miles of solid rock. It's clean, too, and no pilots are risked, and there is absolutely no defense against it."

"Sounds reasonable," McGrath allowed.

"The original calculations indicated the beam would have been over a hundred feet across, but even as the dome was going up we realized we were going to end up with a lethal area less than one percent of that. At that point, I realized we were building a weapon that not only had the capability to knock out bunkers, but to eliminate war by making surgical strikes against those who have the most say in waging it. Think of how many lives could be saved by neutralizing key personnel before any real trouble begins."

"You're talking about political assassination."

"Except there's one big twist: nobody knows it. Say one of our favorite dictators is giving a speech before thousands of his fellow zealots while surrounded by a hundred guards, with not even one American in-country. All of a sudden, he drops dead of a heart attack. As long as no one else is within five feet of him, he would be the only victim. The United States would be absolutely blameless in such a situation."

"How could you be so precise as to time and place?" asked McGrath, slightly intrigued.

"Sir, you know we can pinpoint any location in the world down to a couple of millimeters with our new Global Positioning Satellite technology. Our people could determine the podium's coordinates weeks before the event and enter them into the weapon's database. It would be a simple matter to activate the device upon monitoring a television broadcast of the speech from hundreds or thousands of miles away."

"I see."

"With the technology we have at Pope, the capability exists to eliminate any enemy, on any day, anywhere, no matter how well protected by fortifications or bodyguards. All we need to know is where the target will be around two o'clock in the morning, our time. We can then direct the invisible beam to that point, and death will follow after an exposure of less than five minutes. Right now, the objective has to remain stationary for those few minutes. Within the year, however, we expect to be able to hit a *moving* target by utilizing a small GPS tracker, or the new real-time satellite imaging system, or a combination of both. We'll be able to eliminate the occupants of moving cars. We'll be able to knock planes right out of the sky by neutralizing the pilots. We'll be able to destroy a submerged submarine by incapacitating key personnel over the course of an hour or so."

Not qualified to make a psychological diagnosis, McGrath was nevertheless practiced at recognizing a man under extreme stress. "General Hightower, while I can conceive that your motivations might have been pure, the execution of your plan has been so abysmal that I have to consider your actions criminal. This project of yours is shut down now. Permanently."

"Yes, sir," Hightower said, barely managing to get out the words.

"One more time, General, why didn't you tell me? You must have known you couldn't keep this thing a secret forever."

"Before the last election, the decision was made to inform your successor of the project within the first two weeks of his appointment. Because it would have been one of a thousand things presented to him and because of the extreme secrecy involved, he would never have discovered any discrepancies. The election went badly for us, of course, and you remained on. We didn't know what else to do except to hunker down for another few years."

"Who else is involved in this—this thing of yours?"

"Secretary McGrath, you have me, but I am not about to turn in my fellow officers. If any," he added weakly. "Shit, I'm sure you don't even need my help; you sure as hell have amassed more information than I thought was possible."

"Was the Air Force secretary involved?"

Hightower smiled momentarily. "No, of that you can be sure. None of us likes that snot-nosed kid."

"You are of course relieved of all duties."

"Relieved . . . yes, of course." the defeated general said. "Where did it go wrong?" he asked, his voice directed at the carpet.

"You really don't get it, do you? It didn't go wrong, it was wrong from the beginning, starting with misappropriating—stealing—over a billion dollars. From there, it must have been an easy stretch to killing people you consider scum while you ignored incidental deaths among your own people. Then you graduated to murdering your own and eliminating innocents who just got in the way by means not so remarkable or scientific. Yours was a weapon of assassination, a weapon of terrorism. It was not something this country needed, and it was dangerous in the extreme to have it in the hands of unchecked military personnel. Worst of all was your plan to take this plot international, believing it to be undetectable, when it took a single small-town cop less than a week to completely uncover your scheme."

After concluded their discussion, the general made three telephone calls while McGrath looked on. Hightower then literally slunk from the office as Rockwell Kajor entered.

"Jesus, he looked bad, sir," Kajor said.

"It was all true, Rock, everything Hanlon told us about that neutrino ray and the murdering government agent in New York and the conspiracy of highly placed personnel. All true, with much more thrown in that he didn't know about."

Kajor sat heavily in the nearest chair. "So General Hightower was behind this?"

McGrath lifted his hand to his chin in contemplation. "He says he initiated it, but there are certainly others. Van Valkenburgh has to know, as well as Hardesty, who was Air Force chief of staff when it all started. Irwin and Wainwright down at Pope would have to be idiots not to know, and neither is. It would be premature to guess who the others might be, but we'll find them."

"And do what?"

"Let them retire and live out their lives in quiet seclusion, far away from Washington, or bring the lot of them up on capital murder charges. Or something in between."

"Murder?" Kajor expelled.

"I'm afraid so. The total is thirty: twenty-three test victims, five unexpected deaths due to health hazards, and those two killings in New York."

"Still, sir, these were not crimes of passion, they were carried out while in uniform under some shadow of authority. A trial would devastate the government."

"Perhaps you're right," McGrath said as he stretched, extremely weary. "We can decide that over the next few weeks. I'm afraid I've had it for today. Please call the car."

"It has been waiting, sir."

"Yes, I suppose it is getting late," McGrath observed as he glanced at his watch. "We need to accommodate Mr. Hanlon before I leave, though."

"You're not considering letting him go, are you?" Kajor asked with alarm.

"He didn't kill anyone; he hasn't even hurt anyone."

"Perhaps not, sir, but he was definitely involved in the damage at Pope."

"That place needed damage done to it."

"It was not Hanlon's call."

"What do you see as the alternatives?"

Kajor thought as he spoke. "We could have him charged with perhaps two dozen violations of federal law, including breaking into a high security military facility, destruction of property, and theft of classified documents. The second option is to detain him indefinitely without charging him in the interest of national security. The third option, I suppose, is to cut him loose, but I don't think that is advisable because of his criminal activity and the security issues."

McGrath folded his arms, settled back into his chair, and closed his eyes, silently pondering the situation for a long minute. "None of the above," he finally stated with conviction. "I want to hire him."

"Sir . . ." Kajor began, then trailed off to nothingness in exasperation.

"There are millions of people in our organization, and we have millions of other supporters out there, but no one has done more for the Defense Department over the past week than that young man. What he confronted this week was a cancer, a hidden, evil disease. Against all odds, he recognized it for what it was, discovered its cause, and eradicated it, and I want a man like that on our team. And we owe it to him; thanks to our wonderful free press, as far as almost anyone in the country is concerned Hanlon is a terrorist and murderer. I know he his neither, and publicly putting him on the payroll is the best thing we can do to dispel that notion."

"But sir . . ."

"To top it all off, Thayer says the man saved his life this afternoon."

"But sir . . ."

McGrath showed Kajor a steady palm. "No discussion on this one, Rock. Okay?"

"Okay," Kajor said, trying but failing to hide his trepidation.

McGrath stood uneasily. "Is he still across the hall? I'd like to say a few words to him."

"No, sir, Colonel Powers escorted him to the cafeteria for dinner."

"I'll see him first thing tomorrow, then. Tonight, however, I believe there's something more than a new job in store for Mr. Hanlon. I need you to take care of something for me in the next few hours."

"Of course, sir."

———————

The government sedan pulled up a concrete ramp and moved into the night air, heavy with moisture though it was not yet raining. Inside rode three grim men, a driver and two passengers. Since the beginning of the journey, not a word had been said by anyone, a cool atmosphere of silence that, Joe Hanlon believed, would last for the rest of the expected long trip.

As the receding Pentagon finally came into full view, the driver nosed the car onto Interstate 395, headed south. It was the same road that had brought Joe to the big building, and though chaos did not now pervade the scene, he thought the situation equally as desperate. In the many hours that had passed since his meeting with William McGrath, nothing at all had been said by anyone about Susan.

Joe glanced to his left at the other occupant of the back seat, the special assistant to the secretary of Defense and, for three hours, his co-worker. After abruptly dismissing Powers and with a voice laced with reluctance, Rockwell Kajor told Joe that no criminal charges were forthcoming and dutifully presented him with an offer of employment with the Defense Department. Joe, considering there was little to lose and perhaps a great deal to gain, had tentatively accepted. It was obvious at the beginning that the working relationship between the two was not going to be a warm one, however, and the stiff posture and unblinking stone face of Kajor, eyes fixed on the road ahead, served to reinforce this impression.

Although a job title had not been determined, Joe's duties would initially involve assisting in the investigation of the illicit activity at the B-2 facility at Pope Air Force Base, an assignment that pleased him greatly. Though he knew more about the operation at Pope than all but perhaps twenty or thirty others, he still had a couple of thousand unanswered questions, including a huge, overriding one about the fate of a specific individual who was never out of his thoughts.

Though he was technically free, access to a telephone was denied to him for "reasons of security," probably until the next day. His parents topped the call list, but his boss came in a close second. Though reluctant to leave Sunnyside and Chief Dempsey, he had made the decision several days before that he could never live there again.

After informing Joe they were going to Andrews Air Force Base soon, Kajor made him wait for three hours. As he fought his way through this long, lonely period, initial optimism gave way to dark speculation; by the time he was escorted to the car, he was convinced there was only one reason for such a quick flight back to Pope: to identify Susan's body.

Blurred by darkness, speed, and emotion, the streets of Alexandria passed quickly by. Though well lit, the avenues held little traffic, and no people were to be seen except a group of about twenty gathered outside a brick building. At that time of night—well after eleven according to the clock within the dashboard—it was a nightclub, Joe reasoned, though the structure looked remarkably like a post office and the people did not seem at all festive.

From Route 395, the car negotiated the swirling Beltway interchange and within ten minutes was crossing the Potomac River. The traffic flowed normally across the Woodrow Wilson Bridge; no trace of the day's excitement remained save a few pebbles of bullet-shattered glass that sparkled in the headlights of passing cars. The location forced up unpleasant memories of the close calls he had experienced and images of the deaths of those close to him who had not been as lucky, probably including Susan, whose corpse he imagined had been placed in the adjacent drawer to the one that held Elizabeth.

Less than fifteen minutes after crossing the Maryland border, the driver edged over to the right-hand lane. As the sedan exited the Beltway, a few light drops of rain hit the windshield, making it slightly more difficult to see the bright lights surrounding the main gate of Andrews. After a sentry waved the vehicle through, another, larger car passed the trio, headed out, sporting above its front bumper a small blue placard with four white stars in a neat line.

"Van Valkenburgh, back from Manila," the driver commented over his shoulder.

Kajor acknowledged the observation with a low grunt, the first utterance he had made since leaving the Pentagon.

"You don't like me very much," Joe commented to the man beside him, taking advantage of his traveling companion's sudden effusiveness.

"It is my job to support Secretary McGrath," Kajor stated. "Like or dislike of you has nothing to do with that."

"It would be nice to get along," Joe pressed.

Kajor replied with silence.

Joe turned away and gazed dispassionately out the window, recognizing many landmarks he had passed going the other way less than twelve hours before. Administration buildings, barracks, and warehouses gave way to structures more peculiar to an Air Force base. After another half mile, the car moved out onto the wide plain of concrete leading up to the runways.

"That's it, over to the right," Kajor said to the driver, motioning toward a large airplane three hundred yards away on the damp concrete. As they steadily approached it, Joe could see that wide steps had been extended to the front door of the C-141 Starlifter, and that a figure, a dim shadow in the open door, awaited their arrival.

"Will you be flying down to Pope too?" Joe asked grimly.

"We're not here to catch a plane, we're here to pick someone up," Kajor stated coolly.

"Someone?" Joe asked, failing to suppress a mixture of pained excitement and apprehension.

"One person; other than that, I don't know," Kajor replied. "Secretary McGrath arranged for the flight personally with Generals Hightower and Irwin. We will be here only as long as it takes to complete the pickup, then I will take you to your hotel.

Joe fixed his gaze to the front, attempting to make out more details through the rain. Maddeningly extending the journey, the sedan slowed as it drew closer to the aircraft.

"You can't get out yet," Kajor protested as Joe opened the door when the car was still two seconds from a complete stop.

"Yes I can," Joe said.

Standing sixty feet from the base of the stairs, Joe stared intently through the drizzle at the figure in the plane's doorway. What a first glance could have been mistaken for a statue was revealed to be a person, a female. Having seen Joe exit the vehicle, the woman stepped out of the shadows onto the stairway and he saw it was Susan. Dressed the same as he had last seen her, she looked disheveled and exhausted, but unhurt and gloriously alive. The story explaining her presence and condition would come out eventually, he knew, but for the moment, the past was utterly unimportant.

Joe advanced nearly at a run while Susan's feet beat a quick staccato down the aluminum steps. They met in a warm, wet embrace, holding each other closely without speaking, immobile throughout the faint, slow tolling of midnight by a bell some distance beyond the boundaries of the Air Force base. After a while, still without a word exchanged, Joe gently took Susan's arm and with her walked back to the car in the rain.

EPILOGUE

General Powers, I consider it an honor that my first E-mail to the White House is to you. Congratulations on your new position and promotion.

I know you are being bombarded with truckloads of information, the good and bad and irrelevant from offices worldwide, and I am afraid this is no different. The Pope investigation has occupied almost all my waking hours since last April. As you are one of the few military personnel who enjoys almost daily contact with the President, and because you are among the few who know what went on, Secretary McGrath asked me to give you a personal update.

Through the SECDEF, the President was made aware of the situation immediately and was periodically briefed on the solutions implemented for about six months, but it has been on the back burner since then. This is just a quick summary; the full report is nearly finalized, and as soon as it is ready, it will be available for your perusal at a secure location here at the Pentagon.

Physically, little has changed in the ten months since I first visited Pope. The dome is still open to the sky, though the transparent panels were heavily tinted several months ago to eliminate the glare and to protect sensitive equipment. A secondary power plant adjacent to the dome that was run constantly has been shut down, though it is available for emergency use. All of the facilities below the dome's sub-basement level have been sealed, and the components of the clandestine weapon system have been dismantled and destroyed. Finally, security of the complex has been thoroughly examined and several problem areas have been eliminated. No one else is likely to gain unauthorized access to the site. The 525th Bomb Wing was reestablished at Pope last October; more recently, the unit was certified as combat ready. Happily, the two pilots who ferried me to Andrews are still with the unit, although the letters of reprimand in their files will probably preclude further promotion. True flyboys, both told me if they ever were promoted out of pilot positions, they would leave for commercial work anyway.

It took me two trips to Australia to insure the project's remote station in Albany was thoroughly deactivated. The property and its empty buildings transferred back to the local government two months ago.

Almost all of the several hundred military, government civilian, and contractor personnel who were involved in the neutrino project were unaware of the nature of their work. Of the forty-seven we identified as having even slight knowledge of the capabilities of the neutrino weapon, all but a few considered the secret project to be highly unorthodox, but not illegal. The one person who I would have without a doubt recommended for severe criminal sanctions, Chief of Security Philip Roberts, died on that same memorable day that the weapon was neutralized.

As for the top leadership, seven senior generals having direct knowledge of both the lethal tests and the misappropriation of funds were identified. It was decided at a level much higher than mine that their punishment be limited to forced retirement and a withdraw from public service in any capacity, including accepting work with defense contractors or as lobbyists. These mild sanctions came about after much debate about national security issues, legal considerations, and public perception. Although violations did without a doubt occur, it was felt there exists enough ambiguity in the laws regarding the authority and conduct of senior military officers that the commanders would have escaped all but relatively minor charges. Legally, their worst offense might have been their failure to properly notify the civilian leadership of their actions. Although this particular group of conspirators escaped prison, Senator Alexander Thayer is quietly spearheading legislation to remove the legal loopholes. The sniping incident on the Woodrow Wilson Bridge involving the senator and me is still unsolved, and at this point will probably remain so.

General Parker Hardesty was the only conspirator who was already retired when the project was exposed. As Air Force chief of staff, he initially approved both the project and the policy that knowledge of its existence not go above his level. Because of our restrictions, he had to quit several lucrative consulting positions; he has since moved from the D.C. area to his home state of Wyoming.

Major General Benjamin Wainwright, commander at Pope, and the B-2 wing commander, Brigadier General Joshua Irwin, were retired within a month of each other last summer. Bick Badger and Gerald Sampey were the two generals at the Air Force base during the dome's construction; both were subsequently promoted to lieutenant general, and they retired at that rank last fall.

As everyone knows, Generals Donald Van Valkenburgh, Air Force chief of staff, and his deputy, Ronald Hightower, made headlines last May when they resigned their positions and retired. The stated reason for their actions—dismay over not receiving funding to provide for satisfactory security at all Air Force bases—has never been seriously questioned. Van Valkenburgh hasn't been heard from since he moved back to his home state of Alabama. Hightower, with our grudging approval, recently assumed the position of superintendent at the Virginia Military Institute.

Per our arrangements, the project's chief scientist, Dr. Alfred Zeichner, is now working as the science coordinator at an elementary school in Pembina, North Dakota.

The project's chief civilian contractor, Bernardo Marquez, whom you remember meeting at the Pentagon, was in some financial trouble last year, but he managed to avoid bankruptcy thanks to a generous early termination buyout of his government contract and the sale of his business to a large chemical company. He now devotes his time to charity work in Pasadena.

Confidence is high that the project will retain its secrecy for decades to come. All personnel associated with it have been read the riot act regarding its security, and no one is eager to go to jail. So far, the only person involved with the project to be convicted of anything is a man named Kevin Chandler, a former councilman in the town where I used to work. Involuntarily entangled for two days last April by security people from the dome, he knows nothing; a shady real estate deal sent him to prison.

Thanks to Secretary McGrath's decision to return some stolen research data and to augment that paperwork with a few items of hardware from the project, it is all but certain that Dr. Gabriel Burke of Caltech will receive this year's Nobel Prize in Physics.

Besides you, one other person involved in protecting my butt last year has a new job in D.C.: Special Agent Richard Tobin received a big promotion about eight months ago and is now working in the Hoover Building. You two may be joined shortly by Andrew Weiss, whose name is being bandied about Washington concerning an appointment as a deputy director at either State or Justice.

Tragically, the man who had the most to do with uncovering the conspiracy is no longer around. I know I've told you before, but Eugene Evans was invaluable, both during my time of crisis and throughout the first few months of the investigation. Despite his rapidly failing health, he assisted us right up to his final fishing trip last July.

A few weeks after you saw her at Evans funeral, Susan received a fortunate transfer from Boston and now works inside the Beltway. We decided to get married on Christmas Eve, and just a few days ago, we started talking seriously about setting a date. Expect an invitation soon.

Finally, I am for some reason being heavily scrutinized by the IRS over the tardiness of last year's tax return. Although I eventually filed what I am sure were the proper forms and have since paid three levied penalties, there are apparently still unresolved concerns. I understand that a person from the Treasury Department comes over to your building from time to time for meetings; if you happen to see him, I would appreciate it if you would put in a good word for me.